Band on the Run

Phoenix Rising Book 1

James Weems

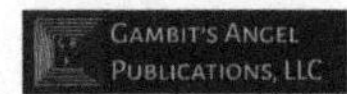

Gambit's Angel Publications LLC

ISBN 979-8-9896681-2-0 (ePub)

ISBN 979-8-9896681-3-7 (paperback)

Second edition published 2026

To my rainbow brothers and sisters:

Live your true life, take care of yourself, and

always love yourself for who you are.

Content Warning

This novel includes consensual same-gender (male-male) sex, explicit language, adult situations, homophobic slurs, mention of off-page hate crimes and brutality, suggestions of sexual and verbal abuse, enough food references to warrant a cookbook, multiple caricatures, and references to historical reports of drug use and violent acts, including the assassinations of Robert F. Kennedy and Rev. Martin Luther King, Jr., as well as the protests against the Vietnam war.

This novel is set prior to the Stonewall riots which marked the beginning of the modern Gay Rights movement, so the terms used in this book for self-identifying homosexual males is "homosexual"—"gay" in reference to non-heterosexual men was not used until around 1969, and "queer," like the term "faggot" or its shorter form "fag" was used by heterosexuals as an insult.

For non-heterosexual women, I have used the term "lesbian," which has been accepted by the community. If there is another term that was used at the time, I am unaware of it.

Contents

•••••••••••

San Francisco, California

June 14 - 16, 1968

ROLLING STONE

Staff Report, April 6, 1968

Sources confirm that the hottest up and coming new rock group on the planet, ***Phoenix Rising***, will begin their first World Tour with two shows at the Fillmore Auditorium in San Francisco, June 14 and 15 this year. Tickets are already on sale for what promises to be a dynamic show. The six-man group recently toppled the Beatles' *Sgt. Pepper's Lonely Hearts Club Band* as the top album worldwide, no doubt adding fuel to this concert tour. Lead singer Ravynn St. John, easily recognizable with his androgynous dress and long black hair, will lead guitarists Todd Ewing and Benji Travers, bassist Clay Brockington, keyboardist Wil, and drummer Sean Alexander on a ten-city "magical mystery tour," according to group manager Greg Thomas. We will have a special correspondent attached to the tour to keep our readers informed.

Fillmore, before first concert, June 14

I close my eyes as the sounds from a packed auditorium surround me. The crowd repeatedly screaming my name washes over me.

"Ravynn! Ravynn! Ravynn!"

Backstage at the Fillmore as we await our first show, five of us nervously pace. That's my bandmates Clay, Todd, Wil, my best friend Sean and me, Ravynn St. John. Together we're most of Phoenix Rising. Currently, I'm also chief worrier and sore nerve, while we wait for things to start—and Benji to arrive.

Twenty-four hours ago, we arrived in San Francisco, the center of late-1960s "counter-culture." Everything's happening here; guys and girls living on their own terms, whether they're heterosexual or homosexual, straight-laced or druggies. I could be real here—Robin Smith as I used to be, certainly as Ravynn St. John, the androgynously-dressed homosexual rocker. Part of me wants to live openly with the man I love, but that can't happen if Phoenix Rising is to become big. We're almost there. We wanna be huge like the Beatles and the Rolling Stones. That means recording the way we want, having extravagant tours and screaming fans. Some mass hysteria like Beatlemania wouldn't be bad, either.

"Where's Benji?" I ask. Benji knows he's supposed to be here; we... I haven't seen him in months. At his birthday celebration, his parents saw this tour would take him away from them for a good bit of time. They insisted, rightfully, on some "real-family-only" time, much as that killed us. We've talked by phone, briefly, so he knows the place, date, and time. So where the hell is he?

"He knows it's the Fillmore, in San Francisco, right?" Todd offers. Shit, I momentarily panic; is there another Fillmore somewhere?

"Aww, G-man, give it a rest," Wil razzes Todd. "Benji's no fool. He'll find us."

These guys cut up like brothers; to me, they are. Even Clay, who's just in the corner with a smile on his face, is family. Sean, though, is my 'brother from a different mother'—the other side of me.

"Take a chill pill, Rave," Sean says. Typical Sean, laid back to my hyper.

As I'm about to fully panic, I hear an unmistakable accent asking an almost-familiar question. "Is this the place for a rhythm guitarist? Benji's in the house!"

I turn to the sound of Benji's voice; the biggest grin splits my face. His hair is windblown, like he's been running, but there's that twinkle in his eyes.

Benji drops the duffel bag he carries, as he sees his costume folded on a nearby table.

"Dat mine?" he asks, but before I can answer, he strips outta his 'travel duds'—no modesty—and begins to change. Matching the rest of the group, he will wear black satin trousers and a red satin pirate's shirt. As he changes, he smiles at me, almost shyly. My cheeks burn. Who is this guy? This can't be Benji. His shoulders have broadened and he must be at least an inch taller than last time I saw him. Suddenly, I wonder if he's worried about what happened between us at his birthday party?

"Sorry I was runnin' late, shay. The bus musta been a local 'cause it stopped about every two blocks, felt like," he says. Shay... there's his Cajun endearment, calling me dear.

"I thought we'd have to play our records to have your guitar...."

"Shush dat, you know it wouldn't work, shay."

It's like he never left, and, momentarily, it's like only two of us are in the room.

Sean clears his throat. "You realize we've got a concert to begin in a few minutes?"

Damn. Almost forgot the reason we're here—Benji's drawing me into him again, already. I gotta stop that. Getting wrapped up in Benji now won't do any good, and could cause trouble. First, he's too damn young. I call him "Baby Phoenix" because he's just so sweet and innocent. There's a more important reason to keep distant from Benji. Phoenix Rising is gonna be bigger than the Beatles, and this tour is gonna make that happen. So I can't have rumors about any homosexual activity getting into the news. That would ruin our chances.

Benji strides over and hugs me tightly; he holds me a fraction longer than is necessary. "I missed ya, shay."

First concert

Backstage, I absorb the frenzied crowd's energy. My long black hair is tied into an extravagant ponytail. My bandmates are pumped, also; Sean's fidgeting with his drumsticks, Wil's playing "air keyboards." Todd and Clay look like they're on some invisible trampoline as they bounce up and down on their feet. Benji, almost vibrating, is radiating his smile.

"This is what it's about, guys," I say. I'm barely able to hear myself over the noise, which continues to swell, from the audience. This is it—the fans, performing onstage.

Over a thousand fans pack the auditorium, making noise for us, Phoenix Rising, the hottest rock group in the world; our second album recently toppled the Beatles' Sgt. Pepper as the top-seller world-wide. Onstage, a local deejay begins the introductions. The house lights lower; a single spotlight illuminates him. I remember our first time on a stage, in what seems a different lifetime—that Valentine's Dance at the school Greg Thomas, now our manager, set up. Was that only 5 years ago? So much has followed; from day one, Sean Alexander, my best friend, was with me as we brought our dream to life. Once we found Wil—never ask his full name—we had a great start.

Since we live in Atlanta, the city that rose from its ashes, we chose "Phoenix" as our group name. At first, it was Sean on drums, Wil on keyboards, Todd Ewing on lead guitar, Tommy Johnson on rhythm guitar, and me on vocals and occasional guitar. Bass guitar was "by committee." Lightning struck when Clay Brockington took the post. The label asked us to record other people's material; Sean and I insisted on ours. The results rocketed us up the charts and into this first tour. Not bad for a twenty-year-old, living behind a front constructed piece-by-piece these past three years.

This moment feels electric; I'm almost overwhelmed. I'm no hugger. My family featured a mother who was arm decoration for her husband and a father so uptight a lump of coal instantly turned to diamond if shoved up his ass. Benji's been open with his hugs and affection for everyone. The guys in the group and the management team of Greg and Diciembre, or DC, get frequent hugs. He's been more expressive with me. I try to discourage his affection without upsetting him. We can't afford to lose his musical ability, and the audiences and everyone around us adore him. I'm keeping it at a nice level like, but he shows emotion with the best of them. While we celebrated his birthday week last October, he was developing an attraction to me. The hugs from him are like "coming home" to me.

With a glance to make sure no one's watching, so no uptight heterosexual can call me out for my sexuality, I hug each of my guys for luck.

The deejay attempts to announce each group member by name. "Here they are! Sean, Wil, Clay, Todd, Benji, and Ravynn...." As we enter, the audience roars approval, the deejay's voice background noise.

I'm in my element. Flamboyantly, I strut the stage, blowing kisses to the audience, prancing as the band members connect their instruments. I'm powerful, the emperor in this domain. Except... I'm a homosexual American, playing a straight American masquerading as a homosexual Brit. The emperor has no pants. Or shirt.

"Welcome to the show, San Francisco!" I shout in my stage-assumed British accent, as the band plays the song *Welcome to the Show*.

Flashbulbs explode; audience members sing along or mouth the words—who can tell? I pour my heart into this; the guys' playing is perfection. The rehearsing has paid off. This group's tight. Our knowledge of the music and each other makes it magic.

Welcome to the Show leads into a string of songs from our first two albums, as well as our recently released third. Throughout the show, I banter with the audience. The crowd enjoys it, but the music is the real star of the show.

In the middle of the string of our songs, as I'm stalking the stage, singing and entertaining the audience, blowing kisses to the guys and girls, I see... him.

It's Dickie Newsome, or as I call him, Dickie Nuisance. He's a reporter, a nosy-parker, as the British would say. I know Dickie from when I was Robin Smith, living with my then-boyfriend Ronnie Kushner. Dickie was a friend of Ronnie's. His only friend. He was a nuisance, showing up at the worst times. Like when Ronnie and I were watching "Bewitched" or "The Jackie Gleason Show" on TV, getting romantic, or relaxing. Ronnie never introduced us; any time Dickie showed up, I faded into the depths of the bedroom, out of sight. Although Ronnie and I never called ourselves boyfriends, Dickie must have figured it out—a one-bedroom apartment, right?

He can't touch me (can he?), but my stomach still twists. I barely pause, then prance back to the group. I try not to focus on Dickie so I don't lose my cool and screw up the show.

We begin *Rock This Town*. The song's a rocker; I "dance" with first Clay, then Benji, then Todd. The guys ham it up with their instruments; I wrap myself around each seductively. The audience loves it. Clay's got a thing for Sean, but Sean's clueless, though I know he likes Clay a lot. I'm hamming it up with Clay, but I gotta be careful with Benji.

There's a spark between us; I noticed it when we met, and it's still there, a live wire waiting to zap us. We were in the garage at Sean's place; the door opened. A kid with a head of platinum-blond hair peered in, and I first heard that magnificent Cajun accent. "Is this the place for the rhythm guitar audition?"

Ever since, I've been fighting my attraction to Benji. I can't risk the group. My record on relationships doesn't give me hope. And being homosexual in the south can get us hurt or killed, not to mention ruining the group.

Once Upon A Dream is our next song. It's not a song for a dreamer, unless the dreamer had a love affair that fell apart.

Sean helped me write the song after my only relationship, Ronnie, ended badly. From that disaster, I created the flamboyant Ravynn St. John, and I'm living the dream. The terrible memories remind me I need to be wary of getting involved again.

As I finish, the audience has lighters swaying back and forth. In the darkened auditorium, it's like fireflies dancing to our music. It's one of those moments I've dreamed about. When the audience cheers, I bow. My hair sweeps around and hits the floor at my feet.

"Well, my pretties, that's cut it—it'll take a while to get this back in control!" I say, gesturing towards my hair, to the delight of the audience. Davey, our road crew leader, appears at the entrance to backstage and I make my way there.

As I pass him, Wil plays a melody which gradually grows into the opening chords of the Beatles' *A Day in the Life*. I return to the stage to sing that masterpiece. Behind us, a screen displays images which blur, melt and mesmerize the audience. That we perform this song proves we're serious contenders to the Beatles and Stones, and it highlights Wil's talents. He doesn't have an orchestra like the Beatles had on Sgt. Pepper. Instead, he's using four keyboards: an electric piano, an acoustic piano, and an organ. Also, a keyboard modified to play specific sounds based on the keys, which he and a friend constructed. The orchestral buildup sounds like we're playing the Beatles' album (we aren't) or have an orchestra hidden (we don't). When the minute-long final piano chord, electronically stretched, fades out, the roar from the audience is bedlam.

From *A Day in the Life* we move to the Rolling Stones' *Mother's Little Helper*. We picked these songs for one reason. The biggest names in music are the Beatles and the Rolling Stones. We are staking our claim to that territory. It's also a blast to start a song with "What a drag it is getting old...."

We follow the covers with four originals showcasing our diversity. *Transformer*, a moderate rocker; *Give Me the Night*, a raunchy rocker, then *Part of You*, a soft-rock ballad. Sean says it's my "emotional coming-out." It was how I felt. I wrote most of the words and the music; Sean added several words to help the flow.

I finish the song—a spotlight on me with the group dimly lit behind me—the audience is silent for a beat, then all hell breaks loose, like no one has breathed during the song, and then everyone gasps as they cheer. The spotlight dims as the stage lights come up, and I turn to the group and blow each guy a kiss before turning back to the audience.

The fourth number is *Just Tonight*, after which I introduce the group, getting the audience's assistance.

I start, "Baby Phoenix, Benji, on rhythm guitar!" A spotlight picks out Benji as he plays a few riffs on his guitar, flashes a peace sign and smiles. Several girls—and a few guys—whistle as the audience applauds.

"Wil, on keyboards," I shout. Again, there's applause from the audience, and a few girls whistle for him. With the spotlight on him, he smiles, plays a nice melody, then waves.

"Lead guitarist, Todd!" The spotlight grabs Todd, who plays a few chords, then smiles and blows a kiss towards the audience. "Cheeky boy," I laugh, as the audience applauds.

"On bass, Clay!" The spotlight surrounds Clay; he smiles, plucks a series of bass chords, and bows. Everyone applauds, and several people cheer. Clay has an aura. Everyone falls in love with him and he seems so bloody innocent.

"Last, my drummer brother from a different mother, Sean!" The spotlight grabs Sean with the full drum kit, then narrows to his face and arms as he punches out a beat. The audience claps, and a woman from the back of the audience shouts, "I'll have your babies, Sean!" Sean does a rimshot on the drums and smiles. I interject, "Sorry to disappoint you, but he's engaged for the next several...."—to which Sean quickly adds "years!" He winks toward the audience (no one could tell unless they have binoculars) as he waves.

After the introductions, we have seven songs remaining, including the encores. We launch into *Hot* from the new album, then *New Orleans Calling*.

As the song ends, I say, "Benji's from New Orleans. That's one reason for the song. We'd hoped to play New Orleans this tour, but we couldn't arrange it."

We play two more songs, then *In Our Dreams* from our newest album.

The song ends; the audience stands, screams, applauds—a roomful of sound telling me we've succeeded. It's mayhem. This is what I've dreamed of. Wil, Clay, Todd, and Benji leave the stage, followed by Sean; I blow kisses to everyone and leave the stage. Within seconds, the crowd begins a staccato chant of "More... more!"

Shortly, Sean returns, beginning a drumbeat matching the chant. Under near-darkness, Todd, Clay, and Benji return and add a melody. Finally, Wil adds his keyboards. As I return to the stage, spotlights pierce the dark. We begin *More and More*, our first encore. If the crowd's response is any sign, we could perform all night.

The song ends and the auditorium lights dim. It's like we're set to leave the stage once more. Applause changes to chants of "More! More!"

A lone spotlight surrounds me. "It's been beautiful! Have you had a good time?" I ask; the crowd shouts, "Yes!"

"Wonderful! All things must pass; goodnight, we love you!"

Curtains is our last song. As it ends, we wave and blow kisses to the audience.

Our first show is history... DC is waiting for us offstage.

"You saw him?" DC asks, handing me a bottle of water.

"Yeah. Dickie Nuisance, Ace Reporter. The fuck's he doing here?" I say, in my normal southern voice. I shrug my shoulders as I towel off my face. It worries me; with Dickie here, Ronnie is certain not to be far.

DC, like Greg, knows some of my past with Ronnie. That includes the fact that his only friend was this guy, Dickie Newsome, the same Dick now bothering me. They don't know how much Dickie knows or has guessed about me. That's scary. For all my bravado, Dickie's a threat; even I don't know how close Ronnie and Dickie are, or what dangers lurk.

Sean and Benji hang back, hearing our exchange. Their being near is the support my system needs. I'm about to begin the crash after a two-hour high from performing live.

"What, that guy who used to bug you and Ronnie is here? Do we need a restraining order?" Benji asks, smiling—he's kidding. He may be "baby" Phoenix, but he's stuck close to me. Protectively, since he heard my embellished tale about what happened before our first-ever concert. When Ronnie broke up with me New Year's Eve, 1965.

That brings up... mostly guilt, because I made Ronnie a total douchebag; the injuries I received were my fault. I lied that he used me, then threw me out. The only good to come from my lies was Benji becoming close to me.

"No restraining orders, guys!" DC is stern—she's serious. "Here's the situation. Mister Newsome—Ravynn, control the urge to say 'Nuisance'—has been assigned to cover the tour by Rolling Stone. They're the music newspaper that's becoming the source for music news."

Sean, Benji, DC, and me are strolling through the backstage area toward the door where our limousines are waiting. It's incredible to say those words. Two and a half years ago, I was the Phoenix born from the ashes of Robin Smith after the breakup with my boyfriend. Phoenix rose from its ashes to become Phoenix Rising.

"Wait, he's assigned to write about us? For who?" Sean's slow tuning in. I love him like my twin, but sometimes he's so dense.

DC explains, "He told them he writes for our Atlanta *Journal* and *Constitution* newspapers, so he has a 'local' angle, even though he's never written about you. 'Who' is *Rolling Stone*. The newspaper, founded in San Francisco last year, 1967, as a counter-culture paper, has become the main music newspaper in the country."

Benji appears puzzled. "How can he have a 'local' angle if he's never talked to us, Deese?" That almost-Cajun, almost-southern accent's delightful, though sometimes you need a translator.

"He's sold it on being from Atlanta, like you guys. Even though you've got an international number 1 album, the world still views you as pretenders.

This tour builds up Phoenix Rising. It also raises Atlanta as 'Capital of the New South' like the city calls itself," DC says.

"So Dickie has sold himself as the guy who can get the truth of Phoenix Rising for Rolling Stone. Great. I gotta put on my smiley face and make nice to the jerk so he doesn't screw us in his articles. Do we get any guarantee he'll treat us fairly, or are we sitting ducks?" I ask DC.

"Rolling Stone assured me we'll see any article he submits before it's printed and have the right to make corrections prior to publication. I'm sure Mr. Newsome will take this opportunity to further his career honorably; I don't expect any issues," DC says, calmer than the ten thousand butterflies dancing in my stomach.

"Okay," Sean says, about half-convinced. "But why's he covering us, when he's never done music before?" My bulldog buddy won't drop it.

"Sean, Ravynn, Benji.... He's an Atlantan, he's got the same 'hick' stigma you guys have. He needs to do a solid job reporting this, or his career's toast before he starts. Once the tour gets to the international phase, the coverage will be crucial to breaking the country bumpkin image people have about the south," DC finishes, as we reach the limousines.

"Wow-wee, that's some car," Benji says, his Cajun threatening to overtake his voice. "Y'all gonna ride with me? There might be enough room."

Todd and Wil are in the second limo and wave to us. DC says, "I'll ride with Todd and Wil; see you at the hotel!"

"Guess it's the fearless four—Sean, Clay, Benji, and me," I say, as I climb inside and settle next to Sean. I watch the driver close the door, then drive us toward the hotel.

Tonight, we're rock royalty. A sold-out concert, screaming fans, limousines. Greg isn't here; we need to thank him. We may be rock stars, but we're southerners with manners. It's a short drive from the Fillmore to our hotel; it's almost unreal.

Palace Hotel

At the hotel, police lines keep people from storming us—another first. I want to get to our rooms and relax. The sight of Dickie at the concert brings unpleasant memories of Ronnie and being played, and dropped, like a fool. I loved Ronnie, and thought he loved me. To find out how wrong I had been about him sucked—more than the scrapes and bruises I gave myself. Ronnie was pissed I continued with the group, and didn't think we stood a chance of getting anywhere. I finally stood up for myself and banged myself up. Now here we are. Ronnie didn't know everything, after all. How that relationship turned to shit keeps me from getting close to Benji—or anyone.

Yeah, we're from what we laughingly (to keep from crying) call the "buckle of the Bible belt" South. The most conservative part of the United States. The fear that some sleazy newsman might make our homosexuality his ticket to "superstar" status doesn't help. Looking at you, Dickie Nuisance.

As we enter the hotel, the ancient-appearing manager greets me. He's gotta be 40 or 50 years old. He holds out his hand for a shake and says, "Welcome to our hotel, Mister Saint John! We hope you and the Phoenix Risings will be comfortable. Our bellmen will show you to your suites and assist you in any manner possible."

I nearly crack up, but hold a convincing smile on my face and thank him. There are three bellmen. I'm drooling at the thought of having their assistance in some rising hard problems. Discreetly, and nothing more than a one-night-stand. Ravynn's Prime Rule: No entanglements. I won't risk success for a boyfriend. A one-off with one of these hunks will help resolve the emotions seeing Dickie caused. Wait; this gets complicated. Benji wants a relationship with me, I sense it from his closeness. Though I can't commit to that, I can't play with a bellman and risk hurting his feelings. That would destroy the group harmony. I won't risk that for the sake of a quickie.

Our "suite" outdoes its billing; there's a central area with three bedrooms. We have two, so Sean, Benji, and I have one while Wil, Todd, and Clay have the second.

As we enter the suite, Sean gazes like he's having a religious experience. That, or he's gone into a trance; his eyes focus around the suite like he's seen nothing so grand. Benji, meanwhile, is showing his youth and Cajun upbringing. His accent's so thick with excitement, I'm ready to call a translator.

"Dis is one fine parlah heah," Benji says. When Sean and I glance at him, puzzled, he laughs and says, "Oh, my goof. I said this is one fine parlor here. Don't get upset; I've never seen anything like this!" That accent is why I'm hung up on him. If I weren't concerned that he's so young... If he hadn't confided to me in New Orleans he's a virgin... If I weren't afraid of messing things up because of my past... If there were no snooping reporters to report guilty secrets... I wouldn't leave Benji single for another hour. But that's too many ifs.

Two of the bellmen take care of Sean and Benji and escort them to their bedrooms, leaving me with the hunkiest; I ask him to show me features of the suite. He tells me that, with the door closed, no sounds from outside the bedroom can be heard, which means whatever happens inside my bedroom will not be heard outside. A brief flirtation kills no one, right? The bellman's badge reads "Erik" so I ask, "Erik, do you have to rush off?"

He smiles—a beautiful smile, two dimples begging to be kissed—and says, "My manager doesn't expect me for an hour." Erik's given me time to indulge myself.

"Could you help me out of my shirt? Two hours performing under those lights practically fused it to me," I almost whisper. It's been a long time since my last encounter... I'd love to see if he has more dimples. He's so quick to help, my shirt is in danger of getting ripped off. Good thing I have several matching sets.

"Calmly, Erik, we have an hour," I tell him—he's puzzled; I realize I said it in my "Robin" voice rather than my "Ravynn" voice. Crap. Not only am I toying around (Erik is gorgeous, but tomorrow, I'll see others as hunky), I'm also slipping out of character. "Our secret, eh?" I say, getting back into character. As my tattoo emerges from my shirt, he stops and traces it reverently.

"I'm human, not a doll," I purr, in my best Ravynn persona. His fingers on my bare skin almost make me forget my decision to avoid sex. He smiles, hoping we're going to spend the hour getting sexual. My sex drive awakens at his touch. I don't need a hotel worker selling his story, ruining the group because I couldn't keep my business in my pants. Besides, after what happened with Benji at his birthday party last fall, I'm not sure where we stand; I don't want to hurt him.

He retraces my tattoo and says, "Remarkable."

"Thanks. Phoenix Rising isn't just the group, it's my life.... Thanks for helping with the shirt. You have lovely dimples." I hand him a $100 bill as I grab a robe from the closet, then walk him to the door. "If I weren't tied up with this tour, I would've enjoyed getting to know you better." My past overshadows my life. I'm trying to be my true self, but I can't come clean about what happened in my past, my real identity buried under layers of deceit.

"If you ever find yourself in San Francisco in need of a decent shirt remover, I'll be here," Erik winks and leaves.

As I close the door, Sean emerges from his bedroom, walks over, and grins. "Someone's got that fresh-fucked glow," he teases me. "Did you add another member to the Club?" In school, the guys crowed about their conquests; we referred to it as the Four-F Club because of the four steps involved: Find-em. Feel-em. Fuck-em. Forget-em. I'd rather not have anything to do with that group; I would prefer the Three-F Club—Find Forever Finally. But I'm in limbo, nearer the first group. Sean isn't close, but I let him think he's caught me after a trick.

"Well, three F's; the last one's in progress," I smirk.

"I hope it wasn't someone who'd tell that reporter," Sean says.

"Y'know how careful I am, Sean. This group's everything. I won't mess it up. Dickie Nuisance won't get anything, I promise. This..." I wave to encompass us, "is the only thing my touch hasn't destroyed. Anything else I've tried has turned to shit—my parents, Ronnie.... I worry I'll mess up Phoenix Rising."

Benji joins us in the living area and, having gotten accustomed to this hotel, speaks slowly enough Sean and I can understand him. "We're here two nights? I'm glad we aren't paying for these rooms!"

"Flash: the label's paying for everything from our sales. Meaning, we are paying for this!" Sean says, making Benji less happy. He squirms so close to me that his arm brushes mine and holds me for a minute. He can't be that upset about the room cost....

“Don’t worry,” I say, “We sold so much of our last album, this tour’s been well-covered.” My words hit the mark; his smile returns. A smiling Benji is the cutest thing.... I can’t go there. For the group, I won’t.

“I missed you while I was gone, shay. How do you like the hotel?” Benji asks.

My mind’s blank from his first comment. I work on a give-nothing answer.

“He finds it very hard to accept we’re only here for two nights,” Sean butts in with a demonic leer. “Don’t you, Ravynn?”

There are times when I would throttle Sean, draw and quarter him, and boil his remains in oil, like now. But, I love him as a brother, so I say, “Yes, very hard.” Hopefully, he sees the daggers in my eyes; he shuts up.

“Guys, we’ve got another show; it’s almost tomorrow. Let’s end the night before DC does a bed check,” I say; knowing her, bed checks would not be unlikely. After the performance, my body’s crashing. Time for a shower and shut-eye.

“Erik, your ass, so tight!” I moan, mostly asleep, thinking my right hand is the ass of the bellman from last night. As I continue pounding into my hand and the mattress beneath, I realize someone’s pounding at my bedroom door. Damn—for a dream, this was real. I’d better see who’s having a stroke on the other side of the door before a new one comes out of my “expense voucher.” I get up, throwing a robe over my naked body, barely covering my still-hard cock.

When I get to the bedroom door, DC stalks into the room, trailing cigar smoke behind her, angry.

"'Sup, DC?" I ask, light-heartedly. It'll be easier to keep things calm if I'm not defensive.

"So, rock gods sleep until 2 in the afternoon when they have a news conference at 4 pm followed by a sound check at the Fillmore?" she asks sarcastically. When DC is sarcastic, it means she's only slightly less angry than a hive full of wasps.

Fuck. I'd forgotten the news conference, or to get a wake-up call no later than noon. That means one rapid dash through the shower and dress. I bet Sean....

"Did you get him awake, DC?" Sean calls from the living area. I hear mumbling, so Benji's also awake.

"Yeah, Sean, he's gonna take a shower and dress in a flash—right, Ravynn?" DC states, rather than asks. I nod as I'm heading to the shower. I complete the process in less than ten minutes, a record for me.

When I stride into the living area, I see my five guys sitting like they're waiting for an audience with the Queen. When DC sees me, she cracks an almost-visible smile, takes a puff on her ever-present cigar, then exhales.

"Damn, son, you clean up nicely," she says, smiling. "We've got a while before the limos arrive, so I'll tell you about the call with Greg this morning."

Greg Thomas, our manager who started as a school principal and got us our first school dance, couldn't join us. He had a business meeting this morning. Greg's been the father I lost when my dad turned his back on me. He wouldn't accept a homosexual son. He hadn't thrown me out, but the result was identical. I could pretend to be "normal" and stay, or I could leave. Two and a half years ago, and I've heard nothing since.

"Please!" I say. The guys nod. DC opens her portfolio. She glances at the pad, then begins.

"The three local channels had extended reports on both 6:00 and 11:00 news last night. You guys are gonna be a smash when you get home. Dickie Newsome has gotten a plum assignment by using the hometown card. He's an Atlantan, as well."

"But, DC, he doesn't know us," Sean says; everyone nods.

"You're right. Greg and I think he'll do his best for his career, and won't write anything sensational. Just don't give him any reason."

"Guess we can't flash our titties at him, then?" Clay says, smirking.

Sometimes Sean and Clay act like that other rock music "S & C" duo, Sonny and Cher. They take turns being the clown, while Sonny is always the clown for Cher.

DC frowns, ignoring Clay. She continues, "Ravynn, don't call him Dickie Nuisance. Do your best shows."

"I'm worried," I say. "With Dickie's connection to Ronnie, something awful could come of this."

"We've just gotta make the best of it for now," DC says; that ends the conversation.

Limousine, Press Conference, June 15

We're riding to the Fillmore for the news conference, soundcheck and second concert. Sean, Clay, Wil, and DC have the first limousine. Benji, Todd, and I take the second.

Three years ago, we played other people's music for several hundred kids and chaperones at a school dance. Now, we've released three albums and started our first world tour. Even if it's ten cities, four international, it's our start.

Last night's audience was full capacity for the Fillmore. Of the twenty songs we performed, two weren't ours. We're in the most "open" city in America, and my life's a mess. Here I am, hiding my being a homosexual from Atlanta, Georgia, behind the facade of a British homosexual. I can't maintain relationships for shit, other than this group. I talk about openness and honesty, yet I'm as far from those ideals as Atlanta is from San Francisco. Dickie Newsome's a connection to a past I have no interest in. His presence is a time bomb that could destroy this group. One reference to my homosexual tendencies and Phoenix Rising would vanish faster than yesterday's TV news. With Dickie here, Ronnie must be nearby. They were always close. I don't need this!

This situation shows I'm right. I can't have music, success, and fame, if I have my genuine life. If I can't be openly homosexual in San Francisco, how can I, in Montreal, Rome, or London? I can't allow my selfish desires to destroy what we've built with this group. My personal life must take a far-back seat to the group.

"Todd, what do you think about these hotel rooms?" Benji asks, the enthusiasm highlighting his Cajun accent. I want to hear more of that. Benji's more than a bandmate, he's a bright spot in my world. I can't risk the group by getting close to Benji, as much as *that* might hurt him. We went too far during the birthday trip to New Orleans last fall. Now I'm trying to sneak that genie back into the bottle. I know he's got a thing for me, which is terrifying and amazing at the same time. It's not good for tons of reasons. The group chemistry is phenomenal, but a relationship could spoil it. Then there's *my* history of disasters in relationships. Most of all,

Benji *is* the youngest Phoenix, a total virgin. Too many landmines, not enough certainty.

"It's amazing," Todd says. "I've stayed in many hotels, but none this fancy. I'm still amazed by police lines as we get in and out."

"True dat," Benji says, smiling.

Our route shows us some of the city as we ride along. There's a cable car in the distance, which reminds me of the trolleys that ran in Atlanta. It's not a long ride. We're staying near Mission Street and Nob Hill, upscale areas. Rock royalty treatment. We pass Union Square, which makes Atlanta's Lenox Square appear like a Saturday-afternoon flea market. I wonder if we can shop some before we leave tomorrow.

"This is what we're working for," I say. Todd and Benji smile like we've achieved our desires of being Rock Gods, the next Beatles or Stones. I'm worrying what Dickie Newsome might do. "We're starting our climb, young enough to have a long stay at the top. But this business can be cut-throat."

Benji seems queasy over that.

"Not *real* throat cutting, Ravynn?" he says.

"I've heard stories about what wicked performers do to get ahead. And some low-class companies will do most anything to keep *their* performers on top," I reply, thinking how lucky we are to have Greg and DC, as honest as they are.

"Years ago, one record company's management got caught paying radio stations to play songs from their artists. When stations refused, the company quit sending promotional material to those stations, black-listing them. The label fired the entire management."

Todd grimaces, like he swallowed something awful. "They were fixing the station playlists? That sucks!"

Benji asks, quietly, "That's illegal. Doesn't it ruin the charts?"

I nod, and reply, "Yeah, but it got their artists more coverage and money, until it crashed. Hey, how was your visit with your family, Benji?"

"It was good, shay," Benji says. "But I thought about you a lot."

I want to respond to that, but the limousine stops. The driver opens our doors, and we're at the Fillmore. As he gets out, Benji's hand brushes mine. Sparks ricochet throughout my body.

Across the street are twelve anti-war protesters being held back by four policemen. The protesters are holding posters like "Make Love, Not War," "Is Love Too Great A Price For Peace," and such. The anti-war effort has united groups opposed to the country's involvement in Vietnam. Males who are legally required to register with the Selective Service System once they turn 18. College students whose avoidance of military service relies on maintaining a certain GPA. The mostly black Student Nonviolent Coordinating Committee. And girlfriends of guys who have registered or are already serving. The press refers to them collectively as "Commie sympathizers." Families are divided. Parents, shocked but in favor of involvement. Kids resent being told they must fight an undeclared war with unclear goals. Vietnam's tearing America apart.

As we head into the Fillmore, one protester yells clearly, "Live your authentic life, man!" Yeah, like *he* knows an authentic life. Probably a college student, getting by on daddy's money. Some *authentic* life! I'm doing *without* dad and mom, period. I flash the two-finger peace sign as we enter the Fillmore. Did I join the anti-war movement? The *conflict* in Vietnam, between the Communist North Vietnamese and the South Vietnamese backed by the United States Armed Forces, grows nastier daily, as protests in America swell. We've escaped being pulled into the war because of our age, our beliefs, and good luck. Greg must've pulled strings for us, because 18-year-old guys must register. It's a waste. Hundreds shipped off to war, a shit-ton come home with serious injuries, missing limbs or mental problems, or return inside a flag-draped box.

We have a news conference to attend. Dickie Nuisance—err, Dickie Newsome—is sure to be prominent for me. I remember when Dickie would show up at Ronnie's apartment. Usually as we were about to eat dinner or watch TV. One of those times I answered the door, he got his nickname. I saw him, and said, "Well, if it isn't Dickie *Nuisance*." The name came in a flash, because to me, he *was* one. Now he reminds me of Ronnie. Yet *another* nuisance I don't want.

There are twenty members of the press, representing local and national news. My eyes focus on Dickie. It worries me knowing he'll be with us this entire tour. Too many things can go wrong because of his presence. In Atlanta, all he ever wrote about was strip clubs, hookers, and the Braves during baseball season. How he got this assignment is beyond me. *Why* he's here annoys me. Dickie and Ronnie were drinking buddies. Then Ronnie started getting pissed over my involvement with the group. He lashed out saying I was a *dreamer* about music. Dickie knows too much about me. Enough, perhaps, to ruin Phoenix Rising before this tour can push us to the top.

The stage has a long table with a dozen microphones on it. They want us all to answer questions, so we've got "assigned" seats. DC is in the middle next to me. Sean's on her other side, then Todd, Wil at the end. Next to me is Benji, then Clay on the end. At the last minute, Greg comes dashing in, gasping for breath, like he ran from Atlanta. He must've flown cross-country. I may have zoned out and missed the memo, or it's a surprise. He squeezes in between DC and me, and the interrogation's on.

Greg peers around the room, then the seven of us, and begins, after a painful squeal of feedback through the sound system (*ouch!*). "Gentlemen, I'm Greg Thomas, manager of Phoenix Rising. My assistant manager is Diciembre Cano Delgado. The group are Ravynn St. John, Benji Travers, Clay Brockington, Sean Alexander, Todd Ewing, and Wil. Let me explain my entrance. I was on a cross-country flight minutes before I arrived. That followed a meeting with label representatives. We'll take your questions." A reporter in the front row waves his hand like a schoolkid desperately needing a pass for a bathroom break. Greg points to him.

"Paul Lafitte, New Orleans Times-Picayune. We understand there were issues which prevented a New Orleans appearance. Can you explain, and will there be a future visit?" he asks.

"Mr. Lafitte, we had several issues," Greg says. "We need a specific number of days between each stop. As busy as your venues stay, we couldn't slot in any performances. We're disappointed, but we'll see you next tour."

"Woo-hoo," Benji beams. Everyone else chuckles.

"Richard Newsome, Atlanta Journal and Constitution, special reporter for Rolling Stone. Will you be performing different songs at different shows?" Dickie Newsome gives the appearance of a professional reporter with his question. He doesn't appear to recognize me as his buddy's ex-boyfriend. I stayed out of the way whenever Dickie visited Ronnie. Maybe he never got a good look at me. Now to treat him respectfully, as DC requested.

"Mister Newsome, thanks for asking. We're performing a set of songs covering our first three albums, so it'll be the same songs every show. Some songs are stronger in Europe than here, so we may switch them around," I answer, in my best Ravynn voice. Greg gives me a "thumbs-up," hidden from the reporters by the table.

Other reporters ask fairly tame questions. One guy asks Wil about his keyboards. He's never outgoing *unless* he's talking about keyboards—then he's "Chatty Cathy." Wil shows his nervousness by answering in a single sentence. Then there are questions about whether any of us are married—*really?*—or if we're "involved" with anyone. That one gets Sean and me giving the tag-team answer we love. Sean says, "Well, actually...."

I finish with, "we're all involved in this group project, very hush-hush." The guys laugh as soon as I say "project." DC and Greg join in, as do most of the reporters, including the guy who had asked the question.

The ultimate question goes to Dickie Newsome, of course. I'm worried he's going to bring up my past. Instead he asks, "What do you guys think about Vietnam?"

Had he seen me as we entered? Impossible, he's been sitting in the same seat all day. He might be trying to stir up an anti-war statement to see how that works for us. This war divides the country. Half the country supports it and half thinks it's a waste. Entertainers who pick a side put their careers on the line. I give him the answer in my heart.

"We know what's going on. Our focus is music. We won't comment about the war and protests. Thanks for asking," I say, forcing a smile on my face. Greg gives another thumbs-up.

"Thanks for your time, fellows," Greg says to the reporters, as they gather their materials. Cameramen take snapshots of us at the table, then we go backstage. The press conference ends. I'm shocked none of the reporters, especially Dickie Newsome, have asked anything awkward. Greg and DC escort the reporters out as Davey and his crew set the stage for our show.

"Those guys asked lame-ass questions, didn't they?" Todd asks.

"Well, I was expecting *one*—Dickie Newsome—to follow up on the relationship question, honestly," I say. "Guys like him never accept shit like what Sean and I said. They keep digging. We should be happy they dropped it."

To put the exclamation at the end of my statement, Greg and DC join us and Greg says, "It'll *always* come up. That's red meat for fans and for the reporters trying to get the fans to read *their* reports. You handled it well, but next time it comes up, because it *will*, one of you handles the full answer. I know you bill yourselves as 'brothers from different mothers,' but that won't fly with the international press."

I remember Greg saying that our humorous phrase doesn't translate well into French and Italian, and likely other languages as well. We need to approach the idea differently. The foreign press may translate the label, if we use it, as *homosexual*. We don't need to combat that.

"Right on, Greg," Sean says, smiling at me. "Ravynn's our leader. He should handle it."

"Gee, *thanks a pantload,* brother," I say, thinking *just what I need... gotta worry about keeping a fake accent and painting a false picture of six virginal guys*. C'mon, I'm 20 years old. I'm touring the US and the world, playing up my British persona as a flamboyant homosexual. At the same time, I'm hiding that the real me is *also* homosexual. It's so well hidden that less than a dozen people really know. Seven of them are part of this tour with me. No pressure, right?

"Don't get bent out of shape, he was kidding," DC gets soft on me, virtually unknown in our situation. She's noticed how much like a father Greg is, so she's becoming Mama Bear. DC's been assistant manager since shortly before the release of our second album. Greg met her through the local label offices. When we met her, we were thrilled Greg had an assistant, and terrified. Her first words were, "Okay, *boys*, no drugs or alcohol, or you'll be pulling weeds at my apartment when you're not rehearsing, and possibly even then, got it?" Though I haven't met a drill sergeant, DC *could* play one on TV. "Davey and the crew should be through setting up the stage, so let's get this soundcheck knocked out, okay?"

On that, she's *baaack!*

Soundcheck, concert

Dickie Newsome's standing near the stage. I go to the edge, my nerves already *on edge*, worried what Dickie's presence means now. In full Ravynn mode, I say, "And what brings you back, Mr. Newsome? The concert begins at 8 pm."

"Robin, someone has been missing you and searching for you." Dickie's words suck the breath out of me.

I hop off the stage and indicate we should talk privately, to one side of the stage. Without knowing *what* he has to say, the fewer ears hearing it, the better. He follows me to a corner where we're obscured from the stage, and I turn toward him.

"You're aware my name is Ravynn, not Robin. I'm not sure why you need to talk to me, but I'm listening."

"I met with Ronnie. He wants to see you; *he* still calls you Robin."

"Dickie, I know you and Ronnie grew up together. I *know* you were friends. I get it, you were drinking buddies. That doesn't give you the right to fuck with me. Look, are we here to talk old times, or is there a reason for this?" I ask.

"Really, *Ravynn*?" He almost snarls. "I know you were living with him after you left your parents. I know he had a crappy one-bedroom apartment. Shall I go further? Let me level with you. I have the job of my dreams, reporting on the up-and-coming group, Phoenix Rising, for Rolling Stone. I travel where you guys go, my expenses covered by either Rolling Stone or the Journal and Constitution."

"Yes, Dickie, I know that, and I'm *happy* for you." Damn, I *really* ought to control my sarcasm....

"Well, *Ravynn*, you might not be. I'm gonna get the scoop of a lifetime—either it'll be how this is a group of faggots, or it'll be the story of how fake the lead singer is, from the name and accent to the pretend-heterosexual lifestyle. I might write the story of you and Ronnie reuniting. If you work with me, I'll present a story of a hard-working, creative bunch of guys who are at the top of their game—for *that*, you'll have to keep me happy, and it'll require your attention to many things these next few weeks."

Ouch. This *isn't* how I wanted this to go. "Can you tell me what you want?" I shoot for center, hoping he'll let me off.

"First, an exclusive interview, one-on-one, you and me, soon. I filed the request with your charming DC."

Fuck me now. Either I play nice with this guy *and* Ronnie, or everything comes crashing down. He's holding the cards, half of them I can't see.

"But—meet with Ronnie? You know we ended badly. If I meet with him, what do *you* get out of it? What can I do to make *you* happy?"

"In our town, growing up as *buddies* meant *blood-brother.* This is a part of that. For my requests, we'll keep in touch. I *will* be watching. Double-cross me and the worst stories will begin hitting newsstands across the path of your tour." Dickie strides out.

The soundcheck should be a formality. We test each instrument and microphone to be certain the levels are correct. The sound crew makes adjustments if needed, then we repeat until everyone's happy. The conversation with Dickie sticks in my mind. I need to be cautious, but I'm not paying attention to what's happening. I miss cues in the soundcheck. Finally, Sean stops the guys and stalks over to me.

"What's happening? You never fuck up a soundcheck! You sick?"

"No, Sean, my mind was wandering; I'll concentrate, sorry."

"Okay, that's not like you—you've *always* been focusing on the future, which is now!"

Sean's right, but my world just got totally fucked. Unsure what to do, I find focus to push through. Luckily, the volume levels from last night's show are good. Soundcheck's done.

Greg joins me heading backstage. I'm happy he's sticking around; he couldn't have gotten much about last night's show from Atlanta's news.

This gives me a chance to thank him for believing in us, helping us get where we are.

"I'm glad you could make it for the news conference, but that wasn't the plan, was it?" I say, trying to change the focus. "I hope there's nothing wrong!"

"No, things are good," Greg says, patting my shoulder. "But something must be bothering you. Want to level with me about what's making you forget the words to your own song?" Greg acts more concerned than angry, and I know I need to be more honest with him.

"When I left my parents, I lived with Ronnie. He was four years older, and I thought he loved me. But when Sean and I got the group going, Ronnie got bitter."

"He was jealous you were away from him," Greg added.

"I guess. First, it was drinking, angry words about how the group wouldn't amount to shit. As we got ready for the dance and show, he got worse. He'd drink more, get drunk. A few times I *thought* he'd punch me."

"You should've told someone."

"I thought he'd drop it. Those two nights before the dance, he cursed me to my face, acted like I was trash. Nothing broken, but I got cuts from his fingernails. Then he threw me out, and I dragged myself to the school where Sean and Clay cleaned me up and got me ready. I haven't wanted to think of him since, but now Dickie shows up. It's freaked me out," I say. I'm ashamed to be hanging onto the lie that Ronnie was the person who put those scratches and bruises on me. There's *still* a show to do.

Greg nods, sensing my emotions, and softly says, "Sean and Clay told me a lot that night. Benji has been so protective since he found out. I figured it was bad, but we can handle this. You've got some time. Take it easy, don't stress; concentrate on yourself. Tonight, give the best show you can. Let your manager..." he points at himself, "do what's needed. We'll talk more, okay?"

I nod in agreement as Benji joins us.

"Hey, Greg, who dat?" Benji asks. He recognizes his slip into Cajun, and says, "I mean, what's up, Greg?"

"I hope you're enjoying the tour so far. How do you like the hotel?" Greg asks.

"Woo-hoo, Greg, that is one fine hotel, tell you what! I'm enjoying this. Of course, the music is most important. I'm happy as all get-up to be a part!"

"Good. Guys, finish getting ready; have a great show. I'll be sitting in the audience with label representatives. That's one reason I flew in. We have news involving one stop on this tour. We'll talk after the show."

"Thanks, Greg," I say.

We finish dressing, flying as high as our Phoenix; we're above the clouds. Time to put on another smash show—even *if* my demons, and those twenty thousand butterflies in my stomach, are trying to derail it.

The Fillmore's packed again. From backstage, I spot Greg. Obviously, the guys around him are from the label.... Wait, right in the middle is Dickie Newsome.

There's that knot in my stomach again. Why is he with Greg? He should be with the press. *Not* our manager and label representatives. Gah. I glue a smile on my face. We wait for the introductions, then head on stage.

As the guys get their guitars hooked up, I prance around like usual, blowing kisses to the audience. After Dickie's comments today, I'm playing to the women. No sense in giving him an easy target. I watch the label executives, Greg, and Dickie Newsome, for any trouble. Greg gives me two thumbs up, everything's okay. Things start off with a few sour notes—not a good omen, but nothing we can't recover from. Once we get past that, tonight's show seems looser, "top of the charts" quality. It's a tough call. Is it because we know the label guys are watching? Or did we get the jitters out last night? We're performing as great as we planned.

The audience is more at ease, as well. We get cat calls from women and men. A woman in the audience, between songs, screams out her desire to be the mother of Benji's babies. Thankfully, we're in low red spots, so the temptress can't see him blushing. It's all I can do to keep from wrapping my arms around him protectively. I turn to him and say, "By *my* count, that makes six potential wives. Can we keep you through this tour, at least?"

Benji lets his guitar speak for him. He strikes a strong blues-slide guitar chord. Everyone applauds, then Benji blows a kiss. He's got his head in the right spot. Benji's the rhythm guitarist for the hottest band in the world. He's in no hurry to do anything but play. Gotta love him (apparently, *many* do).

Tonight's performance of *A Day in the Life* has the label representatives getting into the show. They peer around, trying to locate the hidden orchestra, or where the speakers are to reproduce the sound accurately. As we build into the first orchestral crescendo, I can see Greg talking to one of the label guys. More likely, he's shouting. He's also pointing to Wil. I know what he's saying.

As we finish the song, the label guys stand with a third guy. A man I'd recognize anywhere, mostly from pictures of Beatles' recording sessions. He's been dubbed "The Fifth Beatle" from helping the group achieve masterpieces like *A Day in the Life*. George Martin is a fucking genius, and he's impressed with *our* performance of a song he helped craft. George Martin. Liking *our* performance.

We leave the stage before the encores. I know the guys are jacked. I glance at Sean and Wil and say, "George Martin saw us." The expressions on their faces register understandable disbelief. George Martin is a legend. He's the man who helped the Beatles become the greatest group in the history of recorded music.

"No way," Wil says, shaking his head; his hair flies everywhere.

"Oh my God, really?" Sean asks, peering *over* his granny-glasses. I know he's unsure.

"When we go back, check the guys sitting with Greg. I swear to God, one of them is George Martin. I'd know him anywhere," I say.

I immediately see the surprise hit the guys' faces. As the fans begin to call our names, they peel away one by one. We head back onto the stage for our encore.

As the final encore ends, we say "Goodnight, San Francisco!" as we head offstage. Tonight has been a daze, because of the presence of George-freaking-Martin.

"You guys looked great," DC says, as she dispenses water and towels. "I think you were stronger tonight."

I nod; I've got a mouthful of water, a towel swabbing my head.

Sean picks up the conversation. "DC, it was *awesome*! We *were* stronger, and it's good, because..."

I finish with the towel and pick up the conversation, "George Martin was in the audience!" DC shrugs, like 'George *who*?' "Right. You're not a big Beatles fan," I quickly continue. "He's the guy who arranges most of their music."

DC's eyes grow wide; she says, slowly, "The Fifth Beatle was here tonight, watching my boys perform?"

The evening seems destined to keep going. No sooner have the magical words "the Fifth Beatle" been uttered than Greg strides backstage with George Martin and the two EMI-Capitol representatives.

"DC, guys, meet George Martin from EMI-London, and Tony Southern and Robert James of EMI-Capitol here in the US. Gentlemen, these are the members of Phoenix Rising. DC, Diciembre Delgado, is my assistant," Greg says.

After Greg introduces us, we sit down in a backstage office area. It blows me away to sit here with George-Freaking-Martin, the Fifth *Beatle*. I'm at a loss for words, which allows the others to begin the conversation.

Sean, sometimes diplomatic, and frequent ass-kisser, begins. "Thanks for coming! Thanks for giving us this opportunity!" How's that for ass-kissing?

Before anyone else says anything, Benji adds in, "Whoo-wee, this is one of those nights my mam-maw told me 'bout when I was still a wee baby." That's translated as closely as possible from his Cajun; he was racing full speed. I must intervene.

"Sorry, gentlemen," I say in my best Ravynn voice. "Benji, our young Phoenix from the bayou, gets excited and his accent races 90 miles an hour in a 15 mile-per-hour zone. He's right, though, this is a special night. We appreciate you being here, and we hope we've made you proud."

Benji smiles and, in a slower pace, says, "What he said. That's what I meant, sorry."

George Martin looks at Benji, smiles, and in his refined English says, "Young man, you've nothing for which to apologize. It's a genuine pleasure to meet the lads who replaced our Beatles at the top," then, as he turns to look directly at me, "that is a *most* impressive attempt at a British accent! Not quite spot-on, but certainly close. It's very good." Try as I might not to, I blush full-on.

"No disrespect meant, sir," I stammer out.

"Of course we Brits are aware of how much you 'Yanks' want to be as upper-crust as we," he smiles.

Greg looks inquisitively at the three music company men. There's some question being asked, and answered, without words spoken.

After a moment, Greg turns to me and says, "Barring any problems, George Martin will arrange a recording session for you at Abbey Road Studios while you're in London. How does that sound?"

"*How does that sound*? Abbey Road, *the* place for a rock group to record. *Sgt. Pepper's,* and virtually everything the Beatles recorded, originated there. To record there with George Martin is like a sign saying we've made it." Or a neon one, flashing *Phoenix Rising has made it to rock royalty*, but I'm *not* saying that.

Sean looks at me, Wil looks at Todd, Clay looks at Benji, and, as if we became Cajun, we say, "Whoo-wee! Yes!" We're wearing two hours of sweat from our performance. We shake hands with the music men, then head to our dressing rooms to clean and change into less-sweaty clothes.

We're excited. Clay, who normally is so reserved you wonder if he has a voice, is going crazy. "Abbey Road? Dream come true! Wonder if I'll get to play the Beatle bass? So cool!"

"True dat, Clay, it's gonna be fine as gumbo, smooth as café au lait," Benji adds, making me hungry *and* thirsty.

Sean, carrying his drumsticks, is tapping a beat along the walls as we head towards our dressing rooms. Sounds like he's singing something, possibly he's forming a tune.

"This is perfect. Wil, George Martin loved your keyboards on *A Day In The Life*. I saw him talking to Greg during the performance, and I'm sure he was asking how you recreated the orchestral sounds the Beatles had," I say. Wil is happy, not sure how to process it. His mouth is agape, and he nods. We're ecstatic, walking about three feet off the floor.

We have individual dressing rooms, but we're close enough we can talk without having to shout. The realization of what just happened hits as we change. First, Todd, whose voice carries amazement. "Holy shit, Abbey Road with George Martin! Fantastic!"

Benji adds in, "Whooo-wee, a Cajun boy like me hittin' it big in the best recording studio evah!" I can see the smile, even if he isn't in my dressing room.

"Two years from playing gigs around Atlanta to recording with George Martin in Abbey Road in London? Wow," Clay sums it up.

Wil whoops with glee, then says, "Hot damn, *this* is too good to be true."

"We started Phoenix Rising to become the best. We're almost there.... We gotta take care of this tour *and* knock it out of the park at that recording session," Sean sums it up. With the talking, wardrobe changing takes nearly half an hour.

I finish changing as Greg knocks at the door and enters. "I hope it's okay for me to walk in like this; I should have asked first," he says.

"You're fine. I'm gobsmacked at the deal we just got. How did you arrange it?"

Greg smiles and says, "That was easy. As the show progressed, Mr. Martin told Tony and Robert he wanted to—as he put it—'poach' their talent for a session or two." I'm beyond amazed. He *knows* we want this.

I find my voice. "That's great, Greg, thanks! You, DC, Davey and the crew are fantastic."

Greg smiles. "That's good, Ravynn; you know we're thrilled with what you've accomplished. George Martin is right, you have a huge future. I'm proud of you. Even Benji is handling this well; I hope he's not getting overwhelmed."

"He gets excited, but he calms down. You can tell when he's getting overwhelmed. His Cajun comes through, and you'll need a Cajun-to-American Dictionary."

Greg wraps his arms around me, like Sean's father has done for Sean many times.

"You're welcome. It's going to be fine, son," Greg whispers. He smiles, then adds, "Finish dressing. Tomorrow you can shop, then we'll head for Los Angeles."

Greg Thomas is more of a father to me than my real father ever was. My world is crazy mixed-up lately. I know Greg will keep things on track and make sure we guys are doing okay.

The return to the hotel is serene. Greg is watching me with a look between concern and pride. I've seen it on Sean's father's face when he looks at Sean. That gives me a warm sensation.

Hotel

Entering our suite, it's Grand Central Station at rush hour. No screaming fans or people stalking us. Three maintenance men are in and out of Benji's room. Two housekeepers watch, nervously. A front-desk employee fidgets with her badge, obviously perturbed. The common room is full. Corporate badge lady glances from the door into Benji's bedroom toward us, the grimace on her face unchanging.

"What kinda fool won't call maintenance at the first sign of a stuck window?" The guy walking out of Benji's bedroom spits out.

"What happened?" I ask the maintenance man nearest me.

"Housekeeper was cleanin' the bathroom, using bleach. Didn't dilute it first, spilled a bunch on the floor, panicked." That explains the strong acrid fumes from Benji's bedroom.

The head maintenance man says, "Typical housecleaning, fucking it up for maintenance." He sees us and tries to bring some professionalism. "You guys stayin' here? The one in that room isn't gonna want to sleep there tonight. Window's gettin' dismantled now; it'll be cold."

"I can sleep on a chair in here," Benji volunteers, looking at the seating in the common area.

"That's *not* acceptable!" I immediately protest.

Greg and the management representatives meet in the hallway. The badge lady is doing heavy-duty schmoozing. A moment later, Greg strolls back over. "The hotel is sending up a rollaway bed."

"Where will it go, Greg? How about with you; you've got a room to yourself? Otherwise, there's Sean's bedroom or the other suite."

Sean, hearing *his* name, shakes his head vigorously. "My room's too small for another bed."

Greg nods. "He's right. The other suite's too much moving. Your bedroom is larger than Sean's. Benji will bunk with you. The housekeepers are bringing up a rollaway now."

Fuck me running. Sean knows I sleep nude. And likely the *other* guys know too, thanks to his loose lips. I love Sean like a brother, but don't give him secrets. He can't keep them. In the past, sleeping in a pair of shorts hasn't given me good sleep. On this tour, it's *essential* that I get decent rest. This is gonna be my biggest nightmare.

"Shay, I'll sleep on a chair in the big room," Benji tells me for the third time since we've walked into my—*our*—bedroom.

"It doesn't bother me, Benji," I lie—it bothers me. He's had a crush on me for years, and I'm fighting my *own* attraction. In New Orleans, we got carried away. He wanted his first birthday hug and kiss to be from me. He started it, but I couldn't let it go. I kissed him possessively. The simple kiss became soul-searing-nasty in a heartbeat. "We'll make it work. It's just one night." As I say that, his smile dims a bit. To hurt him isn't my plan, but I don't want to give him ideas.

He's too *pure*. He told me he's never been sexual. I don't deserve him, and he's done nothing but worship me. If I sleep tonight, it'll be a miracle.

While Benji's in the bathroom, I try to get under covers without showing myself. I *had* to wear shoes which won't release my feet. I'm only partially undressed when the bathroom door opens and Benji strides out.

Benji stands beside the rollaway, wearing a nightshirt that *barely* covers his torso. He's right out of *The Night Before Christmas.*

As he pads across the floor, I get my shoes and socks off. When he turns away briefly, I slide my pants off and slip under the covers in my underwear. Somehow, I'm in bed without exposing myself.

Benji lopes over to me, bends down and kisses my forehead. He sees my shoes and pants lying on the floor and cranes around, trying to see my other clothing. He turns back to his bed and slides under the covers without exposing *his* parts. I know, he catches me looking.

"Y'know, if you wanna sleep nekkid, you don't have to hide. I can be as private about my body as you are." He smirks. "'Night, shay."

My mouth goes dry. I'm fighting a losing battle, trying not to fall for someone I've been falling for forever. I can't let this happen. Success is too close.

As I slide my underwear off beneath the sheets, I reach and turn off the bedside lamp. "G'night, Benji!" Damn, this bed's lumpy and uncomfortable. Did I get the rollaway by mistake? I hadn't noticed the buzzing from the neon sign outside the window before.... Crap. How can I sleep?

"I know you're worried 'bout us together. You're afraid folks'll hate the group if they see us that way." I guess Benji wants to talk. Straight to the point. He's always direct about his emotions.

"Yeah.... We went a little too far in New Orleans, and I don't want to fuck things up. I mean, just look at what happened between me and Ronnie...." Do I *really* want to go into that again?

"No, Rave. I don't need to look at the past. I see you better'n you see yourself." I can tell, even in the dark, that Benji's turned, looking at me. Part of my heart is happy dancing. The rest of me screams, *it's built on a pack of lies.*

"You've never been with anyone, Benji. Relationships don't always stay wonderful."

"Yeah, you had that bad 'un. That doesn't make *you* the problem. From the day we met, I saw a guy who needed to be loved for his good heart. *That* hasn't changed." He's so pure, strong in his belief, it *really* makes me squirm. He's building me up as a saint, but I'm damaged, closer to a sinner.

"I'm living a lie. I tell everyone to live open and honest. Here I am, doing the opposite of that in every way."

"Your heart's pure. I know there's more." He's close to some truth. Ronnie and I played house for a year, but he hated my being with the group. Ronnie and I were both wrong. When Ronnie told me we should split up, I tried to fight him and wound up hurting myself. Then I made up shit, because I couldn't stand being abandoned.

Benji's so quiet, I think he's fallen asleep. But he's not ready to sleep.

"Before we went to N'Awlins for my birthday, I wanted to get closer to you...." His voice is nearly a whisper, but I can hear the reverence. "Remember the cake?" How could I forget? He blew out 18 candles, one for each year and one to grow on, with less than a full breath.

"I remember."

If he was *almost* whispering before, now he's really whispering. It's the most vulnerable I've ever heard. "I wished for you."

Union Square, June 16

In Union Square, near the Palace, Sean, Clay, Wil, Todd, and Benji are checking out shops. Above me, the Dewey Memorial stands, Nike watching over the square. It seems like Nike is smiling on us. Even with the messes in my head, I *still* think the group has won.

That I could wake this morning with Benji was nice. His smile being the first thing I saw was incredible. And hearing his voice, the best wake-up call ever... I can't go there.

Benji's confession piles on another problem. To be this close to him for the whole tour, while fighting the attraction to him—it'll tear me up. I want what I can't have. For the sake of the group, I *know* I can't have Benji.

Up ahead, the guys are hunting souvenirs to give family. I've bought myself a keyring with a cable car on it. My mind plays a loop. George Martin offering us a recording session in Abbey Road Studios. Dickie Newsome calling me "Robin," saying someone's looking for me. Benji saying "I wished for you." Constantly repeating. One side pulls me forward, the other, back.

Sean strides up to me, Clay just behind. "So, which of you gave it up?" Sean asks, a gleam in his eyes.

"You won't believe it, but all we did was talk and sleep," I say.

"You're right, I *don't*," Sean says, then shrugs, moving on to a new topic. "We found something. You've gotta see it."

Sean grabs my left hand, Clay grabs my right.

"What's the deal, guys?"

"You gotta see this!" Clay's so excited, he's rattling off the words with few pauses. It *must* be good. Clay is quiet unless he's got a guitar in his hands.

I look ahead and see Wil, Todd, and Benji, sitting together. Wait—these guys, sitting still? Who glued them in place? I *know* my guys. They don't simply *sit*.

We join Benji, Todd, and Wil. Everyone watches as Wil tells me, "We're getting a caricature of the group, the Golden Gate in the background. Your tattoo has to show, so get that shirt off!"

I follow orders well, so in less time than it takes to say, "Caricature in Union Square," I'm shirtless, the guys surround me. Benji's close enough I'm wondering *what* might come up. The artist, who looks familiar, introduces himself as Tobey Jones as he sketches. He's swift. In less than thirty minutes, he presents our caricature, with my tattoo of the Phoenix Rising and the Golden Gate. *This* will be a keepsake for us. I get a card from Tobey, and then I realize. While we were in New Orleans, Benji and I had gotten a caricature by a guy from San Francisco.

"You're amazing! You did a caricature of Benji and me in New Orleans in early November," I tell Tobey.

"I *thought* I recognized you, but I didn't know you were part of Phoenix Rising," Tobey says to Benji and me. "I saw you at the Fillmore. You rock!" We shake hands and autograph a flyer for Tobey.

I pull my shirt on as we take the treasure Tobey created and turn toward the Dewey Memorial. I'm thinking about using this caricature on our next album. This is the start of our flight to worldwide stardom. By the time we return home to Atlanta, we'll have tons of memories. San Francisco to Atlanta, and the World.... Our next album title, I'm sure. The caricature reflects my world. As distorted as the picture is, the Golden Gate melting into our Phoenix Rising logo, our appearances distorted in the caricature, that's how distorted my life is. I'm a rising star in a city filled with people openly expressing themselves, but I'm as bottled up as Jeannie in *I Dream of Jeannie* on TV. The difference is Jeannie gets to come out of her bottle, while I'm *still* bottled up.

As we approach the Dewey Memorial, Benji looks toward Geary Street and says, "I see where Greg and DC will meet us."

Greg's only directions on where to meet him and DC had been "hang around Union Square." I guess he figured we'd know where to meet when we see it. We follow Benji's glance and see two tour buses bearing the *Phoenix Rising* logo. Way to go, Greg, we're *not* leaving town unnoticed in those. Between my long hair and those buses, a crowd of 15 to 20 people gather.

We head to the street. Several people ask us for autographs. Each of us sign and pretty soon the crowd breaks up. We continue to the buses.

"Wow, you boys must be famous rock stars or something!" DC teases, standing next to the front bus.

Buses

"These buses will be our ground transportation. Both have identical interiors; 6 mini-rooms, plus a bathroom. If needed, they could be like hotel rooms," Greg says.

"Stash anything you want down there, guys," DC says, pointing to large storage compartments under the buses. "Then load up on whichever bus you like. Greg and I will switch buses throughout the ride."

At that moment, a medium-sized van pulls up behind the buses. Davey gets out, followed by a crew member named Tony DiMarco. My curiosity gets the better of me, so I pipe up, "But how do we keep in touch and coordinate everything?"

"We'll talk on a CB radio," Greg smiles, reaching beside the steering wheel and holding up what appears to be a microphone on a coiled cable. "So who's with me on Phoenix 1? Climb aboard."

• • • • • • • • • • •

Los Angeles, California

June 16 - 19, 1968

Buses into Los Angeles

I wake, startled. I don't recognize where I am. There's no light anywhere. It must've been a nightmare; I'm sweating like I've been running in a desert. It seemed real. Ronnie and Dickie chasing me to make me return to Ronnie. Parts of the stories I've told combined with fragments of what's happening into one gigantic mind-fuck. I must've screamed, because the compartment door opens, and Benji peers in.

"You alright, shay?" Benji asks me. Before I answer, Todd and DC appear in the opening.

"Rave, you okay?" Todd asks. *Everyone's* freaking out.

"I'm okay. Just a nightmare. Where are we?" I ask, trying to change the subject.

DC takes charge. "We've stopped, another refill, and I'm *not* sure you're okay. We need to talk about this, don't we?"

Damn. We're on tour, and the fear of being abandoned—dropped like a shitty diaper—still owns my mind. I'm putting up a brave face, refusing to talk about it, and it keeps returning. Fuck. I wanna be done with Ronnie, concentrate on this tour and my guys, but my mind says I'm *still* Ronnie's bitch.

Nothing's gotten rid of that sentiment; nothing *can*, because going back to Ronnie isn't just being his bitch. It's also the end of Ravynn St. John; I'd cease being the lead singer for this group *because* Ronnie won't let me be that *and* his boyfriend. That's not happening. I shake my head, and she ushers Benji and Todd away.

Greg joins DC and me, and before either of them can say anything, I plant my feet defiantly, cross my arms, and say, "I don't need to talk, I had a bad dream. If I have to talk to someone every time I have a bad dream, you'll be listening to a lot of nonsense."

I turn to retreat into my compartment, but I'm trapped here already by DC and Greg. My turning away works, because there's a click behind me. I twist to see I'm alone. At least I can catch my breath and compose myself before anything else.

There's a light tap at the door; I open it. Benji's there, looking at me like I'm his hero. "Come on in."

He walks in, gives me the slightest hug, then looks at me like he's worried he broke me. This hug is so gentle that it startles me. Since his birthday, I've known that, in *his* family, hugging is natural. His mother is Queen of Bear-hugs. Because Benji has a crush on me, every touch and every word from him are special, though I know I can't let it grow.

"I'm okay; thanks for the hug. I needed that," I say.

"We love you like our brother, okay? Without your lead, we're another wanna-be band. We need all of you, your swagger, your voice, for us to succeed. You're hurting, shay; Sean and I know that what happened is eating you. You gotta let it go."

This not-yet 18-year-old is comforting me *and* picking my brains.... If I tell him my story, it might help, but I'm embarrassed. Can I do that to this innocent guy—what if I give him most of it and he decides he's not interested in me anymore? For avoiding a relationship, it would be good, but I'm so invested in Benji that if he pulled away, it would devastate me.

Benji looks like he's reading my thoughts. "Don't worry about telling me anything. Remember, I lived in Louisiana before we moved to Atlanta. What happens in the bayous doesn't get talked about in the daylight. Tell me *your* truth."

Benji looks at me, and I take a moment to compose myself and decide *what* to tell him; I can give him the fairy tale I created that New Year's Eve, or bits of that story with bits of the truth, or I can tell him the truth—and watch him leave the group as soon as we get to Los Angeles. The full truth's out. If I tell him some truth with some of the story, I have to remember *which* truths I've told him, so I think I'll just stick with the fairytale; less chance of fucking up.

I begin the story of New Year's Eve, 1965. Such a fucked-up year. My parents made me choose—live a lie with them, or leave if I insisted on being homosexual.

"After leaving my parents, I lived with Ronnie. Things started good, but as I focused on the group, he got mean," I say, not wanting to go any further.

Benji looks at me, a sad smile in his eyes. "Go ahead."

"The night before New Year's Eve, he knocked me out. When I came to, it was mid-day New Year's Eve. He attacked me again, tied me to a chair before I knew what he was doing. Shredded my clothes, gagged me, kept going until I passed out." I'm sick telling this, but the house of cards my character's built on depends on *everyone* believing the same shit. The truth was Ronnie told me we should quit being a couple and sent me to find my happiness. I tried to attack him, because being sent away made me feel worthless; that's a pain deeper than any physical abuse. If I could be Ravynn *without* this lie, I'd come clean to everyone... but that won't happen.

Benji nods, urging me to continue.

"I awoke outside Ronnie's house and started walking toward the one thing left in my life that mattered—our first concert. Clay and Sean cleaned me up; makeup covered the bruises and cuts, and a brand-new Ravynn was born."

My throat's getting tight, my eyes are watery.

I look at Benji, certain he *knows* I've told a lie. What I see is astonishment; more than admiration pours through.

Benji hugs me gently, kissing the top of my head. "That's bad, but you lived through it for a purpose, making folks happy with music. You aren't bad. Your ex is. Your fault is that you're re-living the experience. I'm no shrink, but I know that."

I smile. It's weak to begin with, but Benji's got a way of making me happier. Then he continues....

"I'm gonna talk with Greg, if it's *okay*. He can help you work through it. We need you complete, shay, and that includes a head free of what happened." There it is. I should be angry he's running interference for Greg... wait, let me be sure.

"Benji, did Greg or DC ask you to talk to me? Please, tell me the truth."

"They don't know I'm here."

Scratch anger. I'm amazed. He's the wisest Phoenix; he's taken this on his own. But talking to Greg or DC, not good. Since my story about Ronnie is mostly fabrication, the less discussion, the better—and the less likely I'll fuck it up talking about it.

"Benji, I've got reasons, but you, Sean, and I can handle it best. Tell Greg and DC that I had a nightmare about my ex. I'll apologize soon. Leave it at that."

He hugs me tightly but tenderly, kisses my cheek, then pulls away. That's a present for me—birthday, Christmas, everything. I wait a few minutes to let Benji talk to Greg and DC, then join them in the seating area. DC pats my shoulder, almost motherly, then returns to the other bus.

Shortly, we're on the road to Los Angeles again. Everyone's mostly quiet; things are tense.

After about an hour, Benji says he's going to get a little sleep before we get to LA. I hug him lightly. This falls in the best-friend category, even *if* my cock disagrees. After Benji's compartment door closes, Sean looks at me with a smirk.

"Y'know he's falling in love with you, right?" Sean asks, more of a statement than a question. Greg's grinning. I'm *sure* I'm facing their version of "The Dating Game" with me and Benji as the "bachelorette" and "bachelor number 1."

"Is this the new pastime? Find Ravynn a boyfriend?" I tease. I'm grinning because Benji is the cutest guy I've *ever* met, but I'm not ready for those waters; with the problems pulling me in different ways, starting a romance is impossible.

"You could do worse. You'll never have the problems with Benji you had with that other one," Sean says.

"I agree. One glance at the way Benji looks at Ravynn tells you that, but let's stick with the current situation. You guys are dynamic. Don't change anything. Let's get to LA and go from there. Everything will fall into place."

While Greg's talking, I get behind him and childishly, without a sound, make fun of Sean. Greg senses it, however—he's as good at this Dad stuff as everything. He turns around, catching me during my mocking, and holds a finger up, pointed at my nose.

"Don't make fun of him, because *one day* he'll be the guy helping keep your shit together on the happiest day of your life. We've got another ninety minutes before we get to LA; do you want to grab some sleep like Benji?" Greg asks.

Sean opts for sleep. I decide to put my demons on paper. I can use the writing for a song, or kindling for a fireplace. From how my parents pushed me out and last talked to me after I told them I was homosexual on my seventeenth birthday in January 1965, I write my story.

Greg sits nearby, ready to fight off any demons. We struck paydirt when we met Principal Greg Thomas. He gave us our first chance to perform, then helped us find other gigs. As our popularity grew, he became our manager, sounding board, *and* surrogate father. He rejected none of our ideas, and once we had a recording contract, he fought for us to have our records presented the way we wanted, as if we were the top group for Capitol Records. After our second album, *Phoenix Rising*, took the worldwide number 1 position from *Sgt. Pepper's Lonely Hearts Club Band* for two weeks, we *were* Capitol's top act, and got this tour. Without him, we'd still be working small clubs.

After writing my demons and talking earlier, maybe I can sleep. I yawn at that thought. First, I re-read what I wrote. I've titled it "Ravynn's Lament."

It'll never get recorded or played, but it's decent for getting the demons out of my head.

"Cast aside by those who gave me life.
Dammit! I am worth being loved!
Thrown out by the boy I thought I loved.
Dammit! I deserve a love that's true.
Hiding the true me behind a flashy curtain.
Dammit! Being who I am shouldn't be so hard.
Surrounded by loving friends as a family.
Dammit! The world is so fucked up, hating differences!"

As I read the words, I can almost hear Sean's drums pounding a staccato beat, Wil's keyboards playing a clashing melody, and Clay's bass guitar forming a march tempo. Meanwhile, Todd and Benji's guitars duel, with shrieks and wails, signifying the state of my mind. It sums up my situation, from my parents' and Ronnie's rejections through hiding who I am while trying to be successful and happy someday.

"Hit the sack," Greg tells me, squeezing my collarbone lightly. I pad to my bed; my head barely hits the pillow before I'm out. Blissfully, this time is all sleep.

Troubadour, June 16

I awaken as the bus stops. No nightmares, no bad dreams. Maybe writing those thoughts down was good. At least I got some sleep without my demons chasing me. If I can get through several days without the demons—and Benji—chasing me, *that* would be an improvement. I'm dreading the inevitable moment when Greg or DC tells me that an exclusive interview has been arranged with Dickie and me; I've *got* to figure out what to do about Dickie's threats so he doesn't kill Phoenix Rising or our dreams.

I raise the window shade to a wonderful sight. We're in Los Angeles, in front of the Troubadour.

The Troub, as it's called, is a hot-spot for showcasing talent. In 1965, the Byrds first performed their version of Bob Dylan's "Mr. Tambourine Man," a year after Dylan's appearance. Comedians like Richard Pryor and Lenny Bruce have also performed here—Lenny Bruce showcased his material in 1957 and was arrested for obscenity. The club's unbooked tonight.

It's amazing; *we're* going to be added to a list including those legends! Meanwhile, I'm disappointed to discover the capacity is 500 people.

Have I gotten that excited by enormous crowds already?

These shows'll be more intimate. That's better, though it puts pressure on me to flirt with more women to appear heterosexual. We can interact with the fans. The stage is a flat space at one end of the room. With no differentiation between the stage and the audience, I can get into the audience if the house isn't crowded.

Greg approaches me after talking with the house manager.

"They're allotting two reporters per show, a good thing from our standpoint. Dickie Newsome will cover both, since he represents both Rolling Stone and the Atlanta papers. Also, the manager's offering us two shows a day, 5:00 pm and 8:00 pm. It's your decision, but we need to decide now."

Greg could've spared me the mention of Dickie, which reminds me of the whole meet with Ronnie and do Dickie an as-yet-unknown favor.

I force my thoughts away from the things I can't control back to the one thing I can: the show.

I'd love doing a second show both nights, but that's a lot of energy. I don't just sing—I'm in motion, strutting and dancing, so in one show I get as wiped out as if I'd done six hours of physical work; there's no way I can regenerate that much energy quickly. It won't present us in the best light to do a second show each night.

"Works for me. I'm behind my keyboards, anyway," Wil says.

"It's a great idea, but Ravynn, Todd, Benji, Sean, and I do an awful lot of moving around on the stage, and that would wear us out," Clay says, looking thoughtful. "Can we stick with the planned two shows?"

Wil pipes up first. "It would be kinda rough for me to drag my keyboards around, you know," to which Sean and Benji chuckle. "Still, a second show each night *would* give us more audience exposure," he continues.

"It doesn't bother me to do all the moving around onstage. It's not like I'm rearranging a house full of furniture," Todd says. Obviously there are two of my guys in favor of the idea.

I'm getting ready to make some comment that I haven't figured out yet, trying to avoid having an all-out war within the band on only our second tour stop, when Sean and Benji actually stare them down.

"Look, we gotta do what's best for everyone, and I think that means we stick with the original idea," Wil says, after a moment of thought. Todd nods, and the urge to fight slinks away; battle within the band doesn't happen.

"If that's what you guys want, I'll let them know," Greg says.

Greg goes back to the house manager for a few moments. They talk, Greg shakes the man's hand, and returns to us. The manager waves, we wave back.

Less than an hour later, we walk out of the Troubadour and board Phoenix 1 for the ride to the Ambassador Hotel.

On board, Benji and Sean are waiting, ready to go. Greg grabs the CB and asks DC to join us on Phoenix 1. I sit with Sean and Benji; Benji hugs me like I'm his prize teddy bear, while Sean looks on clumsily, like a leftover. Benji's hugs are like home, as always. That makes my mind think of relationships, and I can't go there; I'm a mess. It's nice to be loved, but I know my luck with relationships will cut anything between Benji and me short.

DC steps aboard and takes a seat with Greg. Once she's seated, Davey steers the bus towards the Ambassador.

"Look, Benji slipped and told DC and me that you've been having nightmares," Greg says, taking the bull by the horns. "We want to be sure you're okay. You need an outlet, so if you can talk with Benji, that's good, but we're available, okay?"

"Yeah, we talked a bit."

"Well, we're glad you can talk to Benji; we want you to be comfortable. No worries. You had a nasty breakup."

"I agree," DC says.

"You're still a victim of that. We won't judge, and we'll be here for you. You're the son I never had. We'll support you in any way we can, as managers or stand-in parents," Greg finishes, causing my eyes to get damp and sting, my vision to blur; shit, *almost* bringing me to tears.

I nod again.

Greg and DC's support is great, but... it's based on lies, so I can't rely on that.

I've gotta figure out how to let *everyone* know more truth without giving up the whole fucked-up mess. If I can, I might save Phoenix Rising, and *maybe* keep Benji as a friend. But finding the easiest part of the mess to unravel is like finding one black speck of sand on a mile-wide beach at low tide. I've got some serious thinking ahead.

The way Greg and DC offer me support blows me away; I'm totally unworthy because of the deceptions they unknowingly accept. If they knew the full story, or the comments Dickie made before the soundcheck, they'd be done with me for good. Given my record of being honest, then losing anyone I care about, it's not encouraging me to open up now.

Still, I have to figure out something, because it's gonna become obvious to them and the guys that things are different. After Dickie's comments before soundcheck, I'm going to be more flirtatious with women than with men. That's gonna put a definite spin on the dynamics with the audience.

"Ravynn, any time you want to talk, my door is open, okay?" Greg asks, bracing himself for rejection.

"DC, Greg, thanks for everything. I love you guys."

Better quit now, or I'm gonna be blubbering like a *real* baby. Not pretty. For the moment, the squadrons of mad butterfly-bombers in my gut have landed, and the bus has stopped rolling. As the door opens and flashbulbs pop outside, Greg turns to me.

"Oh, this came for you earlier," he says, handing me a sealed envelope from Rolling Stone.

Ambassador, June 17

The alarm clock awakens me. The letter, sitting beside it, mocks me—this is Dickie's promised request for an interview, I'm certain.

Rather than dwell on it, I open and read it. The discussion with Dickie a few days before was clear—this is the official request for a one-on-one interview. It's basically a demand: if I don't agree, Dickie starts his "poison pen" stories about us. If I agree but get too cautious, it could *still* blow up in my face. Shit.

As I read the letter, there's some slight relief; Dickie's requested an hour and a half, Tuesday, June 18. He's given a range of topics that he wants to discuss, and asks for approval of them. How we met, how we create our songs, what our private lives are like, who our inspirations are, our personal backgrounds, our goals and dreams. Well, *most* of those I can speak to, but I'm not touching my *personal* background, except in the vaguest way. *Why does he want just me?* I put the letter, folded again, aside.

After spending most of two days inside the buses, then dealing with Dickie's letter, a shower is top priority. As I do exactly that, I consider how to deal with everything. I've barely finished drying when there's a knock at my door. I wrap the towel around my waist, open the door, and see Clay, standing nervously.

"Come in, Clay."

Clay paces the room, looking mostly at the floor, his lips pursed like he's afraid he'll spill state secrets if he opens his mouth. He paces like he's measuring the room's size.

"Clay, you're wearing a rut in the carpet. Why don't you sit and tell me what's bothering you?" Getting him stationary might move us closer to what's going on. After all, we have a show tonight.

Clay sits; for thirty seconds he gives me the fish out of water look with his mouth opening, forming an 'o' for a while, then closing, and repeating the process. I look at him and smile, waiting for him to start. He runs his hands through his medium-length dirty-blond hair, then looks into my eyes and drops his bombshell.

"I should've known this would happen," he begins. "We've been together for nearly three years, and I've spent every day with the group. We're a big family, right?"

"Yeah, we are, but what's that got to do with anything?" I've got a hunch, but I'm not gonna say anything, in case I'm wrong.

"Is it a bad thing to fall in love with a member of your family?"

There it is.

"Do you mean your biological family, Clay?"

He flat-out giggles. "No, not my biological family—that's just mom or my brother, and no way, man. It's one of the guys, and I'm not sure you'll approve, or if it can happen. That's why I'm asking you."

"Look, I'm the worst one to ask. My life is such a fucked-up mess right now. You need to keep this low-key, because the slightest deviation could ruin our chances—but be happy; does your guy know about your interest?"

Clay looks down at the carpet, a frown clouding his chestnut brown eyes. He gives the slightest shake of his head.

"I don't know if I can tell him, Ravynn, but when I fall asleep, all I think about is how my bass guitar and his drumbeats are the backbone of our sound. If he's not into me, then this could destroy our music and career. I don't want that to happen!"

So Sean has a wanna-be lover. I need to make sure Sean's okay with this. Mostly, I need to get Clay to slow down, for the group's sake and for my sanity. If I could do it without having Clay and Sean hate me, I'd throw a monkey-wrench into it, because *nothing* good can come of this now.

"While we're on this tour, it might be impossible to make it work. I'm not telling you no, but it could destroy the group and all we've worked for if you do this now. Can you hold off a while?"

"Got it.... I see how tight you and Benji are, and want something like that myself...."

If it's *that* obvious to Clay, what about the fans... what about Dickie... ohmygawd.

"Well, Benji wants us to be tighter, but like I said, now's not the time for that," I say. "Can we just be six single guys, playing our music? No romance until after the tour?"

Clay's face falls. "But I just need to know if he feels the same. It's eating me up. Getting in the way of me thinking about the shows."

"Fine," I groan. "For now, just be yourself, and get around Sean whenever you can. No romance. I'll see how he feels."

Clay runs to me, hugs me so tightly that I'm afraid my body will snap. For a skinny guy, Clay hides a powerful set of muscles. I walk him to the door, and give him a hug and a friendly kiss on his forehead as he walks out into the corridor. Those butterflies and problems just got a shit-ton of company. Damn. I should've told Clay to forget it until after the tour. My *helpful* mouth. I should find some girl willing to be my "cover" until this blows over.

I need to dress, but I pause, because I think I see Benji's door closing just down the corridor.

Ambassador & Troubadour, June 17

When Greg gets us together for the trip to the Troubadour, I see Benji, sitting as far from me as possible, a frown on his usually-smiling face.

It *physically* hurts to see him upset. I mean, I don't want us getting serious, but I don't want him angry, either.

Could it be so simple as Benji being mad because I didn't act on his comments from our shared night? Possibly he's jealous about me—as flirty as I am onstage, that would be an enormous problem—but one thing is clear. Benji cares a lot about me. I don't know which of those causes me the greatest concern. And with him so far from me, I can't do anything about it. Sean settles beside me, glances towards Benji, then at me, raises his eyebrows as if asking a question.

"What's up with Benji? Usually I can't squeeze a tissue between you two," Sean teases. He's right—Benji loves being as close to me as he can get.

"I don't know, it's got me worried. Ready for tonight? L.A., bay-bay!" I try to lighten the mood, but it's *not* working that way.

"Yeah, I'm ready. I hope we can get Benji smiling before showtime, he's kinda the firecracker."

"That he is, and this *really* isn't like him. We'll get it figured out. You and I might need to hold him and tickle him." *Another* problem.

"Yeah, that's cool. Are we changing anything for tonight's show?"

"Nah. It went so great in San Francisco I figure why jinx it, y'know? If it ain't broke, don't fix it!" True to our nature, Sean joins as I say the last. It feels like we share the same brain. Too bad I can't off-load some of the crap I'm carrying inside my brain to him—that wouldn't be fair to him.

Greg clears his throat and says, "Here's the plan. Tonight we're taking one bus to the Troubadour, tomorrow we'll use the second; wardrobe and instruments are already taken care of. Kick back and rest before we head over for the soundcheck."

Greg sees the frown on Benji's face and goes to his side. I can't hear what they're saying, but Benji shrugs his shoulders and seems to indicate he'll be okay by showtime.

Meanwhile, I turn to Sean, who's also watching Benji, and decide to start my questions, even if I'm not ready for Clay and Sean to be a thing.

"How are you enjoying the tour? Is it everything you thought it would be?"

"Honestly, I'm loving it. The only thing I'm missing is the fun you and I had before the group got started and got so big, but it's a decent trade-off, being able to still pal around with you *and* the guys. I'm so happy we found Todd, Wil, Benji, and Clay. They fit in so well, it's like we were all meant to be brothers."

He plays into my hand perfectly. "Yeah, Wil's the shit, right? We hit it rich when we met Todd and Benji." On purpose, I omit Clay, whose bass is as vital to our beat as Sean's drumming. I want to see if Sean has anything to say; he doesn't fail me.

"Awesome, but you forgot Clay! His bass tracks my drums so well, it's like his brain is wired to mine. He's almost as vital as *you* are," Sean smiles, letting me know he's not *totally* serious, but in his own way, he is.

My brother's got something going for Clay.

As Sean finishes, DC appears, and the entire group heads toward the bus. Benji boards first and makes a beeline into the bus. Given his frowns and avoidance of me, he'll probably continue to the back of the seating area.

With him, I may be setting a record for how quickly I mess a situation up, and that *really* hurts.

When Sean and I board, we're left with the front two rows of seats, given how everyone has spread out. Davey's waiting in the driver's seat; DC's sitting beside Clay, so Sean and I sit a few rows ahead. Greg enters, sits in front of Sean and me, and talks briefly with Davey.

As the bus starts, I turn to Sean. Given the times he and his family stood by me when my life was falling apart, I owe him the chance at happiness, even if I don't *want* to do it.

"So, do you like Clay as our bass player, or could you be interested in our bass player as a boyfriend? I have to tell you, I want you simply as our drummer and Clay as our bassist, and I told him the same," I say.

Sean's quiet for a moment, then says, "I like him—no, *love* him—as our bass player. He's our McCartney. But, boyfriends? I'm surprised you asked. Aren't you the one who refuses to get involved with anyone—*cough* Benji *cough*—because you don't want to 'ruin' Phoenix Rising?"

I *figured* Sean would bust my chops. It's lame for me to refuse to have a boyfriend, yet ask him if he's ready for one. I'd be the biggest a-hole in the world to keep them apart. And I trust him not to mess up.

"Earth to Ravynn, you gonna say *any* of the thoughts you're thinking?" Sean says, peering over his glasses for effect. "I bet he came and talked to you, and you told him you'd scope it out!"

I sigh dramatically, then smile. "Yeah, he came to my room this morning before I'd dressed…." As I tell Sean, my mind replays the morning—complete with the kiss on Clay's forehead at the finish, and that suspicion of a door closing down the hall. "I figured out point two—I suspected Benji saw Clay leaving my room, and *now* I'm sure. Anyway, he's *very* interested in you. Now you know, and now I need to glue a smile back on baby Phoenix's face in short order. We can't upset the situation now, so neither you and Clay, or Benji and me, can happen."

"Leave it to me," Sean says with a grin. "By showtime, Benji'll be back to the smiling Cajun we know and love, and I've got an idea about Clay. We'll work through it. The group and this tour are too important to change things now."

With impeccable timing, Davey pulls the bus to a stop in front of the Troubadour, and we file out.

Soundcheck is fairly smooth, other than a fuse replacement in an amplifier for Clay and a bad mike connection—if everything in my life stays this calm, I'll be happy.

Afterwards, we go backstage to change into our show wardrobe. As I'm slipping off the tee shirt I had worn, Greg taps at the entryway and asks from outside, "May I come in?"

"Come on in."

"The soundcheck was good. You'll be fine tonight. I noticed there was some tension with Benji. Did you two have a disagreement?"

"Greg, our 'raging Cajun' is under the misconception that I have, or had, a 'thing' for Clay." I tell him the story about Clay's visit to my room before I'd dressed, and how nothing other than talk happened. Greg nods, like he suspected as much.

"So I heard from Sean. Apparently Benji's convinced you're not being truthful, because he *saw* you kiss Clay."

"On his forehead. It was friendly, a family thing, I wasn't trying to jump his bones."

"Sean told me he told Benji that. He *also* told Benji that he's interested in a relationship with Clay, which he says you know, and that Clay is also interested. When did this become *Peyton Place*?"

"Sorry. I should've stayed out of it, which would've been my preference, given how I always fuck things up. But Clay came to my door and surprised me. I told Clay *and* Sean they need to put the brakes on any relationship for right now, given the press coverage and the constant moving. It would've been smarter if I'd just told Clay to cool it and never mentioned it to Sean."

"It's okay. You haven't messed anything up. I'm sure Benji will be fine by showtime—as will Sean and Clay. And hopefully you will be, too."

I put on my *sassiest* British accent possible, and extend my arm as if I'm offering him a chance to kiss the back of my hand as I say, "Never fear, my dear; Ravynn St. John is here, loud and clear, ready to take Los Angeles by the horns."

Greg laughs, pats my shoulder, and leaves, reminding me to finish dressing. I guess he's making sure I'm not freaking out. This show's got to be perfect, and I need to flirt more with women, so Dickie loses the scent of *anyone* in the group being homosexual, especially me. Outrageous Ravynn will be kissing "at" the ladies and making them weak-kneed tonight.

The show opens to a standing ovation. Cheesy, given *everyone* is standing. The best thing about the capacity crowd is that all 5 feet, 6 inches of Dickie Newsome is swamped by the crowd between us.

To be safe, I flirt more with the girls than the guys. I'm blowing them kisses, winking at the ones closest to the stage so they *know* I'm winking at a lady, strutting out of the stage area into the crowd towards some of them as I wink and kiss. Being kept away from Benji makes it easier for me to flirt with the women, like I'm telling him no guy could ever take his place.

The show's almost perfect; I catch a few bad chords and missed beats, but the way the crowd reacts, loving us, it's not an issue. I realize only at the end that Benji has been as stellar as in previous shows; if he's upset, he's keeping it well-hidden. His guitar work sizzles, as always; his thousand-watt smile is steady. Hell, he "groped" me back when I was "feeling" him up. When we finish, I note I haven't seen Dickie even once during the show. Part of me finds that reassuring; the rest of me worries what the hell that rat is up to. The oldest southern superstition I remember is, "Think of the devil and you'll see his horns."

As we file offstage to the dressing area, DC hands us each a bottle of water and a towel, the "post-concert" standard, I guess.

As she hands me my bottle, she points behind me, and I know without looking that Dickie is standing there.

I excuse myself and walk over to him; the legions of butterflies in my stomach have already started taking off. What now? Is Ronnie about to show up? Why does Dickie keep popping up in my life, like a terrible dream?

"What can I do for you, Mr. Newsome?" I ask in my *sharpest*, sassiest British accent.

"I wanted to congratulate you on a good *show* here in the Troubadour, Ravynn. You have many hidden talents. I hope you found space in your schedule to grant me the interview tomorrow—I haven't received verification," Dickie says, loudly enough that DC hears it over the noise of the club emptying.

"Our assistant manager is at the backstage entrance. Since she speaks for our manager when he isn't present, she, you, and I should be able to work this out." Outside, I'm confident, businesslike, and in control of myself. Inside, my mind is fighting itself. Dickie and Ronnie, homosexual versus heterosexual, Benji and me and Clay and Sean versus Phoenix Rising, it's all beating up on my thoughts.

DC needs to help me resolve some of this.... *now*.

Dickie and I walk back to DC. Dickie holds out his hand to DC as he says, "Ah, the ever-charming DC, *Diciembre.*" Dickie's voice is a condescending drawl, though whether it's because she's a woman, or he's figured she's a lesbian, I don't know.

"I understand you requested a one-on-one interview, you and Ravynn alone, tomorrow. That flies in the face of all that Phoenix Rising is about," DC says with such ferocity that I know she's in total Mama Bear mode now.

One false step and she'll be ready to get his press credentials pulled, local angle or not. I doubt she would, unless he pulls some bonehead move. This could get interesting, or dangerous, depending on how it plays out.

"It's *not* about Ravynn and a back-up group. The group includes *them all*. Pulling him from the group is as unnatural as it is to remove a petal and consider it the flower," she continues. "As management, I cannot agree to a one-on-one interview. If you pursue this with either the full group, or with Ravynn and another of the guys, we might be agreeable. In *either* case, we would insist upon managerial representation being present to protect the group's interests."

Dickie's face clouds over dusky red. I've never seen Dickie angry, but my father could get that shade of red on his face when he got upset. Oh, hell—why didn't I go along with Dickie today and hope for the best? I may have screwed Phoenix Rising beyond the breaking point. *Why* do I keep doing this shit?

Finally, between DC's bulldog glares at Dickie and Dickie's icy daggers my way, it appears a truce is forming.

"Fine, how about tomorrow, before the show, here?" Dickie smiles, an anemic line on his face. "Ravynn has the letter giving the topics. I would prefer a one-on-one, but I will agree to Ravynn plus one of his bandmates, and one management person, if that's *agreeable*."

I cover my face. No way do I want to seem eager to agree with this, no matter who or what. If the bandmate turns out to be birthday-week Benji, that could play into Dickie's plan to expose us; if it's this morning's Benji, it could get me all fucked up. Right now I'd rather be solo flying a rubberband airplane to the dark side of the moon.

I glance at DC to gauge how she's doing. Her lips are tense. "*Mister* Newsome, it would be best for the entire group to take part, or none at all. So we'll decline your offer."

Dickie's face goes from dusky to overripe-tomato red in seconds. His voice is level, low, and sounds dangerous to me. "Ravynn and I discussed this...."

I gotta save this, *now.* Otherwise, it could get nasty, quick.

"DC, it's okay, I think the idea of two of us plus you or Greg would be good." I look at her with my eyes, *begging* her to agree with me. She holds my eyes for a full breath, then nods slightly.

"Three of us will be here tomorrow at 3:30 pm. You'll have *exactly* one hour to ask your questions; we reserve the right to veto any topic. We'll record the interview in full. I won't allow any bullying of these young men, but we'll *happily* answer valid questions."

To watch Dickie during the exchange is priceless; his face, at first blank until he realizes he's been given an offer, contorts through confusion to bewilderment to resigned. He looks at DC and tries to gather his most professional voice before answering with a less-than-resounding, "Uh, okay."

DC nods; Dickie takes that as a signal, and high-tails it out of the room like it's about to be sealed shut.

Then she looks at me. "Ravynn, I'm not in favor of this interview, either. Phoenix Rising has *always* been about the six of you, so that's why I played it the way I did. Is there something else going on that has you concerned? You've seemed *distant* most of the day."

She reads me like a big-print book. At least she agrees about the interview. As for the other stuff, I can't tell her that Dickie is threatening to ruin Phoenix Rising, or reveal that I'm homosexual, or that he's told my ex-boyfriend he knows where we are. As much as I need some way out of this mess, DC can't fight all my battles.

"I've been worrying about Benji being upset; that's got me distracted, DC. I'm sorry." It's suitable—*hopefully*. If not, it'll have to do. My brain's worked too hard already.

"Okay, let's head back to the hotel and make plans." Oh, joy—instead of numbing out, we're going to plot for the firing sq—I mean, *interview*—tomorrow.

At least I'll have DC and someone to help. I would love it to be Benji, because his presence *usually* makes me happy. Or Sean, because he can read my mind and answer for me. There's a problem either way—Benji's nursing a grudge against me now, and Sean and Clay may be starting a relationship that I'm against; I'll have to smooth some ruffled feathers whichever way.

Ambassador, June 17

To say the bus to the hotel is subdued would be like saying the far surface of the sun is warm. After giving a tremendous first show in L.A., we're exhausted, and I'm limp from the whole Dickie thing. My mind scours ideas about who will join DC or Greg and me; mostly I want it over.

When we return to the hotel, the guys go to their rooms. Greg goes to his after saying he'll return shortly; DC follows, leaving me alone with my thoughts—and that *mocking* letter. To kill time, I pick it up and re-read the topics. How we met, how we create our songs. What our private lives are like. Who our inspirations are, our personal backgrounds. What our goals and dreams are. *Mostly* safe topics, except the private lives and backgrounds. I can't wait to hear what Greg and DC have to say.

There's a knock at the door; I answer—it's Greg and DC. We're ready to prepare for tomorrow's interview. Wonder who they've got in mind for the third person.

Greg must sense my thoughts. "Before we discuss what Dickie wants to talk about, let's decide who will accompany Ravynn. DC, you handled the situation with Dickie so well, you're ideal as the management component. Are you okay with that?"

"Sure. My ability as a bossy-as-hell, *totally* out lesbian has kept our six in line, and handled Mr. Newsome just fine today." DC acts like she's ready to *finish* barbecuing Dickie, if he gives her cause. I'm glad she's on my side.

"Good. Unless Ravynn thinks differently," he looks at me, and I shake my head to let him know I have no objections, "the only thing left is to pick who should accompany you. Any thoughts, Ravynn?"

I've got *plenty* of thoughts, none coherent yet—at least in my mind. I decide to take a chance; it's either Sean, who's been there from day one, or Benji, who makes me calm and happy—*usually*, present troubles aside. "I would choose Benji, but there are issues... so I guess Sean."

Greg is nodding at every point. I'm tempted to ask him when he became a bobble-head doll, but that's probably too cheeky. He turns to DC and asks her opinions.

"Sean knows Ravynn—that's in his favor. But we need someone focused," DC pauses and smiles at me before continuing, "Benji may be just 17, but he knows the group, has a wisdom beyond his years, and usually calms Ravynn with his presence—he's my choice."

"I know you're concerned about Benji," Greg says, probably seeing my eyes getting bigger and bigger. "But I believe, given his devotion to you and the group, Benji is the right choice, assuming he agrees. Is that okay?"

Well, duh. I've been fighting myself for months, trying not to screw up the group as I fall heavier for Benji's charm. Even though I won't let myself form a relationship with him, I crave him as much as an alcoholic craves his next drink. For the good of the group, and for my personal reasons, I agree. "Absolutely, Greg."

Greg leaves to ask Benji—or Sean. The clock seems to have frozen as I think about the possibilities of either Benji or Sean coming through the door. Sean's the brother I never had, so that would be great—*if* he's focused. Sean can "wander off" mentally when it's not something he's interested in, but there won't be tension like with Benji and me. If it's Benji, I have to make sure he knows there's nothing going on with Clay and me, and that if I was going to get in a relationship, it would be him—*whew.* Tall order.

I'm so lost in my thoughts, I miss DC getting up and opening the door when the knock comes a few minutes later.

I look up just in time to see Greg walk in, as always looking like he knows *exactly* who he is and where he is—I hope one day I'll be that certain, off-stage. Onstage, it's never a problem; I'm the center of the show, and I love it.

Greg nods; right behind him is Benji. He's frowning, looking like he'd rather be in a pit full of hungry gators than facing me. God, I gotta *fix* this. I look at Greg and DC, silently pleading for a moment of privacy with Benji.

DC picks up on my silent plea. "Greg, there's some stuff in my room we might need. Can you help?"

Greg nods, and they leave. Thanks, DC... I owe you. Now, to patch things with Benji, hopefully.

Once Greg and DC are gone and Benji and I are alone in the room, I look him in the eyes and begin.

"Benji, you know I'm a mess, right? What I'm about to say is a lot of stuff you'll have to sort out to understand, but I can't have you unhappy.

It makes everyone, specially *me*, unhappy too. And that doesn't help us onstage!"

I pause to collect my thoughts.

Whatever I say, I have to give Benji the truth and satisfaction of knowing that, regardless of anything else, I genuinely and deeply care for him. I'm sure I'm falling in love with him; that's *not* possible now, it's too big a risk for the group. I have trouble accepting he's in love with me—knowing my past luck with any kind of relationship. Just worrying about keeping the group together is enough responsibility for now. As I'm thinking this, Benji's looking at me with a side-eyes glance, like he's not sure he can trust me. And *that* makes it even more important to get my words and emotions right.

"So, you only care about how we appear on stage?" Benji asks, a pouting half-smile on his face, arms crossed; he *knows* he's making me squirm, and he's enjoying playing with my head.

He *again* shakes me to my core.

"Yeah—*NO!* That's not it at all," I say, starting a nod but switching to shaking my head vigorously. My mind is ready for full retreat—if I can't win Benji back, I'm doomed. "The group is the only relationship I can handle, but not because I don't care for you, Benji. I care too much. Don't want to hurt you, or lose you, and I'm scared you'll leave the group if I can't make you happy. I promise you, *if* I was gonna have a relationship with someone, there's no one in the world other than you. I hope you trust me, and can deal with me as a good friend."

Benji looks at me for a moment with a blank look on his face. That's worrying—Benji's face is like an emotional weathervane; you can look at him and see if he's happy, or sad, or angry—but I have *never* seen his face go blank, and that scares me. Then he gets a devilish gleam in his eye and says, "You didn't kiss *him* on the forehead, did you?" He means Dickie.

I blush, and start trying to reject the idea. "Me? Him—Dickie? Kiss? On the forehead or *anywhere*? Eww, just... *no*." Ugh... the idea gives me a nasty taste in my mouth.

"That thing with Clay... I had just...." I'm trying to apologize, but he stops me with his index finger pressed against my lips. I don't know *why* he's stopping me from apologizing, unless he's worried that I'll say something he won't enjoy hearing.

"You don't owe me any explanation, shay, and you don't need to freak out about my use of 'shay' talking to you."

Like that, Benji stands up, wraps his arms around me, and kisses *me* on the forehead. As he does, there's a knock at the door, and he walks over and lets Greg and DC in; they have brought nothing back with them, and they avoid asking what Benji and I said or did in their absence.

Benji, Greg, DC, and I sit and discuss the interview; Benji picks it up rapidly.

"Alright, so tomorrow, it's going to be you three—Ravynn, Benji, and DC, with Dickie. I'm here to help you work through any issues you might have, but I won't add anything unless you request my input. Ravynn, you have the letter; would you like to read it?" Greg starts the discussion.

"I hoped you or DC would," I blurt out. The less I have to look at that letter, the less stressed I am. Greg nods. I hand him the letter; he skims it and then looks up at me.

"This states that you and Dickie Newsome talked in San Francisco and you agreed to a one-on-one interview. I'm concerned about that." He doesn't look angry, just *concerned*. I need to clear a little with him and DC.

"Yeah, Greg; we did. I should've told you sooner. I knew Dickie when I was with Ronnie. This was like a 'friend-helping-friends' thing, but I didn't expect him to follow through.... then the offer from George Martin came through, with all the excitement, followed by the sightseeing and shopping in San Francisco. And the cool buses here, so the discussion with Dickie just got pushed to the back of my mind. I'm sorry." Never mind telling him about Dickie's threats to expose the group as a bunch of homosexuals or his mention of Ronnie; I've given him as much of the truth as I'm comfortable revealing.

"Okay, Ravynn, that explains why you were off your usual game at the soundcheck that day. Let's focus on the letter and the interview tomorrow, but sometime we need to have a heart-to-heart talk about what you do when you're presented with similar situations in the future. Otherwise, why are DC and I here?"

Those words hurt more than I thought possible. Here I go again, making a mess of an awesome situation.

"I'm sorry. I'll be better at working *with* you from now on, I promise." I look at them, expecting to see anger, but see only concern and apparently parental love. Wow, if I haven't fucked this up, I'm really lucky. And yet, even while I'm telling them I'll be more honest with them, I'm holding back three-quarters of the story; I'm ashamed, but I can't bear the thought of losing them—*and* Phoenix Rising—if I tell the full truth.

Greg and DC nod without a word, then he continues from the letter's interview request. "He's requested an hour and a half, and with the topics, it's strange that he requested only you. I think private lives should be out of the discussion, and personal backgrounds are questionable."

DC nods, and says, "Exactly. I gave him an hour, so we won't dwell on the backgrounds. I also think the guys' private lives, given how young they are, *should* be off-limits, so I will veto that. The rest of the questions could easily fill up the full hour by themselves."

Benji looks at Greg, smiles, then looks at DC, the cassette recorder, and then me; when he looks my way, the smile's getting there, but it's less happy. After a few seconds, he asks, "So, we're gonna record the interview, right? I'm guessing that you're gonna use your rights to review the printed article before it's actually published?"

"Sharp, Benji, you been reading all the contracts? We absolutely protect our guys," DC answers in a firm voice.

Somehow, *that* causes the squadrons of butterflies in my stomach to shut down their engines. I look at Benji, smile, and mouth the words "Thank You." He nods, but there's no gleam in his eye, or smile on his lips. I know Benji was hurt, and I *hope* my words have started repairing his feelings, but I know it's going to take some time before he's back to his usual self with me.

Benji looks at Greg and asks, "Any chances he might ask a question that isn't covered by those topics?"

Greg looks at DC, who gets a hungry-vulture grin on her face; she looks at me, then Benji, and says in a calm, steely voice, "Let him try."

Okay, I know who *not* to piss off.

Greg, after a moment of glancing at DC with admiration for her business-like demeanor, gets wide-eyed like he's frightened, then says, "DC covered *that* when she told him any question objected to by either of you or by her would be dropped. I doubt he will push his luck trying that tactic more than once."

"Guys, remember, Dickie and I had a basic stare-down contest before this, and I *won*," DC says. "Besides, he wants this national exposure, so he's gonna play nice."

With that, the meeting is over and DC, Greg, and Benji make their way out of the room. Part of me wishes Benji had stayed behind, if only to talk. Did I say everything I needed to make him happy? The smiles when we were alone tell me yes; the absence of smiles with Greg and DC present tell me I have work to do. I can't afford an unhappy Benji—he's the spice that gives us our special zing; for *me*, he's like a combination of the best friend, kindest little brother, and sassiest almost-boyfriend I *never* had.

Troubadour, June 18

At 3:25 pm, Benji, DC, and I are waiting. The table where we sit is a fancy version of what we call a "card table"—folding legs, heavy cardboard or pressed wood top. This is going to be more intimate than I want, but I have reinforcements. Our session at the hotel last night makes me calmer, and the portable cassette recorder on the table is insurance.

At 3:27, Dickie Newsome saunters in like he owns the place and expects us to bow down in front of him.

He turns to Benji and says, "You're the one they call 'the baby Phoenix,' right? I'm surprised you were selected to be the other member of the group for this interview."

This guy *really* knows how to get a hostile audience.

Benji looks directly at Dickie, saying nothing, but his eyes cloud over, his eyebrows mesh into one, his usual easy-going smile vanishes into a scowl. In the South, we say "if looks could kill"—this is one of those.

"Mr. Newsome, cut the crap," DC says. "To start this interview with insults is an excellent way to have *no* interview—and possibly, no national press credentials. Am I clear? Benji was selected because he clearly understands the group and its members, and *that* should be enough for you. Remember, this is being recorded on the cassette recorder. Shall we begin?"

Dickie's eyes widen with surprise, and he squirms in the chair we left for him—okay, maybe we checked out the chairs and picked the least comfortable one for him; sue us.

DC reaches over, inserts a cassette in the tape machine, and presses Record. Dickie collects his thoughts, then dives in with a rehearsed opening. "Ms. Delgado, Ravynn St. John, and Benji Travers of *Phoenix Rising*, thank you for this interview on behalf of Rolling Stone.. We appreciate your cooperation."

DC nods, but says nothing. Benji smiles. I look at Dickie and say, "Well, let's get this going. How do you want to do this?"

"Let's talk about how you guys met." He looks at Benji, then me, then DC; no one has any objections.

"I met Sean in Atlanta. I don't remember exactly—it was in school, around 1956. We realized we had the same birthday and both of us loved music; that led to us being so close we called each other 'brothers from different mothers.' We met Wil about a year later—he was already nuts about keyboards, so we knew if we didn't get him, someone else would. Todd answered an advertisement Sean and I placed in a music store in Atlanta, played a few songs, and we had our lead guitarist. We met Clay in late 1964, and he fit in perfectly."

"I was born in Metairie, Louisiana, part of New Orleans," Benji says, smiling. "I fell in love with guitars as a kid, finally got my own. My family moved us to Atlanta in 1962 when I was 12, and I heard about this group called 'Phoenix' that I wanted to check out. I was too young, but when I turned 14, I got the chance. I met the guys as they were practicing."

"Benji was tremendous. He got out his guitar and in minutes was playing a song he hadn't heard, as if he'd helped write it," I say. "We asked him to join the group then and there."

"I told them I'd have to ask my parents for their permission," Benji says, smiling. "That's when they realized how young I was. It made me happy as a pig in slop when dad said it was okay, as long as my schoolwork didn't suffer!"

Dickie nods, then refers to the letter and asks how we write our songs.

"Well, each of us goes about it differently," I say, looking at Benji, who smiles at me. "Sometimes I get inspiration from places I've visited or things I have seen. The song 'New Orleans Calling' that we're performing this tour was one that Sean and I wrote together after going to Benji's birthday last year, on the Southern Crescent heading back to Atlanta. We'd enjoyed the city so much we were sure it was calling us back. There are others I wrote just because words popped into my head and a melody came with them. I know Benji's written some blues-inspired numbers, which we'll showcase on future albums."

"My 'bayou country' heritage shows up a lot in my music style," Benji adds. "But I think I can cover any style of music you want."

I notice we've taken about 15 minutes—way too short to avoid those topics I *don't* want to discuss. We've *got* to spend more time on this, just to avoid talking about our backgrounds and private lives—I'm sure Dickie's going to try digging into *my* background and private life most of all. Time to draw out the "song creation" story more.

"Sean can come up with words and a melody simply by tapping his drumsticks against the wall, or the rim of a drum, or anywhere." I remember instances where I was talking through some lyrics and Sean began tapping with his drumsticks—it turned a so-so lyric into a rocking song.

"Wil is such a whiz with the keyboard that you can hum some tune and he can develop an entire melody around it. He's not so much with the lyrics, but his tunes are so fantastic, they could stand as instrumentals—Sean and I have told him so, even as he pushed us to write words for them. Clay and Todd have contributed less, and usually they bring their completed songs to the group for recording. I don't remember ever adding to or changing any of their stuff!" I glance at Benji, who's smiling at the praise his bandmates are receiving. "Then there's our youngest, Benji. He's a guitar wizard, and has written songs in a lot of styles."

"Anything else to add?" Dickie asks, looking at Benji and DC, who shake their heads.

"That brings us to the group's private lives," Dickie begins, before DC cuts him off.

"Mr. Newsome, as we stipulated in the conditions for this interview, if either Benji, Ravynn, or I have any objections to any topic or question, it will be dropped. I believe Ravynn is strongly against discussing the topic, and I suspect Benji is, as well. I know I object, because the group's private lives are just that—*private.*"

"Ms. Delgado, the readership of *Rolling Stone*—as well as the hometown newspapers, The Atlanta *Constitution* and the *Journal*—would love to know how the six guys of Phoenix Rising spend their 'private' time. Is there *any* way we can compromise? I will handle it delicately."

Oh, fuck. I see where this is leading—I'm about to voice my strongest objections when DC glances at Benji, then me, with a look that could be pure sweetness or pure meanness; I've never been good at reading how a woman's thoughts translate to facial expressions. Guess she'll clue us *all* in.

"Well, we have a '*Phoenix Rising* Factsheet' which lists their likes, dislikes, and it mentions what each group member enjoys doing in their 'private' time; it gives their background information, as well. I have a copy of it specifically for you." DC slides the handout from her portfolio and hands it to Dickie, who glances over it and nods.

"Errr, the next topic is who the group's inspirations are. Can we proceed with that?" Dickie seems shaken by DC's quick action regarding one of his prime topics.

I look at DC, who nods quickly to me. "Speaking for all of Phoenix Rising—which I never enjoy doing; I prefer our music to 'talk' for us—our biggest inspirations are The Rolling Stones and The Beatles. But there are others we've met as we got started. There's a group in Atlanta, The Spontaneous Generation, who are so good, it blows my socks off; they should be here with us! Of course, there are other acts like The Who, Gerry and the Pacemakers, and the Dave Clark Five. We find a lot of performers inspiring, but if we name them all, we'll be here for months."

With that answer, plus DC's earlier discussion of 'private lives,' we have ten minutes to finish this interview, and Dickie can't bitch, because *most* of the answers have come from me.

DC jumps in and quickly administers the "kill" to the "personal backgrounds" topic—almost *too* easily, as if Dickie knew he would not get this topic. All she said was, "About the *next* topic, personal backgrounds..."

"That's taken care of by the fact sheet, I believe," Dickie says, then asks, "What are your goals and dreams?"

"We want Phoenix Rising to be as big as any music group evah," Benji snorts. "We want to be bigger than The Rolling Stones or The Beatles. We want everybody to *know* who Phoenix Rising is, and we want most everyone on the planet to love us. Heck, with *my* family, we've got a great start already."

DC grins, and I all but laugh out loud. Meeting Benji's family at his seventeenth birthday was like meeting a town, and being expected to remember everyone a week later. It's easier with Benji's family, because each of them is a genuine character. Benji's mother, Jennifer, is a world-class hugger; she's *never* met a man, woman, or baby she couldn't—or *wouldn't*—wrap her arms around. Benji's oldest brother Adam, the typical jock, is still just as protective of his little brother as if Benji were *really* a baby; he's got muscles that should have their own zip codes. The whole family—aunts, uncles, cousins, and family friends—treated me like I was one of them, and that was *before* Benji started showing feelings for me.

"What Benji said, that's the group's mission," I add.

It's 4:31 pm. Dickie's gotten his interview, no adverse effects on the group or me, and he stands, collects his notes, shakes Benji's hand, then mine, then turns to DC. "Thank you for the time, Miss Delgado. While it was not what I'd envisioned, this will allow me to craft an article for *Rolling Stone* which will no doubt help these young men continue their pursuit of musical excellence. I hope to have the written article ready for your approval within three days. Benji, thank you; Ravynn, thanks. I will see all of you later at the show!" With that, Dickie Newsome turns and walks to the exit.

Soundcheck, second show

Shortly after 5 pm, Greg, Wil, Todd, and Sean and Clay arrive—Sean and Clay practically *glued* together, followed by Davey and his crew, who start setting the stage for tonight's soundcheck and show. If Sean and Clay are keeping things quiet, they're using a different dictionary from mine. When did being six bandmates turn into five bandmates, one of whom is two bodies glued together?

Greg talks to DC quietly, then gathers us together. He looks serious—I don't know if this is bad news from Dickie, or if I messed up by keeping so much of what was going on a secret, but the look on his face has those butterflies in my stomach waking up.

"Guys, a quick 'catch everyone up' here. I know some of you were worried when Ravynn and Benji weren't with the group for the trip today. As you can see, they were already here; there was no mystery, other than the matter of an interview for Rolling Stone, which *apparently* Dickie Newsome had pressed Ravynn for back in San Francisco. Isn't that right, Ravynn?"

Looking around, Sean and Clay are interested in each other, which leaves Todd and Wil. Neither of them seems upset, but from Greg's comments, I think it's time for me to come clean, at least about the interview and other items, to restore Greg's faith in me. "Yeah, Greg. Sorry, guys. I never meant to cause harm for anyone, and I believed it was something I could handle myself—at first."

"As Ravynn and I discussed earlier, none of you should commit to things like interviews and personal appearances—especially during a tour. Let DC and me, as the management team, handle those issues, so you're free to focus on your music and shows." Greg smiles, but I know he's serious, and I know I've hurt him.

"Greg, DC, I'm sorry. Since I left my parents, I've had to be parent and kid, management and employee; I didn't think it through and brought trouble on myself. I appreciate you and will not hide things from you, starting now. In fact, the last time Dickie and I spoke privately, he informed me that Ronnie was looking for me."

If I hadn't been so busy looking everywhere other than at Greg, I might have missed Sean clenching his jaw, Benji looking like he was ready to *hurt* someone, Clay looking sick, and Wil and Todd looking like it was showtime for a fight. Yeah, words about Ronnie don't sit well with *my* guys.

Greg's face relaxes a second—until he realizes what my last statement means—then he tenses up. "Ronnie's looking for you? *That's* what this is about? Why didn't you tell us that first? We need to consider a bodyguard, Ravynn."

That was *not* the response I was expecting. Fuck, my lie keeps messing me up. It's almost driven Benji away, though he won't say it, and I can tell from Greg's words that this is going to mushroom out of control. I figured he'd be angry, that he would tell me to stay out of crowds, or that he'd shake his head and let me worry about it myself. A bodyguard? Wow.... *that's* serious shit.

"Greg, I don't know where Ronnie is. With his history of never having more than two nickels to rub together, he's probably trying to bum a ride to get near us. I have no interest in seeing him, but the small-town-buddy code has Dickie believing that he's got to help Ronnie see me. I have no more interest in that than I have in singing a show of someone else's songs." The guys in the group laugh nervously, because they know I generally *hate* doing cover songs; immediately, they refocus on the implications of Ronnie.

Sean pipes up. “I think we’re a decent bodyguard for *our* singer!” He folds his arms over his chest, trying to look buff, but looking more like an irritated librarian’s assistant.

Todd and Clay stand and join Sean’s pose, and they’re more believable as a protective force. This might slow Greg’s roll on getting bodyguards. Greg looks doubtful.

“Look, this is *our* guy, right? *We* will protect him!” Benji joins the three Musketeers and I’m convinced. I look at Greg, who’s puzzled.

“Fine, for *now*. Since we don’t know where Ronnie is, or anything, I think a bodyguard is a good idea—but I’ll let your bandmates ‘protect’ you. Give them a full description, so they know who to watch for. I’ll check his background to see what else we need to worry about,” Greg says. I should’ve known Greg wouldn’t let it drop. What seemed like a harmless, face-saving lie a few years ago has become a gigantic pain-in-the-ass.

The second show at the ‘Troub’ is as successful as the first, possibly more; it’s been warm, so a lot of the audience are wearing shorts, revealing tan-bronzed skin. Tonight seems like Ladies’ Night—the front row is basically all women. That’s fine for my scheme. I kiss some—discreetly on the cheeks, of course. I’m having a better time tonight, likely because of not worrying... about what Dickie... would ask... oh, fuck. Now I’m worried about that interview, what he’ll print. And about everything else going on.

Why did my mind go down that path? I shake it off; we finish the show strong, no extra issues tonight.

As we bid Los Angeles farewell and turn our thoughts toward Seattle, our next stop, I wonder what Dickie's going to print from our interview, what he's going to ask of me, where Ronnie is and what he's planning, and ohmygod, there go the sixty thousand butterfly kamikaze squadrons revving up in my gut. What can go wrong, I wonder. I'm certain something will, but don't know *when*, *where*, or *what.*

In my dressing area, my back to the door, I've gotten my sweat-drenched shirt off and am hanging it up as my mind plays through the endless loop of my worries. As I get the shirt on a hanger, a pair of arms wrap around my waist and tighten quickly. Just as quickly, I let loose an ear-piercing scream.

I haven't shit my pants, but I'm scared enough to have done so. I hear rapidly moving footsteps and voices approaching. Guess the cavalry heard my shriek. Whoever is behind me hasn't said or done anything, so I'm unaware of how perilous my situation is.

The first person through the door is Benji, whose voice tells me who my assailant is.

"Sean, why are you grabbing Rave like that?" Benji asks in a calm tone. "Is he havin' some trouble?" Damn. So Sean, ever the bad prankster—and by bad I mean his choices were always rotten-egg-stinky, not malicious, but not entertaining—was being playful and grabbed me from behind. That explains why he didn't turn me loose or say anything. He loosens his grip. I slip out and spin around to face him.

"What the *fuck*?"

"I'm sorry, Rave. I guess I didn't think it through; thought it might be a bit... of fun."

"A bit, which *nearly* caused me to soil myself, you jackass."

Greg and DC enter at that moment, and look from Sean to me and back. "Anyone want to tell us what happened?" DC speaks, holding an unlit cigar.

"Sean was bored, or Clay tired of him; he sneaked up behind me and grabbed me without telling me it was him."

I look at Sean, who's hanging his head in a defeated air; Clay is almost glaring. Lover's quarrel? No excuse.

"Sean, you know how much Ravynn's been dealing with," Greg says. "What you did could have gotten you hurt if Ravynn could have moved his arms. You could've given him a panic attack."

"Yeah, I know," Sean mumbles, "I didn't think it through."

"You're lucky I wasn't naked and there wasn't a photographer nearby, or we'd be trying to kill stories about Phoenix Rising's full moon show," I say, *instantly* regretting it. I'm sure Sean will forever refer to this as the 'Phoenix Rising Full Moon Incident.'

It was bad enough when I thought it was Ronnie, trying to embrace me. To find out it was Sean playing around makes it worse. Even Clay is disappointed in Sean, which makes me *somewhat* happier.

DC fires up her cigar. "Gee-zus H. Christ, Sean, you sneak up on *me* like that and you'll be missing a few fingers *and* the 'family jewels' when I'm through with you! Dammit, man, you know Ravynn's been under a lot of stress. Do you remember he told us that Ronnie is looking for him? That alone would be enough to explain that scream."

"You *sure* you don't want bodyguards, Ravynn?" Greg asks, watching me like he's afraid I'll shatter into a million pieces.

"It's okay, Greg. As long as this nut doesn't pull the 'sneak up behind Ravynn' routine, no problem," I say, as I not-so-gently plant an elbow in Sean's belly as a kind of "payback." I didn't jab Sean hard enough to hurt him, but he'll have some soreness for a reminder. A few of the guys snicker, because they know that after a few months, Sean will have forgotten—and be ready to try again.

•••••••••••

Seattle, Washington

June 20 - 23, 1968

Sketchy

Benji and Todd are with Greg and me in Phoenix 1. Benji's a fireball. His infatuation with me translates to "don't mess with *my* Ravynn." Todd could play any position in pro football. Between the two, a mosquito doesn't stand a chance of getting to me, much less a lousy ex-lover. That's my found family—they love me unconditionally; I hate that my lies have turned this into an ordeal. I don't see a way out.

"Dude, what's Ronnie look like, anyway? None of us have seen him," Todd says. I've gotta give them something to go on.

I'm not the greatest artist, but I sketch Ronnie's face—as I remember it—and scribble his details. Dark brown hair, cut so short that it disappears on top of his head. Dull, lifeless brown eyes, lips perpetually set in a grimace. Given his preference for what I call "South Georgia redneck chic," Ronnie'll likely show up in an off-white tee and blue jeans with a beat-up pair of Converse All-Star high-top sneakers, the laces not run through the top two holes—his every-day wear. He's never been a great looker, but when he and I first got together, it *felt* like a match. Now I know better. He's not evil, even if he looks the part, but the way he badmouthed Phoenix Rising—and me for being obsessed with the band—that was like verbal abuse.

I give the sketch to Greg, who looks at it with no expression for a few minutes. Then, he motions Benji and Todd over, slides the sketch to them, and glances at me before he says a word. "Ravynn, that sketch is helpful. The face scares the shit out of *me*, so I understand your reluctance about seeing him. Sure you don't want *professional* bodyguards? I don't doubt these guys' determination, but this guy–" he waves at the sketch, then continues, "is a freaking monster. He's taller than you, bigger than you. Even with Todd's added muscle, Benji and Todd couldn't slow him down."

Restaurant

Somewhere along the ride to Seattle, the buses pull into a truck stop—a place called "Truck'Otel" which claims to have a restaurant, a TV lounge, private rooms with bath, and a barber shop. *And* it's centrally heated and air-conditioned. Modern, but the sign is cheesy. The guys and Greg and DC pile out and head for the restaurant, which looks like a greasy-spoon diner; hungry as I am, it could be Old Mother Hubbard's Shoe.

Inside, looking over the menu, I see lots of choices, and my mouth waters.

The twenty-something waitress, Sandra, according to her badge, takes our orders.

She doesn't bat an eye as six guys, a Latina woman, and a 40-something white guy order just about *everything* on the menu. "Hungry" is an understatement based on the orders. She writes an order for each of us—mine and Benji's are the largest. I can be a big eater, since I burn a lot of calories with all the activity onstage, but *this* may be my eyes talking louder than my appetite. Before she takes the orders to the kitchen, Greg asks the ten-thousand-dollar question. "Will I be able to pay for all these together, with a sizable tip for you, of course?"

The waitress frowns until the word "tip" comes out of Greg's mouth—then she has a smile even the Cheshire Cat would be jealous of.

"Couldn't you have asked that *first*? Sure, hun, that's no problem. Are you a family?"

"Actually, this is the group Phoenix Rising, heading to Seattle for the third stop on tour," Greg tells her, the proud 'Poppa' to the brood. "I'm their manager, and DC is my assistant." DC nods.

"Wow, I've heard about you," she says, her eyes getting a spark of excitement that was missing moments before. "My brother couldn't go to the concerts in San Fran, but he's got friends in Seattle, so he's going with them. He'll be jealous that he wasn't here to meet you!"

"What's your brother's name, ma'am?" Benji asks in his excited-but-respectful way, as he reaches for a flyer from our Troubadour shows.

"Thomas Jeffrey; he goes by Tom. He's twelve, convinced he's going to be a great actor or comedian." She shrugs her shoulders, as if saying 'kids, who knows,' but smiles; she obviously cares about her brother.

While she's talking, Benji has gotten the flyer, and autographs it with the message, *Tom, Hope you enjoy our Seattle show. Looking forward to seeing you in the future, Benji Travers.* He slides it to the guys, each adding their messages and signatures.

At last, it's my turn. I sign *Be who you want to be, who you are meant to be. Love yourself. Thanks for your love of our music, Ravynn St. John. Phoenix Rising, June 19, 1968.* Some advice—I'm a bloody hypocrite; I tell a twelve-year-old to do something I'm incapable of doing. *Some* advice is optional if you fit into a certain category or box. I finish signing as Sandra returns with a couple of helpers, bringing our meals.

"Sandra, from all of us, please give this to your brother, Tom. Thanks for your help and patience!" I hand her the autographed flyer; she glances at it, then looks around the table at us, her smile growing larger by the second.

"Wow, Tommy will be thrilled at this! I'm so jealous that he's going to see you guys play, and I'll be stuck working."

The manager calls out, "Miss Hanks, *if* you're through flirting and delivering meals, could you assist other customers, please?"

"Button your hole, Joe," she says, smiling.

Triangle Hotel, June 20

Our Seattle arrival's subdued. Six young guys and a middle-aged man checking in at what has to be the most ah-maz-ing hotel. It's named "Triangle" because the building is, literally, a triangle. What's truly amazing is that it has only eight rooms. We're taking up almost the entire hotel for four nights.

My "Wall" is intact; the guys surround me going in. Wil points out the bar on the ground floor—he's *almost* twenty-one, so he could *sneak* a drink. Until Greg sees Wil glancing at the bar.

"Gentlemen, that bar is off-limits to anyone in this group under the age of 70," Greg says. "That means *all* of us. Front desk is ahead, rooms upstairs. I'll have the room nearest the stairwell and elevators, so don't get *any* ideas."

While we're still moving like a human wall toward the door, I scan the street out of boredom, until I see a guy leaning against a wall across from the hotel, trying to look casual but failing spectacularly; it's obvious to me he's been *watching* for someone specific—like us—and is now verifying his instructions. I'm torn between bringing his presence to anyone's attention or keeping it to myself when Todd saves me the decision.

"Greg, there's some guy across the street eyeing us. What should we do?" Todd's voice is uncharacteristically loud, as if he's alerting the guy he's been spotted.

"Let's get inside and check in, guys," Greg says, avoiding the topic of the stranger. Hopefully, he'll explain why once we're inside, or I'll drag it out of him.

On the elevator ride up to our rooms, after Greg again stares down Wil about the bar, he finally talks about the stranger.

"Guys, you saw your *first* detective. His orders are simple; watch for us to arrive and ensure our safe entrance into the hotel," Greg says. "By the way, several detectives have previously swept the building and made sure there are no problems inside. Had there been an issue, he would've approached us and started a conversation. That was arranged before we arrived."

As we ride to our rooms, I have mixed emotions. I should appear happy that Greg—and the detectives—have one of my miseries under control, even though it's not a true misery and it's not even something they can do anything about. If the detectives could resolve the Dickie interview, the romances blossoming between Sean and Clay (*and* Benji and me, honestly), the pressures of delivering great shows each night, and staying ready to record in London, plus whatever *else* I put my foot into these next few weeks, *that* would be top-notch help. The Beatles and Stones make it all look so easy—then again, they're older and I'm pretty sure they have help; you know, the illegal kind—drugs. I'm *not* doing that.

Greg takes the room next to the elevator and stairwell. He's *not* gonna let us sneak downstairs. I'm not interested in the bar, which is Greg's biggest concern, and I don't want to think about going outside this hotel alone while Ronnie's lurking. With *or* without my 'Wall,' in a city I'm not accustomed to, I can't bear to take a chance of running into my ex—not because he might hurt me, but because it would be easy for me to get lost and separated from the group. Tomorrow should bring a print of the interview with Dickie, though with my record, I'm not counting on it.

Greg's gotten strategic with room placements. Benji's next to Greg. Todd's between Clay and Wil, and I'm between Wil and Sean. Greg's separated Sean and Clay and Benji and me. With Sean and Wil around me, he's got the "Wall."

We're in Seattle. I'm surrounded, literally, by my bandmates, plus Greg has one *or more* detectives "on the case" around the hotel, and more will be present for the concerts and soundchecks. With this security in place, I should feel like a gold bar in Fort Knox, right? I mean, Greg's got me so well-protected, I don't think a skeeter could take a nip at me without everyone knowing about it.

Triangle & Auditorium, June 21

I'm midway through the final encore when Benji pulls me in for a long, searing kiss; I *feel* his almost-growl of satisfaction as our tongues duel in our joined mouths. Thank goodness there's a long instrumental break....

Wait, there's no bell onstage.

What the hell am I hearing? I wake up, a corner of the pillow embarrassingly tucked into my open mouth. Right, still in bed, erotic dream. Damn.

I jump up and answer the phone. It's Greg, acting as father again, giving us wake-up calls. I've heard other groups talking about how fantastic their managers are, but none of 'em match ours. DC and Greg treat us like a family, not like babies or children or mere employees. Greg suggests we get together in an hour, which gives me time for a good shower. Time to finish that dream the manual way....

After the shower, I dress casually—our show wardrobe will be delivered to the Auditorium when we do our soundcheck, no need to get prettied up. A tee shirt, pair of jeans, and my sandals, and I'm set; checking the time,

I'm ready with ten minutes to spare. It takes less than two minutes to walk from my room to Greg's, where he's waiting with an open door.

"Sleep well?" He asks. I nod, seeing coffee on a table in the room. "Help yourself. I knew you'd need your caffeine. There's juice, plus donuts, English muffins, jellies and butter."

As I finish pouring my cup of coffee from the carafe he's gotten, I find the donuts and grab two glazed ones. Looks like he expects us to be starving; there's three dozen donuts and four dozen English muffins. "It's 10 am, dude. Why so early?"

"First, we need to go over the interview. DC is bringing it soon. Then, we're going to have lunch, so you guys are well-fed. Finally, we'll take you to the Auditorium to do the soundcheck."

"I hope Dickie didn't fuck up our words. That's been bothering me since the interview."

The other guys enter, in a mass, followed by DC, who has a large, thick envelope in her hands, which she gives to Greg and pours herself a cup of coffee.

I look around the room—five pairs of eyes are trained on *that* envelope in Greg's hands.

"You guys *might* consider moving out of the doorway, you know. Grab some coffee or juice, donuts or English muffins, and have a seat. Do y'all want to read a copy, or should I read it and let you hear how it sounds?" Greg asks, shocking me with his "y'all."

"Looks like we've got five more listeners," I say. He holds the interview out to me, offering me first reading; I shake my head. I can't. My hands shake so hard I couldn't hold a microphone if I had to. "Read it, that way I can hear the words and know if it's what we said."

Benji nods agreement, so Greg reads. "This reporter was fortunate enough to land the assignment of covering the new group Phoenix Rising on their first-ever world tour, and during the first stop, in San Francisco, California, I was further fortunate to be granted an exclusive hour-long interview with the lead singer, Ravynn St. John, rhythm guitarist Benji Travers, and assistant manager, Diciembre Cano Delgado. We covered many topics, including how the group formed and how they create their unique music. It's easy to understand how so many young people, women and men alike, find this group so irresistible. I'll allow their words to speak for them."

Greg pauses, looks at all of us, and comments that the introduction is positive. He reads us the questions and our answers, and I am gobsmacked; Dickie Newsome has printed our responses exactly as we gave them, with no editing or commenting. Wow. A great interview to have printed, as the international portion begins—that should help fill seats overseas.

"I owe Dickie an apology," I say. "I figured he was going to do a hatchet job on us, but he's given us a great review. So I'll *officially* try to drop my nickname for him." At least until I know what the fuck *else* Dickie wants. He didn't get everything he wanted, so I know there's a big shoe about to drop.

Greg laughs. "I'll believe it when I see it."

After the high of Dickie's interview, lunch is an afterthought. I know we stop somewhere along the drive from the hotel to Eagles Auditorium, but my mind remains on that interview. At least *this* time, I'm thinking happy thoughts and not dwelling on worries.... Dammit, Ravynn, there you go again. Why do I *always* bring up the negative shit? It kills the mood and starts me worrying again. Fuck me running, I can't persuade my mind to give me a break, so why would I expect anyone else to?

I look around the table. My bandmates are eating, looking round inside this diner and chatting. I'm the one who's stuck in his own head—as usual. Sean chooses this moment to look my way and figures out what's going on; he nudges Clay, who's sitting beside him, and nods my way. Clay nudges Benji, who's sitting beside Clay for once, and Benji looks up at me, figuring out the situation. He gets out of his chair and walks around to me, then kneels beside me.

"A'right, shay, you sitting here like a bump on a log after we got the full honey pot handed to us in that interview. What's running round in that head? Worrying about Ronnie?" Benji asks.

"I'm sorry. I was so happy to be thinking something happy..." I say.

"... and your mind thought it was better than having all your worries, which brought them right up. Then you started worrying about that," Benji finishes.

"Yeah, exactly. Really fucked up, aren't I?"

"We *know* how traumatic your breakup with Ronnie was. The fact he's looking for you, not knowing what he wants, that's eatin' at you, so no, you're not fucked up, you're handling it okay."

I smile. And with the smile, my mind returns to focus on now, eating lunch. My stomach growls loudly in agreement.

"Sounds to me like the demon you need to worry about is your hunger. Eat your lunch, then let's go check out this Eagles Auditorium!" Benji pats me affectionately on my back, then walks back to his seat and resumes his meal. Everyone else is giving Academy Award-winning performances of *nothing unusual here; we're eating lunch.*

After lunch, "Ravynn's Wall" reappears, spurred by my near-meltdown at lunch. Surrounded by the five guys who're my closest friends and bandmates, I'm comfortable returning to the limousines. The ride to the auditorium is no more than two blocks. We *could* have walked the distance from the restaurant. I start to say that....

"No, too much we don't know about the area." Sean reads my thoughts.

"You don't know what I was thinking," I say, knowing better. We didn't become "brothers from different mothers" for nothing—this is a prime example.

"It's written on your face. It's no more than two blocks, we could've walked from the restaurant. Wanna try again?"

"You got me. I understand *why* we didn't."

There's a line of police on either side of the door to the auditorium, in full gear, as if expecting an invasion. The pain from Dr. King's and Bobby Kennedy's assassinations have resonated throughout America.

We make our way into the auditorium.

"The auditorium's safe. Had there been *any* issue, someone outside would've stopped us. That's what the detectives, the police and I agreed upon during planning," Greg says.

Davey and his crew have set up the stage; everything's ready. DC and Greg sit mid-center in the audience area as we hop on stage and perform our soundcheck. Tonight, we'll begin the first concert of our third tour stop; to be sure Dickie doesn't retract the interview, I'll *still* flirt with the women.

We've done this soundcheck enough that it's second nature. Everything's set, the levels, after some adjustments, are perfect; we fly through the routine and head backstage to relax before the show in a few hours. We *still* haven't seen a detective *or* Ronnie Kushner.

The show's a success. From the opening through every number, the audience loves us. The *true* show-stopper is the moment that I "introduce" Benji. He's gotten four or five signs and screams of undying love and affection from women and men.

After the show, Clay teases Benji about the proposals he's gotten. Sean stands nearby, watching Clay and Benji with a smirk on his face. When he sees me looking his way, he tries to hide the smirk. I can't let him get away with it.

"I see you grinning at Clay and Benji, *Granny*. Looking disinterested now is too late to fool me." *Granny* is a playful nudge because of his glasses, similar to John Lennon's.

"Let them have their fun. It's not hurting anyone or anything, right?"

"No, *it's* not hurting anything. I hope you and Clay aren't rushing into anything that could hurt either of you or the group."

Sean looks at me like I've grown another head. I know what he's thinking—when did Ravynn start channeling Greg? I'm sounding stodgy, but this sneaking around, coupled with trying to be sure we have spectacular shows every night *and* my other worries, is boxing me in. It's like I'm one of those containers that say "Maximum Capacity 50 pounds," and I'm at 52 pounds, seeing more coming. Not sure whether the anticipation or the reality of Ronnie is worse, and I'm scared shitless to find out.

Benji and Clay see Sean and me and walk over to us. I decide to lighten up a bit from my comments to Sean, and add some teasing of my own.

"If they ever make it legal in America to have multiple spouses, Benji will need a town to house his. How many women does this make who've offered to birth your babies?"

After our moments of disagreement, it's refreshing when his smile bursts from his face. Damn, I could get used to having that smile around me every day.... Give it up, Ravynn. We're *not* going there. No relationships except the band. No entanglements that could destroy what we've created.

Benji snaps me out of my mood.

"None of them matter. We got this concert tour, right? My place is with *my* guys!" Benji looks directly at me, his emerald-green eyes half-lidded, filled with longing.

Hotel

Roughly 24 hours after our arrival, we see two guys outside the Triangle. I'm worried this might be bad until one leaves. He nods at the other, then at our limousines, and strolls away leisurely. I turn to Greg, sitting beside me watching me and the scene outside.

“Those two are detectives, right?” I ask Greg, excited to think I’ve figured out something. I almost run everything into one word.

“Yes. They were changing shifts,” Greg says.

So far, so good. One night and one day without issues—other than the ones which swirl in my brain, topmost being the tiny lie I told years ago which has grown to the monster which threatens to swallow Phoenix Rising. Too bad detectives *can’t* fix that.

“Ravynn’s Wall” again escorts me from the limousine to the hotel front door. At the door, Greg enters first, then the group allows me to follow Greg. They follow behind me, still forming a shield.

The desk clerk looks up. “Mr. Thomas, there was a call asking for you. He said he would try to contact you later, but refused to leave a name or a message.”

Greg thinks for a moment, then thanks the clerk. We head to the elevators. I’m puzzled. Greg says nothing further. It could be a signal. I know Greg made copies of my sketch of Ronnie and gave them to the detectives and likely every uniformed police officer he’s met, so perhaps one of them has spotted Ronnie. It’s just as likely that it’s someone from the label who didn’t want to leave a message. Why did I think of Ronnie first? Crap, he’s *not* what I want to be thinking about.

The elevators open and we board. Greg, standing fairly close to me, waits until the elevator doors close and then says, “Come to my room when we get upstairs, Ravynn. We have things to discuss.”

During the longest three-minute elevator ride ever, my mind's trying to invent every possible reason why Greg asked me *after* we got in, rather than at any other point in this evening.

Inside the room, I look at Greg with arched eyebrows, as if to say, *Okay, what's all this about?*

I can't say anything before Greg speaks.

"My *guess* is that Ronnie found out from Dickie we're staying here, so he called. It makes sense he would ask for me, because he would figure the reservations would be in my name."

I know Ronnie isn't the monster I played him to be. The likelihood he's gone that bad is as remote as Pluto is from Earth, but I have to maintain this front based on my lie that he was awful.

"Greg, are you sure it wasn't someone from the label calling and deciding not to leave a message? I mean, this sounds more like one of *my* freakouts than level-headed you." True, it *could* be Ronnie, or it could as easily be George Martin from London.

"I think tonight you should sleep in the second bed in my room."

"I'm surprised you haven't suggested that I bunk with Benji again. I'm *not* a scaredy-cat, dude. You make me sound like a little boy," I say. "How about I sleep in my own bed, given the security around here?"

"Go ahead, but if you want to use the second bed tonight, just come back." Greg gently chides, but there's a smile on his face that tells me he cares.

I head back to my room. All Greg's worrying about the ogre-Ronnie he pictured from my lie and the sketch has rebounded, causing me to be as nervous as a long-tailed cat in a room full of rocking chairs, as "Aunt" Pearl, Benji's maternal grandmother, would say.

I get ready for bed, slowing my breathing as I do, then climb into the bed, sliding off my briefs. Once I turn off the bedside light, I'm almost wide awake. I need to sleep. We have a show tomorrow.

I decide to try something Sean's mom once told me to use when I was having trouble falling asleep—I count sheep, starting at 100, counting down. It's never worked, but what the hell—maybe this time. 100... 99... 98... 97...

Eagles Auditorium, June 22

Everyone's keyed up, anxious. We know the soundcheck must be done, but we're focused on how exposed we are when we're onstage doing the soundcheck. There's no one in the audience, and no one backstage, other than two detectives near the dressing area.

I decide to check the cassette recorder that we've hooked into the auditorium's sound system, so I do—along with Todd and Benji as "bodyguards." I replace the cassette cartridge with a fresh 90-minute cassette and set the machine to record. It's foolish, because the soundchecks *generally* run only half an hour, and this cassette will give us three times that.

We return to the stage and begin. What seemed unusual a week ago has become second nature, and soon we break into a spontaneous rendition of "Blue Suede Shoes," complete with Benji doing hip swivels like Elvis, and me doing my best "thank 'ou, thank 'ou verr' much" Elvis impersonation. The guys break up laughing, as do I. The perfect way to release the tension we've been under this whole day.

We put away instruments and microphones and are about to go backstage to relax before the show, when a door at the back of the darkened auditorium opens. There's someone standing in the doorway; since it's dark in the auditorium, I can't see if it's a man or woman. The light in the outer room surrounds the figure with a full-body halo effect. Whoever it is walks slowly, deliberately, about ten feet into the darkened auditorium; the door behind remains open so the figure remains bathed in light.

It's annoying, it's frightening, and although I can't see the person at this distance, the gnawing fear in my stomach is *wailing* that Ronnie has appeared. The way the figure seems to shuffle brings back memories of Ronnie during our last weeks together. As the figure steps a little closer with that distinctive slink-step that I have seen from *one* person, Ronnie, I see just enough to know that my worry is correct. Suddenly, the figure stops moving.

A voice I remember too well, and never wanted to hear again, rings out, "It's time to come home, Robin. We belong together."

After soundcheck

Ronnie. Now I *know* where he is; he's a few yards from me, slowly striding my way. And the longer he's in the same room with *my* guys, the more likely that my lie gets exposed. Fuck.

"*That's* the guy you sketched!" Benji stage-whispers, though with an empty auditorium, I'm sure everyone heard it.

"You sketched me?" Ronnie purrs, if gravel rubbing together can be described as purring. "Seems like you've found your artistic abilities. I wish I could see your sketch of me, Robin."

"It's Ravynn," I interrupt him.

"I know you as Robin, and unless you've legally changed your name, I prefer to call you by the only name I've known for you. Do we understand each other?" Obviously, Ronnie *still* thinks of me as his property, or his subordinate; he controlled me as a teenager, but it's not happening again.

As Ronnie's talking, he strides towards the stage. He's nearly reached the stage already. Instinctively, I back away from the edge. I want *nothing* to do with him. Sean acts like he's ready to go after Ronnie, but I use my head to nod him to move back from the edge. Dammit. Where are those detectives that are waiting backstage? I try a little surprise tactic on Ronnie. I hope I scare him off, or buy some time, with my false bravado. My hands are trembling. I've got them clasped behind my back, dropping them to clinch the sides of my pants—*anything* to keep from showing my nerves.

"You realize we've been recording every soundcheck and every show on this tour, Ronnie? That means you're on tape. If you leave us alone, you'll be okay. I'm not going with you. I'm not your property. You threw me out. *We* are *done*."

That sets Ronnie back... for a moment. He takes a step back and looks around, like he's trying to find the tape machine. He won't. It's in the sound booth, but no one's gonna tell *him* that. In a second, he loses interest in looking, and presses forward. "You got it wrong, Robin. I didn't throw you out. You got mad at me and walked out. I went to apologize, and you were gone. I want us to try again."

At those words, the Cajun firecracker, Benji, explodes. "Yeah, right, *cochon*. Then I guess *Ravynn* beat himself up and scratched and bloodied himself as he walked barefoot away from your place? I may be young, but I ain't no dumb bébé!"

I tell Benji softly to calm down, and he backs away, seething. Gawd, when he realizes that what he said is basically what happened, I am gonna be so *fucked*, and it will be my own damn fault.

"Ronnie, now is not the time. If you want to talk, stay and watch the show. Afterwards, I'll find a place where we can talk."

Well, that goes down like a dead weight—Ronnie's not happy, but Benji, Sean, Clay, Todd, and *even* Wil are ballistic. I understand their anger—hell, I stoked it, with my lie a few years ago, fed with regular booster shots of it. I feel like Lucy on TV, when Ricky says, "Lucy, you got some 'splainin' to do!"

Ronnie nods, glares at my guys, and says, "Catch you later, then, when we can be alone." He turns, walks to the back of the auditorium, and sits.

I wonder what Ronnie has in mind with the "catch you later" routine. Back when we were together and he apparently *loved* me, Ronnie would say "Catch you later" as a way of saying "I love you" to me when there were people around—Atlanta may be moving forward as a city, but two guys living together as a couple? Not accepted. If Ronnie thinks playing cat-and-mouse is going to pull me back to him, he's got another think coming.

Benji and Sean stand on either side of me as I try to figure out what the hell to do now. My story about Ronnie won't survive the night; either I tell the truth now, or it makes itself known when Ronnie and I talk later—because I know there's no chance my guys'll let me talk to Ronnie without backup.

If I tell them now, before the show, it's a good chance that tonight's show will suck, royally. If I wait until after the show, it might wind up being our *last* show. I'm so screwed.

To drive that point home, Benji softly says, “I don’t trust him any further than I would a croc-a-gator from the bayous back home. He’s dangerous, shay, you’ve told us so.”

“He’s not gonna do anything surrounded by these people,” I say as I wave my arms to indicate a full house.

“You didn’t agree to talk to… that cochon, that pig, because you *want* to get back with him, I know you too good to believe that,” Benji says, his eyes flashing lightning rather than his usual happiness.

“No, I have zero desire to get back together with him. In his eyes, I’ll always be a no-good kid whose parents turned their backs on him, an insignificant piece of trash to use and throw away.”

Sean’s fists are tightly balled up. Every knuckle is nearly paper-white. His lips are drawn tight. I don’t know how he manages to unseal them to speak. Clay, Todd, and Wil are showing varying levels of anger or fury, so… let me try to defuse some of this.

“Going back to Ronnie would end my ability to be Ravynn. He won’t let me be a rock star, because that makes me more significant than he could be. But… you guys might want me to; I haven’t been totally honest with you.”

Auditorium

As we get to our dressing areas backstage, Greg and DC join us. Perfect; I can get this out, in one shot, I hope.

“Before we dress for the show, let me clear some things up, and *please*, understand that I never intended to hurt any of you.” Sean, standing so close to Clay they’re almost each other’s shadow, nods gingerly; Benji looks at me, his lips turned up but tightly shut, as if he’s afraid of what might spill out. Todd, Wil, Clay, DC, and Greg all nod. *Time to man up, Ravynn!*

"The breakup with Ronnie wasn't the way I've told you. I'm sorry," I say, glancing around at each of my found family members, before I continue. "The night of our first performance—thanks again, Greg—Ronnie told me it wasn't working, that I would never amount to anything, and that I should take my shit and get out. I accused him of using me and then throwing me out like a shitty diaper and tried to beat him up."

Benji's smile is back, and Sean looks amused. "You? Beat up Ronnie? He outweighed you by at least thirty pounds," he says.

"I was tired of being his maid, his sex outlet. I wasn't a real person with him. So, getting told I wasn't wanted? It hurt like hell. In the scuffle, I scraped myself up seriously—Clay, you and Sean saw that—so I changed the story to make Ronnie the monster."

Whew. Told the whole story, and I'm *praying* that I didn't barbecue Phoenix Rising.

Looking around, surveying the damage, it's apparent that I've messed up. Sean is glaring at me, his mouth open like he's trying to decide whether to scream or cry; Todd slams his left hand open-palmed into the wall with a resounding *smack.* Clay, sitting beside Sean, appears upset, but not as much as Sean. Before I can scan any further, Sean breaks the silence.

"Y'know, I've *always* thought your story was pretty hokey. Now I know why."

Ouch....

I might be able to work through this. Greg is stern-faced but not showing anything. Then I see DC, and I'm worried. She looks like she's ready to cry—as foreign a behavior for her as possible. Ohmygawd, if I've upset the toughest woman enough to make her nearly cry, then I'm messed up. Worst of all, Benji sits tight-lipped until I turn towards him.

"You musta felt real *smug* when I told that *cochon* that I didn't believe you beat yourself up and scratched and bloodied yourself while you walked barefoot from his house!" He says, shaking his head —in anger or disbelief, *hopefully* nothing worse. "How the *fuck* could you put us through that? Is *dat*—what you just told us—the full story, or are you still hidin' something?"

I've managed to tell off my ex *and* alienate the seven people in my "found family" of Phoenix Rising. My history is repeating itself.

"Listen, I know it's shitty to spring this on you like this, but Ronnie showing up backed me into a corner. I knew you'd find out the truth, and I wanted it to come from me rather than anyone else. I'm *sorry.* Really."

I look at each of my *family* members with the same plea in my eyes—*Don't throw me away for useless like those others did.*

Benji walks over to me and says, "This ain't worth a damn, *couyon*! That's so *coonass*, *canaille*...." He's calling me a crazy person, a low-life, a sneak, and I deserve it, but gawd, it hurts. I know how deeply I've hurt Benji, but he isn't done. "*Piké twa*! I knew you were holding something back. Were *any* of your freakouts real, or were they part of the lie? I thought you were hurtin'!"

I've never heard Benji say that last phrase, but one of his friends used it in a way that meant "fuck you." Fuck, that hurts. He's doubting me, and I can't blame him, even if I don't want him upset in that way.

"I *was* hurtin', Benji, even if it was just my mind causing it. I...."

"You crossed a line, Ravynn. You're going to have to get back to who you want to be," Greg says, shaking his head slowly, like a disgusted parent.

"So, uhmm, I think Ronnie's gonna watch the show, then we'll talk—likely here, and I would love to have a few of you here," I give them the last piece. As I finish, I look at the floor in front of the guys, afraid to look into their eyes—afraid I'll see rejection... or *nothing*.

After what seems like a lifetime holding my breath for some good news, I finally hear a slight cough.

"Fine," Benji softly states, leading the four other group members and two management people in grunts or nods of agreement, though not one of them shows happiness.

"I treasure you all." I can't use the "L" word in this setting.

Greg looks from me to the guys. "Okay, show business rule number one is 'The Show must go on,' so go on it will. Get yourselves dressed and ready."

The show goes on, nowhere near the success of previous shows. It's not far from being a total disaster. I *hope* it doesn't ruin our chances to record in London. We pull through—barely, but there've been more problems than we've ever encountered. Todd and Clay suggest before the show that we not do the groping routine, a string on one of Todd's guitars broke, and that was *before* I messed up the lyrics of a song that I had written. Everyone's timing is off. We've had rehearsals that were smoother than this show. Hell, our *first* recording session was smoother, and it took fourteen takes to get the instrumental track recorded. My lie's added another casualty to its too-long list. It's drawn a bullseye squarely on our chance to record in Abbey Road in a few weeks.

We make our way backstage. This has been a fucked-up stop on the tour—the highs of the first show, the low of Ronnie wanting me to return to him. I know our energy was off, and that threw the audience off as well; we owe these fans much better than we gave tonight—and that's *another* one on my list of fuckups.

Greg walks into the dressing area, holding several copies of Rolling Stone with a picture of *us* on the cover; he gives one copy to DC and to each of the guys, finishing by handing one to me without comment. Something about his coldness seems off.

Wow.... Dickie's interview is the *lead* article, and it's printed in its entirety. There's also a letter from a fan in San Francisco who saw our show and loved it. Now, with the love from the press and fans, it's sorta like I'm walking on air. Though Ronnie had said he would stay and talk, his absence is a temporary reprieve.

There's a detective with Greg, Mr. Preston, who assures me that his men will be as discreet as possible while keeping me safe; it's hilarious that he says this *after* I've come clean about how much a non-threat Ronnie actually is. He insists I should call him by his first name.

"You're Robert Preston? The movie star?" I ask. He has a slight resemblance to the character from *The Music Man* that the movie star played.

"I can't hold a tune for all the gold in the world," he laughs.

Greg gives a nervous laugh, then tells the detective, "Considering what Ravynn has told us, Mr. Preston, you aren't needed."

"That may be, but since you paid in full in advance on a non-refundable expense, looks like we're here to keep you safe. You'll be secure in Seattle."

"Guess we'll enjoy your security, then," Greg replies, looking *totally* like he knew it. "Ravynn, Dickie Newsome is outside the dressing area, wanting to speak with you." Greg, you could have just stabbed me; it would have brought me down just as fast.

Of course, my mind *immediately* worries what Dickie wants now. After his one-on-one interview got crushed, and Ronnie's return was such a bust, I'm sure he wants something more from me, or is here to tell me his next article will reveal the real me, since I haven't cooperated with him. Shit, I'm fucked.

"Okay, I'll talk to him. I *promise* no interviews or management-level decisions without asking you first."

Greg hugs me, like a father hugs a son, and I'm reminded that I have the best "found family" a guy could want. Why do I feel like the condemned man, walking to his execution, as I head out to meet Dickie *again*?

Sure enough, Dickie Nu... err, Dickie Newsome is waiting. I go for broke; if I'm about to get fucked over royally, then let it be British royal. In my sassiest accent, I greet Dickie.

"Mr. Newsome, I thought your interview with us had propelled you into the upper reaches of journalism, where you were too busy to trifle with mere rockers."

"You sell yourself short. Your interview *has* increased my visibility with the national press, and that's thanks to you and Phoenix Rising."

"I've seen the Rolling Stone issue with our interview. Thanks, you were fair to us, and we appreciate it, but why...."

"... Am I here now?" Dickie asks, shrugging. "Two reasons. First, to *apologize* to you about Ronnie. I let the 'small-town friends' code blind me to the fact that he wasn't looking for you for any decent reasons. I should *never* have let him know I was following the group. I'm sorry I told him that, and allowed him to invade your privacy. By the way, I saw him leaving the auditorium—he said he'd 'catch you later,' as he put it." I don't know why Ronnie keeps using *that* phrase, like it'll wear me down, but it won't. He may say and do the right things, but I'm *done* with him.

"That's okay, Mr. Newsome. Thanks for apologizing and explaining. You said there was another reason?" I can't believe Dickie is *apologizing* after making me ride an emotional roller coaster. I wonder if he's planning a "gotcha" with this as the set-up.

"Yes, the second reason is to tell you I'll continue covering the concerts, and writing articles for both Rolling Stone and the Atlanta papers, but I won't dig deeper into your life, or that of the other guys." He looks at me with a sad expression—*if* he's setting me up, he's been rehearsing, because it's *totally* believable.

"Well, thanks, I... we appreciate it," I stammer, shocked at the sudden end of the threat.

"Let the magazines take their chances with you, but I'm not helping." Dickie gets an almost-grin on his face, then clears his throat as if he's gotten something caught in his windpipe. "For the record, *before* this tour, I had heard some of your songs on the radio. Not bad, but not earth-shattering, either. I've always been more a Roy Orbison fan. Your first show in San Francisco changed everything. Live, in concert, your music is phenomenal. Consider me a fan." He looks directly into my eyes and smiles.

Oh. My. God.... Dickie is... a *fan*? Okay then.

"Mr. Newsome...."

"Please, call me Dickie."

"Thanks, Dickie."

File this night under "weird, weirder, and weirdest"—*one* will fit. Still, it's too bad that Ronnie chickened out about talking; I really wanted to get everything sorted tonight. The icing on the friggin' shitstorm cake of my demons is that Ronnie is *still* out there, trying to figure out how to lure me back.

Free day, June 23

Seattle's been a roller coaster. I've gained a new appreciation for my found family, who have heard my lies, seen my reactions to them, and stuck by me as I revealed how terribly I had misled them. I'm waiting for that other shoe to drop. It *can't* be as easy as apologizing. I've gotta get started repairing things with *everybody*, especially Benji, DC, and Sean. The first concert was a fantastic high, the second was an almost-disaster. Somewhere between those two, finding out Dickie Newsome is a fan and being boxed in by Ronnie.

The international portion of the tour starts with our next stop in Montreal. We won't have American habits and language surrounding us. The official language in our next two stops is French—a language Sean and I have dabbled in enough to know we don't know much. Before the tour began, Greg assured us there would be "translators" available in both Montreal and Paris. That's good; I can see the disaster of my southern American voice filtering through my put-on British accent to *really* confound any French natives.

As I'm thinking those thoughts, there's a knock at my door, so sharp and precise it could only be Greg. Since I've just finished a shower, I'm wearing a robe. I check myself in the mirror quickly, then open the door. Greg enters the room with a handful of brochures. With them, he motions me to sit. Guess we're going to chat.

"Look, we're under a lot of pressure on this tour, and I know you've had it worse than anyone. Still, it's hard to hear someone you consider a friend, a brother, or a *son*, has told a colossal lie and repeated it. Know what I mean?" He asks, firmly, not angrily. There's disappointment in his voice, like a father.

"Greg, I..." I begin, but he cuts me off.

"No, before you say anything, let me make it clear. You've got a day off today; good thing after last night's show was less than what this group is capable of. Your revelation threw everyone off, so *you've* got to restore their trust. We're going sightseeing, nothing serious, so you've got a chance to correct it. For your sake, for the group, don't blow it."

"I got it. I'm gonna make it up to everyone, I promise you. I'm worried...."

"We *know* you're afraid of being abandoned. The fact the group went onstage last night *after* you dropped your truth about Ronnie should prove that these guys—and DC and I—aren't going to drop you. But you've broken the trust, and you have to repair the bridges you burned with that lie."

"I know I fucked up. Sorry. It was never meant to hurt anyone other than Ronnie. I'm scared shitless at how upset DC got. She's so strong... anyway, I'm gonna talk to everyone. I don't wanna lose the best thing I ever had."

"You know what you need to do, and I hope you know—from the fact we're still here—none of us is going to leave you behind, as long as you own up to your mistake and *never* let it happen again. Now, let's get this day started, okay?"

"Can't we stay here at the hotel? I don't wanna run into Ronnie." Geez, whiny baby much?

"Already considered, which is why Mr. Preston will join us."

"He told me to call him Robert."

"Alrighty. He and Benji will be your close companions for the excursion I've planned—the rest of the guys and DC won't be far. How's a trip up the Space Needle sound?"

"The wha?"

"Space Needle. That tower we've seen. The symbol for the World's Fair in the early 1960s. You might get a kick riding the monorail, and we can start the touristy stuff visiting Pike Place Market, close to the nearest monorail station. To get to Pike Place, we'll take a van ride with Davey."

"Sounds cool, actually. Beats hiding here like a coward." His descriptions make me do a complete turnaround from minutes before.

"Let's have a relaxing day, and you can start rebuilding those bridges while we're at it."

"From your lips to God's ears."

"Then let's get the guys." Greg calls Davey at the other hotel, and we've arranged our tourist day. We've got fifteen minutes before Davey arrives with DC and the van, so I help Greg gather our gang. First stop is Benji.

I knock at the door. It opens immediately. "What, were you waiting for someone to knock?" I ask a wide-awake, fully dressed, *smiling* Benji.

"I might've heard a wee bit of your excitement."

“I wasn’t excited at first, but Greg makes it sound like fun. First, I gotta say I’m sorry about the lies about Ronnie. It wasn’t meant to hurt anyone.”

Benji shows how hurt he still is, looking at the floor, nodding slightly, as he murmurs a short “’kay.”

Damn, he’s not even looking at me as he sort-of accepts my brief apology. Gonna have to go stronger. “Of all the stupid things I’ve done, holding onto the lie about how Ronnie and I split up was the worst....”

Then he looks at me, a glance somewhere between dismissal and hope. I’ve *started* making my apology to him. He’s normally so quick to forgive, I realize I’ve hurt him deeply.

Benji starts to shake his head like he’s going to give me a silent *no*, then stops, looks down toward the floor again, before changing the topic. “I was readin’ this note from my uncle Noah—you remember him, from the birthday party? My buddy John LeBlanc is coming to see *us* in Montreal and Paris.” Benji is almost vibrating with excitement, the subject of an old friend making him happier than I can.

“Your old buddy?” Is that a note of jealousy creeping into my voice? Oh, for fuck’s sake, wasn’t I the one who said Benji would grow tired of waiting for me and find someone else? And after I’ve upset him with the revelation of my lie, he’s pissed off enough to go for his *old buddy*.

“Aw, he’s one of the oldest friends I have.... Le’s go. You get Todd and I’ll get Clay, we’ll be a’most there.” The excitement is creeping into Benji’s voice—I’m *not* complaining.

We follow Benji’s plan. Greg has called Sean and Wil, who join us in the hallway. Sean and Todd are cool toward me as we meet, reminding me I need to repair the trust with them. Sean’s been my best friend, my almost-brother. He knows me as well as I know myself; the fact he’s cool to me now shows how badly I've fucked up. Sean usually lets stuff blow over after a while. Todd is hyper-enthusiastic about seeing the sights—he rarely shows emotion, so the fact he's got a smile on his face, other than when he looks at me, is a giveaway. He's also a "shutterbug" with a camera he's been using to document our exploits; to no one's surprise, it's with him. Clay answers his door slowly, revealing he's slept late. His hair is sleep-tousled. He apologetically asks for five minutes. We agree, we're on no schedule here.

Four minutes later, Clay opens his door, hair brushed into place, dressed for a day out. He smiles brightly in my direction as he exits his room, and I'm confused until I hear Sean's voice behind me. *That* explains the smile.

"Good mornin', babe," Sean says, then quickly adds, "Clay," as if the "babe" hadn't been spoken. I think the "bed-head" has more of a reason than sleep. I *won't* make a stink, considering I'm already on thin ice with the guys. Dickie may be backing off, but there are plenty of scandal rags out there waiting for a hint of something to run with.

Benji looks at Clay and Sean with a knowing smile, then whispers to me, "My would say those two are *de'pouille*—a mess." I nod. Benji knows, I know, and I'm sure the other guys are figuring out those two. Until I get my *own* shit in order, I don't have any place telling them how to live their lives, on tour or elsewhere, even though I wish they would cool it.

Greg joins us in the hallway. We wait for the elevator. He's carrying a set of the brochures for Pike Place Market, the Space Needle, and the Monorail, like we're back in school going on a field trip with the teacher, only Greg is more relaxed than my teachers ever were.

The ride to Pike Place Market is full of discussions about the market. It's a big center of shopping in Seattle, has several places to buy freshly caught fish and seafood, but there are shops of different types. There's a barber shop—I'll pass. Ravynn without the long black hair is *not* another wannabe. Without the hair, Ravynn becomes dull Robin Smith again. There are several shops and restaurants I'm interested in. We'll have fun exploring, even with our shadow, Mr. Preston. It's silly he's joining us, but since Ronnie didn't stick around after the show, it's better to be safe. And he can unwind.

Davey stops in front of a vast building; we get out and Mr. Preston is waiting for us. After we exit, Davey drives the van away. DC, Greg, Mr. Preston, and my bandmates are milling about, rather than gathering around me. It's *not* the "Wall" as it has been, and suddenly I feel naked, out in public without my Wall of guys. I hadn't been *totally* happy about being surrounded by my guys, but with that security blanket ripped away, I want it back. God, that fuckin' lie screwed up my entire life.

We make our way into the Market; one of the first places we see is the Pike Place Fish Market. They more than sell fish—they *entertain*. Guys are throwing fish; not fish you catch in lakes and streams. I'm talking salmon and tuna, big-ass fish, bigger than Sean and me *combined*. They draw a crowd; our mini-crowd adds to it. They flip these big fish from one guy to another like they're tossing tennis balls. Other places in the market sell fish also, but none of them give you a floor show while they do.

Some shops are intriguing. Three Girls Bakery's been in business since 1912; it was the first Seattle business licensed to women. The baked goods smell yummy. We stop in and sample a few croissants and cupcakes. Shit, I need my coffee. The cashier tells me there's a coffee shop nearby. Hope I can move everyone that way. As we continue wandering, we come upon MarketSpice, a shop that began as a tea and spice shop in 1911. The aromas of the spices are comforting and sensual, reminding me of cooking with my mother years ago.

I'm so desperate for coffee at this point I'll take any source; I'm a "coffee-holic." Luck is on my side, because as we pass MarketSpice, there's Lowell's Restaurant & Bar. This amazing restaurant is on three levels in the market. How they deal with customers on three separate levels is beyond me. Glad all I do is sing. We get coffees, sodas, waters, or whatevers. Greg and DC are holding suspiciously colored beverages that *may* be alcoholic drinks. It's their day off, too.

While we're enjoying our drinks, I look at more brochures. There's a place in the market called "Golden Age Collectibles" that I'm *dying* to check out.

"Hey, can we find Golden Age Collectibles next?"

"Isn't that the comics and toy store?" Greg asks, grinning.

"Yeah, so?"

"Figured you *might* enjoy it. That, or be repulsed."

"Does that mean we can?"

"Sounds like fun," Benji stops drinking his cafe au lait long enough. How he got the restaurant to *make* the cafe au lait is a miracle of its own, aided largely by his smile—*and* a New Orleans transplant living in Seattle.

"Of course we can," DC ends the discussion, leaving no doubt about her interest.

We head to the fourth level of the market and find Golden Age Collectibles. I browse row after row of comics and old toys, getting lost in childhood memories. For the moment, I've forgotten Greg, DC, and my bandmates, remembering the fun of my younger years with these old toys, forgetting the pain of what those years led to.

I see a display of early Beatles records and memorabilia near the back, so I walk past the life-size cardboard Elvis standing nearby and mutter, *Thank 'ou, thank 'ou ver' much*, in my best Elvis voice. From behind me, I hear a laugh. Turning, I see Benji approaching, his face almost expressionless.

"I saw you heading back here, and I betcha I can tell what you're thinking. You're wondering if one day there'll be a shop with a section devoted to *us*." He reaches me, and wraps an arm around my waist, instinctively. I'm surprised, relieved, and shocked. This hug seems like an acceptance of my apology, even if it wasn't the best wording. I need to expand on it.

"If I don't fuck us up with my stupid shit, you mean?" I nearly whisper. I can't believe he's so quick to forgive me after dealing with my issues. "Listen, I gotta make sure you know how sorry I am. I didn't do this to hurt you, I swear."

He looks like he's about to say something, so I touch his lips with my right forefinger to slow him down. I gotta mend *this* bridge, now.

"Ronnie was the one who counted, like it was my father who counted. I was the afterthought, the leftover.... I was okay for a cook, or a fuck, but I was never good enough to *be* somebody. So when Ronnie threw me out, it hurt like hell, and I made him look bad 'cause it made *me* look better. I shoulda come clean long before now, but it scared me I'd wind up being a nobody."

"Rave, in case you hadn't noticed it, we're a family here. Might not be blood family, but that makes it stronger, 'cause we *chose* to be family. Families gonna have fights, but ya get over 'em, and come out the better for it." Between his shining green eyes, his Cajun accent, and that devil-may-care grin, he would make a damn good lawyer.

Still with his arm around my waist, he turns us toward the exit of the shop. Sean and Clay are off to the left, looking at old-time games like Chutes and Ladders and Monopoly, their arms around each other's waists. Suddenly I panic; here we are, four members of Phoenix Rising in public, practically *screaming* that we're homosexual. I wiggle a bit, hoping Benji will turn loose, but he's not loosening up.

"You gotta itch or something?" He looks innocent as he asks, except for the grin forming at his lips. Yeah, he *knows* I'm uncomfortable in public like this. Performing is one thing, but offstage, it's another world.

"Or something.... I'm not ready for the closeness, and Ronnie isn't out of the picture." I hope my bluntness doesn't hurt him. He's still got enough reason to be mad at me for the damage my lies caused.

"I gotcha. Okay now?" He asks, nodding slowly as he loosens his embrace—and his smile fades slightly.

I just nod. Damn, I've hurt him again. This is *not* making my life easier.

Greg and DC are standing outside the shop, backs to the entrance, chatting. Benji strides from me to Greg as if he was doing a fast-walk race. DC turns to me at that moment and frowns. Man, I can't win for losing.

"Don't tell me you two are fighting," DC fires off, her eyes narrowing as she glares at me. I haven't gotten *her* forgiveness yet.

Benji shakes his head.

"A little misunderstanding." I say.

The monorail's cool.

I look around. Everyone's in their own situation. Todd's taking pictures inside the monorail and through the windows. Sean-and-Clay, sitting a row in front of Benji and me, are too busy being together to notice the monorail or the skyline. At least they aren't kissing or anything obvious—*yet*. DC sits nearby—these cars have unusual seat configurations, several rows like the train cars we rode in during Benji's birthday trip, but some placed at right angles. It makes it easier for a large group to stay together without having to crane our necks to talk.

With Benji seated beside me, I can pretend for now that everything is fine. We've started repairing the trust I blew up when I revealed the lie about Ronnie, but I know it's going to take time to prove that I'm worthy of being with Benji as a friend. The idea of his buddy swooping in and stealing him bugs me, though I have no right to object to that.

The monorail ride is short, three minutes once the car starts moving. We arrive at Seattle Center and exit the car, walk down the ramp from the platform and there, in front of us, is the Space Needle.

At ground level, it's freakin' amazing. This column of steel and concrete looks like it could be a big industrial chimney until you look up and see the 520-foot "top house" perched above the city. I can't believe there are people who prefer climbing 832 steps—open-air, no less—rather than taking the elevator to the top.

Thankfully, the elevator's large enough for our small army. Benji presses tightly against me. The elevator *isn't* crowded, and Benji's never mentioned fears of heights or enclosed places, so I'm guessing he's giving me a different kind of message that my brain needs to just shut up and enjoy.

If the Space Needle is amazing at ground level, it's freakin' mind-blowing up top. The floors and walls are see-through—a full view of Seattle and surroundings. I'm sure Todd has taken at least two rolls' worth of pictures. It's been a great day. The whole time inside the Space Needle, you couldn't force a tissue between Benji and me. Whatever the deal was in the elevator has continued.

I don't remember how high the top house is, but I'm not thinking about that—I'm not a fan of heights and this one's tiny compared to what's coming next: a flight to Montreal.

•••••••••••

Montreal, Quebec

June 24 - 27, 1968

Airport, June 24

"Bienvenue à Montréal," reads the sign in large letters; smaller, it says, "Welcome to Montreal." If *that* doesn't prove we're in another country, the fact we're checking into Canadian Customs before going to our hotel does. There's a flamboyant guy, about my age, talking to Greg; has Greg gotten himself a boyfriend? There's a lot of that going on with this group.

Greg sees me and brings the guy with him. I get to meet the boy-toy first.

"Ravynn, meet Jean-Paul Martine. Jean-Paul, *this* is Ravynn, our lead singer. Jean-Paul will be our interpreter in Montreal and Paris."

"Nice to meet you, Jean-Paul. I apologize. I thought Greg found himself a boyfriend!"

"Just because Cupid's firing his arrows into you guys doesn't mean he's aimed my way." The tone of Greg's voice tells me he may have accepted the truth about my breakup with Ronnie, but he's not ready yet for business as normal. I still have some work on that front. Todd was so busy with his camera during our day off in Seattle that I couldn't talk to him, Wil was talking tech with Greg, and Sean was too busy with Clay—and vice versa. And DC's been civil, but cold—I gotta talk to her.

"Ravynn, you are homosexual also?" Jean-Paul asks.

Ohmygawd. This guy is so direct. I gotta work on this. I gotta make sure he's not planning to share this with the press. Until I know, the less I say, the better.

"That's not something that we talk about," I sweep my arms around to show my point, "Why did you say 'also' though?"

"Because *I* am homosexual." His French accent's delightful. Wonder how he'll deal with Benji's Cajun.... This could be fun.

Knock *me* over with a feather. Cute, direct, homosexual as I suspected, and he's flirting with me. I'd better be careful, or I'll have Benji pouting again—he's barely forgiven me, I *think*, for the lies about Ronnie. Until Ronnie's really out of my life, *he's* my concern. Though Jean-Paul blurting out he's *also* homosexual gives anyone within hearing enough material to ruin the group. I can't win for losing. At least Dickie Newsome won't jump into that, *if* he's told me the truth.

As we finish going through Canadian Customs, Benji joins Jean-Paul and me. "Hey, who dat?"

"Benji, meet Jean-Paul Martine, our interpreter for Montreal and Paris," I say.

Benji hugs Jean-Paul. He's his mom's kid. If they ever award Olympic medals for hugging, the Travers family of Louisiana will have a lock on Gold. While he's hugging Jean-Paul, our Cajun firecracker's eyeing him like he *might* be radioactive.

Jean-Paul, taken aback, smiles and returns the hug. "Enchanté, Benji."

Benji's eyes widen with surprise. "Hoo boy, you speak *French!*"

"But of course, how else will I be the interpreter for you?"

This'll be interesting; Benji's Cajun is *not* textbook French, but it's closer to French than the rest of us manage. *My* knowledge of French is knowing the French verse in *Michelle* by the Beatles is translated in the song's next lines. I took a year of French because of that song to discover there were no hidden messages.

While I stroll memory lane, Benji and Jean-Paul are having a conversation that can only be called "bizarre." Benji says something in his Cajun-English mix, and Jean-Paul translates it, if possible, into his understanding of English. There are obvious misunderstandings, but the two are becoming friends, though Benji occasionally glances from me to Jean-Paul with what's called "stink-eye," one of those looks that gets the label of "if looks could kill" in romance stories. Benji's jealous.

We wait for Davey and his crew to clear customs. Greg informs us that Jean-Paul will be with us through Paris and reminds us of tomorrow's press conference. "Jean-Paul will translate your answers into French, and the French questions into English. For the benefit of the French-Canadian and French reporters, he will also translate English questions from reporters into French, so be aware. 'Brothers from different mothers' is out."

He stares at me in silent warning; he's still upset over my deception. I'm *still* worried, despite our earlier talk, that Greg will decide it's time to be simply our manager. That scares the shit out of me.

"We got it. What if there's a Spanish or Italian reporter on hand?" I *have* to ask.

"They'll have their own translators with them, so their questions will be asked in English to you."

"Sounds like it's gonna be long," Sean says, and we agree.

"It could be. I'm sure there will be fewer questions than in San Francisco," Greg says.

"What if someone asks about Ronnie?" I ask. At the mention of Ronnie, Benji, Todd, and Sean glare at me—*what the hell are you thinking?* There's more concern about my motives regarding Ronnie than I expected.

Benji spells it out. "Why do you keep bringing *him* up? Are you *that* fixated? Or are you wanting to go back, in *spite* of your denials?" When he spits out "denials," with his accent and rising anger, it sounds like "dee niles."

Shit. I've got Benji angry again, when I was hoping I'd fixed things with him. My squadron of kamikaze butterflies is revving, preparing to torment me through the night. *Why* did I ask that question?

Hotel Nelligan

Perfect. We're staying at a hotel named "Nelligan"? Sounds like a phrase to describe homosexuals: "He's being nelly, again." Was it chosen on purpose, or just a coincidence? If Greg booked the hotels, it's *got* to be a coincidence.

The Nelligan's ritzy. It plays up Montreal's French heritage, with lots of features you don't see in American hotels. For instance, my room's bathroom has a *bidet*—I first thought it was a urinal alongside the toilet, but Jean-Paul's cleared that up for me. The wallpaper pattern, according to DC, is French Provincial, comfortable and stylish. Good thing, since we'll be here for four days. The bed's enormous, at least queen-sized, and looks like I could sink into the mattress. Hmm, think I'll test that theory soon, if Jean-Paul's as willing as he seems to be. But... *if* I play with Jean-Paul, it might hurt Benji, since he and Jean-Paul have become friends—and sneaking around behind Benji worries me. We *aren't* a couple, Benji knows it, but my heart aches like I'll be cheating on him, even *thinking* about fooling around with Jean-Paul. Fuck.

We're each given a room; Jean-Paul has a room next door to me.

Benji's at the far end of the hall, past Clay's room, which is next to Sean's. Greg's given up on preventing those two from being together. I'm hoping they won't have an argument that hurts the group, but so far, it's all lovey-dovey. I'm torn between being glad for Sean, who deserves to be happy, and worrying my ass off for the group, because of my history.

Our group takes up the penthouse.

Once I unpack, I change into my favorite loungewear, then saunter next door to Jean-Paul's door. Either he's expecting someone, or he doesn't believe in closed doors. His door's ajar. I tap at the door, and hear "Entrez—Enter."

As I enter, I see Jean-Paul standing beside his bed, wearing a tight pair of sky blue nylon shorts. Obviously, he's ready to play.

"I'll push your door closed," I say, doing so before stalking to the bed where Jean-Paul stands, drinking me in.

"Tell me, *cheri*, how close are you and Benji?" Jean-Paul goes to the point. My mind struggles with my libido—my mind says "don't do it, remember Benji," as my sex drive tries to get my cock, which had drooped at Jean-Paul's words, to focus on sex alone. My answer's quickly muttered; Benji and I are band-mates and friends. I *know* Benji wants more, and I know he's hurting from my lie. Greg said we should be six band members with no relationships... and Jean-Paul pulls me in. It's *just* sex....

Jean-Paul's eyes have feasted on my torso, clothed in a gauzy long-sleeved top. He scans down my body; his eyes widen when he sees the bulge from my semi-hard cock.

Guys are three types: growers, where the cock becomes huge; showers, where the cock looks huge but doesn't grow as it erects; growers-and-showers, which combines the two. Lucky me, I'm the last one. Hopefully, Jean-Paul's got no problems with that.

In answer to my thoughts, Jean-Paul reaches out with his hand and cups my cock and balls, moaning slightly before our lips meet. The kiss is electric; it could light the Montreal Forum.

As our tongues battle inside our mouths, we're running hands over each other's body. We need to move to the bed, or we're gonna finish too soon.

"Bed," is all I can utter between kisses. We pile onto his bed, a duplicate of mine; a flurry of clothing hits the floor.

I straddle him, finally seeing him fully. His nipples are medium brown, some hair curled around them. A few hairs dust his chest. A treasure trail of pale brown hair traces from his navel to his cock.

After licking my lips, I take Jean-Paul's balls, one by one, into my mouth. He's trying to jerk himself; I move his hand away. I tongue my way up his cock, circle the head—making him moan—then swallow him completely, my mouth and throat suctioning his most sensitive area.

Jean-Paul's delirious. He writhes, grabs the bedsheets like he's trying to ride a stallion, his eyes smoldering sex at me.

He's nearing the point of no return; a few more sucks and he'll fill my throat, but I've got a different finish planned. I let him slip from my lips, raise his legs over my shoulders; with access to his hole now, my tongue teases it, bringing moans from him.

I use my tongue like I'll soon use my cock. I spear his hole, barely opening it; he gasps. I pull my tongue back, circle the hole, then drive deeper. He moans, gasps, wiggles his ass, trying to get my tongue deeper.

My tongue pistons in and out, getting his hole wet and ready. He's moaning, occasionally uttering an understandable "fuck me." I keep plunging my tongue in and out, his hole loosening as I do, while I moisten the fingers of my left hand with saliva. He's again close to cumming, so I pull back my tongue to circle the entrance.

"Lube?" I ask, sliding one of my spit-covered fingers inside.

"Under... bed," he answers, between shudders and moans. I reach down; happily, my hand finds the tube.

I add the second finger, pumping in and out. Thank fuck, the lube's in a flip-top tube, so I open it with my right hand. With two fingers from my left hand plowing him, he's building toward release. "Don't cum."

I get the lube open and squirt some on my cock. Stuff's cold; the horns are intense. I pull my fingers out of his hole and replace them with lube applied by the same fingers.

"Ready?"

"Gawd, fuck me *now*."

I slide my cock into his still-tight hole, taking it slow. I don't want to hurt him. "Is this your first time?"

"Only with you."

I slide more in; he grits his teeth and growls, "Fuck me. Now."

Slowly, I rock in and out, penetrating deeper with each inward plunge, until I bottom out, my balls against his ass cheeks. I pump in and out a few more times, watching his face—he's blissing out.

He's focusing on what's happening; it doesn't faze him when I begin pounding his hole, pulling almost out, slamming back in. I'm hitting his prostate every time I push in. He's sensing me inside him, his climax building. He's falling apart under me.

It's gonna be close whether I cum first, starting his release, or he's first, starting mine. As I think that, his eyelids flutter, his eyes glaze, his breathing comes in gasps as his body prepares for release. His hole begins clenching and unclenching, as his *untouched* cock fires rope after rope of cum, and that's it. I plunge deep and spray inside him, over and over.

We lie still for a minute, my cock inside him. I think he's fallen asleep under me when his voice, sultry and sex-sated, barely makes it past my shoulder to my ears.

"That was magnifique, cherie," he says, then giggles. I fucked this guy and don't know how old he is. He could be a minor; sex between adults and minors in Montreal is a major offense, I believe the equivalent of our felony charge, so that *alone* would put me in jail for a long term. That it's homosexual sex is the cherry on the top.

After cleaning up, Jean-Paul surprises me.

"I want to do this again."

"Jean-Paul, how old are you?"

"I'm twenty-one. Don't panic. I have a full-time boyfriend; we'll be fuck-buddies for a short while."

"You have a boyfriend, yet you have flings with other guys?"

"We have an open relationship. He lives in Marseille. We don't have time to be together often, but when we are, we're *very* exclusive. He knows I'm your interpreter here and in Paris. Afterwards, I will spend time with him in Marseille."

"So, he knows you're with us, but will he be okay about what we did?"

"Here's the thing. He *bet* me you're homosexual. I wasn't sure."

"And...?"

"He told me that if you are, and if there's any attraction, go for it. You are, there is, I did. I want to do it again."

"You're cute, your body is great, but no one knows about me, and I need to keep it that way," I say, almost pleading with my eyes.

"I am discretion itself, mon cher. We play, it's you and me; no one will know," Jean-Paul says, looking directly into my eyes.

"You've met Benji. You probably know he's got a thing for me. I don't want to hurt him, though I can't be in a relationship with him now."

"Your Benji *is* special. He told me the other day he was content to wait until he can 'wear your resistance down,' but he'll grow tired of waiting if you make him wait too long."

Okay, I *could* have a playmate until we leave Paris, but I'm not sure. As tempting as another romp with him is, my mind and heart are telling me that Jean-Paul should stay one and done, and now, my body's listening. I know how Benji feels about me, and he knows how much I care about him—but with my admission about what happened between Ronnie and me.... *Now* I have to make sure Benji doesn't find out about Jean-Paul and me. Given my luck at keeping secrets, I am *so* fucked....

Forum, June 25

We're sitting in the home of Montreal hockey, where the Beatles won over the French Canadian audiences—six American guys, a middle-aged American man, and a 21-year-old French translator. Of our motley crew, I've apologized to Greg and Benji. The rest are a work in progress, but Sean-and-Clay will be a joint effort. A crowbar couldn't pry them apart in a private setting—and I'm sure as hell not apologizing with the press taking notes.

I'm not sure why DC isn't with us for the news conference, and it scares the shit out of me that my lie tore her up. My fear is that I've driven her away from us—okay, from *me*. I must apologize to her soon. She's 'Mama Bear' to us. My priority must be making things right with her.

Our audience includes reporters from Montreal and the province of Quebec, a few from other Canadian provinces, at least one from France, a couple guys who appear to be Italian, and one guy who's obviously British—every hair precise, stiff posture like a cardboard cutout, and the ever-popular bowler hat—he may as well be waving the Union Jack and singing "Hail Britannia." In addition, there's press from America, including our newest "fan," Dickie Newsome, and others. They ask all the usual questions and Jean-Paul translates.

Everything's going great until Fred Thomerson from Vancouver, British Columbia, asks, "Do you have plans to prevent further drops in quality?" Talk about deflating the balloon... one question and we drop from top of the world to the grimy underbelly. Damn. I've *gotta* get this right, and I can't let it go further—this is where I show *everyone* that I'm committed to this group 100%.

"We're *all* concerned about the quality of our shows. Unfortunately,..." Fuck. Thoughts of the near-disaster of that show has me choking up. It's my fault. I've dragged these guys, DC, and Greg, down to the gutter with me.

I see Sean glance my way, his jaw setting in that bulldog manner when he gets determined. He's scoped out that I'm upset, and moves closer to his microphone.

"Ravynn's upset the second Seattle show had problems. We all are." I see Benji, Todd, Clay, and Wil nodding in agreement.

"A lot of what happened couldn't be prevented, but we had backup instruments," Todd continues. "We completed the show, despite the mishaps." My guys are blowing my mind. After my screwups, they've *still* got my back.

"We appreciate the fans in Seattle who attended the show, and we'll return in the future to make it right." Sean finishes the answer. The guys have pulled my ass out of the fire.

Greg nods approval. There are other questions which Greg handles, but I'm stuck remembering how badly I fucked up our last Seattle show—and vowing to myself *it won't happen again*.

When the interview's finally over, we sit in silence as the members of the press, except Dickie, file out. Dickie lingers behind, his shoulders slumped like he's carrying the entire world, turns to me and in a low voice says, "I'm sorry I let Ronnie know where you were; sorry I didn't warn you. If there's anything I can do to help, let me know."

"Thanks, that makes me feel better. Don't beat yourself up for it," I say.

Dickie nods, then slumps out.

We head backstage to allow Davey's crew a chance to transform the platform into the concert stage, and to relax before soundcheck. It might give me time to talk to my guys and repair more of the damage my lie caused. I wish I could know where Ronnie is now, or better yet, know that he won't be bothering me. But I guess that's unrealistic.

Backstage

"That was intriguing," Greg, suddenly master of the understatement, says. We're sitting backstage. I've pulled off my shirt to slip on another for soundcheck.

"I'll just call the detectives to make sure they're alert," Greg adds, leaving.

Sean and Clay walk into the room, almost touching. I've gotta adjust to it, because this *thing* between them isn't going away. They may not be holding hands or looking at each other lovingly, but they aren't far from that.

"Hey, wanted to be sure you're okay. That was crazy out there."

Sean could sum up a situation well. I should be grateful he's concerned about me, but I'm upset he's doing so with Clay practically welded to his side.

"I'm good. You don't know the half of it.... More importantly, I gotta apologize to you for keeping the lie about Ronnie for so long."

He and Clay nod in agreement.

"Rave, you and I have been... brothers... for freakin' forever. I'm the guy who knows you better'n you know yourself. It fuckin' hurts knowing you kept up a lie that long. *Why?*" he asks, almost in tears.

I see how much he cares, how much I hurt him. Clay, holding Sean's waist like it's his lifeline, has a look on his face somewhere between love for Sean and disgust at me.

"I *never* intended to hurt anyone—especially not *you*. It's been us from the beginning. We dreamed this together, and I'm the fuckup who's ruining it. Gawd, I hate hurting you. If I could go back to that night, I'd tell you the story then. I'm a fool, got the best family...." I choke up, unable to continue.

"You hurt him *bad*, Ravynn," Clay makes his strongest-ever comment. I deserve it—I'm so damn insecure I allowed the lie to poison every part of my life.

"I'm sorry for *everything* I've done wrong, for trying to be high and mighty while I was hiding behind a monstrous lie. Your friendship is greater than I deserve after that, much less the family we are. I *need* us to be how we've been. I *want* all of you—especially *you* two—to know you can trust me, and things to be okay between us."

Sean nods slightly. "We'll get there. Promise no more fucked-up stories. And you *gotta* be sure everyone knows how sorry you are."

"I know I fucked up bad, and I'll work every day to earn your complete trust again," I get the words out as my heart breaks over the damage my *little* fib caused.

Sean pivots the conversation. "We need to get another thing cleared up. My relationship with Clay. That's up to us... not you."

The look on his face is typical Sean when he's convinced he's doing what he wants. It's the same look he had when he and I told his parents we were gonna be rock stars. Thinking that, I smile.

"You mean Sean-and-Clay will be around for a while?" I go for humor, but the glares I get in response tell me I misread the situation.

"You've got a helluva lot of nerve, and no room to talk, saying that," Sean fires back. Damn, I'm no good at apologizing. I *always* piss off whoever I apologize to.

"I didn't mean anything, Sean, other than you two have been close. It's *my* personal relationships that turn to shit. If I could, I'd go back to the day I left Ronnie and make sure *you* knew what happened. Since I can't, I'll spend the rest of my life proving I'm never gonna do anything like that."

I turn to Clay, and open my mouth to say almost the same words to him. He beats me to the punch with words that shake me to my heart.

"Sean can *always* count on me, Ravynn. I've *never* lied to him or omitted telling him anything. He's told me he loves you as a brother, and I understand that—my brother's at home dealing with the situation there." Clay pauses, and I start to speak, but he shuts me up again. "You wrecked years of trust with Sean. You're not getting away with a five-minute apology. He's had your back, like at the news conference, forever."

"I know I've messed up. Believe me, I *never* meant to hurt anyone except Ronnie. I felt alone, unwanted, and had to reinvent myself. I was too damn big a coward to tell the truth, and now it's back to bite my ass."

Clay reaches out with one hand and grasps my hand. "We aren't happy, but we can work on it. Sean's told me how fucked up things were with your parents and Ronnie. It hurt that you kept the lie going, but like I care a fuckton about Sean and this group, we know you care as much about us, and we *ain't* gonna let *anything*—Ronnie or anyone—take you away."

Sean gives one of his quirky half-smiles and pulls Clay's hand away. "You've got someone to play grab hands with, Rave. Make sure you give as strong an apology to Benji, and DC, as you gave us. Clay and I are committed to

Phoenix Rising, to *you*—whether you deserve it. We're not leaving, so quit worrying, but keep telling us the truth."

Greg strides back into the room then and looks quizzically at Sean and Clay.

"Davey and his crew have about 5 minutes to complete the setup. There will be a detective in the auditorium."

"Thanks, that's a relief." *Finally* I'm able to relax. With a guy in the auditorium during the soundcheck and the show, there's no way anyone can get to me. If Ronnie shows up trying to charm me back into his bed, he'll be out of luck.

Soundcheck runs almost normally, with an audience of a single detective. As we finish, Sean sings a lyric I've never heard.

"Ask me what I am, I tell you I don't know, Can it be I'm just a person with a cause to show, That I feel a lot for you, and care a lot for you." Ohmygawd, the look on Sean's face as he sings the words, clearly aimed at Clay, is amazing. He's in love. It's beautiful, and I'm thrilled for him and jealous as hell. I want that, but with my history, it won't happen. I hope this love between them, beautiful as it is, won't hurt the group. Those joined-at-the-waist moments, the touching, and his comments minutes ago, add up to tell me he was planning this; the confession to me was the ultimate test, which I apparently passed. This is part of Sean's love song to Clay. Clay realizes it; his face reddens, and he's staring at Sean with a look mixing love and awe.

Todd whoops and says, "Granny's is in love!" He calls Sean *Granny* due to the granny glasses. Sean doesn't flinch, but does a rim-shot on the drums.

Wil gets into the spirit and plays the Bridal March, then Benji laughs and says, "Who gonna marry 'em?"

Before I lose control, I say, "Guys, let's get backstage and dress for tonight's show." I could *kill* Sean for springing this. The guys are taking it in stride, and *my* lie's forgotten for now. Gotta talk to Todd, Wil, and DC.

The Forum's packed. This show must be perfect—no repeats from Seattle. I don't know how many people are in the audience. Looks like the entire city of Montreal, possibly the entire province of Quebec, has squeezed in. If someone figures out how to create seats floating in air, I'm sure *they'd* be packed.

Before we go onstage, I get the six of us together, and deliver a pep talk mixed with a beginning apology for Todd and Wil. "Let's shake off Seattle. We need to show how *tough* we are. Todd, Clay, and Benji, let's get that playful vibe back. It'll be worth it."

Clay and Benji look like they're plotting something, Todd and Wil nod, and I'm positive we can climb back to the top with this show.

"It's on," Benji and Todd say in unison—like they've been rehearsing it. Clay and Wil give smiles and nod. It's showtime. The butterflies in my gut are having a heyday.

In the audience, people are holding signs reading "Je t'aime," with every group member getting representation. *Okay*, Benji and I have more than the others. Shows how much Benji's popularity has risen. I'm the singer—that explains my share.

With no deejay introducing us, we take the stage to thunderous applause and screams. As the guys get their instruments set, I grab my mike and stalk, panther-like, to the edge of the stage. My year of French in school, plus excellent tutoring from Jean-Paul, helps me as I shout, "Bonsoir, Montréal!" All I say is "Good evening, Montreal." With limited knowledge of French, that's impressive, I *hope*.

The audience roars and seems to sing along with some of our songs. Hard to tell in a semi-darkened room. Once I'm onstage, it's me, my guys, and the audience, nothing else enters my thoughts. I spot Dickie Newsome, as well as a guy who could be the detective. Not too many middle-aged guys wearing dark coats show up for rock concerts. The *best* thing, I do *not* spot Ronnie.

The show goes on, and during my English introductions of the group, the audience cheers and screams for each, with Benji getting a few more proposals—hard to tell when it's shouted in rapid French. One woman's voice carries through the hall as she shouts "Je voudrais avoir ton bébé, Benji!" Jean-Paul will have to confirm this for me, but I recognize "ton bébé" as "your baby," so I'm guessing the rest is the woman offering to be the mother of his children; he grins, then looks at the stage floor.

We finish the concert with no incidents, unless you count the women's undergarments (and a few guy's) which have been flung onstage. As we finish our final encore, the crowd begins a rhythmic chant of "Beaucoups! Beaucoups!"—"More! More!"

Soundcheck, June 26

Yesterday's news conference and concert didn't give me a good idea of how large the Forum is, other than massive. As we walk in for the soundcheck, with the lights up, I want to make that grandiose. Four detectives in this auditorium are like four drops of water on a tabletop. You know they're there, but it's difficult spotting them.

DC looks grim seeing me. It's time for the apology she deserves; I can't get over how *broken* and hurt she looked when I revealed the truth. "Uh, DC...."

"Yeah, what's on your mind?" Damn. She's holding her temper, I sense it.

"I need to apologize... to tell you why I let that story live so long."

"So you know, as pissed as I am and was about this, I'm *not* leaving this family of ours. But I don't want to talk about it."

Fuck me running. *Everyone* thinks of the group as a family. That warms my heart.

"Can I say that the explanation I gave everyone was true, if condensed. I didn't intend to hurt anyone. I didn't want it to take control...." Gotta pause a moment. I'm getting emotional, and I don't want DC accepting a half-assed apology because of me crying like that. That thought does the trick.

"Ravynn, it's not easy being the *lesbian* assistant manager of the hottest band on the planet. I thought our shared *secrets* would make it easier for us to stay on the same page." She pauses and stares at me, like if she could hammer a few points into my head, she'd be on it now. "Then you went and messed it up with the Ronnie story. I get it; it seemed to you like he'd tossed you aside, you were useless. That's been nearly two years ago. You and your buddies have worked your *asses* off to become the most-wanted ticket in the world."

"I was only an afterthought to Ronnie. As long as I cooked and cleaned for him, and let him use me sexually, he was okay. But I was *never* an equal. When I made Ronnie the bastard for throwing me out, I became *somebody*. It made me worthwhile. To admit that I caused my own injuries would've wrecked that. I couldn't do it. Then the tour started, and I was afraid to fuck things up if I told the truth at first."

"Then Dickie, a childhood friend of Ronnie's, shows up as the national correspondent for the tour, and *that* messed with your head," DC connects the loose ends.

"Yeah. I was stuck between knowing if Dickie talks to Ronnie, I'm gonna have an unwanted visitor, and wanting to erase that lie. I was backed into a corner, no escape, my own fault."

"I'm disappointed you couldn't level with us until you knew Ronnie wouldn't vanish, but I understand. You've got to quit beating yourself up, Ravynn—there are seven others who can do *that* for you." DC just cracked a joke at my expense. Maybe I *can* salvage this.

I start to open my mouth for another apology, but she shuts me down with a look before continuing. "Look, you're lucky the guys hung with you after that. I'm *committed* to this tour, even if I left my girlfriend behind for it. I haven't been able to reach her since we've been on the road, though I told her I'd call whenever I could. You're not to blame for *her* stupidity; God knows you've got enough issues."

I must look like she jabbed me with a red-hot poker. "Did that get through? I don't want to be a bitch, but you brought it on yourself. Nobody appreciates how hard you've been working more than I do, but you *needed* this wake-up call. You can't tell that story for years and expect people to accept a quick *I'm sorry* as the apology."

She's right, though now I feel like a five-year-old who's been told that he can't have his dessert without eating dinner first.

"I hate that I fucked everything up. I'm gonna show you how much I respect you and how much I want to be worthy of your trust."

"This is a good start. You've gotta be open and honest. We're a family, strange as it may seem; you can't tear through families like you go through tricks." Ouch. She's stung me again. It's not enough for me to think that she and I are *even*. I nod my agreement. My throat is feeling dry—gotta save my voice. I'll go with that.

"I'm going to be totally honest from now on, DC. I owe it to you."

"*Totally* honest? Tell me what you think about Benji, and I don't mean as a musician."

Fuck. She knows exactly how to put me in a corner....

"Uhmm,... well,..." I try to answer. She cuts me off.

"Listen, you were doing what you thought you needed. Just talk to Greg or me in the future before you build any more houses of cards. Be honest with everyone. You're a good guy, even if you *are* a mess sometimes. Now, don't you have a soundcheck?"

"I gotta be sure I'm making *us* right."

"You are. Apology accepted. Get on that soundcheck and make this show a peak performance. You're gonna be brilliant tonight."

Concert

Since the soundcheck, we've been able to unwind. I'm keen to get onstage for this show, twitching with anticipation. Last night's show was normal—from all angles. I'm ready to get onstage. We're not doing anything unusual or different. I want to get performing; my adrenaline is ready to be used.

We leave the dressing area, me leading the way. I stride toward the stage entrance, where DC stands waiting.

"Ready for the show? You look like you're *itching* to go on, bud!" she teases me, as if my lie never happened. She's preoccupied. I'm guessing it's the show.

"I got an adrenaline rush, so I'm ready." As I say it, I look at her.

With that, she pats me on my back and moves to her usual pre-concert position, offstage, where she can watch us and the audience.

Benji, Sean and Clay are standing nearby, ready. I look toward the dressing area and see Wil and Todd are on the spot as well.

I lead the group onstage. Tonight, I'm the master of this house. I reach the front of the stage and peer into the crowd as the guys connect their instruments. "Bon soir, Montreal! Good evening, Montreal!" With the microphone close to my mouth, I whisper, yet my words ring out with sensuality and temptation.

The audience is already under my spell. As the guys begin the first notes of *Welcome to the Show*, I slink across the stage, a pansexual dancer. My words swirl out and mesmerize; I out-snarl and out-prance Jagger throughout the show. With each song, the group and I tighten the connection to the audience, like the spider weaving the web. It's mystical, sensing how strongly our music affects our audience.

As we begin our last songs, the audience sings along; some swaying in their seats, others dancing in the aisles. There are women *and* men holding signs expressing their love for one or more of us—though Benji gets many signs declaring undying love *and* a desire to give birth to his children. Montreal loves us—Wil, behind his keyboard array, gets a number for himself, and low-key Todd has a bunch. Sean and Clay have a few—ohmygawd—as a couple, and each of them has a couple dozen individually. I can see close to thirty signs for me; Benji *easily* surpasses that when you add in the 'signs' which are his face, double-life-size.

The audience is on its feet, waving lighters or anything else to create light, as we finish our final encore. I grab the mike one last time. "Merci, mes amis—au revoir, Montreal.... Thank you, my friends—until we see you again, Montreal...."

Since we've survived our first international stop with only minor technical problems, I'm cocky. If the remainder of the international dates go this well, we'll be flying higher than the stratosphere when we return to the States next month. I *hope* the rest of the tour doesn't feature Ronnie. This is gonna end; Ronnie doesn't own me, I don't owe him a damn thing—other than several well-placed kicks to his butt—but he and I are done otherwise.

After concert

I stalk into my dressing area and peel off the shirt I wore for two-plus glorious hours. You could put out a fire using my shirt. I give each show everything. I'm as limp as an overcooked strand of spaghetti, so I park myself and guzzle the quart bottle of water on the table. There's a mirror trained on the doorway, so I won't be surprised.

I'm confident no one other than Greg, DC, Jean-Paul, or one of the guys will disturb me. As I swab myself with the towels left for that purpose, I notice the door opening slightly. Whoever is entering is being deliberately slow—could Ronnie have snuck in somehow? I don't think so, but he's surprised us previously.

The door opens further and reveals Benji *and* Jean-Paul. Uh-oh. Possibly the two of them have talked and Benji knows about Jean-Paul and me. Or maybe Jean-Paul is going to force me to tell Benji.

"How do you manage that stalking and dancing every night, cherie?" Jean-Paul asks, the concern over my state of near-exhaustion causing his sparkling eyes to be darker, almost hooded.

A copy of the sketch I drew of Ronnie sits on the table. Jean-Paul glances its way, does a double-take. "Dieu, that... *bête* is Ronnie?"

I love his description for Ronnie—*beast*. He's not truly a beast, just annoying the *hell* outta me.

Benji and I have told him about the breakup. He's heard the talk regarding my lie about Ronnie, but I'm beyond exhausted by the subject of Ronnie-freakin'-Kushner.

"That's him. Let's not dwell anymore." I *truly* have had more than enough, and don't need the instant replay, *especially* from a cute, short-term outsider. "I'm limp from the show. Everybody's been good to me after my lies about how Ronnie and I ended. Now if he'd be as kind and leave me *the fuck* alone."

Jean-Paul and Benji nod.

"Shay, you were *superbe* tonight, what I mean!" Okay, Benji's not angry with me, because the smile on his face, directed at me, could blind a person. *Why* are the two together, I worry. I'm like the convicted man waiting for the sentence to be pronounced, but I can't look gloomy when Benji smiles my way.

"Everybody was terrific, and the audience gave us huge energy. It was *easy* for me to be my best." That's totally honest. The energy from the audience kept raising my energy levels all night. But I gotta give credit where it's due. "You guys make it easy for me. With your guitar wizardry, and the other guys playing so well, all I gotta do is remember the words and sing. Piece of cake."

Jean-Paul and Benji are both scoffing at that statement; Jean-Paul is shaking his head. I'm afraid he'll give himself a concussion; Benji gets that bull-dog-like look where you *know* you've said the wrong thing.

"What? It's true, babe, and you know it." That 'babe' slips out before I realize it. Can't take it back; gotta play it as it lies. Of course, as soon as the word slips from my lips, Benji lights up like an overdone Christmas tree; the grin on his face is probably the largest ever.

"No, you entertain the audience, you walk, you strut, you dance, you're a one-man show. *And* you sing and write amazing songs. That's *hardly* a 'piece of cake,' though you *certainly* make it look that way."

"Certainement, Ravynn.... certainly. Benji has, as you say, laid his finger upon the truth." Jean-Paul does well translating French to English, but he needs help with our sayings.

"Lookit, tomorrow's free day, Jean-Paul and I want to spend with you. There's a little French Bistro near here, and Greg has okayed the three of us going there with a detective."

"Wow, I love French food, even if I barely have the skill to pronounce the names." The idea of French food sells me, but the way the two are enthusiastically pushing this, it seems like a trap. I wonder if Benji knows about Jean-Paul and me, or if Jean-Paul is putting this together to force Benji and me together.

As Jean-Paul and Benji appear ready to tell me *more*, Sean pops the bubble, unknowingly, as I hear him exclaim from the hall outside the door.

"Hot damn, I get to call Mom and Pop tomorrow!" He comes in smiling, which dies when he realizes I heard him. In an apologetic tone, he stammers out a sort-of apology. "Everybody... is... fuck, Rave, I forgot. I'm *so* sorry." He's blown it.

I take mere seconds to compose my face *and* the appropriate reply. "That's okay. I have a date with two of the nicest guys on the planet at a sweet little French Bistro, so no worry."

Jean-Paul exchanges looks with Benji, apparently relieved by my reply to Sean, but I could be missing something. These two have gotten too close since they met. I have no idea how secure the secret of my night with Jean-Paul is. Meanwhile, Benji does his best *taking-care-of-Ravynn* move by hugging me and planting a kiss on my forehead. Sean blushes, stammers out another apology, and leaves the room rapidly.

Benji places one hand on each of my cheeks, then turns my head to face him, keeping my face in his hands. The power I feel from his touch seems like I'm connected to a generator. I *feel* currents passing from his hands into my cheeks and then into my body. He looks directly into my eyes, his gaze pulling me into his aura as if he was a magnet and I was a chunk of steel.

"You're okay with this?"

"If you're willing to give up talking to your family—a process which could take *several* days, if they're all present—to keep *me* company, I'm more than okay."

"Don't forget Jean-Paul."

"Okay, then, to keep *me* and *Jean-Paul* company...."

Jean-Paul laughs, and I smile. If I'm about to be double-teamed about a one-night-stand, there *are* worse fates. I can keep things moving so no one spills anything about Jean-Paul and me, unless Benji knows and is waiting to play it at the right moment, or unless Jean-Paul is going to press the issue himself. I'll trade the *rest* of my 'found family' for these two for a few hours, no problem.

Hotel, Bistro, June 27

Benji, close as he is with his family, has given up the chance to talk to them to spend time with me; I'm dumbfounded. It reminds me how strong his emotions are for me, that he can substitute me for his entire family. I get a lump in my throat. The "kid" gets to me *every* time. Why do I call him "kid" when he's more mature than everyone except DC and *possibly* Greg?

The guys are excited about calling their families. DC's also excited—she's so reserved that most of us know nothing about her private life. She let me know she has a girlfriend back home; that's got to be part of it. It might be interesting to be a fly on the wall during her call, but I'll stick with my dates.

Jean-Paul is wearing a skin-tight black satin shirt and blue velvet slacks with matching blue suede shoes. Should I break into a chorus of Elvis now, or wait until later? The guy looks good enough to *be* lunch.

From down the hall we all hear "Well, it's a one for the money, two for the show...." and everyone laughs as Benji "promenades" from his room to join Jean-Paul and me. Benji's wearing a white jumpsuit. As he joins us, he pulls a flashy gold ring and red bandanna out of his pocket.

"Are you supposed to be Elvis?" I tease.

"Absolutely," he croons.

"Where's the rest of your jewelry?"

Benji bats his eyes like a Hollywood starlet.

"I'm waiting for *my man* to give me the pretty stuff," Benji replies in a voice so sultry that parts of me respond immediately. This could be a *strange* lunch.

Jean-Paul hugs Benji, who hugs him back—if I get caught between the two of them, I'm going to be a piece of paper printed with my image, nothing more. And just like that, Jean-Paul hugs me.

Then Benji hugs me and kisses me… on my cheek. Wow. That kiss travels all the way to my toenails. I think a few hairs on my head curl as well. After watching the two hugging, then having both hugging me at the same moment, I'm worried there's more going on. Perhaps it's a case of them being so jealous that if one hugs me, the other has to as well, or maybe it's darker—like Benji knows that Jean-Paul and I have been together and he's determined to have his chance. I'm waiting for *that* shoe to fall. As amazing as that kiss was, it's time to remind myself, *again*, that getting into a relationship with Benji is not a good idea.

The detective, our escort, joins us, doing a triple-take at the blue suede shoes *and* Elvis-Benji. Damn, wish Todd was nearby with his camera. It would be *epic*.

The flash from the camera in Todd's hand surprises me—slightly. Jean-Paul and Benji have been planning this for days, *and* thought about everything. It's working. I'm happy, relaxed, looking forward to lunch, and I can't wait to see the pictures Todd has taken. Now I understand why Benji suggested I wear the red satin pirate shirt and black satin trousers from our first concert in San Francisco. The three of us shine.

Lunch at the Bistro is magnificent. We sample many delicacies. Seated across from Benji and Jean-Paul, I'm developing whiplash trying to keep both my dates in my conversation. It's tricky watching them without becoming a swivel-head doll; I desperately want to know if I'm in trouble from my one-nighter with Jean-Paul. The detective refrains from having wine, *claiming* he's on duty. We aren't interested in alcoholic beverages, so we're served bottles of sparkling white grape juice. Fresh warm bread with butter, French onion soup, and then a tray full of shells is placed in front of us. The shells look like those I've seen hermit crabs crawling out of. I'm leery. I don't want something with claws going into my mouth, cooked or otherwise.

Jean-Paul looks at me staring at the tray of shells and asks, "You've never had *escargots*, mon ami?" I'm glancing at Benji as Jean-Paul begins speaking, or I might have missed the little stink-eye he throws Jean-Paul.

"Had *what*?"

"Escargots. It's a delicacy," Jean-Paul says.

I'm watching Benji's eyes grow large as his grin grows larger; *he* knows something.

"Since we're in a *French* Bistro, I would expect it to be a delicacy; but what the blazes does 'ess-car-go' mean? It wasn't in my one year of French."

Benji almost bursts, trying not to laugh, as he tells me from his Cajun viewpoint. "Shay, you gonna get a kick outta them. It's snails raised for being eaten, specially prepared." With that, he grabs one, takes a forkful from the shell, chews it, and swallows before I can say anything.

I watch him chew, then swallow; I wait. He doesn't get sick, doesn't turn into a snail-creature, but sits there, beaming. If Benji can do it, so can I.

I grab a shell, take a forkful, and bring it to my mouth. I hesitate; there's no odd smell, though I'm about to put a snail in my mouth. Buck up, man; it's been chopped up and roasted, it's not gonna *eat* you.

I put the fork in my mouth, slide the escargot off the fork and chew. Wow, very tasty. I swallow and want more. Benji's right.

After my first shellful, I'm a fan, but I allow the others to have their share. The tray held six shells and there are four of us, so that leaves two....

"We invited you; it's your choice who gets the final escargot, mon ami," Jean-Paul says. That "mon ami" gets a glare from Benji.

"True dat."

"I enjoyed it, but I don't want to eat the last one by myself. Can we get another tray?" As I ask, the server appears with a second tray of six escargots. That gives each of us three—I'm happy.

The rest of lunch progresses with small plates and shared portions; we sample almost everything the Bistro offers, except alcohol. No problem there—the food is, as Jean-Paul says, *incroyable*—incredible.

Toward the end of the feast, Benji gets a serious look on his face, glances at the detective, and says, "Everything you've tried to get rid of Ronnie, he's not gettin'—he's not takin' the hint. Like my Pappaw would say, ya gotta get his attention with a two-by-four to the stomach."

"Huh?" I ask, stumped by this down-home bit.

"Hit him where it hurts. Show Ronnie you aren't available."

The look on Jean-Paul's face matches the way I feel.

"What do you mean?" I ask.

"Simple. Get yourself a fake boyfriend, one Ronnie won't mess with."

If the idea wasn't so comical, I'd consider it; I can guess where it's heading—either Todd or Sean, big as they are, would scare Ronnie off with muscles. I can't stop my laugh, which gets a frown from Jean-Paul and a full Cajun stink-eye from Benji.

"Who?" I ask.

Jean-Paul looks at me, then Benji, and they almost split their sides laughing. What's their game? Is this a build-up to springing Benji knowing about the hookup? Perhaps they're playing, and they're gonna suggest a detective. I'm not sure what's funny, and I say so.

"Cheri, the answer is obvious," Jean-Paul croons. Benji frowns, probably at Jean-Paul's use of the term "cheri," then smiles; it's obvious he's *still* jealous of Jean-Paul. He can't mean a detective or himself....

"Wait... you mean Benji?" As I say his name, I hope I'm wrong.

Wordlessly, Benji and Jean-Paul vigorously nod their satisfaction that I've realized their genius.

"I'm not sure," I say, my weakest-ever argument. "We're leaving for Paris tonight, and that's a long distance for Ronnie to cover. He's *never* had a shit-ton of cash, so flying to Paris isn't likely in his plans. There's no need for a fake relationship there, because he won't be there." That's better; it's true.

"What if Dickie bought him a plane ticket? He might be on a different flight."

"He's right, mon ami. Better safe than sorry." Jean-Paul and Benji aren't gonna let me squirm out of their plan.

"Next, you'll be suggesting Ronnie might backstroke 4,500 miles across the Atlantic Ocean."

"Is he athletic, shay?"

My snicker ends that. I'm facing the fake boyfriend idea, nothing to counter it.

"Cheri, it makes sense. Right, B?" Ohmygawd, they're talking like long-time friends.

"You were too nice to him in Seattle. It didn't slow him down." Benji glances at the detective, so rigid he could pass for a crash-test dummy, before continuing. "He ain't gonna give up with you sayin' *I don't wanna*. You gotta show him you can't. Best way to not be able to go with him?"

"Be with Benji instead, tres simple," Jean-Paul says, pronouncing the last two French words like "tray sam-pluh." I remember "very simple" from my year of French. This plan is *anything* but very simple.

"I know you guys are doing this to help, but this can fuck up in so many ways. If we do this, the press or fans could get hold of it, and there goes our chance at the top." Benji and Jean-Paul look from me to each other and back again. Benji's smile hasn't faltered.

Jean-Paul jumps in. "The fans in Montreal were *crazy* for Sean and Clay."

"He's right. Not gonna be an issue."

"The fans think it's fake. Greg doesn't want boyfriend entanglements on the tour." That's my weakest defense. Greg's given up on separating Sean and Clay's rooms. Benji knows I'm grabbing at air, because he stares at me. "Besides, you know *none* of my previous relationships have worked out."

That *last* line has me laughing at myself. Here I am, pathetic, trying to use the "relationships don't work" defense for a *fake* relationship.

"Blah-blah-blah-blah, blah-blah, blah-blah-blah," Jean-Paul and Benji recite in unison.

"I'm not sure about this... it's difficult. I wish Ronnie would vanish. But... help me out, give me something to work with, some idea. *If* we do this, how do we become *fake* boyfriends?"

"It's easy-peasy. We hold hands, we hug, we kiss. Play it like Sean and Clay. We show up together, we leave together. We did more in New Orleans on my birthday, and you were fine. This'll be a replay."

"But not in public, right? Nowhere that the press or people can see us, right? Like, during soundchecks and backstage, and at the hotel for practice?"

"Should I call my pappaw, get a legal bill done? It's us holding hands and huggin' and kissin'—ain't gonna be any funny stuff."

Damn, here I go, upsetting him again. "I want it to work without my suck-ass luck hurting you or the group. I think we can handle it...."

When I say that, he turns to me and beams. After his pursuit, my deception, and my "no relationships" stance, he's backed me into a corner, no way out except *in* his arms. He's buying lunch. This lunch was a set-up *date*, for crying out loud. I'm caught. If *anyone* had told me before we left that I would return with Benji as my fake boyfriend, I would've doubted their sanity. Benji wants me for real; I can't believe he's okay with *fake*.

I remember his birthday in New Orleans. We spent a week as almost-boyfriends. On his birthday, he wanted his first kiss and hug to be with me, so he started it. I *had* to take charge. The kiss became a lip-lock that threatened to get "down and dirty" in his grandmother Pearl's house. *Would* have, if she hadn't walked out of her den and caught us. That day was followed by three more, filled with holding hands, hugging, and kissing. New Orleans weaved its spell.

We're gonna recreate the togetherness from that week. This could get troublesome, because I remember how tempting Benji was then—and he's grown more so. I've gotta be careful, because this *fake* boyfriend bit might cause harm to the group, or Benji. Or to me....

"So, we're gonna spend lots of time together. Are there rules? Are we making this up as we go?" The biggest step is getting the boyfriend bit in place. Ronnie never liked competition or confrontation, so this *might* get rid of him.

"Mes amis, might I suggest, you take it in baby steps? Don't put the racecar before the mule." Benji and I look at Jean-Paul with questions on our faces.

"You tryin' to say don't put the cart before the horse?" Benji has stumbled through Jean-Paul's mixed-up idiom.

Jean-Paul nods, and I hazard my thoughts. "We should act like a new couple and do a lot of hugging and kissing. I like that."

Benji looks at me with a grin, shaking his head like he can't believe it took so much effort to persuade me to play fake boyfriends. "Rave, we gonna be fake boyfriends. We'll do what seems right whenever it happens. I'm not pushin' for anything." He grins, then continues. "We just let the others know we're doin' this so they buy it. Other'n that, we hug and kiss when we're alone or with the guys onstage during soundchecks, or backstage, maybe in our rooms."

"That's good. I'm worried about the press. I would *never* be ashamed of being with you."

My fear—other than getting into a relationship with Benji which screws up the group—is hurting him, because he's inexperienced. I know Ronnie isn't big on confrontations. So seeing Benji and me together, confirmed by the group, should be enough.

"Well, nothing else has worked, so fake boyfriends can't hurt. Do we need to sign a contract?" Jean-Paul and Benji smile. I don't know why, but I'm okay with this.

Benji pays the check, and we walk back to Hotel Nelligan. Lunch relaxed me, but damned if our conversation afterwards hasn't tied me up. As good an idea as it seems, the press finding out and smearing it worldwide is perilous. Other than that, all I've thought about has been food and being with Benji. And Jean-Paul, of course. And we were ourselves, three guys, having a great time. No evil people to ruin it. It was a glorious afternoon with a weird twist at the end—one I did *not* see coming, and certainly wasn't expecting. Just the matter of a *fake* boyfriend. No pressure, right?

We walk into the hotel's communications room where the telephone calls have been happening. It's a room off the front desk with two separate telephones, more like a small office. Once we're inside the hotel, Benji grabs my hand. I'm worried, then I realize he's taking the lead to begin our fake boyfriends bit. After that, it's as pleasant as when we strolled through the French Quarter eight months ago. It seems like another lifetime, though; this time, there's more involved, much more at stake.

"We're doing this?"

"You're silly sometimes. Course we're doing this. We gotta get comfy being a couple *before* we go 'live' in front of Ronnie, so he'll believe us, right?" Benji sets it out plain as day for me to understand it. I decide to enjoy it, awkward as I feel. In my life, I've never experienced romance. With Mom and Dad, it was quick hugs and kisses on the cheek. Ronnie was the driving force; I got a quick kiss after *he* got off. Now I'm like a frog with one leg pinned to a board, hopping around in circles—it's *that* kind of awkward for me. I'm as new to romance as Benji; I'm moving through uncharted territory.

"I'm not sure I'm ready to show the guys *another* relationship." As I say it, the strength of his grip on my hand remains steady, reassuring. That sends shivers of happiness through me.

"You jes' gotta worry 'bout something, don'tcha? Well, chaw on this. If we *don't* get the guys okay with us, and your stalker-menace shows up, he'll see through us in a heartbeat, even if he's dumber than a doorstop." Shit. Benji nails it; if the guys aren't in on the plan, and we start acting like boyfriends in front of Ronnie, he'll have the four other members of the group on *his* side, rather than them on our side.

"You could be right. It can't hurt to practice…." I'm *still* not sold, but having the physical connection with Benji is worth the fake label.

As we enter the room, Sean is on one phone and DC on another; DC is tense, making sounds I can't understand, but they *aren't* happy—this call isn't going well. Clay and Wil are sitting, waiting; we join them.

"Where's Todd?" Benji asks.

"He and I were first. He finished and went back to his room," Clay replies. That means Clay's waiting for his "baby" to finish *his* call. Sean gestures for Clay to come to the phone. This is "meet the parents, telephone version."

Clay speaks for a few moments, before handing the phone back to Sean and rejoining us. He's upbeat as he sits and says, "That went well. Sean's parents seem nice. They told me it's good he's met someone *else* to keep him busy." I can see Sean's mom saying those exact words. She likes me, but she's never believed I was a stable influence on Sean.

"You're good for him, Clay. I'm happy for you."

"Why are y'all holding hands?" Clay's noticed Benji holding my hand, as I see Sean staring at Benji's hand grasping mine. This will travel fast.

"We're trying something to get rid of Ronnie," I sputter. "Did your parents meet Sean on the phone?" Why the *hell* do I ask that? Am I so into self-abuse I have to know everything?

"I spoke to my mom, who said Sean sounds like a lovely guy—her words, but I agree with her. Don't change the subject! What the heck are you doing? Why are y'all holding hands like Sean and me? Are you mocking us?"

"We're *not* mocking you. Benji and I are gonna be *fake* boyfriends to get Ronnie to leave us—me—alone." Clay's home life is like what I went through. It hasn't been as smooth as others. I can relate. His mom, who sounds sweet, has given her blessing to Clay and Sean with a brief conversation? I shiver, remembering my father making me choose to live a lie to stay home, or insist on being myself and leaving. Of *course* Clay gives me grief about the boyfriend bit, after the times I've tried to get him and Sean to cool it.

"*Fake* boyfriends? You *sure*? Y'all got real close in New Orleans."

I shoulda seen *that* coming. Benji and I weren't exactly sticking to our hotel rooms when we were hugging or kissing. I hope this doesn't blow up in my face.

DC slamming her phone down interrupts my thoughts. "Dammit to *hell*, the bitch!" Someone's call didn't go well. I rush to DC, offering support. She's gone through hell for me. I persuade her to sit down, which she reluctantly does.

"I called my girlfriend. I told her before we left I'd call her whenever I could. We've talked occasionally; things seemed okay. Today, she says we should see other people. She's *never* expressed interest in other people before. The bitch has *met* someone. Dammit!"

I've never tried to console a woman—those skills are non-existent, but I'll try after all she's done for me. "Sorry *my* bad luck rubbed off on you. Is there anything I can do—other than stay a thousand miles away? That wouldn't work with this tour." Shit, I mess up my relationships, and it looks like I've fucked up DC's. And I have a *fake* boyfriend. As I'm attempting to comfort DC, Benji is here with me.

"Thanks, Ravynn." She doesn't notice Benji, but looks at me with a sad smile and watery eyes. I know how bad this hurts her, and it worries me—if her relationship could collapse that easily, what'll stop Benji from ending our *fake* relationship when something better comes along? With that sinking emotion, I lead Benji, Clay and Jean-Paul as we escort DC upstairs to pack for our flight to Paris.

••••••••••••

Paris, France

June 28 - July 1, 1968

Flight

I'm not crazy about heights, other than occasional roller coasters. But compared to the roller coaster of the past several days in Seattle and Montreal, this seems like the train we took to New Orleans for Benji's birthday last fall, smooth and easy.

Since this flight will take seven hours, it's good these seats are comfortable—they have pillows for us, not as fluffy as Hotel Nelligan's, but they'll do for in-flight. Don't *I* sound like I know what I'm talking about? My first long flight and I'm claiming expert level.

Greg must've worn off on me—the need to check that everyone is here is strong; I scan the cabin around me and see almost everyone.

Wait. All accounted for... except Benji. Where's Benji? Gotta be sure he's on this flight. I look across each aisle. I'm ready to find someone to turn the plane back toward Montreal to find him when he saunters from the tail of the plane, followed by Jean-Paul. *What??* Why are they so close? I hope *they* haven't been playing. I can't believe myself; I tell Benji I can't handle a relationship, then have one-nighters, and *now* I'm jealous he might play with the last guy I played with. Such a hypocrite—I'm unworthy of him.

They walk up to me and call me mother hen. Am I that obvious? I'm glad Benji's here.

"We were exploring the plane. The stewardesses said it was okay." I know how strong Benji feels about me, and seeing nothing in his face to tell me otherwise, I believe him, but Jean-Paul's a tease. He looks like he'd make out with me right now. He's under no restraints. He could as easily be ready to make love with Benji, and *that* bugs me, though I've told Benji I can't be in a relationship. Benji can use the *same* argument to have a fling or just sex with Jean-Paul, and that bothers me more than I like.

"I was afraid they'd left you!" I blurt out, a schoolkid to his crush. My demons remind me about my bad luck in relationships—my parents, Ronnie, and DC breaking up with her girlfriend, even *if* she claims my luck didn't affect her. Damned if I haven't topped it all off by falling for Benji, despite myself. Fuck, I'm *so* screwed.

Benji makes me sit, then joins me, giving me a hug and a kiss on my cheek. I sense my blush beginning. Jean-Paul sits a few rows back.

Benji opens a compartment, produces a blanket which he hands to me, then takes a second one for himself. "Let's get some sleep, gonna be a long flight." Guess he's flown before; he never stops amazing me.

I awaken; we're still flying toward Paris, early Friday morning. Soon we'll land at Orly Airport, where six years ago, a plane with most of Atlanta's arts community crashed on takeoff, killing over one hundred. It traumatized Atlanta. I'm surprised any Bond films were shown afterwards—the plane that crashed was flight 007.

The memory of *that* scares the crap out of me. Rock 'N' Roll history is littered with crashes that killed stars like Buddy Holly, Big Bopper, and Richie Valens. I'm *not* ready to join them. We haven't gotten famous enough, and I haven't told Benji how I feel about him. To die now would suck ass in the *worst* way.

Why do I do this? Here I am, a new flyer, and as we're approaching landing, I think of a plane crash.

Benji wakes up, sensing I've thought myself into a panic. He's got an instinct.

"Take it easy. Breathe slow. This is gonna be easy-peasey." Enough Cajun to remind me it's him, the right words to calm me down.

At that moment, the plane hits turbulence, and I'm panicking again. Benji snuggles me into him. "A little turbulence, just relax." As he speaks, he rubs one hand in small circles around my back as the other hand caresses my face.

Benji knows how to restore my sanity when I'm melting down. He knows where to touch me to calm me. I've got no freakin' idea what being in love is like, but given the way my body reacts to his voice—my heartbeat flutters—I'm falling in love, if I'm not there already.

I follow Benji's instructions. It's not advice after the fifteenth time of being uttered. And it works.

Perfect timing; the stewardesses remind us to fasten our seatbelts for landing. Benji takes my right hand in his and squeezes it gently—for luck, he says—then the plane drops slightly. Benji's hold on my hand reassures me. It hasn't tightened, so I assume it's normal for a plane landing.

Soon enough, I see the lights along the runway, then there's a gentle bump as we touch down. We're in Paris, sometime Friday morning.

Arrival, Hotel, Friday, June 28

Once the plane stops, the flight crew help us exit. As we walk the few yards from the plane to the check-in desk, I take a moment to look around.

I'm not sure in which direction to look for Paris, so I scan a circle. To the north, there's a good deal of light, so either the City of Lights goes dark at night, or we're south of Paris.

Greg figures out what I'm doing, and shows me his map of 'Paris et Environs'—Paris and Surroundings—which shows Orly Airport is south of the city, "13 kilometres" south. That means every distance here will be in kilometers; we'll have to convert to our mileage. This could get hairy. Greg saves me.

"We're about 8 miles south of Paris; we'll have a relatively short drive to the hotel. Most of the guys will sack out for a while once we get to our rooms, I guess."

When we arrive at the hotel, the doorman opens the front doors of the hotel and greets us. "Bonjour, mes amis. Bienvenue à l'Hotel Paris France!" Jean-Paul translates for us, though my modest French tells me the doorman has said, "Good day, friends. Welcome to the Hotel Paris France!"

Check-in takes mere minutes; we get room keys. There's a table with a platter of croissants and eclairs. I'm standing near it, and the smells are inviting. The desk clerk tells us, through Jean-Paul, to have a pastry of our choice. He recommends the croissants because they are freshly baked and, he says, taste "incroyable" with a touch of fresh butter on them. One bite and I totally agree.

Our rooms are on the top floor; there's an old-fashioned "lift" that can take three or four people at a time, or beautifully elegant marble staircases. The top floor is the seventh floor, it's not like climbing the Alps. I opt for the stairs. Almost everyone follows. Sean and Clay want to experience the *romance* of the lift.

Benji and I reach the top floor slightly ahead of Jean-Paul. After Todd and Wil arrive a moment later, the five of us head down the hall in search of our rooms; the lift arrives with Sean and Clay. I have to razz them. "So, did you guys stop on *every* floor?"

"*No*. We got inside that contraption, pulled the gate shut, pressed our number and the Up button. It shuddered, shook, and when we were ready to get out for fear of our lives, it started moving upwards." Clay's *still* holding Sean's waist so tightly, we might need reconstructive surgery for him, but Sean somehow gives us the blow-by-blow on the lift. So much for romance.

Theatre, Saturday, June 29

The Olympia Theatre, where the Beatles performed for several *weeks* in a row in their early days, is our stage for the next two nights. To me, *this* is where we prove we're comparable to them, or admit we're second-best. As we enter the Olympia for soundcheck, it hits me full-force. Top that off with a case of fake boyfriend nerves as Benji-and-Ravynn debut to a group of four musicians.

Benji and I enter the foyer; as soon as he sees there are no reporters or outsiders, he wraps one arm around my waist and pulls me into his side like a tow-truck pulling in a car.

"Ummm, I'm *not* a sack of potatoes," I sass in my best British persona.

"We gonna do this, or we gonna play word games?" He's grinning as he says it, so I go in for a kiss. Of course, as I do, the outer door opens, and he turns, so I kiss the side of his right cheek. That draws a laugh from Sean and Clay, who've entered the foyer, followed by Wil and Todd.

"Sheesh, y'all are such cock blockers." All that gets is a round of snickering and wolf whistles, so I try again.

Benji's ready. As I move toward his lips, he places his free left hand behind my head and pulls me toward his lips, his head helping close the distance. As our lips meet, the wolf whistles and snickering vanish. I think I've tuned out sound, until I hear a noise outside. Nope, my guys are struck silent by us.

His fingers trace through my hair, his lips against mine. I know our tongues are dueling inside our mouths, and I feel his heartbeat pounding a crazy rhthm against my chest, as surely as he must sense mine. Finally, we break the kiss; whether it lasted a minute, an hour, or a lifetime, I could not tell. I felt his lips even as he removed them from mine. If *that* was a fake kiss, I've *never* been kissed for real.

It takes us a moment to remember that we are in the Olympia Theatre to do a soundcheck before our first show in Paris.

"You guys've been holding out," Todd says.

"I taught him everything he knows," Sean says, humorously, pointing at me.

Clay just blushes silently.

"Damn," Wil whispers.

Dammit, I gotta get into ready-for-show mode, but my brain is *still* processing that kiss, and dealing with the guys' reactions.... This isn't *any* show—this is for the right to say *we're* as good as the Beatles. A great show does that. A good show both nights also does that. No fuck-ups or mistakes allowed.

As for how Phoenix Rising stacks up against the Beatles, I *know* the answer; I sense it every performance. We *aren't* the Beatles, but we're as good as they are, as innovative. I may suck at one-on-one relationships, but with this group, I struck platinum, gold, and diamonds, all at once.

When Benji and I enter the auditorium, arm in arm, Operation Fake Boyfriend remains in effect. Once we're on stage, Benji turns my head and gives me a kiss that I feel all the way down my spine to my toes and back, by way of my crotch, to my face.

As we're kissing, though my brain and body focus on Benji's lips and body, my ears pick up a comment which I remember for later.

"Now *that's* how kissing is done, guys," Todd says, obviously to Sean and Clay, because they make negative-sounding noises. I'm surprised they aren't trying to out-kiss us.

Like they could.... Benji's the sexy Cajun I kissed in New Orleans in November, but *day-yum*, either he's been watching videos, reading books, or.... Ohmygawd, I *hope* he hasn't been practicing with Johnny. He's had his tongue teasing my teeth, my lips, and mapped my mouth. While he's doing that, his hands have been caressing my back, my sides, my arms, my head, rubbing my chest, stroking the sides of my neck. It's almost like he's memorizing my body with his hands. I'm turned on; thank goodness I wore looser-fitting pants today. At last I pull back, because it's clear Benji won't. I try not to meet his eyes for too long.

Dazed from the kiss, I hear a throat-clearing from the back of the stage, behind the four statues who are my bandmates. Davey coughs to get my attention, then shakes his head in the direction of the instruments and mike stands.

We're here to do our soundcheck. Davey and his crew have worked their magic and assembled our stage. The *two* detectives—for me, a reminder of Ronnie, though it's the policy of the venue when rock groups are performing here—will sit midway through the auditorium during the shows. No one expects Ronnie to show up in Paris; it's mostly for general security.

We're loose; the music and vocals flow naturally. There are a few minor hiccups with the soundcheck, but nothing to stress about. If the show tonight goes well, our first night in Paris will be a smash.

We begin filing backstage, DC handing out towels as if we'd done a full-fledged concert. Since she got the Dear Jane phone call from her girlfriend—shitty way to break up with someone, but less painful than how Ronnie broke up with me—DC has been very attentive to us, like she's substituting us for the ex-girlfriend.

She looks from Benji to me like she's about to say something. I take the lead and ask her how she's doing after her girlfriend broke up with her.

"I don't really want to talk about it, but I'm alright. Are you guys ready for tonight?"

Benji wraps his arm around my waist, beaming.

"Better believe it! Tonight we're gonna give Paris a rock show they'll nevah forget."

I simply nod. I couldn't have said it any better myself. DC looks at us, Benji's arm still around my waist, and smiles broadly. For some reason, she seems happier than she's been in a few weeks.

DC joins Benji and me as we walk toward the dressing room, Benji's arm still wrapped around my waist.

"Is this something new?" She finally asks, pulling out one of her cigars.

"Benji and I are playing *fake* boyfriends to persuade Ronnie to leave me alone."

"Fake, huh?" DC says, raising her eyebrow suspiciously.

"Yeah, at the lunch at the French Bistro the other day, Benji pointed out that detectives hadn't slowed Ronnie down and proposed a clever solution—we pose as *fake* boyfriends. So we're trying that. Ronnie really isn't as tough a guy as he acts, though—I'm pretty sure he's never had much and is a lot of talk and little action."

"Like my mammaw says, an old bulldog with a lotta bark and no bite," Benji says.

"Your *mammaw*?" DC asks.

"Oh, sorry, my grandmother on my mother's side. I forget that y'all aren't *blood* family, we all are so close."

Greg's standing in the hallway to the dressing areas. He sees us, cocks an eyebrow to say, *what's going on now?*, then beckons us over to him. As Benji and I walk over, I arch an eyebrow.

"You two seem lighthearted today. Soundcheck must have been good," he says.

"One of the best, I think, almost no problems!"

"That's good. You're all holding up well under the stress of this first tour, which is definitely a positive because the label is already talking about the future."

"As long as that future doesn't remove the recording session in Abbey Road, no sweat."

"I think he's talking about next year or later, shay," Benji brings me back to the present.

Greg suddenly notices Benji's arm around my waist, and gestures toward it. Benji doesn't turn loose and I don't try to pull away; it feels too comfortable as it is. Besides, we're just *fake* boyfriends, right?

"Is there something going on here? Something in the water, or some drug or something?"

"Greg, chill, dude... Benji and I are playing *fake* boyfriends to persuade Ronnie to leave me alone."

"Fake boyfriends? I don't see how that helps."

"He's never been as evil as I portrayed him, honestly; I think he's all bark and no bite, as Benji has said. I *know* he has never liked confrontation, so this could be the simplest way out."

"Okay; Ronnie has, frankly, worn me out. With this fake boyfriend idea, you may be on to something. The chemistry between you should sell it. Remember, this is a concert tour, not a wedding march," Greg says. He looks like he's trying to decide whether to be happy, worried, or uninvolved, and none of the three choices is winning.

At that moment, DC walks in with Jean-Paul, who's been reading a French newspaper.

"Are you okay, Ravynn?" DC asks, acting strangely maternal.

"I'm better than I've been in a long time," I say, startled to realize I mean it. I *am* feeling good.

"Really?" Benji grins.

"Yeah... really," I say.

On that, Benji leans in to give me a kiss on the cheek—but I turn and our lips meet. It's nothing like the other kisses. It's not passionate or forceful. It's tentative... it's awkward... like we're both kids, doing this for the first time.

I pull away, flushed and breathing hard. Benji is staring at me with big, innocent, hopeful eyes. He sensed the difference too, and I know I've made a big mistake.

Olympia

Backstage at the Olympia, waiting to go onstage for our first Paris show, and all my mind is dealing with now is *that kiss*. Benji's attempted peck on my cheek as we talked to DC became a face-to-face full-on kiss, and it was *my* doing. I turned my lips to his, knowing what I was doing—I thought—up until I didn't. That kiss short-circuited my brain in too damn many ways. Soon as we pulled apart, good as it felt, I knew I'd fucked up. This is beyond the lie of the Ronnie mess. Even after a bit of time has passed, I can sense the electricity from that kiss. We're supposed to be playing *fake* boyfriends, right?

That kiss was anything *but* fake. For either of us. Had I planned it that way? Not originally, but as the kiss began, it seemed right. I dunno; it was like Benji's lips were meant to fit mine, and vice versa, but damn, I fucked up. I wouldn't trade it for anything, except *now* Benji doesn't see the *fake* part. To be honest, I don't either, but we can't start a relationship on this tour—not with Greg's resistance, not with John's and Ronnie's presence, not with my disastrous history, not with the possibility of being found out by some reporter, and not with the prospect of losing a chance at recording in Abbey Road Studios with George Martin and becoming as big as the Beatles.

I don't regret it. I'd do it again, a million times. The *only* way I'd regret it is if Benji regrets it, but... I don't see that happening. In the back of my mind, and in my heart, there's a thought growing which simultaneously thrills me and scares the ever-loving crap out of me—namely, that Benji Travers means more to me than anyone I've ever known.

We're standing backstage, gazing out into the semi-darkened auditorium. I'm getting jazzed from the excitement in the air, helped by the electricity *still* buzzing in my system from Benji's kiss. I can't look directly at him, or I'll want another lip-lock—the guys will have a field day with *that* — instead, I'm playing the game of peeking his way every few seconds. No matter when I look, Benji is watching me with those emerald-green eyes at full intensity, a Cheshire cat-worthy grin on his face. He's happy as can be, so we can scratch *regrets* from the potential side effects. In a few moments, the house lights will go down fully, and a single spot will illuminate the stage as the six of us enter and begin the show. The audience seems excited, even at this early moment, and that's a great sign.

I'm trying to shift my thoughts from Benji to the show—I can't tell if the auditorium is full. My mind keeps drifting back to that kiss. Focus, Ravynn. My focus has got to be going onstage with such energy and electricity that the entire audience—10, or 10,000—senses my energy, and feeds off it, feeding it back to me and the guys. That's how I do it, anyway; no stimulants other than loving the music, loving the crowds, and loving being there with my brothers.

The house lights flicker, then dim; the spotlight illuminates the stage. Sean climbs the drum riser; following Sean, Wil goes to his keyboards, then Todd, Clay, and Benji with their guitars. As they connect to their amplifiers, I prance onstage, blowing kisses to the audience indiscriminately. We have another standing-room-only crowd, and they're loving it.

"Bonsoir, Paris! Bienvenue à l'Olympia!" I half-shout; the microphone will amplify the message: 'Good evening, Paris! Welcome to the Olympia!' Even a bit of squealing feedback doesn't dampen the enthusiasm, and it passes quickly enough. The roar from the crowd thrills me. It sounds like some audience members are saying "Good evening."

We go through our numbers, sung in English—amazingly, many in the audience are singing along. How *cool* is that? When we get to the introductions, I begin by telling the audience, again in English, that these guys are my brothers.

When I introduce the guys by name, everyone gets a fair amount of applause; then there's Benji. I introduce "Baby Phoenix" and the audience erupts in screams and rhythmical chants of "Ben-ji, Ben-ji!"—two separate women plead to be the mother of his babies, if my basic French gives me *any* help. Again, he replies with his guitar, letting loose a nice bluesy riff, which gets a further round of applause. I save Sean for last, and tell the audience in English how important meeting Sean was to the formation of the group. I hope that gets told to everyone in whatever language they speak or understand. Without Sean, there wouldn't *be* a Phoenix Rising.

The rest of the concert goes smoothly, and soon we're finishing the final encore and leaving the stage. Olympia night one is in the books, firmly a success. DC greets us with towels and bottles of water. As she hands me a bottle of water, I'm wrapped in Benji's arms. As he moves in for the kiss, I hear DC chuckle—then a towel lands over both our heads; like giving us a semi-private room.

Benji leans in and kisses me; it's like a combination "welcome home, sailor" and a "guess what I'm going to do to you tonight" sultry kind of kiss, yet sweet and hesitant, like a schoolboy. I'm as hesitant and awkward with my responses, partially because half my hair flopped over my eyes; I'm trying to kiss through a wet shaggy dog-cover, and partially because we're in the middle of the backstage area, which I hadn't scoped out for running around in the dark. There's no doubt about the kiss. It's real. My body, having been through the rigors of a two-hour-plus show, reacts like I've been sitting around doing nothing other than waiting for this moment. Shit, I may be moaning a little. Please, let the others be away from us. I may call Benji a Cajun firecracker, but this kiss has *me* ready to explode.

Between the heat of the towel draped over our heads—we've been too preoccupied to think about something that simple—and the fact that our clothes are soaked from the show, we *reluctantly* break the kiss and head toward the dressing area. As we do, Benji kisses me quickly on the cheek again, and then heads to a doorway to the audience area.

Backstage, Greg's beaming; either he's had some champagne or he's as thrilled by the show as I am. He walks to me, pats me gently on the shoulder, and walks with me into my dressing area.

"You were magnificent! I've got an idea—we can put together an official *Phoenix Rising* book, using your introductions tonight as the starting point. It could be multilingual, so that anyone could read your introductions in their language."

That floors me. I tell Greg, agreeing with his idea. To think my introductions of my found family could introduce people everywhere to these guys is wonderful.

"Thanks, Greg! I'm glad we've been recording the shows, so we've got what I said on tape."

As we're talking, Benji walks up with a familiar-looking guy. I've seen him... it hits me. It's *Johnny*, his childhood friend; we met back in October. They aren't touching, but Johnny's eying Benji like Clay was looking at Sean a few weeks ago.

"Johnny, you remember Ravynn from my birthday party, right? Shay, this is Johnny... John LeBlanc." Benji re-introduces us, nervously.

"Who dat," Johnny says, then remembers he's not among Cajuns. "I mean, hey." He's nervous, too. This guy's known Benji all his life, and could walk in here and steal him from us.

"Glad you could finally join us, Johnny; we missed you in Montreal." Yeah, like you miss a hangnail. I'm being nice to Benji's *friend*.

"Whoo boy, he missed some fine shows, didn't he?" Benji says.

"I wish I could've, but between family and work, there was no way. Glad I can slip in Paris and Rome."

Damn, he's gonna stick around for Rome? Fuck. *Not* what I wanted to hear. "I know Benji's happy to visit with you," I say, as enthusiastically as you'd welcome a visitor bringing a brand-new puppy into a house with wall-to-wall *solid white* carpeting.

"You guys are great! I loved the show. I didn't know y'all were as popular here as you are." John's words are friendly, but his eyes are on Benji. *Of course they are; he wants Benji for himself.*

Hotel

At the hotel, showered and casually dressed for some after-show relaxation, I'm over the moon by how well the show went. I believe we showed everyone we're serious contenders to the Beatles. My mood's heightened by *no* Ronnie.

The *downside* is Benji's friend Johnny showed up; he's with Benji now. That's got me more upset than Ronnie or Abbey Road. What the *fuck* is he doing with my—our Benji? The show was outstanding, but what if Johnny persuades Benji to leave the group? What if Johnny wants to stay for the rest of the tour? That fucks up our boyfriends bit. And who knows what'll happen with the group's dynamics? Why can't Johnny go home alone?

I can't keep worrying about Johnny and Benji, though part of me wants to. We've got this tour to finish, and the possibility of recording with George Martin in Abbey Road Studios—*that's* what I'll focus on. Sure... and Paris is *just* a humble little town.

We may not have played a lot of places while we were forming like the Beatles did, but we've played around Atlanta for years and gotten tight as a group; we're not letting anything slow us down in our pursuit of being the best group ever—including ourselves, and that means not upsetting the group dynamic with romances, real or fake. So far, Sean and Clay being together has strengthened it.

Sean and I have talked a few times about our next album; since we started recording the soundchecks and shows, we've gathered a collection of good live performances. Driven by Dickie's comments, we want to include good-quality live recordings on future albums. We *also* want to include new stuff, so we've got to figure out the balance. Another benefit of having Greg and DC as our management; most groups in our position would have a label guy telling them what to do. There's the difference in having a superb manager and having scored a world-wide number one album; the label loves us, and is giving us *almost* everything we want.

When we first mentioned doing a double album, including live recordings from the tour plus new material, we expected the label would ultimately refuse; instead, the label's given approval for what we requested. The bosses at Capitol Records even pass along a memo from the home office, EMI Records—a hand-written message reading *Suggest you name it 'San Francisco, Atlanta... and the World.' Best, G. Martin, London.*

This is wild. G. Martin at EMI in London could *only* be George Martin, the same George Martin who saw us earlier and who'll be overseeing a recording session with us in London—*if* we don't fuck it up. His idea for a title is *almost* the title I had thought of. I'm so *jazzed* about the idea of working at Abbey Road Studios; it's going to be a dream come true. If we keep Benji and lose Johnny, that is.

I'm about to slide into bed when there's a knock at my door. Who's knocking at 12:15 Sunday morning? I stand at the door without opening it and use my normal voice, "Who's there?"

"Shay, it's jus' me, okay?" Benji's voice is muffled, but unmistakable. I open the door, and a sleepy-looking Benji shuffles in. He's wearing that same nightshirt and matching sleep cap from the San Francisco sleep-over, as I remember it. He looks like what you'd expect from "The Night Before Christmas." Totally precious... Sheesh. Ravynn, do *not* go there. I wanna ask what happened with Johnny, but I don't want to seem jealous.

My "resistance" to Benji continues wearing away. Though we're playing fake boyfriends to drive Ronnie away, I'm convinced a relationship with him, other than just within the group, will cause disaster, fracturing the group. I can't chance it. But, when he does something like this, walking into my room virtually ready to crawl into my bed, my ability to resist him drops.

"Babe, *why* are you dressed like that?" I ask. I've got a sinking suspicion I won't appreciate the answer.

"I'm ready for bed, what do you think I'm dressed for?" Straight to the point, but avoiding the *real* question.

"I see that; is there a problem with *your* room?" I hope I don't sound as whiny as I think I do.

"No, just big and lonely. After Johnny and I visited, the room seemed empty, y'know?"

Wait—is Benji telling me he brought Johnny back to *his* room? "Did something happen, Benji?"

"Uhmm, not... really...." *Not really*? What the crap?

"I don't wanna push, but that's not reassuring."

"See, me an' Johnny's been friends forever, shay. He's a nice guy an' all, but...."

"He wants you to leave the band and go back to Louisiana with him. Right?"

Benji looks at the floor silently, but nods. At least I've got the beginning of the picture.

So there wasn't anything horrible. "So, is there more you want to tell me?"

"He's afraid if I'm out on the road, it'll make me into another washed-up druggie rock star, an' he sounds like he wants to be boyfriends."

"That's stupid; the *hardest* stuff you've ever done was that thimble of alcohol on your birthday," I say, rolling my eyes. I'm not happy with Johnny. "But you told him you're committed to our group, right?"

"I told him I was with Phoenix Rising for as long as you guys want me."

"Johnny better be prepared to wait until he's eighty then," I laugh, and Benji joins in.

"So, is it okey-doke for me to stay?" After our discussion, neither of us want to be alone, so my answer is swift.

"Late as it is, let's go to bed."

Benji's eyes go shiny and wide-open, he's so happy. Have I stuck my foot in it?

He heads to the bed. This is *not* how I picture my first time with Benji; I don't intend for this to *be* that kind of first time. If possible, we're going to fall asleep, side by side, *possibly* a hug and a few kisses....

I turn off the desk lamp and cross to the bed. Benji's lying in the bed on his back, that sleep cap still on his head. I slide in beside him, expecting to feel his flannel nightshirt against my sleep shorts. Yeah, and Custer expected the Indians to surrender to his superior force. The thing about sleep shirts is they can slide up your body easily; Benji's *not* as 'sleepy' as he appeared.

"You know I'm not ready for a relationship," I begin, but he shushes me.

"Shay, having a good time one night isn't a relationship. If it is, you had a relationship with that bellman, and with Jean-Paul." Ouch. He *knows* about my one-nighters? *And* he's still in bed with me? Maybe this *is* how I pictured my first time with Benji.

Before I can say anything, he rolls over closer to me and plants a kiss directly on my lips. He's not fooling around. We kiss. It's the hottest I've *ever* experienced. My mind's shutting down, but sends a last whimper of protest to my heart; yes, Benji's a cute, sweet guy, and he's a wonderful potential boyfriend, but there's *no way* this can happen now.

Some corner of my mind registers the protest and snaps me to my senses.

"Love, I don't want to hurt you—can't stand the idea—and I am definitely far from uninterested. This isn't the time or place for us to start something."

Benji looks into my eyes. I can see he's unhappy with my words, so I need to make him understand why I'm saying it. "Baby, it's not because I don't want you. You *are* the guy for me. Not as a one-nighter. One-nighters are just physical, getting off. I can't do that to you. It's crazy saying this. I want a relationship with you, but I can't handle it now, with the craziness in my life. Is that okay?"

He's quiet for a few moments—*too* quiet. Finally, I look at him, in time to see a single tear slip from his right eye. "Shay, I'm sorry," his voice trembling as he tries to control himself. "I know you've told me, but it never made sense. I figured if I got you in bed I'd make you see it's me you need, and you I've been wanting since I first saw you."

"Shhh, baby, it's okay. I've known you want me for a while, and I'm flattered, though your choice says you need a mental exam, picking the most-damaged one of us."

"Can I ask a favor?" I don't know where he's going with this, but I take a leap and agree. "Make love to me tonight, as if we were lovers." His last words are so softly spoken I have to strain to hear them.

I'm *so* fucked. If I don't do it, I'll hurt Benji. If I do it, it could ruin the chemistry of the group, including the bond Benji and I are developing. I can't win, regardless of which answer I give. To make love to Benji as if we're lovers, then go back to friends, will destroy us both.

I remain silent for what seems like ages, trying to figure out which of two impossible choices to pick, unsure of what to say or how to say it.

I start to give Benji my excuse when I notice his eyes are closed, his mouth slightly open... a very soft snore escapes. He's fallen asleep.

Travel to theatre, Sunday, June 30

Benji in my bed when I wake up is like a dream coming true. Momentarily, I'm surprised, until I remember his knock at my door and our discussion. Do I *want* Benji in my bed, as my lover? Only as much as I want air in my lungs, coffee in my cup... in fewer words, *damn right*, I do. But I'm terrified of my record; that'll ruin Benji and Phoenix Rising, so I can't allow it.

I know Benji wanted at least a quickie last night, but *that* wouldn't be fair to him. I'm thankful he fell asleep.

Benji waking up is the *second* most adorable thing I've seen. (Duh, *the* most adorable is Benji, fully awake.) This morning, he stumbles out of my bed and rushes into the bathroom. After a few minutes, he emerges, awake and refreshed—he's showered. His eyes sparkle, his smile is huge.

"Did I make a fou-fou of myself, shay?"

I pat the bed beside me, wanting him to sit. I'm wearing my sleep shorts, and I haven't had even a thimble of coffee, but seeing Benji has awakened me better than *any* coffee ever did. In that sexy nightshirt, he sits next to me, so close I feel the warmth radiating from his body.

"You've *never* made a fou-fou of yourself, babe, unless a fou-fou is someone who wants something and asks for it. Am *I* a fou-fou, with my melt-downs?" Benji shakes his head, as I knew he would. "If I'm not a fou-fou for *that*, which is crazier than anything you've said or done, there's no way you're a fou-fou."

Benji looks relieved but then a pout turns his lips. "But... but didn't you want it even a little?"

I sigh.

"Of course I did. You waking up next to me this morning made me realize what I've been missing. To see your smile first thing every day will keep me going better than all the coffee in the world. But I can't start something with you if my mind and body aren't ready for it, babe, and now isn't the right time."

"You don't have to explain. I gotcha. Y'know, last night, after Johnny left my room, I was lonely, so I came here." His eyes are twinkling mischievously as he's talking, so he's happy, and he's *probably* about to spill a secret. Somehow, this explanation seems off, like he's trying to judge how I feel about him, and as he continues, I'm certain. "It was my idea to come to your room in my nightshirt and cap. I added the sleepy act, so you'd let me in rather than send me back to my room. Clever, huh?"

"You're clever, and I should probably go British School Headmaster on you and cane your naked bum, but I won't, because I can't do anything that cruel," slipping from my normal voice into my British for the school headmaster talk. It has the desired effect; Benji giggles, and I laugh. "But, we have something serious we need to settle; I can't have you as a boyfriend, fake or real, without a pet name for you…. I've been thinking, since you came from bayou country, I might call you my *salamander*, 'cuz they live in the bayous and streams, right?"

Benji was quiet and almost downcast when I started the 'serious' talk, then perked right up. "Long as you don't call me something bad, I won't mind."

I shake my head, because I can't say anything around the lump in my throat caused by the loving gleam in his eyes. Shit, I am *so* fucked.

"I better get back to my room and get ready to go to the Olympia, huh?" Benji hugs me, a solid, 'you-belong-to-me' hug, kisses my cheek, and winks.

"Yeah, and I need to get myself ready and add some caffeine to my system, since I won't have my Benji beside me…." I try to act sad, but it's the lousiest acting since Sean tried to impersonate Yoko Ono the first (and, thankfully, *only*) time.

Benji opens my hotel room door, then turns to me and pulls me close to him. "You'll always have me, shay," then kisses me again, firmly on the lips, half in the hall, half in the room.

The burst of applause following the kiss has both of us reddening. Sean and Clay are standing there, leading the applause. So much for the romance discussions with them. Right behind the two lovebirds are Todd, Wil, DC, and Greg. Fuck, there's Davey and his crew… and Jean-Paul. *Everybody's* just seen the kiss, and now it's gonna be a long and winding road of denials and unwindings. And the likelihood *any* will be believed is absolute zero.

Benji makes his way through the mob of well-wishers—it's like we got married, the way everyone's acting—and gives me a wave once he's on the other side, heading to his room. I turn to get back inside my room when Sean and Clay block me from closing the door.

"That was some parting kiss, brother from another mother," Sean oozes sexual innuendo, with a little hip-rocking motion. Clay is beside him.

"For the record," I begin in my British voice, "Benji *slept* in my bed last night. He and I did nothing more than talk and sleep."

"And I'm the Queen of Sheba," Clay joins in.

"You can be Queen Elizabeth *and* any other queen you choose, because nothing—abso-freakin'-lutely *nothing*—else happened. Yes, I care for Benji. I think I'm falling in love with him. But I'm not gonna have a one-night-stand with him, because I know how much he cares about me. That wouldn't be fair to him!"

"And it would be like shooting fish in a barrel," Sean adds.

"Huh?" I'm stumped. What the hell do fish have to do with Benji and me?

"It's easy pickings, no challenge, *that's* what it means."

"Well, for *your* information, oh brother from another mother, if I were going for easy pickings, I could've had you dozens of times since we first met, right? And *did* I?"

Clay and I are watching Sean; I suspect Sean's never told Clay that he had thrown himself at me several times when we first met, but I didn't want to mess up our friendship by trying a relationship with *him*.

"No, you didn't want to lose our friendship," Sean says. Clay hugs him, and all's back to normal for them.

"Exactly, Sean. And henceforth, it's brothers for *all* of you. Now, I need to dress for the trip to the Olympia."

Olympia Theatre

As we enter the Olympia, curiosity about Johnny finally drives me to act. It's been eating me up since Johnny first showed up; he joined us briefly backstage last night, and visited with Benji in his hotel room. Beyond that and a few crumbs Benji gave me, I know nothing else.

"So Johnny's still in town?"

"Yeah, he's still here, gonna watch us tonight and our first show in Rome, then he's gotta fly home." At least he won't be tagging along all the way to Nashville, thank heaven. Guess I need to ask a bit more about how this'll work out.

"He's gonna fly with us to Rome? Or is he getting there on his own? I mean, it's not my business...." Like I didn't just sound like the flight manager. Next I'll be going, *tickets, please.*

"You don't need to worry; he bought his *own* tickets and hotel rooms. Just happens he's gonna be stayin' at the same hotel in Rome with us—I know *that* makes you happier 'n a fully-fed gator!" Oh gawd. Johnny'll be in *our* hotel in Rome, even if it's one night. Not a happy thought.

Tonight's our farewell to Paris, and our last goodbye to Jean-Paul. I said goodbye to him earlier, because I know the end of the show and the airport will be too crazy. I'm sure Benji and the guys have said goodbye as well. Back to business; soundcheck and the show.

The soundcheck is again a formality; we've done enough that it's like an assembly line. Other than Sean breaking a drumstick and Todd misplacing a pick, nothing much happened out of the ordinary. Microphone 1, check; guitar 1, check; and so on. Bloody monotonous. Now I know why groups come up with insane melodies *during* soundchecks—otherwise, we'd go friggin' nuts.

We head backstage to relax, then change for the show, and Greg tells us we're going to have pictures made. But once we see our wardrobe, the "rest" period shrinks drastically because it's gonna take almost two hours to get dressed.

Wil and Sean, hidden by their instruments, get cream-colored slacks and shirts; from there it's direct to kitsch-land, do-not-pass-go, do-not-collect-two-hundred-dollars. Clay, Todd, and Benji will create a French flag theme onstage, wearing red, white, or blue satin shirts and trousers—Todd with the American flag on the front and the French flag on the back of his otherwise-white shirt, and Benji sporting the black satin top hat I gave him for his birthday. I'll be a walking French flag, wearing a red sequin-covered top with a deep vee neck, a pair of electric blue satin trousers, and a wide white satin sash around my waist, topped with a sequin-covered red, white, and blue tricornered hat.

We change into our wardrobe. Johnny comes backstage and takes one look at Benji; his jaw hangs open. Johnny's got a case of the lusts for *my* Benji.

"Damn, son... you look *fine*," Johnny says to Benji, who doffs his top hat while wearing the bracelet with his name engraved on it (the one *I* gave him).

Johnny notices only Benji, like a gigantic hole sucked the rest of us into oblivion. I'm steaming. Benji's as sweet as always; he towels down his chest and back, then turns to face me. Johnny's slightly to my right, so I'm watching both of them. Benji smiles at Johnny, then oozes sexuality when he faces me, sliding his shirt on seductively. He's mastered putting clothing on being more seductive than taking it off. Finally, he's dressed. Benji shoos Johnny back out to the audience, and we're ready for the photographer.

The photo shoot takes longer than we thought, and the audience is left waiting for nearly 10 minutes. Finally, I speak up. "Why don't we break, let mister photographer move out front and catch us as we enter the stage for a few shots, so we can *perform* the concert, our *original* plan for tonight?"

Greg realizes the time. "Let's do it." The cameraman huffs, takes his equipment, and moves onto the stage to a light round of applause. The audience is so tired of nothing, they'll applaud *anything*.

We stride onstage normally, paying no attention to the photographer—*except* Benji, who looks at the cameraman and doffs his top hat as the shutter clicks. *That's* gonna be the prize picture of this tour.

Once I know my guys are set, I stalk to the front of the stage and tell the cheering audience, "Bonsoir, Paris! Nous sommes arrivés! Good evening, Paris! We've arrived!" The crowd *roars* its approval as we begin the slightly-delayed show.

With the outfits we're wearing and the flashbulbs going off as cameras record our every move, the auditorium is full of light. Like last night, the audience seems to sing along; a few places near the stage I see people dancing in the aisles.

When I introduce the guys, I start with Sean; he taps out a slinky rhythm on the high-hat and snare as I tell the audience he was the first guy to suggest our group. Wil's next; he plays a bit of *La Marseillaise*, the French national anthem, as I introduce our keyboard wizard. With Todd, I turn, nod his direction, and he plays a wicked riff on his guitar as I introduce him as our lead guitarist. The sturdy bass lines begin and I introduce Clay as our bass guitarist; he finishes with a flourish.

The audience knows who's left and begins chanting "Ben-ji, Ben-ji," as Sean and Clay add a little bass and percussion. Wil and Todd join in and add a hint of keyboards and lead guitar to accent the chant. I simply say, "Our rhythm guitarist, Benji." He's beaming, his playing pure wicked; he upstages the entire group with a few chords, then stops, tips his top hat, and struts back to his spot. The audience adores it. As the chant grows louder, I turn to him and motion for him to take another bow, which he does—to another *roar* of approval from the crowd.

While the crowd remains upbeat, we launch into the rest of the show. We have a finale which hopefully won't piss off our French audience. We'll find out.

Finale

We finish our first encore; usually we'd wait onstage as the stage lights darken a few moments, but tonight, we head backstage for our extras. Here, I'm carrying a large French flag to a stand just beside the front microphone. Davey and his guys help Wil carry out a replica Statue of Liberty; how cheesy can we get? The replica *looks* heavy as lead, but it's paper maché on chicken wire; a breeze and Lady Liberty would be gone with the wind. We begin our final number with an extended instrumental as I wish our Parisian hosts *au revoir*.

The effect is cheesy, but cute; I'm standing in darkness as a single spot illuminates the French flag. As the instrumental blends with the opening notes of our final song, Lady Liberty gets illuminated with a single spot, bringing out a rolling laugh in the audience. I take over and begin singing *Curtains* as the crowd gives us its love. Reaching the ultimate moments of the song, I lift the flag from its stand and wave it back and forth as the crowd joins my guys singing the last words. The entire house is on its feet. Our homage to French and American relations has been as big a hit as anything else.

We strut off the stage, waving and blowing kisses to the audience. DC greets us, as always, with towels and bottles of water. I tease her we're going to name her "goddess of the waters" if we ever do a show in Greece.

"I'll make sure Greg avoids scheduling any concerts there," she says, the smile on her face telling me she's *not* taking anything seriously. Though I *may* have to think about that title more; she deserves recognition for the help she's given us, and the hell she's put up with on my account.

Backstage's an excited blur. We're changing out of our costumes into clothing suitable for traveling back to the hotel; everyone's happy that our farewell gesture went well, and I'm relieved that for several days I've been *mostly* Ronnie-free.

As I think that, a clock chimes twelve. It's midnight, Monday, July 1, 1968, and soon, we'll be leaving the City of Lights to fly to the Eternal City, Rome. No Jean-Paul, no Johnny, and no Ronnie. I had to think about *him*. Shit, I can't get away from Ronnie, no matter how hard I try.

Benji and Clay see my reaction to my thoughts and are by my side immediately. Clay takes the lead. "Yeah, it's July 1, but we haven't seen *him,*" like Clay doesn't want to say the name for fear Ronnie will appear.

As Clay finishes, Johnny LeBlanc reappears. If it's not Ronnie, it's Johnny. They even rhyme. Johnny has the decency to stand back as we finish talking.

"He's right, shay. I think our boyfriend act will run him off. We're gonna keep it goin'."

"Am I interrupting anything?" Johnny asks, either ignoring or misunderstanding Benji's comment to me.

"Just our after-show wind-down, Johnny," Benji says. "We're always so jazzed after finishing a good show."

"I thought it was a great show! It was different tonight."

"It was our last night in Paris, so we went for a bit of flash, but the songs were all the same," I say, like a parent to a small child. I'm condescending, very upset and put-off by Johnny trying to steal Benji from us.

Johnny suddenly swoops like he's wanting to kiss Benji, or swallow his head. The move is so sudden, I couldn't be sure.

Sure enough, Johnny's swoop is for a kiss, which I don't like. It's over almost as soon as it starts, so there's that....

"John, boo, that's sweet, but not in front of the guys, okay? They get enough of that from Sean and Clay. Besides, I'm focused on this tour, ya know?"

"'Kay, B. I don't mean to upset ya, just can't resist."

"Are you kissing him, or trying to eat his face?" I say.

"Damn, son, you attracted to sweaty men or somethin'?" Benji smirks. I'm trying to find a hole in the wall I can crawl into.

"Just one in partic'lar, I guess," Johnny's eyes are undressing Benji.

"You so crazy, boo... I'll catch up with ya in a few, okay?"

John hugs Benji, and Benji hugs him back with little hesitation. In spite of just saying *not in front of the guys*, they kiss. I guess I don't count as one of *the guys*. I'm about to go over and break up the kiss-fest when Benji pulls back.

"Tete dur, boo, hard-headed as heck," Benji says, smiling.

John just nods, then leaves. I'm tempted to follow him to be *sure* he's really leaving, but I prefer the scenery here.

Benji and John together has me tighter than Sean's snare-drum head and worried the way they're going at it may kill the group's dream before we get to London. I'm scared shitless I'll never be Benji's *real* boyfriend.

• • • • • • • • • • •

ROME, ITALY

JULY 1 - 5, 1968

Airborne

We're airborne, flying straight up it seems; suddenly, the pilot levels the plane and we're parallel to the ground, a very unsettling beginning to this flight over the mountains. I wish I could somehow leave Ronnie and Johnny on the other side of those mountains.

The seatbelts light blinks off, so I unfasten mine until my mind helpfully supplies the thought that the pilot might decide to flip the plane and fly upside-down; on that thought, I refasten my seatbelt. Benji, who's left his fastened, looks at me and smiles. Better safe than sorry. On amusement park roller coasters, you *know* you're gonna get whipped around, perhaps turned over; this pilot's determined to keep us guessing.

Sean's less worried than I am; he and Clay walk up the aisle to our row. "Some takeoff, huh?" He asks, as they sit across the aisle.

"Was that what that was? Perfect for a roller coaster. Not sure how it qualifies for an airplane. Maybe the pilot had a liquid lunch, y'know?"

"Don't give them ideas," Benji adds, snorting with laughter.

"You two ready for the Eternal City?" I ask, changing the subject. I'd *rather* be asking Benji about Johnny.

"I'm *stoked*, been looking forward to Rome since I knew we were going to play here. I wish we could perform at the Colosseum, but I know the authorities shot that down."

Clay's right. We *wanted* to do an outdoor show, with the ruins of the Colosseum as the backdrop, but the Ministry of Conservation of Antiquities, whatever they call themselves, shut the idea down. They wouldn't let us do a show there for fear the vibrations from our music would cause damage to the Colosseum, and that was the end, but it would've been damn amazing.

I look up and see the seatbelt sign's lit again; we must be approaching Rome. The plane makes a tight right turn, followed almost immediately by a tight left turn, as if the pilot's following a mountainous road with an ess-curve on it. After the turns, the plane heads directly toward ground, or in this case water; we're over the Mediterranean Sea, near Italy. I hope the pilot knows what he's doing. Benji, sensing my near-panic, touches my arm, grounding me.

As I'm worrying I may have to swim out of the plane, the pilot swings the plane ninety degrees, parallel to the surface of the water, and suddenly I see buildings and what appear to be lights to guide planes to the runway. The plane bounces a little, then I can sense the runway underneath the wheels on the landing gear. If they'll put the brakes on, so we don't run off the other end.... My life's full of zig-zags, like this flight—the highs of the group; the lows of busted relationships, and what those mean for the group, and for Benji and me, *all* of it has left me up in the air.

Free day, Tuesday, July 2

We arrive at Leonardo da Vinci Airport on July 1; the name itself places you among older cultures. Atlanta's only airport has recently been named after a well-loved politician. No contest; Rome wins. A short drive takes us, via two limousines, to the Hotel Napoleon, where cheering fans restrained by police lines greet our arrival.

Our first day in Rome is free, beginning with a discussion of whether we should venture outside the hotel, with many "security questions," as Greg puts it. Of course, *one* of the first things mentioned is Ronnie, after Greg lets me know that Dickie might stop by.

The room phone rings, and Greg answers it, talks for a minute in a low voice drowned out by the buzz of my five bandmates all trying to one-up each other about what we should do on our day off. When Greg returns the handset to the base and turns to face me, it's like someone flipped the volume switch to "mute" on all of us.

"Dickie Newsome is on his way up, seems he has some interesting news for you," Greg says.

The hell? Greg couldn't just put me on the phone with Dickie? I gotta see him and deal with whatever it is in front of everyone? Oh, joy.

In a few moments, there's a light rap at the door; Greg opens it, and of course it's Dickie.

"Sorry to cut into your free time, but this might be important for you to know," Dickie says, looking more uncomfortable than I have ever known him to be—kinda like he'd prefer to be *anywhere* else but here. "I wanted you to know that Ronnie's aunt Lizzie, a distant relative, passed away some time ago and left him a fairly substantial inheritance, enough that he might show up in Rome or London to try to buy your affection."

"He's wasting his time and money, and pissing me off," I say. I want to go sightseeing, not argue over Ronnie-*fuckin'*-Kushner.

"Man, do *not* tell me we've gotten jacked up about seeing Rome and now we can't," Sean says, mirroring my own thoughts.

As the other guys look just as upset as Sean and I have stated we are, Greg gets on the phone again. After several minutes of talk, which we again can't overhear, he hangs up and turns back to us.

"The venue has agreed to send two of the plain-clothes detectives assigned for your shows to accompany you."

"Dammit, we're going sightseeing." I glare at Greg, daring him to object.

Greg arches his eyebrows. I'm prepared for a verbal battle; I will *not* spend another minute hostage to my fears. Surprisingly, he nods, saying nothing.

If *every* battle was this easy, I wouldn't be worrying about anything now. Time to check out Rome. Greg and DC remain at the hotel working on management things, so it's the six of us plus two detectives as bodyguards.

Sean's been studying his map and discovers we can ride the subway to get to the Colosseum and other sights. It's the way to go, rather than taking limos. We *could* walk the distance—it's a few miles at most—but that's not smart, for many reasons. The subway will get us there and back easily and inexpensively. The fare's a couple hundred lira each, less than two dollars a person. A bargain.

Our small horde—six band members and two detectives—heads towards the Manzoni station, a block from the hotel, if Sean's map is accurate. Benji and Todd are at my sides, one detective behind me, and one leading the way. I see the guy in front scanning left and right constantly; I know he's got my sketch and description of Ronnie, as well as pictures of him. If Ronnie shows up ahead of us, he'll be spotted before he sees me. For the first time, I'm worried more *for* Ronnie than *about* him.

We arrive at the Manzoni station—basically a doorway between two shops, with a red "M" above. We enter and descend a flight of stairs to the platform. Sean points toward the platform marked "MA Battistini." We follow him.

"We'll take the train to the terminal and switch to the 'MB' line heading towards Laurentina. Two stops later, we're at the Colosseum stop, or we can go one more to the Circus Maximus stop." Damn, sounds like he's channeling Greg now.

We hop on the train when it arrives, and follow Sean's plan. This ride is fun. It points up *another* thing our hometown Atlanta lacks, a rail transport system.

In minutes, we're leaving the train and finding our way to the "MB" line. Given that none of us speak or read Italian, and the signs are Italian, we're relying on Sean having read his subway map correctly. That leaves me queasy—Sean's great, but his patience with reading maps—*especially* written in a language he neither reads nor speaks—is not reassuring. We may be in Rome for the duration of our lives.

As I'm about to surrender to my gloom, Sean points to a sign denoting a stairway to "MB—Laurentina." He found our way. I would kiss him, but... no.

We practically gallop down the steps, in time to see a train pulling in. *Perfect* timing. The eight of us climb aboard—it's not really climbing; the door on the subway car opens level with the platform. We could *body-surf* in.

When we get to the "Colosseo" stop, we exit, heading for street level. We expect to be a couple blocks away from the Colosseum, but as we top the stairs, the first thing we see is a huge, old stone building—it *has* to be the

Colosseum. It's like every picture we've ever seen of it, only larger, way more impressive. This building's survived for nearly two thousand years; that's amazing itself. That it dwarfs most of the "modern" buildings nearby proves how advanced Roman civilization was. But what truly catches our eyes is....

"Caricatures!" Clay sings out. We laugh. This tour's destined to be immortalized by caricaturists. Of course, we pose; this time, the artist captures my tattoo alongside the Colosseum. Once we're shirtless, he makes us Roman Legionnaires, Benji and me at the center of our own legion, including my tattoo a second time on my chest. I'm not sure how realistic it is—I don't recall many Legionnaires embracing or gazing at each other, yet that's how he portrays Benji and me, our arms around each other's neck, our eyes focused upon each other.

When the caricature's completed, we replace our shirts; we wander around the Colosseum, find several souvenir shops nearby and purchase trinkets and mementos. As we're wrapping up our purchases, several stomachs express their *own* desires—time for food and relaxation back at our hotel.

The trip back is a simple reverse of our trip to the Colosseum. We walk back to the subway station, ride the trains, then finish walking back to the hotel, with another caricature under our arms—okay, under *my* arms.

Greg and DC nearly split their sides laughing when they see a second caricature. DC, who has a dry wit like mine, breaks us up. "Guess we'll call this the Carica-Tour."

Too bad we're halfway done—it would've been *boss* calling the tour that. Maybe next time we'll have a good name *before* the tour begins.

"Greg has news for you guys, don't ya?" She looks at Greg, who looks like he's been working a jigsaw puzzle with missing pieces. He's smeared ink on his nose, his hair looks like he's pulled it in twelve different directions. Six empty styrofoam cups surround him and his paperwork. As Sean's mom would say, he's *frazzled*.

"Well, I have some things I can share, and things we're still working on. We've confirmed two stops for the next tour. Miami, Florida, May 1 and 2 next year, and New Orleans May 6, 7, and 8." As soon as Greg says 'New Orleans,' Benji lights up.

"How long a tour?" I ask. Not that I have any plans next summer....

"Probably four to seven months. There'll be more international stops, plus more US cities."

"You're gonna work us to death, then?" I joke.

"No, we hope you'll have as much fun next time, if not even more, so you *won't* be worked to death."

If we could get to the "having fun" part....

Travel to theater, Wednesday, July 3

As we get into the limousines for the ride to the theater for tonight's soundcheck at the Teatro Brancaccio, I suggest to Greg, who's riding in the second limousine, that they discuss dressing as Roman Legionnaires for tomorrow's show.

Benji, Todd, and DC join me in the first limousine. The scowl on Todd's face tells me *he's* not in favor of dressing as a Legionnaire. DC is *barely* suppressing her laugh; there's a grin splitting her face. I look at her, cock my head to one side. "Well? Whaddaya think?"

"Sheer lunacy, but it'll be fun. You'll have to get the guys to agree, *and* Greg... and *then* we'll have to find six Roman Legionnaire outfits." DC ticks points off, *still* bursting from laughter.

Benji has been calm during this. I turn toward him.

“Shay, the Roman Legions wore those red skirt things, right? Over boots that looked more like sandals, with straps up to their knees?”

“Yeah, with brass breastplates over a plain white tunic,” I add.

Todd jumps in. “So, *basically*, you want us all in sandals and dresses? Do you *know* how much that’ll make us look like a bunch of girls? I’m against it, but if most of the guys say yes, I’ll do it, I just *won’t* enjoy it.”

Benji looks at me and smirks. “You’re *already* picturing it, aren’t you?”

I nod.

“Don’t tell me you’re thinking of saying yes to this idea,” Todd says to Benji, but he’s smiling; I think his *not really* is softening.

“Not thinking. It’ll be fun. I’m in.”

Good. Benji’s *yes* makes it easier to sway Clay, Sean, or Wil, if I have to.

Perfect timing; we stop in front of the Teatro Brancaccio, with the police line from the building to our limousines on either side of the theater’s front door. The marquee over the door has a lot of Italian words on it, but spelled out in the middle in large red letters is “Phoenix Rising.” So cool. Someone’s gotta get a picture.

Greg, Wil, and the “twins” as we’ve started calling Sean and Clay (since they’re always touching) join us. Greg looks at me, then at Sean and Clay and throws his hands up; he’s given up. As long as they don’t fuck up the group, I won’t say anything.

“We talked about the Legionnaires idea,” Greg starts.

“Oh, Gawd,” Todd moans in agony.

"Long story," I tell Greg.

Greg nods, and looks like he's about to continue telling me about the discussion, when Clay abruptly fills in a few blanks. "Me and Sean are *all* in favor!"

Not to be left out, Wil adds, "Well, if everyone else is saying yeah, count me in. I don't wanna be left out."

"Benji and I are definite *yes*, Todd is against it but will go along if the majority says yes. That means we've got 4 yes votes, one sort-of yes, and one reluctant participant," I finish, smiling.

"Okay. I'll see if we can find Legionnaires' costumes to fit you, and I'll make sure it's not violating any laws. Don't need y'all hauled offstage in Rome on American Independence Day," Greg says.

We start toward the stage, Benji's arm around my waist, when a voice comes from behind me that I had no desire to hear.

Soundcheck

Benji and I haven't made it to the stage when Ronnie makes *another* appearance, wearing a pasted-on smirk above his white tee and blue jeans over black tennis shoes. South Georgia redneck chic appears in the Eternal City. Benji's grip on my waist tightens, painfully, as he sees the unwelcome visitor.

"Enough of these *impromptu* interruptions, Ronnie," I bite out, clutching Benji nearly as tightly as he's holding me.

"I've come to see if you're ready to come back to me. I'm not *pressuring* you," Ronnie tries for a smile, but winds up closer to a snarl. Benji's almost growling.

"You and I are done. Sorry you wasted your time and money pursuing this."

"I told you I'd be back. Here I am."

"Yeah. The thing is, I've realized that you aren't the guy for me. With you, I was an afterthought. It was *your* life, *your* choices, *your* everything. It's *my* turn."

"You're pretty confident. Not the guy you were."

"I've grown, discovered who I am, what makes me happy. I've learned I'm worthy of being loved for who I am, no matter what anyone thinks. Benji gets that."

"He might, or he's along until something better happens. Sure you wanna throw away our past for *nothing*?" Ronnie sneers.

"He's more mature than *either* of us. He's also more considerate of everyone than you ever were... yes, I *am* willing to throw away whatever our past was."

Direct hit, based on how Ronnie's face darkens and his fists clench.

"*Fuck* it, Robin. I'm outta here. You were never worth it, anyway." With those words and a dual single-finger salute, Ronnie turns toward the door and strides out.

Teatro Brancaccio is a grand theater, used for live shows—operas, theater, and concerts. It resembles the music halls you see in movies about the wild west of the US—multiple levels of seating around the sides and back; plush seating on the main floor, and blood-red curtains which appear to be velvet. Finished with lots of blood-red tassels and braiding with gold cording.

Ritzy and upper-crust looking; maybe I should learn the Italian to use John Lennon's quip from the Royal Command Performance in London several years back—"those of you in the cheap seats, applaud; the rest of you can rattle your jewelry." That might be *too much* Italian for this southern boy with the fake British accent to handle. I'm struggling enough with "Buonasera, Roma! Benvenuto allo spettacolo!"—"Good evening, Rome! Welcome to the show!"

I reach to hug Benji, then stop.

"I guess the fake boyfriend act is over, huh?" I ask, thinking I should've let Ronnie dangle a bit to keep this going.

"Shay, we don't need to rush dropping the boyfriend act. You sure that couyon ain't hangin' around?" Benji asks, not using the word *fake*. He's hesitant as he says it, like he's stepping on a lake in winter, unsure how solidly frozen the surface is.

"I was thinking it might be too soon, salamander," I smile, awkwardly using my pet name for him in front of the guys for the first time.

First concert

We've finished soundcheck with minor adjustments; everyone's upbeat, a lot of clowning around. Greg gets in on it and tells Todd his "O Sole Mio" is *almost* opera-worthy. There are the usual hijinks: towel battles, using towels to "pop" each other; trash-talking; six guys acting like they're almost invincible.

Benji and I stride over to Greg. Time to put the specter of Ronnie to rest, hopefully. Greg sees us and realizes something's up.

"Who dat, Greg," Benji starts with his now-recognizable greeting.

"Hey, guys, what's up? Problems?"

"No, not really...." I start. I should *kick* myself; that's the best way to make Greg think something's wrong.

"Ronnie?"

"Uh... he *was* here. I don't think he'll be a problem anymore." I tell him the story.

Greg stands thoughtfully for a few moments, then says without hesitation. "Okay."

"I'm 98 percent sure that Ronnie will head home. He doesn't wanna see me with Benji, and he knows the guys aren't gonna put up with more shit." I stare into each of my guy's faces, sending them a jolt of raw power.

Concert, after

The show goes on to a *packed* house.

Through the show, I prowl the stage, singing and talking to the audience, loving them. They're loving us, loving me. While I'm prancing and strutting, I'm watching for signs of Ronnie. We finish the show without seeing him, and I'm *not* complaining. I want it over.

Backstage after the show, there's an enormous arrangement of flowers for Benji. It's signed *With love*.

"Woo-hoo, Baby Phoenix has an admirer!" Sean hoots. If he notices I'm *not* happy, he's not showing it.

"Babe, don't tease him," Clay jabs Sean lightly in the ribs. Benji smiles, a slight blush on his cheeks. I'm starting to steam.

DC takes one look at me, one quick glance at Benji with the flowers, and decides. "Guys, give Ravynn and Benji space, okay? Try changing out of your outfits, instead of gawking like *schoolgirls* in love."

That does the trick. Sean, Clay, Wil, and Todd clear the room. DC stays, watching from a corner, distant enough to give us privacy without being too far if we need her.

"Those are beautiful, Benji." I start in neutral territory; I've got a hunch who sent the flowers, but I don't wanna say the name and sound jealous as hell.

"Johnny sent them," Benji whispers, confirming my fears. He's not even looking at my face; I can guess what he's thinking.

"Shall I leave?" I ask. I don't know what else to say. This seems like Ronnie, version two. I'm crushed, like I got run over by something unexpectedly huge, heavy, and slow-moving, like a fucking gigantic snail.

I turn to leave, not daring to look at Benji. I'll go to my dressing area, try to compose myself and change. Not sure why; my life ended with those three whispered words.

"Wait, shay," Benji's voice is back full force. Is this the new game, get me happy, crash me to the depths, then start again? I can't handle it.... Benji wraps an arm around my waist, like nothing has happened and we're playing boyfriends. I look away momentarily because I've gotta paint a smile on my face, so he believes me. This is unreal. A few days ago, I was worried this *thing* between Benji and me would get out of hand, or get into the press and ruin our chances at being the next huge group. Now,

I'm worried this thing with Johnny is gonna take Benji away from me *and* the group.

"C'mon, now, you don't need to be down like that. We had a great show, didn't we?"

"You little show-stealer, you know we did." I can't help myself; the way he says it makes me happier. And he's got those emerald-green eyes trained on me with his smirk.

"That's bettah," he emphasizes his Cajun accent. He *knows* what that does to me.

"What about the flowers, babe?" Do I *really* want to know?

"Hey, I knew he was gonna send 'em; he told me. I was hoping to have DC or someone get 'em so you wouldn't see 'em, but I couldn't. Don't matter none, we keep doing our boyfriend bit."

"But Ronnie's left, and..."

"You're 98 percent sure he's gone. We can't risk that 2 percent! We gotta keep going, unless you're tired of playing boyfriends...."

"Oh, *hell,* no way!" To prove my point, I grab him in a hug that borders on a decent touch football grab, or maybe even a bear-hug. Must've worked, because he returns the squeeze and adds a bone-melting kiss.

Benji's kiss and that hug effectively wipe my mind clear. What was I worrying about?

He smiles, and I sense he's figured out what I was thinking. He *probably* has—he's so good at it. Sometimes it seems like my thoughts print on my forehead for him to read.

"Shay, we gonna show up in London as the top guys. An' I betcha we'll find a bunch of songs to record, long as George Martin doesn't turn us away. But first we're gonna be the best damn Legionnaires Rome's ever seen!"

Oh, yeah. I forgot about that. I can't wait to see how sexy Benji's gonna be in that Legionnaire's outfit. Almost makes me sad Johnny's gonna miss it....

Celebration, Thursday, July 4

After yesterday, I wake up this morning, Independence Day, excited and looking forward. Tonight's our final Rome show—I am kinda itching to see the guys as Roman Legionnaires. I hope Greg knows how to use Todd's camera. We've gotta get pictures of everyone. Todd will try to avoid being on film in the outfit. No way.

Today's the holiday back home, so we'll have our own celebration before we get to the soundcheck and concert. Not sure what—we can't launch any fireworks without going through all kinds of paperwork. Greg's checked; it was six inches' worth of forms for a few firecrackers. Not gonna sign away our lives for that. We'll do something else. Greg and DC claim they've got it; we'll find out.

A rhythmic tap at my door interrupts my thoughts. Based on the pattern, it's either Sean being funny, or Greg's upped his game. I swing the door open to find Benji.

"Thought I'd be first to wish ya a happy *quatre juillet*, shay!"

"Thanks, but what's *cot-truh-jwee-yay*? I've got no clue," I say, in the dark what he's talking about.

"It's the Fourth of July, in real French. You've never heard that? Here I thought I was being cool!" Benji says with a smirk. I ruffle his hair to mess with him.

"You scared me with words I haven't heard. Next time warn a fella!" I'm not upset, just something's odd. The urge to kiss him is strong; when he does something thoughtful like this, it knocks me over. The idea of kissing him pops into my head any time I'm near Benji, even onstage. One day, I'll probably fuck up and do it. I'll enjoy it, and he will also, but the cost afterwards will be more than we can bear.

After my comment, Benji gives me a kiss. He must've been thinking the same.

Thank goodness I'd pushed the door closed securely behind Benji when he entered. While we're kissing, there's another knock. I break off the kiss, giving Benji a solid hug as I do.

Benji hears the knock as well, and sits at the desk in my room, like he's been writing the whole time. I'm about to open the door as another knock sounds. Someone's impatient—pretty sure it's Sean, probably with Clay.

"Well, it's 'the twins,' coming to visit," I tease them. They've heard the nickname plenty of times from Greg and DC and the other guys.

As they enter, they see Benji sitting at my desk; he grins and waves.

"We were gonna ask if you knew where Benji was, but apparently he's been here all along." Clay says, even as he looks from Benji's lips and tousled hair to me. We're *busted*. Though who knows how much they're going to imagine we've been up to.

"Having private Fourth of July celebrations?" Sean leers, wiggling his eyebrows as he insinuates that Benji and I have been carrying on.

"We kissed, that's all," I say.

Benji looks at them and grins. "True dat. We're *still* fake boyfriends til we're sure Ronnie is gone. We have to stay in practice."

"Yeah, tell yourself that," Sean says, beaming. "But practice like that is different from soundcheck, because you get more out of it than you put in."

Just then, Greg knocks on the door and steps inside with DC, Wil, and Todd.

"Hey, Greg! I was wondering if you'd given up on us," I tease.

"No, DC and I found a green spot near here; we're going to celebrate the Fourth of July picnic style there, then head to soundcheck at the theater."

"Cool beans!" Todd, usually low-key, is excited. I am, too.

"Then, Davey will ferry us to the spot shortly, then to Teatro Brancaccio. The Legionnaires' costumes are waiting for you," Greg looks directly at Todd with the last words, and Todd shrugs like a condemned man, preparing for his last hours of freedom.

"Whoo-wee, a pic-a-nic in the park, what I mean!" Benji is sliding into his Cajun, safe to say he's excited. Everyone seems the same. I have the *best* found family.

On the way to the van, we stop at DC's room to collect what looks like two baskets of laundry; at least, they're covered with large fluffy towels. I realize these baskets contain our *pic-a-nic* lunches, as Benji called it.

In minutes, we stop next to an incredible green space in this ancient city. There's plenty of space to stretch out a couple of blankets, which we work on. Davey and Greg bring out the baskets and the picnic begins. DC and Greg have found hot dogs, potato salad, green beans, carrots, everything we needed. Topping off, we've got Coca-Colas, like we're home. And, schmaltz alert, there are little American flags for everyone. No fireworks, but plenty of American pride.

For twenty minutes, the *only* sounds are swallowing Cokes and chewing and swallowing the food. It strikes me; this is the first Independence Day we've spent anywhere other than in America. It chokes me up somewhat.

"You thinkin' about bein' away from home the first time, shay?" Benji reads my mood, partially.

"You've got me figured out, *salamander*," I smile. I want to tell him to forget Johnny, but I can't offer him a reason. I clam up instead.

"Salamander, huh?" DC teases, smiling like she's *in* on the secret.

"They come from the bayous, like me," Benji explains. DC's smile gets larger, and she just nods.

Wil, usually the silent one, suddenly softly sings, "Oh beautiful, for spacious skies, for amber waves of grain..."

That's all it takes. The rest of us join in, singing the remainder of *America the Beautiful*. It's *not* our usual style, but it fits, on this day, in this place. We draw a small crowd, who applaud politely. They're mostly Romans, and probably have no idea what we're singing.

Back in the van heading to Teatro Brancaccio for our last soundcheck, Benji's hand grasps mine, seeming to promise everything will be fine.

Soundcheck

As we enter this magnificent theater again, I pause, admiring its beauty. Given the mess with Ronnie previously, I didn't appreciate its majesty. From the outside, it blends into the surrounding buildings, like a row of nondescript buildings. Once you enter, you realize *this* is no ordinary building.

The Beatles *never* performed here. *We* have and are. Game, set, match. Yeah, I'm hung up on the comparisons. A shit-ton of people will find ways to *keep* the Beatles the best group ever. *Only* four of them, and look at the diversity of their music so far. My answer to that is simple; the Beatles used a 40-piece orchestra to accomplish the sounds on *A Day in the Life*; Wil used four keyboards to do the same. George Martin produced the album that featured the song by the Beatles, heard our rendition, and was thrilled with it. In my mind, that evens the playing field.

Tonight's show is *Arrivederci, Roma*. Until we meet again.... Appropriate, because this group has staying power. *If* we don't fuck up.

Soundcheck's smooth, almost *too* smooth, but we chalk it up to being an added bonus on Independence Day. Sean, picky about *everything* concerning his drums, is quick to say it's good. He hops off the drum riser and is immediately hugged by Clay, like they've been apart for weeks.

I can't talk; soon as Benji puts his guitar away, he races to me and hugs me as if I'm the source of life.

My brain again asks, *Are you sure this is a 'fake' boyfriend relationship, or are you fooling yourself?* I don't answer. I have lips that must be kissed.

"If I can interrupt you," Greg says, as I realize we've kissed our way backstage. Oops.

"Sorry, staying in practice," I mumble.

"Yeah, whatever," Greg says. He steps into one of the adjoining dressing areas and wheels out a rack of six Legionnaire's costumes, complete with the metallic chest covering and the sandals.

Todd chooses that moment to walk in, sees the rack of costumes, and reacts as he had previously. "*Fuuuck*, I was *hoping* this was going to be a poor joke. Looks like the joke's on me."

Greg shows each of us our chest plate—they're different sizes for our differing body shapes. He's also got six pictures of how to get the sandals on properly. The sandals look like they could be the real bitch.... Until Sean points out that the main part of the costume is kinda like a miniskirt. Now we've got an issue for real.

"Any of you who are worried, the bottom of the costume has a built-in brief, so it keeps your 'stuff' tucked away." Greg answers my unasked question perfectly. With my prowling around onstage, I imagined giving the first few rows a free show of the wrong sort.

"That's a relief," Sean says. Damn, I'd forgotten him sitting at his drum set in that outfit.

"We're not wearing headgear of any sort, are we?" Wil asks. Shit, I forgot most pictures I've seen of the Legionnaires show them with helmets with a red brush-like center. Now I *hope* Greg didn't go that far.

"No headgear. Just your hair." Greg smiles, and I relax.

We've got a couple hours until showtime, so some relaxation before stressing into those sandals sounds like a plan, until Greg tells us he's got *another* bloody photographer coming to take pictures of us before we go onstage. Fuck me running. There goes at least an hour of relaxation time....

"How soon is the photographer due?" I ask, figuring we might get an idea of how much relaxation we're going to have. Tomorrow's a news conference, then the flight to London, so it'll work out.

"He'll be here at 7:15. The show starts at 8:00, and I want to give him time to get enough pictures of you. He might get some once you go onstage."

"Cool. That gives us almost an hour and a half before he gets here; will half an hour give us enough time to get dressed?" I'm concerned. I don't want to volunteer to dress already, but half an hour may not be enough.

"Rest and relax for half an hour, then we'll see," Greg says, obviously concerned about getting six of us dressed as Legionnaires in half an hour. Some day, *someone* should stop me when I get a *cool* idea. It backfires, usually eating up our relaxation before a show.

To make things weirder, Wil suggests we *keep* the costumes and appear unannounced, as *Suzy and the Redskirts* once we get home. That'll go *grand*. We'll look bizarre, and the costume company will probably put out an international hit on us for stealing their costumes.

"That's a hard pass," I say, cutting it off, as Greg focuses on us.

"What's a hard pass?" Greg's puzzled, so I tell him. He shakes his head.

"No, no, no.... That's *not* a possibility. I'm surprised Todd didn't shout against it, or has he tuned out?" Greg looks around, and Benji and I join the scanning. No Todd.

"One of the costumes is missing," Benji says.

We check; Todd's outfit isn't among the *five* costumes.

I'm almost panicking. We're nearly through the half-hour, no sign of Todd. Sean and Clay decide to search backstage for Todd or his costume. That relieves me. Benji's accent in my ears, his hands on my shoulders, keeps me calm as he guides me to a sofa in the common backstage area.

As Sean and Clay begin their search, we hear a shuffling sound from the hallway to the dressing rooms. It sounds like a wounded bird walking on a beach, dragging a broken wing in the sand.

What the...?

I'm not sure if I should laugh, cry, whistle, or sit with my mouth open—so I do a little of each. It's Todd. He's changed into his costume, and damn, Sam, he looks hot, for being so against it.

Greg looks at me and grins. "There's your answer. It took Todd less than 15 minutes to become Fierce Legionnaire Todd." Todd snarls for effect, but it doesn't *completely* work.

"Yeah, don't give up on music yet," I tease him.

"This isn't as bad as I thought," he admits, grinning.

Final concert

We enter the stage in our Legionnaire costumes. The audience gives us a *standing* ovation. Cheers, applause, everyone's on their feet. When I say good evening in Italian, it's official—these people *love* us. I glance at the guys. They're all smiling. This makes it worth the haggling over the costumes.

The show progresses, the audience singing along some. I'm over the moon at how well the Rome audience has accepted us; there had been rumors American rock groups weren't well-received. Maybe it's my British persona that's winning the crowd over, but I really believe we're damn good.

During a few of the more up-tempo numbers, Clay, Todd, and Benji form an impromptu chorus line, not missing a note. They're playing so skillfully you'd think we've been touring for years instead of a few weeks.

Of course, there are signs in the audience.

The Rome audiences are democratic—there are signs for Todd, Wil, Sean, Clay, Benji, and me, almost evenly distributed. Okay, evenly distributed if you took half of Benji's signs away. He's become a superstar. There are *also* pictures for most of the group; I see Sean, Clay, Wil, Todd, Benji, Sean and Clay together, me, and—

Fuck me running, there's a picture of Benji's face with my face, *almost* like we're kissing. The picture the fan is holding is obviously two pictures glued together, the backgrounds slightly different, but it's close enough a quick glance gives the impression that we're kissing.

It catches me unprepared—like a two-by-four to the gut.

I forget the words of the song I'm singing.

Gah.

After a total mind freeze, I flash back and manage to catch up with the music. I *might* get away with the fuck-up… then I glance at Benji and Clay. They're playing, their jaws set so tight their teeth may turn to powder. I've fucked the song, maybe the concert, possibly the recording session in London, and now I've got at least two bandmates absolutely furious with me.

We finish the song. It's introduction time. Maybe I can salvage this somehow…. I start with Todd and Wil, then Sean. Sean appears okay, but I can see he's concerned about what just happened; he knows my lyrics as thoroughly as I do. We'll have a meeting after the finale… I hope. Clay gets a round of applause, then the audience chants for Benji. I look at him, silently begging him to do this for the group. This'll probably drive him straight into Johnny's arms, and it's because I got weirded out by one picture of our faces together—from a *fan*. I *know* that he's pissed about my reaction to the picture—that by rejecting the picture, I'm rejecting him, but that's as far from the truth as we are from home. He shoots a look at me that, had his face been a double-barrel shotgun, would've left two gaping holes through my chestplate. Fast as that look hits me, he turns toward the audience with his brightest smile. Gawd, I'm in *deep* shit.

I keep myself calm; there's a group of guys and a recording session on the line here. The remaining show goes smoothly—to outward appearances. But I'm a wreck. I can almost *hear* the words Benji is going to hurl at me backstage.

After the show, it's apparent the moment we get backstage that things aren't *okay* with Benji and me. Benji's flexing his fists—opening and closing them, repeating the process, like he's deciding between slugging me or choking me. No hug or kiss, no gleaming eyes looking into mine. In fewer words, *Ravynn fucked up.*

"One. Just one dam' pitcher," Benji spits words at me like a machine gun.

"One damn picture that could rip our world, this group, *and* everything we've worked for, apart," I say, looking at the floor. He's so mad I can't face him.

"Look. at. me. Dammit," more word-bullets fire from Benji's mouth, as the guys stay well out of arm's length from both of us. *Where* are Greg and DC? Not like I want to be *further* humiliated, but we need a mediator.

"Babe, I'm sorry. It caught me unprepared. I'm not perfect; I've told you that before, but I didn't mean this to hurt you."

I should've gotten a can of gasoline, poured it on myself, and ignited it, because my comments make Benji even angrier. His face is now somewhere between a dusty rose and a ripe tomato, and getting closer to the tomato every second. Oh, fuck.

"So, you're sayin' you want us to stay hidden. Is *that* your idea of living a true life? Because if it is, I got nothin' more to say. There *are* people who don't have that hangup." He's thinking about Johnny, even if he's not saying the name. What the fuck do I do?

Sean chooses this moment to add his two bits. "You've always bitched about having to hide who you are. You always say you wanna be real. I gotta tell you, watchin' you and B these past days, you've been happier than I've ever seen, and more like the guy I first met."

Now I know what being gang-tackled in football feels like.

"I'm goin' to my room to change," Benji spits out, "and I *don't* want company." He storms out of the common area. I've just lost my last, best chance....

"Look, you gotta realize this: your reaction to the picture of you and Benji was like telling Benji you didn't want him. You better figure out something quick," Sean says.

"Sean, Clay, I need your help. Can you find Greg and DC?" I'm lost and panicky as I ask, needing to hear Benji's Cajun to calm me.

Sean and Clay agree. I've gotta figure something out. My mind's telling me twenty different things, but my heart says the group—and I—need Benji happy. I need help from cooler heads. As I'm mentally scribbling dozens of thoughts, cataloging options, to see if any make sense, Greg and DC *finally* show up. Greg looks around cautiously.

"Did something happen?"

"Greg, I messed up bad. Benji's changing *alone* and doesn't want visitors."

"Okay, Ravynn, spill; is this about the picture of you two?" DC goes for the kill.

"You saw it?"

She nods, but says nothing; Greg stands, his mouth open like he wants to say *something*, but hasn't thought of the words.

"I totally fucked it this time. I saw it, singing one of *my* songs, and forgot the words—just before an instrumental break. The audience was fine, Benji and Clay weren't."

"Then *why* is Clay here, but Benji isn't?" DC asks the question I've been trying to form.

Clay, usually quiet, fills us in. "Because *my boyfriend* and I know how you're hurting. So we're gonna help fix it."

"Ah-ha. I suspected," DC nods, like a doctor confirming a diagnosis.

"Tell me this is *not* going to destroy the group before the end of this tour..." Greg says, shaking his head. "I've received two cables from London in the past three hours. The first confirmed that Mr. Martin has reserved two half-day sessions in London before your first show there. The second came moments ago, tersely worded, reading *perhaps pressures of touring are too great, should recording sessions be canceled?* It's obvious he got reports about the problem and is offering us an out." *Wait*—recording sessions?

My first reaction is to freak out or throw something. My second reaction is to fight back tears at the thought of getting *this* close to what I've craved all this time, only to lose it a little more than 24 hours before it was to happen. I catch my breath, steel my thoughts, and push on.

"Please, don't let him cancel us because of my fuck-up, Greg, if you can prevent it.... Here's what I want to do, if you, Sean, and Clay can help me."

"To keep you guys together as a group, I'll do anything, if it's legal," Greg says, and DC nods.

I'm scrambling, because I've never been in a situation with this many parts and so many things that could get horribly messed up with the slightest error. I fucked it up, so I gotta fix it.

"Benji's in his dressing room changing. I know he doesn't want to see me, because of my stupid reaction to that picture in the audience. I need him to understand that I'm the same guy I was in New Orleans, in San Francisco...."

Sean cracks the tension. "The same lovable fuck-up as ever." He smiles at me and *almost* offers a chest-bump, except for Legionnaire costumes.

"Can you and DC arrange something at the hotel for me?" I ask. DC is giving emphatic nods of agreement, without hearing my request.

"Get out of your costume before that chestplate fuses to your skin; DC and I will get in touch with the hotel now."

I trudge to my dressing room, hoping my plans will get Benji to realize my reaction was shock, nothing more. Shit, I know it was more than that. Shock, yes, but fear of being rejected, of being abandoned, fear of losing out on passing the Beatles, and fear of losing the best family I've known, because if this band breaks up, we'll go separate ways.

Meet the Press conference, Friday, July 5

After our final Rome concert, I'm sitting in a private alcove in the hotel's fanciest restaurant, table for two. On the table, set with china and silver utensils, sits a vase with a dozen perfect red roses. Totally wasted; I'm alone. Sean and Clay can't get Benji to calm down. My grand gesture—my attempt to win Benji back, if I ever had him—has flopped.

As I sit thinking I'm doomed to being alone, I look up, and there he stands, gazing at me guardedly. No smile, no frown. I settle for that. I stand as he approaches, but he motions me to sit back down, his lips tight. He hesitates, finally sitting.

"You can't drop what happened and expect me to like it. I'm not your lap dog. I ain't no pet you keep hidden."

"Benji, I...."

"No, you're lis'ning now. We're alone, like *you* want, so I'mma sayin' my bit. Then you can think on it, *alone*, and maybe figure it out."

I'm here to listen, not talk; I nod. Tears threaten. Somehow, I hold them back.

"I let you *think* we were playing boyfriends, and then you blew up over that damn picture. You talk about livin' your authentic life, but you can't handle being *fake* boyfriends. It won't work. I'm goin' back to my room now. Don't fret, I ain't leavin' the group, an' I'll still smile at the shows an' play wicked music. But things are changin'. You can't have me if you only want me in secret." Before I can say anything, he stands and leaves. My face begins to flush with embarrassment. Thank gawd I'm in a private alcove, no audience to my shame.

Well, almost no audience. Once Benji stalks out, the waiter walks over carrying two plates of fresh frutti di mare with mussels, spaghetti, and a magnificent sauce. I manage a few bites, but the lump in my throat—courtesy of Benji's visit—makes eating or drinking anything difficult. Gawd. Benji's been *playing* fake boyfriends—no wonder it's seemed real. Shit, I've really fucked up. I have to show him how much he means to me and how much I need him, not *just* as a guitarist. First, I persuade the waiter to send the arrangement of roses, with no card, to Benji's room; he agrees, and even packages the frutti di mare to send along. After a sip of water, I leave a decent tip and return to my room, too devastated to think.

We're back at Teatro Brancaccio for our farewell press conference. No surprise, Benji's at the far end of the table, hardly glancing my way. He's put the group between us.

We've got an Italian translator today. I'm so distracted I haven't heard his name. He could be Leonardo da Vinci XIV or just Leonardo Pomodoro. He's a nice guy, jet black hair with olive skin Italians are famous for, a nicely-trimmed mustache—I think they're called "pencil-thin" mustaches—and the slightest goatee.

There are twice as many reporters as we saw in Montreal. Criminey, are we getting *that* well-known? There's even one with an Australian flag on his hat.

The news conference covers the usual stuff; the responses coming from everyone in the group—except Benji. He's quiet, and though there's a smile on his lips, it doesn't make it to his eyes. He's angry, and I've got to make it up to him.

Mister Australia gives me the opening. "I say, we've been noticing pictures of the group members at a lot of the shows, and since around Montreal it seems pictures of Sean and Clay together have been added to the mix. Last night we saw one of Ravynn and Benji. Can you elaborate?"

Greg looks at me, and I grab the opportunity. "We're gobsmacked at the love our fans give us, whether it's signs or pictures. We're not doing this—we were as amazed as you when the pictures started. Last night's sighting of a picture of me and Benji was the same. At the risk of going on too long..." I pause, hearing Sean, Clay, and Todd mutter *as if*, or similar thoughts, "I was so gobsmacked at the picture of Benji and me together I momentarily forgot the words to a song I wrote." There, it's out. I'm *sure* there'll be a follow-up.

Dickie Newsome nods. He knows what I've admitted, and he couches his follow-up delicately. "Does it bother you? It appears you two are kissing." There are murmurs among the reporters, but no hostility. I glance down the table. Everyone except Benji is looking at me with what could be panic in their eyes. Benji's still unreadable; he's built a wall I cannot penetrate.

I look directly at Dickie and answer him directly. "No. It's a picture. It doesn't mean anything beyond the fans loving us." I've written headlines across the world either that we're a bunch of homosexuals, or that we're the most honest group of guys ever. I hope it's the last.

. . . . . • . • . . . .

London, England

July 5 - 10, 1968

Flight, Friday, July 5

I'm glad the flight to London is smooth, because Benji's nowhere near me. He's still hurt from my reaction to that picture of our faces together, and I haven't been able to explain to him it wasn't rejection; just panic at being labeled a homosexual. It's hard to explain when he won't get near enough for me to talk to him, and I'm not prepared to shout it. I hope that Todd, Clay, Sean, or DC will persuade him to talk to me.

Possibly my prayers have been answered. I turn my head to look out the windows on the left side of the plane and see Benji coming up the aisle. As he approaches, I see he's not smiling. That worries me; an unhappy Benji is not good.

He sits across the aisle from me, within talking range, but out of reach. Damn. Gonna have to win this with words.

"I've been thinkin'," he starts, his face expressionless, which is worrisome. Benji without an expression on his face is the *rarest* of occurrences, in the worst possible way—like finding you've locked your house key in the house on a hot day with a gallon of ice cream in the car, the ice cream has a hole in it, and you've also locked your car, and the car key is on the key ring inside the house. *That* kind of bad.

"Benji, I...." I begin.

"No, just listen. It's not gonna work. You can't get past your fear of people finding out about us. I don't like it one damn bit, but I understand. I'm gonna do what I gotta."

"Please, Benji,...."

"No. You can't ask me to keep puttin' myself last. I been there for you since the beginnin', shay, and it kills me you wanna keep *us* a secret. I can't do it. I *thought* I could, but I can't, and I won't. I'm leaving. Gonna get a ticket back home, I'll get my stuff later."

"You and I were just *fake* boyfriends, and you kept me confused because Johnny was in the picture. I thought we were *playing* boyfriends. When did that change, because I didn't get that message."

"You gotta be kiddin'. With the way you were kissin' me, I thought you *knew* it had gone real. And Johnny's always been *just* a friend. He was helpin' me get your fire lit. But I get it now. Nothin's gonna make you jeopardize the thing you really love, fame. I need to go home, 'cuz I can't be *just* friends with you, an' I can't hide, neither. So maybe I'll stay with Johnny for a while to figure things out."

Johnny was never a threat? They were *playing* me? How did I miss that? As I'm turning this new information over in my brain, Benji turns to leave, nearly knocking Sean and Clay over. Clay looks at Benji quizzically as Benji heads toward the rear of the plane. Sean sits where Benji had been, but Clay leaves, following Benji. Shit, I'm a one-man sabotage unit.

"Where's Clay?" I ask, sniffling, realizing I've been crying for some time. My hands are damp; my shirt has become a towel.

Sean waits until I compose myself some; I'm a mess. "He's gone to talk to Benji, for you," he tells me. "He'll fill Benji in on your feelings about the picture *and* him." I'm sniffling like I have a cold, tears threatening to erupt. Other than tears, I'm hollow, most of me ripped away.

"Feels like you've been kicked in the nuts, doesn't it?" DC asks.

"I... I don't know, never had this feeling before," I say.

"Don't worry. I'm sure Clay can calm Benji enough to keep him from leaving," DC says.

"If I could, I'd tell him the truth, to his face, but he won't let me get a sentence out," I tell DC.

"What *is* the truth? Before you tell Benji, you'd better be certain yourself," she smiles, reminding me how important this is.

"Truth... I need Benji. He's a part of my life I can't live without. Every time I'm near him, it's... right. I don't know how else to explain it, 'cause I've *never* felt this before. Not with my parents, Ronnie, not with *anyone....*"

Sean looks at me like he's sorry for me. I'm not sure. I know I'm fucking pathetic, crying my eyes out over a *fake* relationship.

Clay returns from talking to Benji. I look at him, hoping he'll give me good news, but he looks away immediately. It's not good news. I'm screwed.

DC moves beside me as Clay sits next to Sean. The two of them talk quietly; I can hear their voices, but I can't make out anything.

"Look, Ravynn, you know Benji's on the plane, so he's not leaving now, right?" DC focuses me on one fact I can be sure of. I nod.

"We've got time before we leave the plane. There's a chance. Don't give up." She's too perky. Wasn't she the one who got broken up with by telephone? Still, I can't find fault with her comment.

"I'll try, but it's like my chances are down to Slim and Nunn, and Slim's halfway out the door," I try smiling, but it seems more like a grimace.

DC gives me a friendly hug, which only reminds me of Benji's bearhugs. Damn.

DC returns to the seat in front of Sean and Clay, and Clay takes the seat beside me. What is this, babysit Ravynn day?

Clay looks at me, then at Sean, and takes a deep breath, like he's steeling himself for an unpleasant task. Fuck. This isn't looking good.

"I sat with Benji. He's hurt and confused, more than anything. You'd been going along so good, he thought you'd realized things were the way they should be. And then you flipped over the picture, and that blew his mind," Clay says.

"I was trying to save the band." I wipe my eyes; tears threaten again.

Clay waits until I'm composed and resumes. "He got angry when you dismissed the picture as 'just a picture,' like it was nothing. That was too much a denial of you two, so I told him you weren't denying him. I *may* have overstepped, but I needed to get through to him. I told him you're sick about it, because you're in love with him."

"You told him that?"

"I had to. I'm *desperate*. We're getting closer to London by the minute; if I don't persuade him, he *will* follow through and go home," Clay says.

"Did it help?" I'm not sure I want to hear the answer, given how grim Clay's expression has been. It isn't saying *he's staying*.

"In a way, yes. He dismissed the statement about you being in love, out of annoyance mostly; he thinks you should've said it yourself. But... I got his promise he won't leave the group; he enjoys playing music with us *all*." Clay takes a breath, like he's gotta refill his lungs. I feel a *tiny* bit better. Clay continues, "He's disappointed you're not living up to your own ideals. He's not gonna hide himself, and if you can't accept that, you *will* lose him."

There it is. I've got my choice. Live openly with Benji, or lose him. Be the real me and have the most wonderful guy I've ever met, or hide behind a mask to be the biggest rockstar in the business and risk it all. My stomach drops.

Actually, the entire plane drops; we've begun our descent to Heathrow.

Arrival, limousines

When we land at Heathrow, Benji is true to his word. He *doesn't* book a flight back to the States. Instead, he's twenty-five feet away from me, like there's an invisible barbed wire fence around him. Greg and DC both stop to ask him if he's okay, and he acts with them like he always does, smiling, *normal*. Only around me does he become sullen, *withdrawn*.

Greg goes through customs for the group. Three limousines arrive to take us to the Royal Albert Astoria Arms. Greg points to the first limo and says, "You and Benji in that one."

"Uh, Greg...." I start.

"Deal with it, Ravynn. You're grownups, act like it, talk."

Fuck me running. I'm screwed here. Alone with Benji, no plan of what to say, I'm a sitting duck. He's mad as fire, and one misspoken word could seal the fate of our on-and-off relationship, *and* the band. Maybe he'll decide that he and I are done as boyfriends and we're just bandmates. Or, that third choice, Benji wants me for real, the way I realize I want him, and damned if I know how to get there from here.

The other two limos have filled up with their assigned passengers, and I'm stuck where I was when Greg gave assignments. Benji is *also* where he had been, staring at me like I'm a new species of insect.

Finally, he walks to the limo, opens the door, then turns to me. "You gonna stand there all night?" No anger, no emotion of any form in his voice; he could be talking to the pilot or to any of the other passengers.

That hurts more than his threat to fly home; tears threaten again. When did I become such a whimpering fool? I hesitantly walk to the limo and climb in. Benji sits and makes sure the privacy window is closed. Obviously, we're going to talk.

"Clay told me you weren't freakin' out about us, but your reaction to that picture seemed like it. I ain't playin' here. Either you an' me are together, or we aren't."

"I… I've *never* felt anything like I do about you. When we were playing *fake* boyfriends, it was more real than any other relationship I've ever had. I'm sorry I laughed it off in the news conference…." Pausing to collect my senses, because I'm getting choked up, and there's a million things I want to tell him. "There's no way I can make up for that stupid move. All I can do is tell you I'm sorry I hurt you, didn't mean to, and I'm gonna make it right, *somehow*."

"You tell everybody to live their authentic life, yet you hide *yours* under a mountain of lies and insecurities. That's no way to go. I want to live *my* authentic life, too… and I won't wait forever to start."

"You told Clay you wouldn't accept my words—through him—that I'm head over heels in love with you, right?"

"You haven't showed me reason to believe it, so I figured it was Clay tryin' to hit me with something to keep me around." I know he's upset with me, but saying I haven't shown him a reason to believe? That hurts.

I lean forward, cup his head in my hands, and bring my lips to his. The kiss begins tentatively, uncertainly; I'm not sure he'll allow me to continue or if he assumes I'm kissing him to end the discussion. My tongue traces his lips, asking permission to enter; after a few agonizing moments, he allows me to push my tongue through. His tongue does its own tracing of my tongue and back to my lips before pulling back.

"I'm not kissing my *fake* boyfriend," I whisper, close to his ear. "I'm kissing the man I'm *crazy* about."

Benji sits silently for a few seconds, tracing his lips with his fingers, like he's making sure they're unharmed. Or, is he tracing the kiss, thinking it could be our last? "It's nice to do that and say it here, where no one's gonna see us. Are you gonna be able to hold my hand in public?"

I know what he's asking. I've been thinking and worrying about it. As I prepare to answer him, he gently places his right index finger over my lips and says, "Look, you can't jump to us being open together suddenly. You know it, I know it, heck, *most* of the people we're around know it. So don't tell me you're gonna start tomorrow. I won't buy that load of crappadoodoo, regardless of how pretty you package it."

I can't just switch off being the *proper* British rocker and become the homosexual version of myself. But I can't stay the same. It's not an option to hide Benji, and skipping down the street holding hands isn't either. There's gotta be a third choice that works....

I stew over this. Benji and I have become the most difficult, most important, issue in my life. I know I've got one last chance to get it right, and my best effort in Rome was a flop. Somehow, I gotta top that.

Hotel, Saturday, July 6

As much as I'd hoped to have Benji smiling and hugging me, I'm settling for Benji smiling and happy with Sean, Clay, Wil, and Todd. Like a sailboat cut loose from its dock, I'm drifting. I'm happy Benji's still part of the group, but he's not ready to commit to me again. That's why I'm lost.

Greg's gathered us for *big news*. I tried to get some idea, but I might as well have been trying to play a record backwards for all I got. What kind of answer is *all will be revealed soon*? It sounds like something from one of those Magic 8 Ball things.

We're waiting in Greg's room for "big news." Whatever that *big news* is, the way my last few days have gone, it could be the cancellation of the recording sessions and the rest of the tour, the termination of our contract with EMI-Capitol, and good luck getting home because the label isn't paying for anything else. 'Scuse me while I get totally depressed.

DC's here, and she's either a damn good liar, or Greg hasn't clued her in, because she doesn't know. Right now, I'd kill to have Benji's mamere Pearl tell us something with her Sight.

After what seems like hours, Greg comes walking in.

"Everyone's here, boss," DC quips. Greg raises an eyebrow at the "boss" comment, then smiles.

"Great. Here's the deal. After a lot of time discussing the tour and the recording sessions...." Greg pauses and looks at each guy, beginning with Wil and ending with Benji, then turns to me. It kills me the way he mentions the tour, the recording sessions, and then pauses like he's suddenly a drama queen. I roll my arms with the signal to speed up. He chuckles, then continues, "Mr. Martin and I are happy with how the tour's going; the two problematic shows aren't major. In fact, the press in London covered the show in Rome, and there are comments you'll see shortly."

"What about the recording sessions?" I ask.

"George Martin's looking forward to having you work with him and some local musicians and singers. He's selected some songs, and he wants you to bring any of yours to record. You'll be working in the main studio—the same one where...."

"...The Beatles recorded *Sgt. Peppers Lonely Hearts Club Band*," Sean and I almost shout.

"Uhmm, yes. Try to be less enthusiastic once you're around the equipment, perhaps," Greg deadpans. As if. You wouldn't go into a shrine to Buddha and break the statues, and we won't go into Abbey Road and mess up *the* recording studio.

"Limos will be here in 20 minutes, so make sure you're dressed comfortably but decently," DC reminds us.

"Yes, mother," Sean teases. DC ruffles his hair.

"What about the show in Rome?" Call me a glutton for punishment; I want to know what the world is saying. Who better to tell us than the British press?

Greg hands me a copy of yesterday's London Times, with an article talking about the Rome concert. It's very positive. He hands me the Friday Daily Mirror edition. Front-page pictures, *including* one with *that* picture of Benji and me. The story says that Rome has gone crazy for us all, "especially the charismatic lead singer Ravynn St John and the handsome rhythm guitarist Benji Travers." There's mention of the fan picture of us, and a reporter suggests that fans want us to be together. Similar stories in other area papers. I need to check with Greg—I've *gotta* be missing something.

"Uh, are all the reports like this? I mean, these are almost like they're saying the fans *want* to see us in a relationship," I look at Greg, begging him with my eyes.

"I haven't seen reports from everywhere, but if the Times in London says it, bank on it. That's a conservative paper, not given to flights of fantasy."

Benji's reading the Daily Mirror story. I can tell, because every few minutes, he lowers the paper enough to glance my way over the paper, a smile in his eyes, even if I can't see his lips. He's reading the same story. Ohmygawd. What a fucking *fool* I've been.

Recording

To walk into this building is surreal. Outside, it's so unassuming that someone with no musical interest would hardly guess the significance of the structure; to Beatles fans, this building is as culturally important as the Tower Bridge, the Houses of Parliament, and Buckingham Palace. Abbey Road Studios has a low-key exterior but a high-energy interior.

As I enter the lobby, a guy wearing white linen trousers reading a copy of the London Times sits next to an Oriental-looking woman wearing a white dress. Damn, I'm in black jeans and a navy-blue turtleneck. Someone forgot to tell me it's "Dress Whites" day.

As I approach, the guy dips, then lowers the paper. He seems familiar; I blink a few times. Then I realize... it's John Lennon.

"We've got company, Mother," he says to the woman. "Hello, mate, we've been waiting for you! This is Yoko...."

I'm quick-frozen in place. My tongue and vocal cords have shut down. They must think I'm some kind of nut, standing here speechless, motionless. Finally, my brain clicks back in.

"I… I'm happy to see you," I stammer out. John clasps my hand like we've been buddies all my life, then Yoko demurely takes my hand. I bend and kiss the back of hers; she giggles.

"You lads snuck up on us. I'm fuckin' amazed at your talents, mate. George—Mr. Martin—told us your performance of *A Day in the Life* was spot on."

"I'm floored he invited us to record *here*," I say, still in awe.

"Man, you're good enough to record *anywhere* you want. You deserve it, and *Taking Flight* from your *first* album? That's better than stuff we've done since *Pepper*."

"I've got a good group, thanks." I'm blown away with the praise.

"We've got company, George," John calls out.

Two voices reply—one an older, more distinguished voice which I recognize from San Francisco as belonging to George Martin. That means the *other* voice belongs to….

George Harrison, the youngest Beatle, the guitar phenomenon. He walks into the lobby and smirks, "Guess you meant the other George, huh? No skin off my fingers!"

As my mind melts into mush from being in this place with *The Beatles*—or at least *half* of them, Benji, Todd, Wil, Sean, and Clay spill into the lobby. Like me, they react in a mix of awe and disbelief when they see John Lennon and George Harrison standing there.

When John sees Benji, he looks at me, then back to Yoko. It's obvious the two of them are in love. He simply says, "Y'know, mate, who you love and who loves you is between you and that person, and the public isn't always gonna be on your side—but the love of your life will be. It's been like that for Yoko and me, too. People don't always see that." How the hell did he look at Benji and me and figure us out like that?

George Martin joins our crowd, bringing along Paul McCartney and Ringo Starr, plus two guys I couldn't have imagined being in the same room—Mick Jagger and Keith Richards of the Rolling Stones. In American papers, the rivalry between the two groups is a war; yet here are the Beatles and two Rolling Stones, acting like buddies. It's confusing; even newspapers can't figure out the relationships and goings-on with famous musicians.

George Martin leads us to the main studio, where instruments are ready; there are enough guitars and basses here for dozens of musicians. There are three "isolation booths" with full drum sets ready. Wow, we really *could* have a rock orchestra here.

"So. We're going to record a few tracks. I've a few ideas we'll try on for fit," George Martin says, as I watch the Beatles, my guys, and Keith Richards "gear up" with guitars, basses, and drums. Charlie Watts, Bill Wyman, and Brian Jones—the *other* Stones—join us, and suddenly there are three bass players, three drummers, one keyboardist, six guitarists, and one multi-instrumentalist, Brian Jones. That leaves me and Mick Jagger watching.

"Right, today and tomorrow, we're going to see what the top three groups in the world can produce. You newcomers, just call me George," Mr. Martin starts. "I've got several pieces that should work well. First off, we'll have a few from our American visitors, I think. Mick, if you and Ravynn will join me in the control booth, we'll get this underway."

Sean looks like he's just been awarded drummer of the century. He's gazing around the studio, drinking it in. If he were a camera, he would've taken at least three dozen shots in a few minutes. Benji's reaction is subtle; I'd expected his Cajun "Who-wee," but instead got shy Benji, then curious Benji. While Sean's drinking it in, Benji is memorizing every corner, every inch of space—the placement of every instrument and amplifier, and where the control booth is in relation. Both are totally gobsmacked, as are Wil, Todd, and Clay—who gets to play a Hofner bass like Paul McCartney, standing less than two feet from his idol.

If you'd told me, that day we first performed in Atlanta, Georgia, that a few years later we'd be recording in Abbey Road Studios with The Beatles, The Rolling Stones, *and* George Martin, I would've been calling for mental evaluations for you.

George escorts Yoko, Mick and me to the control booth, so we can chat while the instrumental tracks are "laid down," the term for recording the basic track that vocals are dubbed onto, or recorded into.

I watch as my guys give the Beatles and Stones guitarists an instrumental version of several of our songs. When the superstars nod toward George, he flips a switch and says, "Right. We'll try a take now. Tape rolling in 5...."

The three drummers—Sean, Ringo, and Charlie Watts—wait in isolation booths with their drums. Benji hits the first notes of what I recognize as *You're Not Alone in This*, and the other instruments follow. It's just the music, but sitting in the control room, with that talent, I'm getting goosebumps, ready to go full teeny-bopper fandom.

In a single take, those talented musicians transform Clay's response to my "Lament" into a helluva rocker, then move into the song that *always* rips my heart out. They capture the full anguish, musically, that I relived writing the words to *Ravynn's Lament*.

The guys take a break, and John pops into the control room—little more than a booth, actually. First, he gives Yoko a kiss, then looks at me and says, "I meant what I said, mate. Love the person who's right for you, and fuck what the world thinks. You *might* lose a few fans, but in the end, you'll have what counts." On that, he gives me a "bro hug" and then heads back into the studio.

Mick looks from me to Yoko. "John's right, man. You gotta live your own life—you only get one shot. If you can't be happy, what the hell's the bloody point?"

Yoko smiles. Everybody's got me figured out, except *me*, but I'm getting there.

Next up's a song called *Abraham, Martin, and John*. Again, it's just the instruments, so all I know right now is the title and melody. It sounds like a cross between folk-rock and an old-time gospel song. Interesting. After that, the next piece is a song from the Stones, *Street Fighting Man*; Mick tells me he's proud of the song. The "supergroup" instrumental version sounds fantastic, but I'm *itching* to sing.

George tells the instrumentalists that it's time for the singers and backing vocalists. Time for me to do as good vocally as my guys did instrumentally. Clay *has* to be lead singer for his song.

There's an army of female vocalists; George calls them his "Angels Chorus"—rightfully. Petula Clark, Lulu, Marianne Faithfull, Dusty Springfield, Cilla Black, Helen Shapiro, Sandie Shaw, and a girl barely older than our Benji, Mary Hopkin, truly form an angelic chorus.

Clay duets with Paul for *You're Not Alone in This*, and the two lead voices get Mick, John, the Angels Chorus, and me on backing vocals. Then I join Paul, John, and Mick on *Ravynn's Lament* and I admit it sounds fine, better than I ever imagined.

We take a few minutes to read through the lyrics for *Abraham, Martin, and John* before we record. I split lead vocals with John, Paul, and Mick. Everyone else is singing backup. It's a tribute to Martin Luther King, Jr., Robert and John Kennedy, and Abraham Lincoln.

The last song, *Street Fighting Man*, Mick starts, then brings me into a duet, then John and Paul join in. The Angels Chorus provides a wall of female voices. The effect is mesmerizing, haunting, and *damn,* I wish I'd written it.

George tells us that's a wrap for recording; he's thrilled with our efforts.

I'm overjoyed to have had the opportunity, though a lot of that's because Benji's here. Somehow, it's more important having Benji here than to be here. I mean, the studio and the recording session are real, but it doesn't seem as *real* as Benji sitting beside me. We're all milling around in the studio: four Beatles, five Stones, six Phoenix Rising, and a slew of female singers. Benji and I are closer than we've been since that concert in Rome with the picture. And talking to John and Mick made me realize that, as Sean's dad would say, it's time to fish or cut bait.

Hell, Sean and Clay, lovebirds that they are, have been so low-key about their relationship that nothing's registered. That worries me; am I their reason for being so? I hope not. I know I'm far from perfect, but I'm learning; they've gotta live their true lives. But I'm damn proud of how well Benji handled himself... I'm still worried he'll decide to cut his losses and run to Johnny.

As soon as I think that, it bounces from my brain to my lips. No filter in this head. "You talked to Johnny recently?" I ask.

“Nah, shay,” Benji answers, shaking his head.

“Guess it would be kinda soon for him to get a letter to you,” I say. It’s only been a few days; mail between the US and Europe is notoriously slow, unless you pay a small fortune for what they call *speedy* delivery. Even that takes nearly a week.

“True dat.”

Without thinking, I go on, “Say you don’t love him, my salamander....”

Benji smiles at the pet name. “Aww, you *know*...”

Paul McCartney’s been standing behind us the whole time, but leans in at that moment. “Kind of a catchy phrase, that,” he says as he scribbles it down. I stifle a gasp of astonishment, then just shrug and smile at Benji, whose eyes are huge after Paul’s comment.

“Whoo-wee,” Benji says, smiling.

There’s *my* Cajun firecracker. It’s good to have him calm, at least for now. I know I still have to prove to him I *need* him with me.

The Stones say their goodbyes for the day, and the ladies of the Angels Chorus follow them out. After the departures, I start to thank George Martin and the Beatles, but they stop me before I get the words formed.

“We should be thanking you, mate,” John Lennon says, clapping me lightly on my back as we head out.

Back to hotel

In the limousine back to the hotel, Benji’s relaxed, seated next to me; it’s almost like “old times,” if a week ago qualifies as old. This is my opportunity to clear up the mess and get us closer to where we were. I’ve gotta be careful, because I don't want to upset Benji, but I've gotta say something, so he knows I'm trying to make this work.

"You were fantastic, salamander," I start easy to build into what I hope I can say to make things right.

"You know I love playin' music, shay," he replies, and hearing the term of affection makes my heart beat faster and stronger.

"I wanna keep you playing music for years. Seriously, babe, you're our special ingredient, the spice in our gumbo."

"You love butterin' me up, don'tcha? Or is it the food ya love talkin' about?"

"What I'm saying.... trying to say...." I'm stumbling, trying to find the words, hoping like hell Benji doesn't get pissed at my taking so long, or at the words I settle on. "Look, I'm gonna lay it all out, and trust that you'll see what I'm saying. Because I can't come up with anything fancy for this."

Benji's gazing into my eyes.

"The first moment I saw you, when you were trying out for the group, there was *something* that pulled me toward you, like you had hooked me already. I fought it hard, because I didn't think it was right. You were so young, it worried me. When you became our guitarist, I had a powerful attraction to you, and it got stronger every day. Still, after my past, I was afraid, because that had warped my idea of love, and I couldn't do that again...." Shit, even now, remembering how messed up I was after Ronnie, I'm not sure I'm worthy of Benji, but damned if I won't at least offer.

Benji's still looking directly into my eyes, a tiny smile on his lips. Either he's caught up in my words, or he's feeling my emotions as I say this.

"Then we went to New Orleans for that crazy party for you, and you treated me like I belonged to you, in the best possible way. You made me experience things I'd never known before. With your family, it was like a *real* family for the first time. And it started with *you*, babe. I guess I'm saying my emotions for you are so damn deep I'm not sure what to call them, but they aren't going away—they get deeper. It scares the crap outta me. I've *never* felt this way; seeing that picture freaked me out. I wasn't rejecting the picture, I wasn't rejecting you, and I wasn't rejecting us. I can't picture my life without *you* in it."

For a minute, Benji says nothing; I worry I've gone too far, said too much, put too much pressure on him. Finally, he breaks the tension. "You're great when everything's private. I'm not doubting you, shay, just you're giving me these moments where it's you an' me, so it doesn't mean you're ready to live openly and authentically." Ouch. He softens the words, a little, with a quick kiss on the cheek.

The limousine stops in front of the hotel, and we emerge to a throng of thirty or so fans holding posters of Phoenix Rising. Just like before, there's a poster that has our faces together almost like we're kissing.

Benji's watching my face and eye movements, so he figures out why I break into a huge smile. Childish, but a win's a win. I instinctively take his hand before we exit the limousine. I'll never be ashamed or afraid of him and me. There's a squeeze back, and what feels like a little tremble—hopefully happy. But the biggest thing? The sly grin on his face.

Second session, Sunday, July 7

Back in the limo after a quiet night; Benji and I talked on the way to the hotel, so we didn't push things. I've got some ideas in my head, from talking to John and Mick yesterday, and I want Benji to commit to me, knowing I'm fully committed. Today's ride is quiet, the six of us in one big-ass limo.

At the studio, we're greeted by the musicians and friends from yesterday. Almost immediately, George pulls me aside. Uh-oh, what's up?

"I understand your Fourth of July celebration turned musical," he says.

"Yeah, it was our first time away from home, and Wil did an a cappella version of *America the Beautiful* which we joined in on. Greg wanted us to record it, but I thought it would be in poor taste...."

"Because it shares the tune with *God Save the Queen*? Far too sensitive, Ravynn! That's why rockers exist! I think a rave-up of the two would be *simply smashing.*"

From the sly grin on George's face, I guess we're gonna do it.

"You'd left music for a few other songs as well, so we'll plan on adding *Fool*, *We Own This Town*, *We Own This Night*, and your Benji left *Dark Night*, which simply *must* be recorded."

Wait... Benji wrote a song and I haven't seen it? Damn..... I *know* it'll be great, but what if it's about our problems—or what if it's a breakup song?

"Sounds like a full day."

"It'll go fast, I'm sure, and there are two more seasonal numbers to add. Again, your Benji gave me those ideas." As George says that, I look at Benji, who's giving the *best* not-me-I-didn't-do-it look.

Again, the non-instrumentalists—Mick, Yoko, and I—join George in the control booth while the others get their instruments. The women are remaining in the lobby.

After the instruments are connected and tuned, thumbs-up signs are given, and the first take begins on what I recognize as Sean's song to Clay, *Fool*. With the instruments, it seems like a romantic symphony.

Next up is *We Own This*, for which Sean and I had written two sets of lyrics—one titled *We Own This Night* and the other *We Own This Town*. So we'll record both versions using the one instrumental track.

A brief break follows, and John dashes into the control room for a kiss with Yoko—it's reassuring to see that he's open with his affections with her, knowing some people don't understand—the next song starts as unrecognizable, then becomes Benji's arrangement of *Silent Night* from our trip to the bayou at Christmas last year. Next up is Sean, Ringo, and Charlie Watts' lead-off for *The Little Drummer Boy*. I get chills listening to the three drummers drumming and the guitars and keyboards, fleshing out what had been Benji and me fooling around on Christmas Eve.

Another brief break, and then the instrumental of *God Save the Queen* and *America the Beautiful* is recorded—George says he'll record full versions of each, then edit and splice, like he's done with many Beatles songs, to get one long version of both together. Finally, a song I've never heard, which must be Benji's song *Dark Night*. It's orchestral in its sweep—Brian Jones is playing a flute, Wil is playing his electronic keyboard, and the guitars sound like a shimmering wall. I can't wait to hear the words of the song.

Pinch me. I'm dreaming, recording in Abbey-freakin'-Road Studios with a ton of women vocalists, the Rolling Stones, and the Beatles. It's my greatest dream come true, *plus* extras.

"Before we record the vocals, I want everyone to be ready after the vocals are done. I think a Supergroup Jam session is in order, including all the musicians and vocalists, though it might get a bit tight in there," George says to us and the instrumentalists, using the microphone into the studio. This will be epic.

As we return to the studio, we're joined by the Angels Chorus.

We record *Fool*, with Sean singing. Sean and John sing lead on *We Own This Night*; a short break later, *We Own This Town* has Paul, Mick, Benji, and me singing lead. For *Silent Night*, Benji begins, I join in, and everyone else follows—with the women's voices, it truly is angelic. On *Little Drummer Boy*, Sean, Charlie, and Ringo sing the first line, everyone else singing the "pa-rum-pa-pum" bits, then Mick, Paul, and I take over lead vocals.

The mash-up *God Save the Queen* features the Angels Chorus and Paul, with backing vocals from Mick, Brian, and me; *America the Beautiful* features all of Phoenix Rising, just as we had done in Rome—Wil leads off, then the rest of us join in. Amazingly enough, the Angels Chorus *also* joins in.

"We've got one more song to complete, but I think you lot are creative enough to come up with something spectacular off the cuff," George says through the microphone. "Let me load a fresh reel onto the machine, then we'll see what kind of Supergroup Jam you can make, right?"

For some reason, George is holding Benji's song until last. I don't know how to interpret that; could it be due to what the song is about? I'm scared shitless to hear the words.

Anyway, the tape's changed, and the Supergroup Jam—the world's top three rock groups, plus the majority of British women pop singers, becomes a nearly twelve-minute rave of drums, guitars, driving beats, pounding keyboards, and vocalists singing all kinds of nonsense. Basically, pure fun. When it's done, we're drained, so we go to the lobby, grab soft drinks, and gradually return to normal energy levels as we move back to the studio.

Which brings me crashing to earth—we've recorded *everything* except one song....

Dark Night. Benji runs into the control booth and talks to George; I can't see either of their faces. As they finish chatting, George nods and Benji leaves the control booth.

"Ravynn, could you join me in the control booth?" George asks through the microphone as Benji returns to the studio, hugging me briefly as we pass. What's happening?

I get to the control booth and George lays it out. "This song's special to Benji, and he's worried your presence in the studio will cause a problem. So I told him you could sit here and listen."

Fuck me running. Is this a love song to Johnny? A breakup song to me? I'm ready to fall apart....

"Tape rolling in 5...." George says into the microphone, and in 5 seconds Benji's guitar leads the instruments into the song he wrote, then *his* voice, solo, double-tracked, begins.

In your dark night, as the storms crash all around,
I've got your back, I'll never let you down.

The roads you've traveled haven't always been smooth,
Decisions you've had to make haven't always been easy;
You set your goals and stuck to your chosen path,
Your brilliance and persistence amaze me.

You've had many folks come and go in your life.
They have used you and thrown you away without thinking;
In spite of the hurt you remained on your path,

Your trusting and faith in others shrinking.

The day we met, what a glorious event,
The intensity of your eyes burned through my defenses.
All I could do was stay calm enough to play,
As your aura melted all my senses.

In the dark night, as the storms crash all around,
I'll never leave, I'll always stand our ground.

Oh. My. Freaking. Gawd. As the song ends, I'm trying my *best* to keep it all together. Those words, written in the early days of the tour, were about my demons and his determination to be my knight in shining armor. As soon as George has finished the recording, I race from the control booth to the studio and wrap my arms around Benji like I'm afraid he'll vanish. I bring my lips to his, and our kiss is at once fierce, tender, needy, uncertain, and determined. I forget where we are and just shower him with all the love I can, short of finding us a bed.

"You're fantastic, baby! That song needs to be featured in a live show," I tell Benji between kisses. He shakes his head, emphatically, then starts another searing kiss. Out of the corner of my eye, John Lennon's smiling at Benji's reaction to my comment, or maybe at our openness. Maybe both.

"Cut!" I hear, from an amused British accent. I reluctantly break the kiss with Benji and realize that we have an audience. *Fuck*—have I just told a slew of women singers, the Rolling Stones, the Beatles, and George Martin I'm homosexual? Better yet, who cares?

I kissed Benji. In front of the Beatles, George-freakin'-Martin, the Rolling Stones, Yoko Ono, and a ton of vocalists. Benji's standing there like he got hit with an electric pulse, Sean and Clay seem *totally* shocked, but everyone else seems unfazed. Sean and Clay seem *most* affected, like they never expected it.

For several seconds, nobody moves or says anything. Finally, George clears his throat and says, "Let's get things sorted and put away, shall we?" And that's it; everybody gathers equipment to put away, while talking about the recordings.

Crap, have I blown our chances by kissing Benji? Dammit, *my* authentic life is more than just a shit-ton of fame and gold records. I deserve to be happy, and happiness for me *is* Benji, the love I have for him, the love he's been giving me, and that kiss.... Fuck it, it seemed right... but I hope the guys don't hate me....

To my surprise, as people begin leaving, no one looks at Benji and me weirdly—well, *other* than Sean and Clay, who act like we've been replaced by pod-people or something. Still, neither of them say anything. We say goodbye to the women of the Angels Chorus, then the Stones head out.

Mick stops at the door, the last of them, looks at me, and says, "Remember, mate, life's too short. You gotta live it the way you want it."

At the hotel, Benji joins me in my room. We've been inseparable since the kiss after his song. I told him, in front of everyone at Abbey Road, that he should perform the song in a live show. He shook his head. I wouldn't pressure him.

Now, here, alone, he opens up.

"Shay, when the time is right, the right audience, I'll perform it live."

"Baby, I won't ask you to do anything you don't want to do."

"How 'bout askin' if there's anything I *want* to do?"

I've got a feeling where this is heading.... We've danced around it before. This time, everything seems right. I play it up first.

"Okay, salamander, anything special you'd like to do?" I smile.

"How 'bout we get rid of some clothes and get in bed?"

We reach for each other's shirt, resulting in a collision of grabby hands midway between us, as we both dissolve in nervous laughter. Finally, he lowers his hands, and I start unbuttoning his shirt. After a few heartbeats, he slides my vee-neck pullover loose of my pants. Soon, we're down to our briefs.

"This dream's finally coming true," Benji says so softly he's almost mouthing the words. His smile, half-lidded eyes focused on my chest, and soft voice instead of his usual excited tones, show me he realizes what's happening.

"I've wanted you since I first saw you, babe, but I don't want to hurt you. Will us being together mess us up?"

"I been wantin' you since forever. You ain't gonna break me, 'kay? We been playin' boyfriends, and it hasn't messed up the group. Easy." His voice is stronger, more certain, but there's still a current of uncertainty. He's entering unfamiliar territory.

"I wanna make you happy, baby," I say. For a few seconds, he stares at me with a look that combines admiration, love, and lust, then he goes quiet; his eyes focus on the bulge in my briefs.

"We gonna play cute, or get nekkid?" Benji asks, a sly grin on his lips. His fingers are *already* at the elastic of his briefs.

"Babe, with you, it's cute, regardless," I answer honestly, as I slide my briefs down, seconds behind Benji.

In the time I take removing my briefs, Benji's pulled back the covers and sheet and is lying on the bed, eyeing me like a panther surveying its prey. He reaches a hand to me, and I place mine in his.

Shit, this kid's got a grip. He manhandles me into bed beside him. Before I can help him, I'm lying there, my head next to his, our shoulders touching. No nightshirts, no pretenses. Two guys, for the first time.

Oh, *fuck*. The *first* time, and there's no lubrication other than the hotel soap. That *ain't gonna* happen. Tried that once—it was awful.

"Uhmm, baby, we have a slight problem here...."

"You don't have slick stuff, right? No problem. I wanted to taste you, anyways." Benji surprises me again.

My boyfriend—it's strangely *right* calling Benji that—swallows my cock like he's been doing it most of his life. After a few near-gags, he figures out how to give a mind-blowing blowjob. I slow him long enough for us to lie side by side on the bed, with his cock where my mouth can reach it.

Benji may be inexperienced, but he's a natural at arousing me. I focus on getting him as worked up as he's got me, and soon we're taking a *quick* break in sucking to warn each other how close we are.

He surprises me again when one hand sneaks to my balls and teases my taint, enough that I sense the beginnings of my orgasm. Benji snakes a finger inside me, and that finishes me.

In seconds, he moans around my cock, then fills my mouth with his cum. And keeps shooting. It's like years of stored-up desire gets released at once. I swallow rapidly, but my baby's still shooting; must be some serious vitamins in that swamp water.

When he finishes, his eyes are so glazed over I think he's fallen asleep... until he smiles, bends toward me and kisses me.

"Your eyes are so beautiful."

"I'm sorry I didn't have any lubricant so we could get more romantic if you wanted, baby," I say.

"I ain't goin' nowhere, shay. We got time."

Rainbow, Monday, July 8

This amazing place, sometimes called The Finsbury Park Astoria, is known to music lovers as The Rainbow. The Beatles have played here frequently, so we gotta be sharp.

I find the lighting director and make my request about the lights during *Fool*. He's okay with the idea; he's probably had crazier requests.

It hits me—after London, we're down to *just* three American stops. This tour's flown. We've survived my near-collapses about Ronnie and my nearly screwing up the group because of the picture of Benji and me in Rome. The fans are still crazy about us. Tonight *hopefully* won't change that.

Soundcheck has become almost a formality—other than the usual small things, like tonight's broken strings on Clay's bass and another blown tube on an amp, this one Benji's. I tease him that it's the Louisiana blues that killed the tube and get a puzzled look from Todd for that. Once we're done, Sean descends from his drums to the now-usual hug and kiss from Clay. Benji refuses to be outdone; he struts to me at the front, grabbing me in a hug that could squeeze the air out of you if you weren't expecting it. Fortunately, I was. That's followed by a kiss, which begins as a peck on the cheek, then moves to the lips. We're out of synch as we try to connect, like we're hiding the *real* relationship after flaunting the *fake* one. It doesn't take long; soon we're exploring each other's mouths as we kiss, making *all kinds* of noises. Thank goodness we're not near a microphone; I can imagine our moans echoing throughout the auditorium.

Todd teases us, saying, "They're *baaack*." He draws out the last word like it's a line from a horror film. *Nothing* horrible.

We've got time to relax before the show, and, thankfully, *this* time, there are no photographers.

Wil has some battery-operated game that makes annoyingly shrill beeps and trills, like it's designed to numb your mind. I tease him it's a zombie that'll eat his brains once they're mushy. He nearly throws it at me. Ten minutes later, I *still* hear the game; he's in his dressing room. I hope he remembers our music tonight.

Benji heads to his dressing room, and I worry we've moved too fast and he's having regrets. I hope not, but if he does, tonight should fix it, or I'm gonna take out full-page ads in major world papers announcing my love. It could get expensive, but he's worth it—I figured *that* much out.

As I'm pondering full-color ads in twenty major newspapers, the object of my desire strolls in, similar to his 'Elvis' swagger back in Montreal. Benji struts to me, gripping my waist with one arm, and uses the other to trace my hair away from my eyes. *No one's ever* done that, and it's so good, so right. I'm still so insecure. Ronnie's last words in Rome didn't help; being told that I'm basically worthless settled heavily in my brain.

"*We* are okay, right?" I ask. "I still feel unworthy of you, baby."

Benji gazes at my face, like he's seeing and loving it for the first time, then nods. "*Everyone* who's been around you was too stupid to deserve you, shay."

"I can't believe I almost lost you with my stupidity, babe."

"We *all* make mistakes. The trick is backin' outta them at the *right* time."

As I'm about to offer the millionth version of "I'm sorry," our lips meet, pulled together by an invisible force. It begins slowly, timidly, as if both of us are totally new to kissing; it progresses rapidly to a gently passionate kiss of exploration and discovery, reclaiming lost connections and finding new. We're so swept up in the moment we forget we've left my dressing room door open—until Sean and Clay "remind" us.

"Y'all need a cold shower?" Clay smirks.

"Jeez, give us a warning, would ya?" I huff.

"Uhmm, you *know* that's what doors are for, right?" Sean asks.

"We're just catchin' up," Benji offers. This *won't* end well.

"With what? The week's kisses in every high school and dance hall in the world? I think ya got 'em beat," Sean laughs, crossing his arms.

"Don't pay him any mind, Benji, he's jealous!"

That gets a glare from Clay, and a quizzical look from Sean. I swear, he's not the sharpest tack in the wall. Better rephrase it before I have to apologize again.

"We've been kissing. As Benji noted, we're catching up. What's up?"

"Sean's *worried* that he'll fuck up tonight. I keep telling him he'll do fine." Clay looks at Sean with love, even while he's talking about worry.

Benji jumps in, as he does so well.

"So, the song's about Clay?" Benji asks.

"You better believe it," Sean says, a proud smile on his face.

"You'll be good as gold. Think about Clay as you sing, it'll come through like it did at Abbey Road." True, Sean had been thinking about Clay as he sang the vocal at the studio. Benji's right.

"I'm gonna be there in front of you, love," Clay says—the first time anyone's heard Sean called anything *other* than his name, Granny, or babe.

"I'm gonna do my best, baby. I owe it to you and the guys." Sean's eyes are glued to Clay as if he's the only person in the world. I understand how Sean's acting.

"Have we got it sorted?" I revert to my *very British* accent.

Sean, Clay, and Benji are nodding. Benji doesn't have a clue what I've got planned for *him*. I hope he likes it.

In just over a week, we'll be home. The tour ends July 19, the second Atlanta concert. Before that, we've got Boston and Nashville. This tour has been fun, even with the *shit* from my lie. We've had a few less-than-perfect shows, but it's been mostly great. The fact that I had my head up my ass about Benji most of the tour wasn't my best, but I've figured myself out.

It's a question how not one, but two homosexual couples in the group will be handled in the States. Boston's liberal; we likely won't get any idea there, but being in America will give us a chance to see news from closer to our base. I know Nashville, the home of country music, and Atlanta, our home, are deep in the Bible belt. There's a good chance we'll be walking into a full-on dumpster fire in either. I've been focused on not losing fame, but fame is nothing compared to living my authentic life with Benji. For me, Benji is top priority. After he dealt with the shit I put him through, he's earned that.

Not the time to get sentimental. We've got a day in London before flying to Boston. Time to take my *salamander* shopping.

I'm wearing a vee-neck white shirt and blue jeans with my leather sandals, and I've pulled my hair into a ponytail, so it's less noticeable. Benji wears a plain white tee, blue jeans jacket, blue jeans, a baseball cap to conceal his platinum blond hair, and *boots*. I've never seen him in boots.

Greg's arranged with off-duty taxi drivers so we can go shopping or sight-seeing without forcing Davey's crew to work, giving them a day off. Benji and I meet our driver, a woman named Bobbi, who would have a grand time with DC. I sense she's lesbian immediately. DC joins us. Benji and I can relax, and DC and Bobbi might find common ground.

We do tourist stuff. We hit the shops—Carnaby Street, the "Mod" head-quarters of the world, among others. I purchase a pair of English wool bell bottoms and a pirate's shirt; later, an English tweed jacket. Now, my accent doesn't seem so fake.

Benji buys some clothing as well, some kind of shirt and a pair of pants. He's secretive, so I haven't seen them. He also buys a tweed jacket.

"I say, moving the bayou to London, mate?" I tease him with my best fake accent. He laughs, but won't show me his purchases.

"I'm gonna show these to my boyfriend after this tour," Benji says, then kisses me before I can worry.

My stomach growls, followed moments later by two more. Bobbi states it's luncheon; there's no debate. DC's smiling, stronger than I've seen in days.

The place we stop is literally a window in the side of a building. Bobbi goes to the window and raps three times; the window slides open and a man with three days' worth of five o'clock shadow peers out.

After some discussion, she brings us four servings of fish and chips, a small shepherd's pie, and four packages with plastic utensils and napkins; she had paid what appeared to be a handful of change for it all.

She *insists* we try a bite of the shepherd's pie first. I've never heard of it, but yum. There's cheese, mashed potatoes, veggies, some kinda meat, and I'm in heaven. Everyone's having the same reaction.

Then we dive into the fish and chips. Since I've been playing a British persona, I know that *chips* are what Americans call French fries. Paired with fried battered fish fillets, the combination is fantastic. I have a new favorite food.

"You should try it with malted vinegar," Bobbi says, after seeing my expression. "It adds another level."

"Is it usually so cheap?" I blurt out.

"Nah, I've known Mac for years. He looked out for me when my parents threw me out for being a lesbian. Since then, he *always* cuts me a deal, but I bring him business, like today."

She and I share similar pasts.

"I'm glad you're our driver," I say, honestly. Benji, who's been quietly devouring his fish and chips, squeezes my waist as he nods.

We finish our meals, and Bobbi stops at a "Petrol" station to discard the trash. We resume sightseeing, before it's time to head to the airport—which Bobbi informs us she'll *also* handle. Thank goodness we packed our suitcases this morning; the extra packages shouldn't require much extra space, unless someone buys Piccadilly Circus.

After thinking that, we drive past it and Trafalgar Square and many highlights in the city. Our last, and to me most impressive, sight is Buckingham Palace.

"Hey, can we go see Queen 'Lizabeth?"

"I doubt she will allow us that honor, unless it's been scheduled in advance," I say, hating to disappoint him, as I notice we're already heading toward Heathrow.

"Well, *foo*," he says. DC lets out a laugh, Bobbi smiles, and I—well, I do the best thing I think of to calm my Benji when he's disappointed.

I turn my face to his, pull him gently to me, and our lips meet in a kiss that promises everything will be alright for us *both*.

By the time we are airborne over the Atlantic Ocean, heading for Boston, my stomach starts to twist with nerves; my mind is focused on getting the six of us to Atlanta intact. *Maybe* I'm freaking out about our stop in Nashville, the home of Country Music, and the *other* buckle of the Southern Bible Belt. If the group is still loved once we get to the South, we're good; if not, Benji and I can move to London and sell fish and chips.

•••••••••••

Boston, Massachussetts

July 10 - 13, 1968

Buses to hotel, Wednesday, July 10

We land at Logan International Airport late. Greg and DC guide us through our first return to the United States and Customs. The questions they ask are ridiculous. Do we have *contraband* in our luggage? I mean, it's silly to ask; only a world-class numbskull would bring something illegal in his luggage and tell the agent, "As a matter of fact, while I was in London, I picked up a couple kilos of hashish that I tucked in my jammies."

None of *my* lovable numbskulls do anything stupid, so eight of us, plus Davey and his crew, leave the terminal building.

And there they are. Our fuckin' beautiful buses.

Davey and two of his crew head to the buses and the van. We're standing near the entrance waiting for them to pick us up. Benji is to my right, his left arm around my waist. We're wearing the outfits we wore during the London cab ride. It'll be nice to get to our hotel, have a shower and change.

Greg chooses that moment to drop a bomb. "Since it's apparent six rooms are overkill, we're getting single rooms for Wil and Todd, and double rooms for Sean and Clay and you and Benji. Please don't destroy the rooms, guys." What does he think we're doing, playing cowboys and Indians?

"Don't fret, Greg, we won't," Benji says.

DC points out the newspaper box outside the terminal. The Boston Globe.... There's a copy of the paper, from the day after our first London concert, which we grab. There's a small article about the concert, mentioning the upcoming appearances at the Boston Tea Party. It gives a detailed description of the *Fool* performance, with no negative comments. DC is scanning the "Letters to the Editor" section; there's nothing about us.

In the Want Ads section, however, there are *hundreds* of ads, *wanting* tickets. Apparently, we could have set up a dozen shows and *still* sold out. There's not one negative word anywhere.

"Remember, this is a liberal area; there's less likelihood of rejection because of sexual identity," Greg reminds us, just as Davey and the buses and van arrive. We board; the equipment and luggage is loaded. Shortly, we're on our way to the Fairmont Copley Hotel.

"Almost every president since 1912 has stayed in this hotel," Greg says.

"So, they're *finally* getting culture, huh?" Sean teases.

"I'm not sure they'll see it that way, so let's keep that to ourselves," Greg smiles.

"Well, given some of the presidents we've had since 1912, I agree with Sean," I say with a smirk, as Sean, Clay, Benji, and I join Greg on Phoenix 1.

Davey waits until we're seated, checks through the CB radio with the van and Phoenix 2, and slowly heads us toward the hotel.

Benji is sitting next to me, beaming. It's like our exploration of each other reinforced the bond between us, not simply repairing it.

Last time we rode these buses, I was freaking out over Ronnie trying to get me back. I'd convinced myself there was no way anyone could love me because I was damaged. Now, I have a boyfriend who thinks I'm the greatest. Every day, Benji makes me happier, and every day, I fall deeper in love with him. I've realized my truth about living an honest life is more important than achieving a goal which might bring happiness or fame; for me, living an honest life *must* include Benji.

I mean, *if* I can have Benji *and* huge success, I'll take it, but of the two choices, my salamander, my Cajun firecracker, is the most important.

"Ya gotta be thinkin' 'bout *us*, shay," Benji says.

"What gave me away? The smile on my face, the glazed look, a combination?"

"I know you, shay. When you start thinkin' 'bout us, your heart beats faster an' you breathe diff'rent. Like now," he smiles.

"Guilty as charged. Amazed at how lucky I am, to have so wonderful a guy..."

"Watch out, they're about to start suckin' face again," Clay says with a giggle.

Greg shakes his head, like he can't figure out *what* to do.

"Can you guys at least stay decent until you get into your rooms? Please? Should I grovel and say pretty please, with a marshmallow on top?" Greg teases.

"Awww, dude, don't give 'em any ideas about new uses for marshmallows," Davey says, and we're all stunned into momentary silence.

"Marshmallows, huh? Hmmm....." Sean, ever the prankster, *has* to get his two bits in. I hope Clay is strong enough to squash that.

Benji leans against me. At first, I think he's going to snooze on the ride, or he's being romantic, until I hear his softest whisper.

"Wonder if we can find some slick stuff near the hotel."

"We'll figure something out, baby," I say, softly as possible.

As we slow in front of the Fairmont Copley Hotel, I see a drugstore across the street. From the smile on Benji's face, it's obvious he's seen it, too.

Free day, Shopping, Thursday, July 11

After arriving in Boston late last night—I didn't notice the time. I was busy fixating on being back in the States; it was nearly midnight by the time we checked into our rooms. Perhaps not terribly late, but between sightseeing, boarding, flying across the Atlantic, then taking buses to the hotel, it had been a taxing day. Benji and I put off getting lubricant until today—*that's* how tired we were.

We wake up mid-morning, refreshed and ready to take on things. At least, that's how *I* feel. Benji looks like he's got some things on his mind, and I can guess.

"Shower, coffee, drugstore, then *maybe* some shopping or sightseeing, babe?"

"Ya got three right, shay. The first three."

"Let's take care of the shower together, okay?" I'd scoped out the shower; we could hold a recording session there. Fucker's *huge*.

"Thought you'd nevah ask," Benji says, putting on a bit of Cajun-turned-Bostonian accent. We giggle as we walk naked.

While I'm getting the water started, Benji is scouting through the cabinets—this bathroom's stocked like a swank home bathroom. After he opens the second cabinet, he's laughing.

"What's funny, babe?"

"They've got enough space in these drawers to stash away half my souvenir collection and all the stuff from my last birthday, that's all."

"Water's good," I say. He pads to where I'm standing, gives me an adorable good morning hug and kiss, and we enter the cavernous shower. Once we're inside, I make sure he's getting his share of the water, then I return his hug and kiss, with more spice to the kiss. I'm amazed he's here, after all I put him through. From now on, I'm gonna show him he's above everything else.

Shower time is *mostly* showering, though we hug and kiss. I soap my hand and wrap it around our cocks—we're always at least half-hard when we're near each other; after a few strokes, we're erect, a few *more* strokes and we shoot.

We've just finished showering when there's a knock at the door. This is becoming a pattern. We grab the biggest, softest towels ever to wrap ourselves in, and go to the door.

Opening the door reveals Greg and DC. They're looking relaxed, so I take that as a good thing.

"Who dat, Greg?" Benji says, smiling. Still wrapped in just a towel.... I can *almost* guess what Greg and DC may be thinking.

"Hey, Benji. Y'all doing okay? Sleep okay?"

"I slept so good, like I was a peeshwank again." Benji's pouring on the Cajun charm.

"Sleeping like a peeshwank is good, right?" Greg double-checks.

"True dat!"

"That's great. Hey, we ran into Dickie in the lobby. I'm guessing he's going to drop in on us shortly," Greg says, calmly, but I momentarily wonder why Dickie's coming here now. Maybe he wants me to tell *him* the story of Ronnie and me, or something.

DC looks bemused by us in towels, talking to Greg as if nothing has changed. I look at her and nod, hoping she understands everything is okay.

"Today is free, but be careful, okay? Just because we're in America doesn't mean we're free," Greg says. Has he heard or seen something?

"We're planning on getting coffee, after we dress, then a little shopping, but not much. Have you seen or heard something we need to know?"

There's a knock on the door. Benji opens it; oh, shit, that's him. Dickie Newsome walks in.

"I hope I'm not interrupting anything important," Dickie says. We shake our heads and motion him to come in and sit. "I heard the end of your question, Ravynn. That's actually why I'm here; there's an item in this newpaper you might find interesting." He hands a copy of a Nashville newspaper to Greg, who's closer to him.

"This letter to the editor from some conservative Baptist minister there states the group *Phoenix Rising* is bringing Sodom and Gomorrah to Nashville and should be banned from the city," Greg says, after a quick read of the article. "We *knew* from day one there was likely to be negativity about the shows."

"Sorry to be the bearer of bad news so often," Dickie says, shaking his head in disbelief.

"There *will* be police, right? Out of the Ronnie frypan, into the religious fire," I say. Shit, I remember a few years earlier, in Atlanta, going out with friends. We were all dressed nicely—nothing flashy, but a car full of rednecks pulled up beside us, yelled "Queers!" and threw a drink at us. The drink was in a paper cup and missed us, but it shook us up. But, gawd, we were just *walking*, so what could happen now that we're making music and performing? Fuck me running, if just walking while being homosexual was enough to get the rednecks fired up, what kind of target are we painting on ourselves performing music while being homosexual? I hadn't thought about that, and now I wish I hadn't remembered it.

"We've had security planned, and lined up, for Nashville *and* Atlanta since before the tour began," Greg says. He arches his eyebrows. "You okay, Ravynn?"

I nod.

Dickie looks at me with a sad expression.

"Ronnie wanted me to print a story describing your relationship with him in intimate detail, and I mean scandal-magazine trash level detail. I refused."

"Thanks for not helping him, Dickie. I guess he's pissed off that I wouldn't go running back to him." It shocks me to hear Ronnie is actually *worse* than my lie had painted him.

Dickie hesitates like there's something he wants to say, but isn't sure if he should. Finally he says, "I'm afraid he'll try other papers or some other way to get back at you."

"There's no way any honest newspaper would take the word of some guy coming in off the street claiming he used to be my lover, is there?" A knot forms in my stomach. If Ronnie finds a paper that will print the story, what will that mean for the band? "He's always been so quick to talk a big game, but I've never seen anything come of it." Now I'm worried he might even try to hurt Benji to get back at me. Dammit!

"Thanks again, Dickie, you're a good guy. Greg, the shows go on, unless security says otherwise, right?" I try to act calm, like I'm asking for a piece of paper, but I'm messed up. Meanwhile, Dickie waves and leaves.

"Exactly. If you see anything unusual while you're out, find a safe spot and call the hotel; Davey, DC, or I will pick you up, got it?" Greg's firm, but he's smiling.

"We will," I say, a bit nervous. "I'm not letting Benji out of my sight."

DC pats my shoulder gently like she knows what I'm thinking. She probably does. From what she's told me privately, she's dealt with more than her share of threats and violence just being a lesbian. I remember her mentioning a good friend of hers, another lesbian, being forced to deal with a redneck asshole who was hellbent on "straightening her out" his own way. DC assures me her friend got away unhurt, but the redneck "wasn't quite as lucky."

A second later, she waggles her eyebrows, and tousles Benji's hair.

"Y'all make a cute couple, you know?" DC says, trying to lighten the mood. It works. Benji turns his smile my way... and I melt again.

"I think I'm the luckiest guy on earth, messing up the way I did and *still* having this guy hanging on me," I say, grinning like a fool and not caring.

"You just shush and let's get ready," Benji says, right before he plants another mind-melting kiss on my lips.

Greg is looking around the room as if he's inspecting the paint job for cracking and peeling—*anything* to avoid watching our kiss.

"We'll let you guys dress. Just remember, be careful, and call the hotel if there's *anything* that worries you, okay?" Greg's in principal mode.

When Greg opens the door to leave, *of course* Sean and Clay are outside, about to knock. Damn, I may wind up going shopping wearing a towel and a smile.

After Greg and DC have left, Sean eyes Benji and me and makes his usual miscalculation.

"Had y'all just finished fucking when Greg and DC got here?" If the smirk got any larger, it would consume his face.

"You got a one-track mind, dude," Benji says with a smile. "Just 'cuz y'all are like a couple rabbits in heat doesn't mean *everyone* is. Because we don't have any slick stuff. I wanna find some flavored or scented stuff, like yesterday or sooner!"

Five minutes later, the four of us are dressed as inconspicuous as possible and cross the street to the drugstore. We get to the door as a middle-aged guy in ripped jeans and a faded flannel shirt is shuffling out, holding a small paper bag against his chest.

He nearly bumps into me, then recoils, looking from my tight pants to my long hair. A sneer forms on his face.

"What're you supposed to be, son?"

"Excuse me?" I ask, my words as tight as Benji's sudden grip around my waist.

"You one of them hippies or queers, *boy*?" The emphasis he places on the last word is followed by a swift spit which lands inches from my feet.

"You always insult people randomly on the street, dude? Don't see any restrictions on who's allowed to shop here," Clay says, quietly but firmly.

"Four long-haired troublemakers from out of town in *my* neighborhood, giving *me* lip," the jerk replies. This isn't going well—Sean won't put up with Clay being disrespected.

"Listen, man…." Sean begins.

"Oho, four-eyes *speaks*!" The jerk retorts. This is gonna get ugly.

"Dude, we're just visiting here. We aren't attacking you, you're attacking us. Can't you take your paper bag, your attitude, and *leave*?" Clay speaks more forcefully, and the jerk turns toward him like he's ready to punch Clay. Sean clenches his fists tightly enough that every knuckle is almost white.

The jerk looks at each of us, like he's cataloging everything, staring daggers. It's giving me creeps and pissing me off. The fuck? This is Boston, not Backwater Bayou, Mississippi.

Sean steps toward him, fists still clenched, his face as darkened with anger as I've ever seen it. Benji steps in as our savior. Without looking at the jerk, he turns to Sean.

"No need to waste time and energy over a *couyon* like that, Sean." As soon as Benji says it, Sean relaxes, though he's staring at the guy like he'd as soon kick his ass as look at him.

The jerk looks at me and says, "I guess they'll let any *fruits* wander the streets of Back Bay these days, dammit!" He again spits in our direction before storming away.

Sean takes a step forward; he's ready to go after the jerk, but I pull him back. We don't need to leave Clay and Benji alone.

"He's not worth it. We don't need that kinda trouble," I say.

We enter the store; I'm on edge and worried what we might run into.

Once we're inside the store, one of the cashiers near the entrance asks if she can help us with anything.

Benji jumps. It's obvious his cool appearance during the exchange with the jackass outside was a front; he's rattled.

All the upsets of the past few days and hours have gotten to Benji. He's out of his normal mode, so Sean jumps in, pushy sort he can be.

"Where would we find slippery stuff?" Sean asks. Benji nods his agreement with the question.

"What kind of slippery stuff, hun? We have household lubricants like WD-40 and oils on aisle 8, we have a small selection of motor oil on aisle 9, and we have personal lubricants on aisle 4."

"Thank you, ma'am," Sean pours on the southern charm.

When we get to aisle 4, there are six shelves of lubricants, including five different-sized tubes of K-Y jelly, Vaseline, and enough varieties of flavored lubricants to make your head swim. Who would think of using *peach margarita* flavored lubricant for sex?

Clay tentatively grabs a couple of flavors that have Sean looking like he's ready to try them immediately. Yeah, he's a *true* horndog, even while his boyfriend is *still* shaken from the events of the past hour.

Benji is nervously alternating between scanning the store, expecting another showdown and browsing the flavored lubricants like he's in a grocery store buying ingredients for a special gumbo—except *this* gumbo is gonna be us.

"Shay, you're not allergic to anything like strawberries or bananas or plums, are ya?" His voice wavers slightly, telling me he's still quite upset about what happened.

"Nah, babe, no problems there." I lower my voice to nearly a whisper before continuing, "I wouldn't be much of a homosexual if I had a problem with fruits." Sean, Clay, and Benji groan at my *terrible* pun.

Benji grabs enough lubricants, we could start this whole tour over and never use it all up. I can't see all the flavors, but there are several reddish containers, so I'm guessing strawberry, plum, watermelon. Clay has *nearly* as many as Benji. Looks like there's a lot of lovemaking soon.

At the checkout, the same cashier who had talked to Benji checks us out.

"You're those rockers from Phoenix Rising, aren't you? I thought you looked familiar. Let me apologize for that jerk who insulted you outside. I didn't catch it all, but what I did was enough to tell me you guys were not wrong."

She speaks loud enough that anyone in the store can hear her. I'm shocked—what if her comments bring out another jerk? But she isn't done.

"That doesn't happen around here much. I don't know why that turkey thinks he can act that way. We keep hoping he'll move to Nashville or Atlanta, somewhere in the south that fits him, you know?"

"We're from Atlanta, and we're going to be performing in Nashville after we finish here," Benji says, softly.

"Oops, I guess," the cashier says, with a grin. I like her.

With that, she gets back to checking Clay and Benji out. Benji's still nervous. I don't blame him. It's mostly the earlier confrontation, though around fifty dollars' worth of lubricants in the bag he's holding may add to the nerves. He keeps shifting his weight from one foot to the other and back again, scanning the entire store and occasionally glancing at me with a tight smile.

The cashier looks at the quantity of lubricant, but says nothing.

"Got a few hot dates this week," Clay says calmly, picking up on the cashier's look.

"You guys have fun, then," she says, handing the guys their change.

Benji strides confidently toward the exit, then stops short of opening it. It's like he's worried what might be outside the door; finally he cracks it open slowly, peering both ways to be sure nothing bad is in sight.

"Let's just go back to the hotel, please?" Benji asks.

Benji and I walk into *our* room. It thrills me thinking or saying that; I never expected to have anyone else in my life. Now I need to focus on Benji, and calm him, because he got more than a little rattled by that jerk.

I pull Benji into a kiss that starts off, as usual, soft and romantic. Almost like you'd see in a Hollywood movie. You know, Doris Day and Rock Hudson. On those films, the kisses *never* get down and dirty; with me and Benji, they usually do. Tonight's no exception. Within minutes, we're mapping each other's teeth and mouths with our tongues. I'm thinking the slick stuff got purchased at the right time. Except, I sense some hesitation from Benji.

And as I think that, Benji breaks the kiss.

He smiles at me, wistfully, but it's there.

"What, baby?"

"Shay, I... I don't... I can't do it now."

"Babe, I know the first time...."

"It's not that, it's...." I follow his gaze to the bag holding the lubricants. I get it. He's remembering the confrontation before we shopped, and possibly all the other negative shit.

I decide the best way to get rid of the bad energy from the jerk is to talk about it, so I start to bring it up. "That guy was just...."

"No, let's not, 'kay?"

"I just don't want that jerk to—"

"No. I don't wanna talk 'bout it, at all. Not now, maybe not ever."

Shit, he's scared about the guy or mad, but I can't push him. Dammit, that *fucking* jerk at the store stole what should have been a *beautiful* and romantic first from Benji and me.

Concerts, Friday and Saturday, July 12 and 13

We're in one of the oldest cities of our nation, our first concerts back in America after the recording sessions and shows in London which basically said, "Hey, world, Phoenix Rising has four homosexual members." So far, the press has been quiet. These two shows will tell us if we're once-and-done on touring, or if the fans love us, regardless. A week ago, I'd be on nails worrying what the press and fans think. Today, I'm happy, but worried about *my* Benji. In *my* mind, he's the greatest thing I could possibly have. And he's *definitely* got me, even if the lube remains unopened.

Our concerts are in the Boston Tea Party, a stately red-brick New England mansion on the outside, but inside it's a concert hall of the top level.

The place gets its name from an incident that helped spark the Revolutionary War, when the colonists in Boston rebelled against paying a tax on the tea which England had shipped to America and then demanded payment. Like if you were sittin' home, and the postman gave you a box of stuff you hadn't ordered, and told you to pay for it, plus the packaging, plus the postage, and *oh yeah*, there's a tax on top of that. I think I'd be shooting some redcoats too. *Maybe* I shouldn't use my fake British accent here?

Nah, shouldn't be a problem. The Yardbirds, Procol Harum, and The Who have played here and lived to talk about it. I'm good.

Benji sidles up to me and gives me a top-notch hug and kiss, "for good luck," he says.

Soundcheck is the usual. A few sour notes and Todd and Clay have a couple of minor disagreements on Sean's drumming, but otherwise all is good. This building holds lots of people, and the managers have told Greg, DC, and me if we'd stayed another week, they could've filled every night to overflowing. Sounds like Boston loves us, and we haven't played a note.

The first night begins like every show. We stalk onstage, flashbulbs all around, spotlights picking us out as we stride to our places. The energy from the audience is raw electricity, mixed with animalistic passion. These people are showering us with their love before we get started. I'm gobsmacked again, and blow kisses to the audience.

There are signs and pictures throughout the building. Clay and Sean. Benji and me. Todd, in his Legionnaires costume—what? Wil, at his keyboards, with a Sgt. Pepper-like collage behind him. And one poster with the six of us above the four Beatles and the Stones. Obviously, news has spilled about the recording sessions. And then I see one poster that turns my blood cold; thank goodness we're getting ready to start the show. If I'd seen this during the show, like what happened in Rome, would I have a meltdown, or could I play it cool? I'm hoping I can stay cool tonight.

The poster reads "Die, Queers."

I try to shake it off, ignore it. If the others have seen it, they aren't showing it. We start the performance strong; all seems great. While we perform the second number, there's some kind of disturbance coming from where the poster *was*, and I see the poster in the hands of a guy being hauled out of the audience by security. The rest of the audience, like the guys in the group, seem oblivious to what was happening.

When we get to *Fool*, Sean does the vocal. In the moment the song begins, with no previous plan to do it, I decide I'm committing to Benji for everyone to see; it might throw kerosene onto an already-blazing bonfire—hello, Nashville and Atlanta—but it's my life, mine and Benji's, whatever happens. I speak the words to Benji—with my heart caught in my throat, full of love for him, but remembering that hateful sign; it takes me a few moments to realize that the audience is joining in. How the hell is *that* possible? We haven't released the song as a single, but there it is—the audience is singing along, like it's one of our earliest songs. And if they're singing this very obvious love song from one guy to another, then *some* of our fans support Sean and Clay, and Benji and me. We *just* recorded it in London a few days ago; if it's been "leaked," what *else* has gotten out?

We're toweling off backstage after the last songs. Greg's smiling like a combination of a Buddha, a hyena, and a drunken clown. He's not *any* of those, but he's definitely as happy as I am. Looking around, make that "as happy as we all are." Because Sean and Clay are all smiles—between the hugs and kisses—and Wil, who's *usually* so calm you want to hold a mirror under his nose to make sure he's still breathing, is smiling so broadly that he may forget how to look serious again. Even the soundcheck griping about Sean's drumming is forgotten, at least for now.

"If we finish this tour with five more shows like this one, this tour will be the highest-grossing 'new artist' tour of the decade, guys," Greg says. "That means—"

"Another way we top the Beatles *and* the Stones, right?" I almost shout. I'm *that* jacked.

"Yes, Ravynn. Another win over your idols."

The second show, the pressure's on. After last night's audience acclaim, our great performance, the expectations tonight are astronomical. Benji reads my mood.

"Shay, don't get frazzled. We *got* this."

Those words are so full of conviction, how could I doubt him?

Before I met Benji, I had heard the term "fated mates" tossed around, but I was never a believer. Now, I think there might be something to it.

Five minutes *before* showtime, the Boston Tea Party is at maximum capacity. The manager informs Greg and me he's allowed a "limited" number of standing room only tickets to be sold; when Greg asks how many, he says a few hundred, meaning there are about two hundred more audience members tonight than last night.

Two minutes before, the audience buzz is as noticeable as a fluorescent purple line painted on a solid-yellow wall. My guys are jacked; this stop has brought home how much we love being in America.

As I stride onstage, followed by the rest of the guys, the roar from the audience is the loudest we've heard. Wolf whistles, screams, applause; we haven't played a note. Once the instruments are connected, we launch into our numbers. When we start the third song, *Taking Flight*, the song John Lennon had complimented back in London, it seems half the audience is singing along while the other half sits mesmerized. I don't know if John's words have been reported here or if this audience is in tune with our music, but it makes the moment special. I glance back at Benji. His playing is perfect, his eyes are sparkling.

To say this show outdoes the previous show is like saying the Empire State Building is taller than the Washington Monument, not a fair comparison.

Fool is again a highlight, and we do it the way we did in London, or last night. I may lose lead vocalist duties to Sean from this one song, but I don't *bloody* care.

When we get to the introductions, the *audience* leads the way. They demand, and get, *Benji* first. He's blown away; he reacts with a wicked riff, bows deeply and blows kisses to the audience, getting many professions of undying love while he looks at me. Clay, Wil, and Todd all get a ton of love from the audience as well. That leaves Sean, who simply beams from all the applause he receives as he taps out a rhythm on his snare drum and high-hat. Clay joins in with his bass, and there are more than a few "aww's" from the audience.

We finish strong; the audience is screaming for more, even as we leave the stage after our final encore. Boston has been such a high. Next stop, Music City, USA, Nashville. On that, I start worrying; are we gonna get met with burning crosses and pitchforks, or are we gonna be run out of town without playing a note?

•••••••••••

Nashville, Tennessee

July 15 & 16,1968

Municipal Auditorium, Hermitage Hotel

"What the hell's their problem?" Benji's face scrunches up; he points to a sign in front of a Primitive Baptist Church which reads "Only Christ Rises, False Prophets are Sinners."

We've arrived in Nashville, sliding in under cover of darkness, and I'm bored dull from so many hours of staring at the highway.

I blink at the sign for several seconds.

"So?"

"That means *us*, dummy," Sean says. "*We're* the false prophets."

"The sign references 'rising,' right?" Greg adds, driving home the point.

"Yeah, *now* I get it." Fuck me running. Remind me again why we wanted to perform in Nashville.

"Look, we knew from the start there could be issues playing here. That sign is rough, but it could've been worse; at least it wasn't a mob of rednecks in flannel shirts spitting and cussing at us."

Yeah, like *that* thought makes us all calmer—though I notice Benji, Sean and Clay cracking grins, so maybe it worked.

Downtown Nashville is a trip. The street the Auditorium is on is one way heading south, so we go to our hotel first. It's a ritzy place called the Hermitage. We're ready to get off these buses, much as we love them. As soon as Davey slows the bus down to park, we're at the door, like kids waiting to get out after being cooped up too long.

"Did we just tour the whole original thirteen states, shay?" Benji asks as we jump off the bus like we're diving feet-first into a swimming pool.

"Seems like, huh? But no, just about half."

"I need... uh, *we* need... showers," Clay deadpans.

With those words, we head for the registration desk. We're all about brain-dead and numb from the waist down. Once we get to our rooms, showers and beds are likely all that any of us will think about.

It's our next-to-last stop on the tour, the heart of Country Music, Nashville. When the tour started, we were thinking this was the real biggie, because the Beatles *never* performed live here. And then reality poked its nasty sniveling nose in, reminding us that some of the biggest burnings of Beatles albums after John Lennon was misquoted took place right here in Nashville.

Just a few years ago, Nashville had joined the rest of the South in record-burnings when those reports stated John Lennon had claimed "The Beatles are bigger than Jesus." Of course, the press got it wrong; John had said that, in terms of influence, the Beatles were bigger than Jesus to most teen-agers, which is as true today as it was then. It makes me sick to think of those records being burned because of a messed-up quote. Crap. Or, as Benji would say, crappadoodledoo.

So, we're about to go onstage for our first show. We've kept the lowest profile in town since we've been here; hell, I'm not sure the housekeepers at the hotel even know we're here. Backstage at the Municipal Auditorium, we don't have the same views of the audience as we've had in other locations. Here, we're blocked from a direct view of the main area by the curtain and a wall. We're off to the right of the stage, so instead of entering from the back, we enter nearest Wil's keyboards. I'm nervous about what kind of reception we might get once we're onstage.

Greg and DC are doing their best to reassure me it's all fine. *Easy* for them. They're not gonna be standing in a bright spotlight for two hours with everyone in the place *knowing* I'm in love with Benji. Cripes, what if someone tries to do something to Benji?

Just as I'm about to work myself into a full-blown panic that the auditorium is filled with homophobic assholes out for Benji and me, and possibly Sean and Clay as well, DC nods toward the stage. It's showtime. I summon my inner swagger and stalk out like I'm a cross between a big game hunter and Mick Jagger. The audience is roaring its approval. *Wait*—no homophobic assholes?

While the guys get their guitars hooked up to their amps and prepare for the first song, I stride across the stage, surveying the audience. It's a full crowd; maybe not as many pictures and signs, but the screams, applause, and every other kind of noise of approval makes me completely forget all the worries from moments ago.

We go through our songs, like every show, feeding off the energy from the fans and giving them all our energy in return, a perfect transfer from them to us and back. It builds a strong bond, even here in the heart of country music. Maybe there's a sour note here or there, but the audience doesn't seem to notice, and overall, it's nothing to get worried about.

We make one slight change to the show; for *Fool*, Sean does the lead vocals, but without playing it up. We figure our fans will know the story of the song, and the group members are fully aware. Like Benji's grandmother would say, you don't go jabbing a wasp's nest to see if they're paying attention—no need to stir up the anti-homosexuals.

Even the introductions are as routine as every other stop. Why was I worrying about being here? We get as much love from the audience here as at most of the other shows, so I'm feeling a lot like king of the mountain or something. We've conquered Music City.

We finish the show strong, exit the stage to huge applause, and are greeted backstage by "the goddess of the waters," DC.

Benji wraps his arms around me.

"We did it, shay! We did Music City!" I start to nod in agreement when he clinches me tighter and pulls my head in for a mind-melting kiss.

Greg clears his throat loudly.

"So, obviously there's still a huge audience for y'all here," Greg says. "Tomorrow's show is SRO—standing room only. But we're going to head for Atlanta as soon as the show is over, *assuming* we do the show."

"Wait—what do you mean, *assuming we do the show?* If it's SRO, why wouldn't we do it?"

Greg fills in the blanks. "Reports have been forwarded to me from the sheriff's department that a well-known hate group has plans to *greet* us at the hotel tomorrow night."

"Uhh, a *hate* group, greeting us?" I ask, a bit confused by the contradictions in his words.

"You guys probably don't even remember the story of Buford Pusser, the guy whose wife was killed and who became sheriff in McNairy County, not far from here. He's familiar with a lot of these hate groups, some of whom are long-time KKK sympathizers. They aren't the type to take chances with. These groups change to fit whatever hatred is top of the roster, whether it's against blacks, women, homosexuals, Jews, native Americans, or whatever. The suggestion was to avoid any meeting with the group, and I agree, which is why I was all in favor of simply canceling the entire Nashville stop."

Damn, Greg, way to kill a post-show buzz.

"Fuck, I remember hearing some of that shit," Sean says. "Pretty rotten bunch, I guess."

"If by pretty rotten you mean shooting pregnant women, black or white, with double-barrel shotgun blasts at close range, castrating or burning alive black men and homosexuals, then, *yes*, pretty rotten," Greg comments. Wil and Todd are ashen-faced. Clay looks ready to throw up or cry, or both. Benji is as pissed as I've ever seen him—but also frightened.

"You for sure they won't be showin' up tonight?" Benji asks the question I was *just* thinking.

"Well, the 'good old boys' of the Klan want to be able to say that whatever happens to you didn't happen while you're in Nashville, so their plan is to wait until you finish the second show and return to the hotel, then *help* you leave. That's the rumor, anyway. That's why I think we should cancel the second show, cut our losses, and hit the road in the morning. By the time they realize what's going on, we'll have a good head start on them," Greg smiles grimly.

"I don't like it. It's cowardly. We've got security, and we can still leave from here like you said. I vote we do the show," I say, putting forth more bravado than I really feel.

The guys agree with me, and I glance at Greg, arching my eyebrow as if to say, "Your move."

Greg looks at each of the guys in turn, eye to eye, as if he's doing some kind of mind scan or something; everyone just looks right back at him. "I still think our smartest, safest move is to cancel the second show and leave in the morning. It won't hurt anything, guys; Ravynn, you *know* the final figures on this tour will be higher than what we've seen."

"We didn't have any trouble tonight, Greg," Benji says, his jaw clenched.

"I don't give one fuck about the numbers, Greg, I give a damn about our fans who bought tickets to see us. I say we do the show."

This time, the guys are muttering their agreement, so it's obvious we're six headstrong musicians against our cautious manager, and Greg reluctantly agrees.

I guess we'll be doing the show as planned and then slinking out of town under cover of darkness, kinda like we arrived.

Benji and I are in our hotel room, in bed, clutching each other because we're worried what the darkness outside might be hiding. We both *want*

to get sexy, having just had a fantastic show at the Municipal Auditorium. But... that church sign on the way into Nashville, followed by the warning of the hate group. Kinda rough to feel sexy in the face of not one, but two big bad wolves, and we got nothin' but straw houses.

"Shay, this ain't fair."

"No, babe, it isn't." I'm wrapped around Benji like my arms and body can shield him from the evils of the world.

"We ain't hurtin' nobody, we just livin' our own lives. What's so *wrong* about that?"

"Baby, some folks can't be happy until everyone else is as miserable as they are."

"Is it really worth it to live our lives openly?" Even in the near-darkness of the room, I can see the frown darkening Benji's eyes, even as I can feel him tensing at the thought. Not many weeks ago, I would have been the one thinking those thoughts. I can't let him doubt how right we are.

"No, baby. Don't let them make you question yourself; if you do, they win."

"It ain't fair; they get to be with their lovers and everything. Why can't we?" Benji sniffles a little, trying to stop tears.

"Some of them believe we are going against nature and God. They think we shouldn't exist."

"I'm scared, Rave. I just got you. I don't want to lose you." As I hold Benji, I sense every tremble and shake. He's close to falling apart from all this, and I can't let him feel that way, not after he rescued me so many times.

"I don't plan to lose you, either, babe. And I'm scared shitless, honestly."

"But… that guy in Boston at the drug store…." His voice has fallen to virtually a whisper, like he's afraid to say anything too strongly.

"Was a piece of shit, love. Don't let him ruin your life."

"And all the mean signs…."

"Small-minded people will always try to hurt you using words when they can't get to you any other way, baby. We just gotta look past them and see all the love around us."

"You can say that after we just got told the KKK is comin' for us? They do really fucked-up things to people, like cuttin' off body parts for fun." He's barely mouthing his words now, the weight of all the bad things—the jerk in Boston, the signs, all the negativity—threatening to cut off that wonderfully expressive voice I adore, and *that* both pisses me off and hurts me.

"I know, my love, but we've got good people around us, looking out for us, and as scared as I am, I promise you, no one's gonna get to you without getting through Todd, Wil, the security Greg has hired, and Sean and Clay and me." Though I'm a mess of nerves myself with this KKK thing, I force my voice to be strong and sure so I can project an air of confidence, a vision of hope and safety for Benji's sake.

But he's quiet, extremely so, and he's still trembling, though a little less. He's fighting tears, he's so frightened. I am nearly as frightened, but for my Cajun baby, I gotta be strong.

"Shhhh, salamander, you're not going to lose me, and I'm never going to lose you, either. I will protect you for the rest of my life."

All this tour, I've been chasing fame, thinking it was the goal. It's not. I have my goal here in my arms, right now, and he's scared shitless, but finally calming enough to sleep a little.

I think I'll write a song called "I Don't Like Mondays" because it *always* seems like the bad shit hits on a Monday, like last night. At least we didn't run into them at the hotel. Benji and I were way too tense about what might happen, so we just clung to each other in bed like we were each other's life raft, and eventually we both slept.

Now we're back in the Municipal Auditorium for what Benji, Sean, Clay, and I have been calling the "Show and Go" concert. Gallows humor from the four of us with the biggest targets on our backs. What's cool is that Todd—who looks like a short pro football linebacker—has already stated that he'll defend *his* guys with all his might. Wil and the road crew have added their support as well. I hope it doesn't come to that, but I'm again gobsmacked at the love my family gives me constantly.

Outside the auditorium, our buses are loaded with our wardrobes and collected souvenirs from the tour. Once the show ends, Davey and his crew will break down the drum riser, pack it into the buses, then load our amps, drums, guitars, and the remaining equipment. Finally, we'll board, and the van and our two buses will be southeasterly bound for Atlanta, home.

But first, there's a show to present. Like last night's show, there aren't a lot of pictures, but there *are* signs, some discreet, some not so much. I mean, *Benji + Ravynn 4 Ever* isn't exactly tricky to figure out... even when the flip side reads *Phoenix Rising 4 Ever*. Guess the owner isn't hedging their bets.

Musically, the guys are perfect. To watch them, you'd *never* guess that we are all performing with a threat hanging out there.

All too soon—seems like two hours have compressed into a half hour—the finale is happening. As the last notes reverberate through the auditorium, I shout, "Good night Nashville! Until next time!" Then, I stalk off the stage.

• • • • • • • • • • •

Atlanta, Georgia

July 17 - 25, 1968

Downtown Atlanta, Wednesday, July 17

Ho-lee shit. We're home. Peachtree Street, downtown Atlanta, en route to the new Regency Hyatt House. And oh my god, they've got traffic diverted both directions. The only vehicles on Peachtree Street? Phoenix 1 and Phoenix 2 and the van. And about three-quarters the population of the state of Georgia, from the looks of it.

It starts on a down note, as we pass the Baptist church. There's a banner hanging across the church that was *meant* for us to see. "The Phoenix: a myth that was consumed in its own fire, reduced to ashes." What a fucking letdown to get home to *that*. If one of their deacons or whatever the fuck they're called asks for a contribution, my answer will be a quick, caustic *sorry, fresh out*.

I grip Benji's hand tightly, and he squeezes mine right back.

As we continue down Peachtree Street, the crowd increases in size. There are people on both sides of the street holding up our album covers, posters, signs, pictures. Every face I see is beaming at us, screaming our names.

Suddenly, I'm smiling, too. I loosen my grip on Benji as the tension in my shoulders relaxes.

"They must've closed town for business today, shay," Benji beams at me, and I think he's right. This place is rocking, and it's fuckin' unreal.

Davey is driving us down the middle of the street at about three miles an hour, and I'm about ready to tell him to slow down because there's just So. Damn. Much. to take in—Benji and I are bouncing from one side of the bus to the other like manic tennis balls. Clay and Sean aren't much better.

It's amazing—this love for the six of us, coming home after a quick world tour. I'm getting a little emotional because *most* of these people probably never knew who we were until this tour began.

It doesn't even kill my happiness when I see *one* sign off to the side of all the revelers which reads "Queers Burn." At least there's only one, bad as it is. Thank gawd Benji is beside me; I don't think he's seen the vile thing, because he's too busy cataloging album covers, posters, anything the people have brought out to celebrate our homecoming.

"This is the best, babe," Benji whispers, his Cajun threatening to take over. He's as touched by all this love from our home as I am.

"The best, babe, is having *you* by my side while this happens." With that, I kiss him, just a promise of more for now.

"Lookit! This hotel is wild!"

We've arrived at the Regency Hyatt House. 22 stories, making it currently the tallest building in downtown Atlanta. Atop the hotel is the Polaris Restaurant, a futuristic-looking blue dome which rotates. Every diner who sits in the restaurant for at least an hour sees a panoramic view of the city of Atlanta and parts of Georgia around the city, including Stone Mountain off to the east, the largest exposed chunk of granite in the United States, if not the world.

Walking into the hotel lobby is surreal. There's a banner that greets *everyone* entering the hotel: *Welcome to the Regency Hyatt House Hotel, Official Home Hotel for Phoenix Rising 1968 World Tour*. It even has our logo on it! Todd has his camera, thank goodness, and we get one of the hotel desk personnel to take several shots of all of us—Greg, DC, Davey and his crew, and the six of us—under the banner.

After the pictures, we get checked in. We've got the *entire* twenty-second floor to ourselves. Greg gives us our choice of rooms, and Benji and I pick room 2222. Sean and Clay are right next door, in 2221.

The elevators are in a central area of the hotel, which is open from the ground floor to the roof; the rooms are around the four walls, with an open wall overlooking the courtyard below. I wouldn't want to be looking over the wall much, with my fear of heights. Still, this place is amazing. There are plants growing in planters throughout the hotel, so it's like you're in a natural setting, rather than in a concrete box in a city.

And the room? It's heaven. Of course, it may be because I'm with Benji, but the king-sized bed is almost large enough to have the entire group there. Almost, not quite. And the shower in the bathroom? Ohmagawd, I wanna take it home with us. Big enough for Benji and me to play in, hot water for days, and a shower head that doesn't require a mathematician to figure out how to get water where you need it. I know, 'cause Benji and I showered for about half an hour. Well, guess I shoulda said *used the shower* because a lot of the time was kissing and hugging and getting sexy. Maybe before this tour ends Benji and I can *christen* this shower in our own way.

Municipal Auditorium, Thursday, July 18

August 18, 1965, I saw the Beatles in Atlanta-Fulton County Stadium. It was a freakin' madhouse. Sean's mom went with Sean and me because we were too young to be in downtown Atlanta by ourselves, she said. And now, here we are, a few hours away from our first show back home after a world tour. We can't do the Stadium because the Braves are playing, so we'll just rock the Municipal Auditorium. It's okay; Bob Dylan, The Who, the Mamas and the Papas, and a load of others have played here, to good crowds. Before this tour started, my priorities were screwed. I've learned that nothing is worth having if you have to hide who you are to get it, and Benji has gone from being part of the group to the most important part of my life.

I remember coming to the Municipal Auditorium for the Ringling Brothers Circus when it came to Atlanta. In a way, that makes me want to say, "Whoa.... You sure there's no elephant shit left?"

It's soundcheck 19.... Too bad we don't have a recording of every soundcheck we've done. They'd sound pretty much like we've recorded one nineteen times. Other than when Ronnie and I had our dust-ups, nothing much ever happened, except the occasional busted string or such, that is. Now we're on the next-to-last day.

Predictably, Sean checks every drum and every cymbal, every bit of his percussion equipment. He's anal-retentive, but I don't want him any other way. His drumming and Clay's bass form the spine of our sound, much like Ringo and Paul's drums and bass form the Beatles' core sound.Every instrument and every microphone checks perfectly. We're set for tonight. My adrenaline is surging. It's just after 5 pm, and in less than two hours, the seats will begin filling with people from our hometown, eager to see *us*.

Backstage, Sean's mom and dad, my *adopted* parents, are waiting, along with Greg, DC, and a nervous-looking young guy who resembles Clay, with a thinner face and black hair. He's glancing around at all of us like he's witnessing history or something special; guess he's a little star-struck by us.

Sure enough, Sean's mom hugs Sean like it's been years since she last saw him. When she turns him loose, she hugs Clay just as tightly; she's adopted the boyfriend already. And *then* she turns to me. She's not as strong a hugger as Benji's mom and grandmother, but she's close.

Meanwhile, the dark-haired kid approaches Clay. His behavior reminds me so much of me from my early days with Sean's family—nervous, but excited; quiet, like he's afraid to draw attention to himself. I've never met Clay's family. I know he and his mom keep in touch. That's about *all* I know about Sean's favorite person. Clay spots the guy and smiles.

"Bro, I can't believe you made it! Is mom here?" Clay rushes the words out, like his brother will vanish in a cloud of smoke if he takes too long asking the question.

"She... doesn't... know," the brother replies.

"*What?*" Clay asks.

"She and... him... were arguin', so I left. I couldn't take it no more. He was always yellin' about something. Something Mom had done. Something I had done. Even something you had done. One day he acted like he was gonna clobber me an' I double-dog-dared him to do it. I told him I'd make sure I got a good bruise an' then swear he'd beat the fuck outta me to the cops. He kept away from me then."

"Fuck, that sumbitch, I wish to hell she'd never married him. Dougie, did he ever hurt you, for real?"

"Just my ears, with all the damn yellin'. And my eyes, watchin' him hurt mom's feelings. I don't think the asshole's got balls enough to physically hurt her."

"He ever does, he better find a way to turn invisible, 'cause I'll find him, and my guys and I will make him understand what real pain is," Clay says, a grim smile on his face. "C'mon, you gotta meet everyone."

Clay introduces Douglas—Dougie, he calls him, though I think Douglas prefers the full name or *just* Doug—to Sean, Sean's parents, and the rest of us, once Sean and his parents finish their sudden hug-a-thon with Douglas.

As Douglas and Todd meet, I notice a sudden sparkle in Todd's eyes—and a corresponding gleam in Douglas's dark brown eyes. Maybe it's just the lighting.

With the introductions complete, Greg and DC take over. It's unusual for Greg to have anything to say before a show, so part of me is in "uh-oh, what's up" land, while the *rest* of me is still buzzing about the fact that we're *home*.

"Guys, we've got the attendance for all the shows through Nashville. If tonight's show has *just* a dozen people in the audience, this tour will go on record as the number one highest-attended debut world tour by a new group since records started being kept, meaning...."

DC takes over, before I can. "Meaning, guys, you've beat the Beatles *and* the Rolling Stones again."

I want to squeal in happiness, but before I can do anything, Benji hugs me and kisses me like there's no tomorrow.

"So, we've got two shows as gravy, that's what you're saying?" I finally say, after I recover from the kiss. Greg looks at me as if I've just learned to speak English.

"That would be a safe assumption, yes," Greg replies with a smirk. I gotta hand it to him. For being all "no-relationships-on-the-tour" at the beginning, he's handled having *two* romances bloom under his nose well. I think he's only blushed a few times.

"We've got a splendid dinner being delivered, enough for all of us *and* our guests," DC says. Magically, three delivery guys show up bearing what appears to be enough food to satisfy a starving horde. We're talking huge disposable pans with fried chicken, potato salad, cole slaw, baked beans, salisbury steaks smothered in mushroom and onion gravy, macaroni and cheese, and *one* guy stays behind with something that looks like a deep fryer.

We devour virtually every edible thing. When it's all gone, the guy standing by the deep fryer has heated it up and has turned his attention to preparing a batter of some sort. He looks up, sees everyone watching him, and says, "Ready for some dessert?"

I look around even while nodding my affirmative. Everyone else is nodding. Benji is gleaming, like he's figured *something* out.

"You didn't see it, but I did. The batter he's workin' came outta a *Café du Monde* box."

"You mean...."

"Exactly. Beignets, shay, gotta be."

The man at the deep fryer smiles. He's heard us, and nods. "Yes, beignets with powdered sugar for everyone who wants them, three at a time, like in New Orleans."

We have beignets—Benji and I persuade the guy to make each of us three more, which he does with a smile.

Best. Homecoming. Ever.

DC takes her usual position near the curtain at the stage entrance, turns back to us, smiles, and says, "Welcome home, boys. Now go kick ass!"

We head onstage. Like in most of the other places we've performed, we're entering from the back of the stage, so Sean goes first to climb up his drum riser. I'm right behind him, followed by the other four.

The crowd is huge. And vocal. As soon as they see me—or Sean, I'm not sure which—the applause, screams, and pandemonium begin. Once Benji and Clay are onstage, you can't hear anything; it's like a wall of sound has descended around this building.

As the guys are hooking up their guitars, I'm surveying the crowd. Having been in this auditorium on the audience side, I am now getting a view I never really expected—as the performer sees the audience. If there were *any* doubts about Atlanta, this crowd erases them all. Scattered throughout the hall are signs stating "Atlanta Heart Phoenix Rising." There are a few signs towards the back that aren't so nice to us—the usual "Queers Suck" and a few more creative, like "Fags Go Down" and "Penis Rising? Not for Me!"—but they're outnumbered ten to one. Our hometown loves us. Period.

"Good evening! It's good to be home again, Atlanta," I shout. "We love y'all!" I start in my British accent, then drop to my regular southern voice for the final bit. If anyone caught my slip, no one's saying anything.

The guys begin playing, and the show begins for real. Here at home, with family and friends in the audience, it's phenomenal. The best show by far; every peak moment of every previous show is rolled into this show.

The energy from the crowd is so strong it feeds us, and we give our energy to the audience. This show could last for hours and I wouldn't argue. It's that energizing. That we're doing all this at home makes it even more special.

When we get to the introductions, I decide to get a bit more personal since we're playing for the home crowd. I start with Sean, but this time, I give him a proper introduction.

"Several years ago, after I was tossed out of my house, I met this guy who wore wire-rim glasses and played drums. *Not* a solo instrument. He also could write a mean set of lyrics and had a good ear for melodies, even if he couldn't always write one. Turned out we shared a couple of things—a birthday and a desire to form a damn good group. Sean, our drummer, helped make this whole thing happen." The spotlight shines on Sean as I'm talking, and he looks like he's for once trying not to boast.

"Then there's Wil. The man's a total genius with keyboards, even if he's shy about admitting it. No less a musical genius than George Martin called Wil one of the greatest keyboard players he's ever seen or heard." Wil is sitting at his keyboards, looking like he's ready to run for an exit—he doesn't take praise very well.

"Todd came to us from Gatlinburg. He's been a helluva guitar player and a good sport since the beginning. I believe if I'd told him he'd wind up at some point dressed in a Roman Legionnaire's costume as he played onstage, he probably would have said thanks, but no thanks." Todd nods at the end of my comment, followed by a twangy slide-guitar sounding chord, but he's smiling.

"Clay joined us from South Carolina. We'd been doing a bass-by-committee thing, where Todd, our original rhythm guitarist Tommy, Wil, and even I played the occasional bass bit. Can you imagine the Beatles with no Paul? That was us without Clay. Anyway, Clay fit in like he'd been part of our group forever." During my statements, Clay is turning toward the other guys, looking bashful almost, until he looks at Sean, who blows him a kiss right there onstage. Well, if *that* doesn't get the churches here screaming for our blood, nothing will. Clay plays a nifty little bass riff that sounds very much like something he might have picked up in London.

That leaves Benji. And, like multiple other stops on the tour, the crowd starts chanting "Ben-ji! Ben-ji!" before I start.

"Yes, Benji. Our youngest Phoenix, our rhythm guitarist. The newest member of the group, he's originally from Metairie, Louisiana, part of New Orleans. His guitar style won us over when he auditioned for us two years ago—shortly after he'd turned *fifteen*. He's young in years, but wiser than that. He's been there to keep me smiling." I pause. "I don't know what I'd do without him by my side.... And like I said, pure wicked on the guitar." As I finish saying that, I turn toward Benji, who plays a monster riff on his guitar with the most angelic smile on his face. And finishes by blowing *me* a kiss.

The audience loves it all—the applause and cheers are strong throughout. We launch into our final numbers, riding a tremendous high from all the love this crowd has given us.

After first concert, Atlanta streets, A local hospital

We've finished our first "homecoming" concert, in front of a jam-packed audience in the Atlanta Municipal Auditorium. I'm still floating in the clouds. I know we rode limos back to the group hotel, but I really have no memory of anything other than the cheering and screaming from our fans. My guys did a great job tonight; every note was perfection. Maybe times *are* changing, even here in the belt-buckle of the Bible Belt South.

"Benji, you were terrific tonight," I tell my guy shortly after we've closed the door to our hotel room.

"Shay, everybody was, but you... what you said in the introduction, that was so sweet," he says as he gets out of his shirt and shoes.

"I just said what I felt, love. I am *still* so jazzed from the show!"

"How 'bout we go for a little walk, huh?" Benji says with a grin.

"Yeah, we've been cooped up in buses or planes or hotel rooms for freakin' forever. Let's get dressed so we don't stand out, and get some air." As I say it, Benji nods in agreement, and in a few moments, we're dressed like two young men, no glam or glitter, just jeans for me and jeans shorts for Benji, and plain tees for us both, with my hair pulled into a ponytail and Benji wearing an Atlanta Braves baseball cap.

We hit Peachtree Street at a little after 11 pm, and though it's late, there are still some people out. We walk about a block away from the hotel, talking quietly about our memories of the tour.

"Can you believe we ran into the same guy who did our caricature in New Orleans while we were in San Francisco, Rave?" Benji asks, smiling at both memories.

"And then the caricature in Rome, don't forget," I added.

"This really *has* been the 'Carica-Tour,' hasn't it, shay?"

We both smile at the memory of telling Greg and DC about calling the tour that while we were in Rome. There's a side street, and even though it's darker than Peachtree, we don't worry about it; there are likely less people to recognize us.

"The entire experience has been a blast. I wouldn't change much, unless...." I pause, because I'm suddenly aware there are other people in the shadows with us. Benji senses it too and gets closer to me, though we refrain from holding hands or touching.

Suddenly, a strong flashlight beam in front of us momentarily blinds me before it moves to Benji's face. I have a queasy feeling in the pit of my stomach, and it's not from the beignets we ate before the show. A passing car shows at least three big shapes ahead of us—guys, certainly. There's probably many more. We're kinda caged here, at a distinct disadvantage.

"What do ya know, boys? We're in the presence of royalty here—they're from that queer group Phoenix Rising. ***Ronnie*** sends his regards. Bubba, give the blond queen a royal salute," a nasty voice says from the direction the flashlight had come. Ronnie? What the fuck does *that* mean?

At that moment, to Benji's right, an arm swipes out and crunches into his right eye. Almost simultaneously, I hear a sound that worries me.

Click!

Shit. That's some kind of weapon, probably a knife.

"Fuck! What the hell?" I shout, shaking. I'm pissed *and* afraid. They're messing with *my* Benji. These are street thugs, not KKK hoodlums, but the end result is that we're getting targeted for being homosexual. And apparently Ronnie is somehow mixed into this.

Things happen quickly. Benji clocks whoever punched him, but that draws more of the gang in. For a few moments, I'm able to help by attacking the guys who are trying to hit Benji.

I'm doing my best to keep them from hurting him, kicking, punching, clawing... anything. Our early efforts are strong, other than the punch to Benji's eye; my sense of bravado lets me feel like we're winning. Maybe Benji and I will get out of it okay, and a little bandaging and makeup will cover up our misadventure before our last concert tomorrow night... seconds later, something hard hits the back of my head and *everything* goes black.

Later, I open my eyes... wait, other than feeling like I got run over by a couple of dump-trucks, I've got no idea what's happening. I'm groggy, like I've awakened in the middle of my sleep, but I'm sure that's not right, either.

What the....? As my eyes and senses decide to try functioning, I realize I am in a hospital room. Why? I don't remember....

Oh shit. Oh fuck.

I remember Benji and me deciding to go for a walk around downtown Atlanta. And I remember we turned off Peachtree onto a dark side street....

Where the fuck is Benji?

That there's no sign of my boyfriend anywhere in this room hurts more than all the aches and pains in my body. It's a fear of having lost him, of never seeing that smiling face again....

There's a machine that appears to be monitoring my heartbeat and pulse, and there's some IV drip connected, and there's all kinds of different-colored tanks like for gases around me, but I can't tell if they're actually connected to me. Maybe it's my anxiety peeking through, but I can't help worrying how much of my "normal" functions are being handled by a machine. I mean, am I gonna be hooked up like this for life? No thank you. I can't handle it. Right now I'm freaked out too much from the lack of my Benji... gawd, he's *got* to be okay....

Regardless of anything else, if I still have Benji, I'll be okay.

Just as I am about to call out for someone, anyone, there's movement behind me and a very recognizable head of platinum blond hair comes into my field of view. The smile is missing from Benji's lips, but the gleam in his eyes at least partially makes up for it, even with a painful blackening around his right eye. His right eye makes me cringe. I hope he's okay....

"I must have died and gone to heaven," I tease, "because there's a really cute angel hovering around me."

"Hush talking like that, shay. You ain't dead, no-sir. Thank the Bon Dieu, thank the Good Lord," Benji says.

"Are you okay?" I blurt out. Benji's well-being is more important to me than anything else.

He flashes me a smile and nods. I gotta be sure.

"Are you *really* okay, baby? Your eye looks awful."

"The guy who did this got the worse of it. His hand hit bone, so I got lots of bruisin' but no harm to my eye, *and* I'm purty sure I clocked him a few good times on his face."

Benji glances at the door—to be sure no one's entering, I guess—and kisses my forehead quickly. When he pulls back, his smile is back in full force. "You scared me shitless, Rave. I was afraid...."

"Baby, are you really okay? I mean, like physically and everything? And how did we...?" I have to ask him because I'm so worried he's being *brave* in the face of all my issues. I need him to be healthy....

"Doctors checked me over fully. Other than this nasty black eye, I avoided any harm. I'm sorry it didn't work that well for you, Ravynn. And thank the Bon Dieu that a police car came along when it did; the gang scattered, the police called the medics and got you here in time."

Shit, I could've lost *him* before really having him, before we *really* got a chance to know each other. All my big talk about being open and honest, and I've *still* been hiding. I can't hurt him by hiding who I am, *any* longer. "It's *not* Ravynn."

"Of course you're Ravynn, shay."

"No, babe, that's a stage name. For you, I'm Robin Smith, forever *your* Robin Smith, *if* you can handle the real me—the insecure, broken, messed-up me."

As I finish, I look at Benji. He's smiling, a mirror image of his grandmother Pearl from his birthday, an almost all-knowing smile. He grasps my hand gently, squeezes it lightly—just enough that I can sense it, really, bends over and caresses both my cheeks, a promise of more to come. He pauses, looks directly into my eyes, and nods.

"I'm really lookin' forward to getting to know *that* person," Benji says slowly. He's looking at me, lying here in this hospital bed, like I'm a prize catch. He's always looked at me that way. "But, shay, the truth is... only you see those problems. Most of 'em came from that couyon you were with before I ever met you. I get that."

"I can't use that as a crutch. I'm responsible for how I behave in the world. You and your family accepted me for who I was right off the bat, no questions. You deserve the best, and I'm going to do my best every day to be worthy of you, soon as I get outta here...."

"Shush, love. You gotta heal. We gonna get you healthy! Then it'll be good, my *Robin*, I promise you that!"

"I will do *anything* to make you happy, Benji." If I could, I'd pull him into this damn bed with me for a cuddle, but there are so many tubes and things running around my body that there's no chance of that. I wink at him, and he winks back with his uninjured eye. I hope the bastard that socked him got run over by a couple buses, then backed over by a garbage truck. He damn well deserves it.

We may not be able to cuddle yet, but we can kiss. And Benji leans over and gives me the sweetest, tenderest, gentlest, most caring kiss I've *ever* had—like a mere brush of lips, promising more with a sense of eternity. At least, to me, that's how it seems, and it curls my toes more than most of our sexiest kisses have. "My lips, mouth, lungs, and throat aren't broken, that I'm aware of, baby," I tease him.

"I know that, shay. I just don't wanna get you too worked up before we know what the doctors are gonna say. Don't want my baby hurtin' 'cuz he's getting' blue balls from a kiss." No, Benji *didn't* just say that, did he? Maybe my ears were affected by the assault.

"Come here, babe," I ask, in a low, almost feeble voice. It does the trick. He gets close. I pull his face to mine, being careful with his eye, and proceed to give him the most scorching kiss I can. After a few seconds, he joins in, and we're getting into the range of "eating face" rather than just *kissing*.

All good things must end, usually just when they're getting good, and this hospital bed kiss is no exception. Our lip-lock is interrupted by the sound of two throats clearing.

Greg and DC are standing inside the room, gazing at us. DC looks like she hasn't slept in a week; her eyes are red—wait, has the fiercest Mama Bear ever been *crying*?

"Ravynn, are you okay, ba—kiddo?" I'm shocked, DC has *never* been so nice. Gawd, she must've been worried.

"I knew we should have just canceled the concerts in the south, after everything else happened," Greg adds, and the stubble on his chin tells me he's been so worried about us that he's neglected himself.

"No way, Greg. I'm sorry if I've worried everyone, but I'm fuckin' *glad* we went through with the concerts. I'm done with apologizing for who I am, and I'm never hiding from bullies or bigots again. I'm living my real life, and *that* will always include Benji, no exceptions, no apologies."

When I finish my rant, Greg and DC stand silently, and I worry I've said too much, gone too far. Finally, Greg speaks.

"I'm proud of you, son. You're standing up for your beliefs and yourself, and that's great. After Dickie's revelations, we hired a private investigator to check into Ronnie, unfortunately too late to prevent this. We found out that he sold his story to a really sleazy scandal paper, then persuaded the thugs who attacked you two to do their worst—they were actively scoping out the area waiting for you. Fortunately, their worst was *not* realized."

DC nods, then adds in a strangely subdued voice, "What he said."

Man, Greg and DC blow me away... and Ronnie has turned out to be more rotten than even I had painted him. Instinctively, I clutch Benji's hand tighter. He must understand what I'm experiencing, because his grip on my hand tightens as well.

While that drama has been going on, my "attending physicians," two doctors, enter the room and look at the four of us.

As the doctors step closer to my bed, Benji reluctantly steps an arm's length away—I won't turn loose of his hand *unless* the doctors instruct me to do so, and from the looks of things, that's not happening. Greg and DC join Benji's side, DC wrapping an arm around his waist.

The doctors identify themselves as Dr. McKee and Dr. Park. Neither seems particularly warm or friendly. With no experience with hospitals, I wonder if this is normal, or is this the hospital where everyone has suck-ass bedside manners?

Dr. McKee begins. "Mr. St. John, I ordered a battery of tests upon your arrival here; you were unresponsive." Way to make me feel warm and bubbly, doctor. At least Benji squeezes my hand, like he's reassuring me I'm *still* among the living.

"You've suffered several instances of blunt force trauma to multiple parts of your torso and outer extremities," Dr. Park continues. "We identified at least three cracked ribs, fortunately no breaks, but the potential is there for internal organ damage, which is why we'd like to keep you here for several days so we can monitor you, and why your diet is going to be pretty bland for several days until we're sure you're out of the woods." Eww... I've heard about bland hospital diets, not a fan. Bring me a burger, please.

"We will keep you here for observation and any necessary treatment for the next few days," Dr. McKee adds. Oh, joy. There goes my cut of the tour profits, right to the hospital and doctors.

"Will I be able to visit him, doctor?" Benji asks.

"I'm sure he would like that *very* much," Dr. Park smirks. If I could get outta this bed.

Dr. Park is a younger guy, probably in his early forties, and he's definitely looked over Benji. Like, *totally* checked him out.

Atlanta, Benji Travers' family home, Thursday, July 25

Our return to Atlanta and the first concert ended the tour. That night, I could've died. After Benji and I were attacked in a dark side street in Atlanta, I spent a week in the hospital on the blandest diet this side of soda crackers and tap water, eww—being monitored for internal organ damage, which fortunately didn't seem to have been the case. Benji suffered a nasty black eye, which has now mostly faded away. The last show of the tour was canceled, but we'll make it up to our fans eventually.

As of today, I'm staying with Benji at his family's house, until we go to the coast. I had protested that being here was too much of an imposition. That was met with answers I could have almost seen coming.

"No way, shay," Benji stated.

"Since Charlie moved out with his Emmie, we've got a spare room," Benji's mom Jenny said.

"Another guy around here will be nice," Benji's dad, Justin, added.

Don't these people *know* that I'm so much in love with their son that it'll kill me to live under the same roof with him and not be able to do more than kiss him? Gawd, being in that hospital room with him, I wanted to pull him into the bed with me.

So, of course, I moved in. Sean was upset; he and I have been like brothers for so long, I kinda understand. Moving in with his family after Ronnie and I broke up really cemented the image of us as brothers. But he's got Clay now; things are changing. Besides, he's always gonna be my brother from a different mother.

Benji and his mom set me up in Charlie's old room, which is right across the hall from Benji's room, in a part of the house away from his parents. Adam's bedroom, when he's around, is right next door. But Adam is off at some sports camp or something, so it's private here. Benji knew more than he was letting on.

But I'll only be staying here at Benji's house for a few days. After that, he and I will be heading to the coast for two weeks. Benji's birthday gift from Greg and DC, two weeks at a private resort on one of Georgia's Golden Isles, will allow us to complete my recuperation and finally start our real relationship, without machinery or tours or *any* other interruptions.

Anyway, I'm playing patient, Benji is the doctor, and he's being very thorough in making sure that I get plenty of rest. I am. I'm friggin' bored to near death. All I've done is lie in this bed, watch TV, kiss Benji every chance I get, drink what seems like the equivalent of the Atlantic Ocean in juices and water, and been escorted to and from the bathroom to pee every time I need to go—which, given the amount of liquids I'm consuming, is a frequent occurrence. At least I get to kiss Benji whenever I go to the bathroom, because he's my escort to and from the toilet.

Benji's mom and dad treat me like one of the family, just like Pearl and Hank did in New Orleans every time we were there. It still catches me unprepared that there really are decent people who will treat a person kindly for no reason other than he's a fellow human being. Jenny, Justin, and all Benji's family accept he's homosexual, and that's another thing that amazes me. I don't do it often, but now I'm thinking of my biological parents, or as I prefer to think of them, my sperm donor and incubator. Neither of them seemed to ever have much interest in me as a person, and even less once I told them I was homosexual. Those cold-as-ice doctors in the hospital were actually nicer to me than my supposed parents had ever been. Well, I've moved on, and I like to think I'm a better man today for being true to who I am.

During my recuperation period, I've been told I'm not allowed to do anything more strenuous than think about music. Benji's figured me out. Music I can handle; anything else and my brain starts short-circuiting. Right now, the short-circuiting involves the fact that my *boyfriend* keeps showing up wearing some of the tightest, shortest outfits I've ever seen on an adult.

He struts into the room, wearing a pair of shorts that appear to be spray-painted on him. I wonder how he's breathing. Did I mention, *short*? Like, I'm not sure where he's hiding his junk. *That* short. The top isn't much more than a tank top that covers his nipples, but leaves his belly bare.

"If you're trying to kill me with overstimulation, babe, mission accomplished. Are you taking that outfit to the beach?"

"Naw, I got a few shorter ones."

"Please tell me you're talking about the top, not the shorts."

"Dang, shay, I can't find *nothin'* shorter than these. I *barely* fit into 'em as is."

"I noticed. How *do* you do it, anyway?"

"A friend of mine's a drag queen, told me about tucking, and showed me how. That's why you can't see anything, but I'll be straight up with ya, no way I'll ever do drag, no-sir. This hurts worse than bein' a baby gator's first taste of Cajun."

"Love, do me a favor. Go change into something baggier and looser, and be ever so careful untucking. I want you unhurt when we get to the coast!"

"You're not mad?" Why would he think I could *ever* be mad at him? No way. I guess he's worried about the tucking thing, or maybe the drag queen friend talking to him about tucking, but none of that's going to get me upset.

"I could never be mad at you, baby. Frustrated that I can't pull you into bed right now, but.... All in good time, babe."

"Okay. Don't go nowhere, 'kay?"

"I promise."

Benji runs to my side, gives me a scorching but brief kiss, then tears out the door. Moments later, I hear all kinds of noises from his room across the hall. I'm tempted to get out of bed to see what's up, but I promised Benji I would stay right here. In my mind, I can hear Sean's voice laughing at me, saying "whipped" over and over, like he did once when I was still with Ronnie. No, *this* is different. This time, I am truly in love.

Seconds later, Benji walks back in. Now he's wearing a pair of pants made of nylon or some synthetic fabric, with snaps down each leg. Handy; a guy could be totally respectable and become totally *un*respectable in just a few moments. I like that.... Then I see the top. It's a basic white athletic shirt, like a tank top. In that outfit, he looks decadent, yet refined. *He's all mine*.

"You thinkin' 'bout us again, shay?"

"Yeah, how could you tell? And I hope you're bringing that outfit to the coast!"

"You got a goofy but determined look on your face, so I figured it was us you were thinkin' about. And if this outfit affects you like that—" he points at the rise in the sheet over my crotch before continuing, "I'll bring two or three like it!"

• • • • • •• • • • • •

Epilogue: Georgia's Golden Isles

August 8, 1968

Two weeks later, August 8

Benji and I are using his birthday present from Greg and DC—two weeks at a resort in Georgia's Golden Isles. We've gorged ourselves on seafood, strolled the beaches, played tourists. We're doing our best to avoid the press—one particularly stubborn newshound, namely Dickie Newsome. Good ol' Dickie wasn't buying Greg's announcement that the second show was canceled due to me being totally exhausted. He had apparently gotten some juicy tidbits from the hospital about my *condition* when I was admitted.

We arrange through Greg for Benji and me to meet with Dickie for an interview. DC joins us in Brunswick, the "home port" for Georgia's Golden Isles and a sizable shrimp fleet, and we then sit down with Dickie at the Conference Center at the resort where we're staying.

For *this* interview, Dickie is waiting for us. We show DC our accommodations with a magnificent view of the beach and the Atlantic Ocean, let her freshen up a bit, then the three of us walk half a block to the Conference Center. Dickie stands from his chair and shakes our hands as we enter. The entire interview is low-key, comfortable, like old friends chatting. He starts by apologizing again about Ronnie.

"You were doing what you thought was honorable for a friend, and he took advantage," I reply.

"Thanks, I still worry that I betrayed you somehow," Dickie admits.

DC glances at me, then at Dickie, then adds her perspective.

"You were Ronnie's friend. You grew up together. *He* took advantage of you, and turned out to be the bad one. You tried being a nice guy and helped, and we appreciate that."

I'm amazed. DC has said what I was thinking, better than I could have.

"Exactly what she said."

"Still, if I hadn't told him I was covering your tour...."

"He woulda found somebody else to get to Ravynn," Benji says.

"So, you guys are doing okay, no bad after-effects from the attack?"

"Just letting the bruises heal, the nightmares recede, and trying to avoid particularly stubborn newshounds, but *you* wore us down," I say, smiling.

"Anything else you want to add, Ravynn?" Dickie asks. He *knows* I have something to say.

"Ronnie's story obviously was an attempt to hurt me or to ruin my life. Most of what he told the scandal rag was made up or exaggerated nonsense," I say, while I hold Benji's hand as almost a lifeline. "He surprised me at his level of anger; he'd never been that nasty while we lived together, so it was a shock when that thug uttered his name before the attack started."

I pause to take a sip of water, because the memory of *that night* still haunts me at times. Benji's gentle squeeze of my hand snaps me back to today.

"Lying in the hospital bed, surrounded by everything, but mostly by my found family represented by Greg, DC, and Benji, I realized again that it's more important to stand up for what you believe, and live an authentic life, than it is to be rich and famous. For me, that means having Benji in my life, and standing up against bullies."

"If I get a chance at Ronnie, I may show him how gators bite," Benji says, smiling. I'm not sure how serious he is, but hopefully Ronnie won't press his luck to find out.

"Let's focus on getting the two of you healthy, okay?" DC says, mock-sternly. She's smiling, so she can't be too stern.

"Thanks for everything, Dickie. You've been a great help," I say, honestly.

"Actually, thank you, Ravynn, and DC and Benji. It's been an honor covering your tour, and I wish you all the best. I will write a version of this interview that will tell your truth without revealing too much," Dickie says.

Dickie nods, shakes our hands again, and we all leave; the interview is done, and DC can get back to her vacation while Benji and I resume ours.

Through it all, Benji's been by my side like it's his responsibility to get me healthy. That hasn't slowed our hugging and kissing, but I know he's as antsy about certain parts of our *new* relationship as I am. We haven't even broken into the stash of lubricants he bought back in Boston, other than to sample flavors.

I worry I'll hurt Benji. But his attitude, and the way he looks at me—like a predator looks at its next meal—makes me think he's not as fragile as I think. When we kiss, he takes charge as often as he lets me lead. He *might* be the youngest member of the group, but he's an equal partner in this relationship. I told him that was the *only* way; the *one* thing missing is his song being performed live in a show. He's assured me that would happen when the audience was right.

We take a leisurely bike ride, stopping for a late lunch of local seafood before I suggest we return to the room.

"I was beginnin' to wonder if that stay at the hospital screwed up your sex drive."

"You know I'm worried I could hurt you, salamander."

"Do you see me bein' made of china, shay? 'Cause I promise ya, I'm not easy to hurt." The smile on his face proves he's not upset.

"I know you're not breakable, babe. But there are things that can hurt, and I don't want to."

"I'm good. I know you're gonna be careful with me, that's your way."

I grab a mouthful of shrimp, because he's made me blush again.

We finish our meals rapidly. Benji pays our bill and we race to our bikes to make a beeline for the resort.

Parking the bikes, we dash the five steps to the entry. As I'm trying to open the door, Benji is hugging me, kissing my arms, and distracting my concentration. Finally, we're inside.

After months of tip-toeing around, going through the tour with enough electricity between us to light up most of the world, we're giving in. I think everyone has expected this since Benji's grandmother Pearl talked to us back in New Orleans.

My past and insecurities tried to stop us. Nothing could stop us.

But now we're alone. We've been hugging, and we've kissed so much that our lips look like over-inflated balloon lips—not to mention chapped as hell.

Benji's hugged and kissed, but he's never done anything sexual with another person. I remember how nervous I was the first time I was with someone and *knew* that we were going to have sex before the night was over. Nervous? I was scared shitless.

By comparison, Benji's just sitting here.

It's not sex or getting our rocks off with Benji and me. I've sensed a connection to him since his earliest days with the group, like *nothing* I've ever experienced before. I know now I was falling in love.

As I'm thinking, Benji is tracing his fingers across my shoulders, up my neck, around my jaw.... I sense bolts of energy when he touches me. He gazes into my eyes, his emerald green glowing.

"Shay, relax, get comfy. We're alone; you're sittin' like you been carved outta a tree. You'd be a lot calmer without that shirt." Now he's gonna undress me; he devotes himself to me and I'm *still* afraid I'll hurt him. He pulls off my shirt.

I want to kiss him, only him, forever.

Benji lets me lead into the kiss, making me believe the shy virgin routine. Almost. As I'm about to get more passionate with my kiss, his tongue tickles my lips, *demanding* access. After a moment, I open my lips and our tongues do a mating dance of their own.

The room is quiet except for our kissing and occasional moans.

I slide one hand down, trying to act sophisticated while finding the zipper and button. Instead, I act and *feel* like a high school freshman trying to impress a more experienced date. Finally, he takes one of his hands away from my body and undoes the button, and starts unzipping his shorts. I slip my hand in and finish unzipping them as his fingers loosen mine. Again I feel like the high school freshman—Benji's gotten his pants and mine loose in less time than I spent trying to find the damn button on his.

As he slides my shorts down my waist and legs, I'm still all-thumbs, trying to slip his off. Am I that clumsy, or that worried that I won't be good enough for Benji?

"Shush, babe," Benji reads my mind, and calms me enough that klutzy me vanishes. Thank goodness we had stepped out of our shoes earlier, or this would be a friggin' nightmare.

Soon we're shed of clothing. Benji pulls back long enough to sweep his eyes from my head to my legs; I do the same thing with him.

"Beautiful, shay." Benji's voice is so soft, yet aroused, that I *almost* think someone else has spoken. He's licking his lips, a hint of a smile creeping around the corners of his mouth.

"Beautiful, shay," I repeat his words. It's the first time he's been called "shay" by anyone other than a family member. His eyes light up, his smile takes over his face, and the look he gives me is enough to melt pure steel.

He *is* beautiful. From the shocking platinum blond hair, the expressive emerald green eyes, all the way down his body. Seeing him openly displayed for me alone is the best early Christmas present ever.

Benji leans forward, kisses a trail down my neck to my chest, then lightly sucks each of my nipples before moving to my navel, which he kisses and then tongues, making me squirm. It almost tickles. He doesn't stop there; he goes further down my body, kissing my left and right legs where they meet my torso, and then shocks me as he kisses the head of my dick and both balls. I'm harder than I've ever been in my life.

I coax him into lying on his back on the bed, then I kiss him. He *knows* this isn't simply sex. His eyes are still gleaming, but half-lidded now; the gaze he gives me is pure heat. I trace my fingertips down his neck, along the veins, his pulse racing under my fingers. His cock, which neither of us has touched, is engorged, wet with pre-cum.

I lean into him, so close, completing the journey with a kiss to his full, pouty lips. My hands trace his arms, sensing the curves of muscles and the points of his elbows, all the way to the ten fingers I will never release. Benji sighs, a contented sound barely escaping his now-swollen lips. I trace my way back up the underside of his arms, then down his chest, tweaking each nipple lightly.

"Shay...." Benji draws the word out like it's the longest stretch of letters he can remember. I kiss his Adam's apple, then each nipple, before sliding down his body.

He's about to say something when I take his hardness into my mouth. Whatever he was going to say comes out as a long, low moan of unintelligible syllables. I haven't even moved my mouth or tongue, just swallowed his shaft in one movement. Inside my mouth, it's leaking already; he's primed to shoot.

I let him slip out of my mouth, a gasp escaping from his mouth as I do. "I want to make love to you in every way, babe," I whisper softly. He nods, as ready for this as I *finally* am.

"You are so damn hot, baby. I just want you to enjoy what we do, but if you want me to stop, just say so, okay?"

"Just... stop... talkin'. I ain't no dumb bébé, y'know."

"But... you're still new to this. I don't wanna fuck it up for you."

"Kiss me, then make love to me, shay. I'm yours, I ain't goin' nowhere without you."

I may be the group's leader, but I'm following Benji's orders. Our lips meet, then open to allow our tongues to join the party. The kiss goes on forever, electric jolts as our bodies touch.

Benji isn't lying there; his arms and fingers are playing my body as skillfully as he plays his guitars. He instinctively slides his fingers across my body, hitting all my "spots" just right. My nipples, but also the sides of my neck, along the veins, the inside of my legs, and even my sides get touched, rubbed, or caressed.

My hands, which had been cupping Benji's face, now attempt to keep up with what he's doing to me. Even with me lying on top of him, he's thrusting up at me, our cocks trapped together between our bodies. It's a good thing that I'm not heavy, because we go at it for a while, kissing like we can't get enough.

Eventually, we break for air. Benji's beaming. With all our kissing, his lips *still* manage to smile.

Wordlessly, he hands me the bottle of lubricant he has selected for our evening. I almost burst into laughter when I see it's cherry flavored. Subtle hint, I guess; he wants me to use cherry lube to "take his cherry."

The bottle has a flip-top cap, which makes it easy to use. I pop the cap open, squirt some onto my fingers, then carefully, I slide my index finger into his virgin butt, sliding past the ring of muscle. He's watching me with his half-lidded eyes, even as he spreads his legs further apart to give me access.

I slide my finger in up to the second joint, watching Benji's face for any sign of pain or discomfort. None, pure happiness. I pump the finger in and out slowly a few times.

"Shay, I'm not a china doll, I ain't gonna break." Smiling with an air of satisfaction, or at least happiness, he's finally got me where he wants me.

I add a second finger and pump both in and out; he looks at me with a hungry smile. I add the third finger, and he's got a look of determination on his face. He's not as comfortable as he was.

"Don't. Stop. What. You. Are. Doing." Each word said bluntly, but I can sense the love and lust behind them. I'm stretching him more than *that* part of him has ever been, and yet he wants more. I pump my fingers brisker now, and after a few strokes, he's back smiling.

"If this hurts too much, we'll stop when you say," I tell him, worried that he would let me hurt him just to be sure he loses his virginity to me. No fuckin' way.

"Are ya gonna yammer all day, or are ya gonna make love to me?"

A few more plunges with three fingers, then I add the fourth. He grabs my left arm, holds it still for about ten seconds, then s-l-o-w-l-y slides my hand in and out twice. I expect him to delay any further penetration, but he surprises me yet again.

"Get the lube on your cock and do it, Rave. I'm ready."

Nothing like a bossy virgin bottom directing the show. I know he's eager to get to the "real deal" so I slide my fingers out, add a good bit of lube to my cock, and move into position, lifting his legs as I guide my cock into the tightest, sweetest spot it's ever been in.

I stop after the head gets through the ring of muscle. Even though my four fingers are pretty big, my cock is larger, as hard as it is now. And he's got about eight inches yet to feel.

After a brief pause, he pushes his ass back toward my cock, so I slide another inch in. The look on his face is somewhere between dazed and pure bliss. As gently as possible, I pump in and out a few times with no further penetration. When he tries to work more of me into himself, I pump with greater intensity, more of my cock sliding into his tight passage.

When my balls tap his ass cheeks, he lifts his head, glances between his legs, and looks from his hard cock to my eyes. A smile somewhere between "at last" satisfaction and "I'm the big bad wolf, gonna swallow you whole" devilishness spreads across his face.

At this point, we are as tightly joined as is possible. I've never been so hard and so snugly surrounded. We're made for each other. I pump into him forcefully, and the wolfish grin, impossibly, grows bigger.

"Fuck me, Rave, I'm yours."

My brain translates that into *fuck me into the mattress*. I start pounding into him, and he's still trying to get me deeper. He reaches to stroke his length, but I get my right hand there first and begin sliding my hand the length of his cock, slowly at first, then faster, until I'm jerking him off as rapidly as I'm pounding into him.

"Gawd yes... fuck me, babe... nnngggh," his words begin falling apart, which tells me he's close to having what hopefully will be a mind-blowing orgasm.

He's not the only one getting close, either. I'm hammering Benji's butt, and my balls are drawing up—I'm so close to cumming, it's *almost* painful.

I want to make him cum first. To move things along, I jerk him a little faster, swirling my thumb over the head at the peak of each stroke.

That does it. Benji's ass muscles clinch as he shoots the first jet between us, and those tight walls and the vise-like grip on my cock send me over the edge. I pump him full of my cream as he weaves his head back and forth on the pillow behind him. As I finish, I gently drop onto him and our mouths seek each other.

The kiss is sloppy, but more romantic. As we break the kiss, he opens his eyes fully—even though the lids try to remain hooded—and stares into mine as if he's looking into my brain.

"You're everything I ever wanted, shay."

I sense the blush rising to my cheeks. Even lying here in the aftermath of his first time making love, he amazes me with his sweetness and goodness. I'm still half-hard, but I don't want to wear him out.

Later that evening

Wrapped in each other, with a sheet covering us, the glow on Benji's face must match what I'm feeling. He turns and pecks my cheek, then starts humming a tune I remember from London. I'm about to ask if he needs his guitar, when he begins singing a cappella.

In your dark night, as the storms crash all around,

I've got your back, I'll never let you down.

The roads you've traveled haven't always been smooth,

Decisions you've had to make haven't always been easy;

You set your goals and stuck to your chosen path,

Your brilliance and persistence amaze me.

You've had many folks come and go in your life.

They have used you and thrown you away without thinking;

In spite of the hurt you remained on your path,

Your trusting and faith in others shrinking.

The day we met, what a glorious event,

The intensity of your eyes burned through my defenses.

All I could do was stay calm enough to play,

As your aura melted all my senses.

In the dark night, as the storms crash all around,

I'll never leave, I'll always stand our ground.

Damn; it's almost impossible to speak. Benji had promised me he would perform the song live at the right time, for the right audience....

I grin at him, letting his voice settle over me.

Benji was there to help me through my dark night, and all along, he was the one who helped me find myself when I was losing my shit left and right. I couldn't have made it without my salamander, and I damn well don't want to ever try.

"I love you, Benji."

"I love you more."

~ ***The End*** ~

Author's Note

December, 2025

Wow. I've got to thank so many people for making this book a reality. Each person listed here is incredibly important to me, and to getting this project finished. Extra-special thanks to you, dear reader, for picking up this book and taking a chance on a first-time novelist. I hope you'll stop by Goodreads or Amazon and leave a review!

Thanks to my guide, mentor, book coach, and sounding board, Dr. Heather Davis. You told me, about two years ago (in what feels like another century), that we'd bring to life a book I would be proud to call my own. With your guidance and persistence, *we* did it. I think Ravynn, Benji, and the "cast of thousands" really developed their own personalities and voices with your help. You focused and steered me, and even figured out what I was trying to get on the page more than once. For that alone, you deserve a gracious thanks and my eternal appreciation. And you don't have to edit this part, so anything I screw up here is strictly on me! Thank you for helping me rejuvenate my love of writing, and for allowing me to wander aimlessly at times during our sessions.

Great thanks to an unsung hero—my beta reader, Lilian Zenzi. With her input, the words of the original story got wrapped in warmth, care, and realism. Without that input, many of the passages would have been missing or not fully developed. I cannot thank this "word warrior" enough.

Thank you to my maternal grandmother, who encouraged me to try so many things which worked, and a few that didn't, and always acted like I was a tremendous success either way. Even though she's no longer with me, I feel her presence—and I'm pretty sure I inherited a dose of her sense of humor as well. She always encouraged my writing, though she would "tsk-tsk" me at a lot of the words in this book. Sorry, Nana, but they fit the guys. My grandmother and grandfather raised twin daughters during the Great Depression and World War II, and kept them fed, clothed, and well-educated. My aunt became a librarian, further instilling books in my life, and my mother was both a homemaker and a businesswoman long before it was fashionable for women to be "higher ups" in business. My father died when I was ten, and I was never a sports-oriented guy; I retreated to my world of books, and found plenty of friends and adventures there. Soon, I began writing my own stories, poems, and attempts at plays, all fostered by my mother, my aunt, and my grandmother.

Thanks to the members of **The VERY Thing!** writer's group for their input and insight in helping me craft the book you are currently reading, as well as others yet to come. Michael Halfhill, Thea Nishimori, Nathanael Starr Key, Miles Navaro, J. Alan Shipton, Luke Wilde, Sharon Hancock, and Bernard Morin are voices you need to explore.

To the people of Louisiana, thank you for giving me a "home away from home" which helped inspire so many of the characters in the prequel, the Christmas short story, the novel, and a few more that may yet be lurking. I hope my liberties with your language, customs, and lifestyle are not too overbearing.

For those of you in the Volunteer State of Tennessee, I do not paint you all with the same brush. Know that I appreciate the differences in cultures, and though Nashville gets a bad rap in this novel, I don't hold it against the city one bit. I have enjoyed many visits there.

To every person who identifies as an ally of the LGBTQIA2S+ community, thank you from my community; please keep being an ally. We may not all thank you, but we appreciate you. Your efforts are helping, especially in these troubled times.

On a serious note, the attack on Ravynn and Benji *almost* didn't occur. Ravynn made a decision about his life, and one consequence of that decision was the attack. If the scene traumatized you, or caused you flashbacks, I'm sorry. Living while being gay is not a sport for the light-hearted; I've been at it for many years now, and it's never easy, but the rewards of being yourself are immense. Ultimately, isn't that what *all* of us want?

For the members of the "rainbow alphabet," the spectrum of LGBTQIA2S+ existence, never doubt yourself. Never accept being an afterthought. Stay safe, and know there are thousands of people worldwide just like you, and thousands more allies and supporters. 'Equal Rights for All' doesn't mean anyone gets less; it's not a pie getting carved. Find your community and be happy. As Ravynn, Benji, Sean, and Clay found their happiness in the novel, you must find yours—and it starts by knowing and loving yourself. If you're lucky enough that your family accept you as you are, great! If not, find accepting substitutes; just be cautious with your trust.

Find local LGBTQ+ organizations in your area, or a national hotline. Excellent resources include the TREVOR Project, which is partnering with RAINN to prevent sexual assault on LGBTQ+ individuals. The Trevor Project is online at www.thetrevorproject.org or by phone, call 1-866-488-7386 or text 678678. The Trevor Project can talk to younger people about gender identity issues, suicidal thoughts, mental health in general. Showing my age, there's also The Matthew Shepard Foundation, www.matthewshepard.org, founded in 1998 after 21-year-old gay University of Wyoming student Matthew Shepard was beaten and tied to a fence outside Laramie, Wyoming, on October 7 of that year. He lay in a coma in hospital for 5 days before dying. The Foundation's mission is simple: to "erase hate."

If you have been the victim of sexual assault, or know of anyone who has been, please contact RAINN—the Rape, Abuse & Incest National Network—online at www.rainn.org or by phone at 800-656-HOPE (800-656-4673). From the minute I started planning this novel, the original backstory for Ravynn and Ronnie was much darker, and I decided I was going to use my novel to help draw some attention to the good work RAINN does.

Finally, if you want to talk to a sympathetic ear, you can always email me or find me on my social media platforms—a luxury we didn't have in my younger years.

email: authorjamesweems@gmail.com

website: https://jamesweems.com

ABOUT THE AUTHOR

James Weems is a writer who has a unique sense of humor and a world of experience.

James graduated from college with a Bachelor of Arts in English; he focused on broadcasting and creative writing while in college. He has written several short stories and hundreds of poems, and has been published in his college literary magazine, *The Erskine Review*, as well as in the literary magazine published by an Atlanta group, *The Unknowns*. Most recently his short story, *The Case of the Hanging Chads*, was published in the anthology *MOSAIC: A Gay Anthology*, from Gambit's Angel Publications, LLC.

James loves the beach and visiting favorite places like New Orleans, the Golden Isles of Georgia, the Great Smoky Mountains, and a return trip to Europe wouldn't be bad, either. He loves to cook and explore new dishes. He also enjoys listening to a wide variety of music and watching movies and television shows. James enjoys swimming—or at least splashing around in a pool or the ocean. When he's not writing, James loves to read, watch favorite movies and TV shows by way of DVDs, and occasionally he plays games on his phone or computer.

James lives in Avondale Estates, Georgia, part of metro Atlanta.

To learn more about James, visit his website at jamesweems.com (https://jamesweems.com). You may also find him on Facebook, Bluesky, and other social media platforms.

Also by...

If you've enjoyed this novel, I invite you to join my newsletter mailing list! I won't bombard you with tons of emails (usually one newsletter every three weeks), and it's an easy way to keep up with what's coming next! Plus, you get the prequel to the novel absolutely free (other than the price of your email address), and you can unsubscribe any time.

Benji's Bayou Birthday Bash – a **Phoenix Rising** prequel

https://dl.bookfunnel.com/az2gwlwxju

Also available: **Christmas Bonfires** (regular and special illustrated editions, ebooks only) and **Benji's Lost Weekend** (ebook only)

Available Spring/Summer 2026:

Phoenix Rising Book 2: It's All in the Family

The hottest rock group on the planet returns to action in a longer world tour with *new* romances springing up! Benji's homecoming (of sorts) to New Orleans, and *Phoenix Rising* in Phoenix, Arizona? Almost every continent catches Phoenix Rising mania!

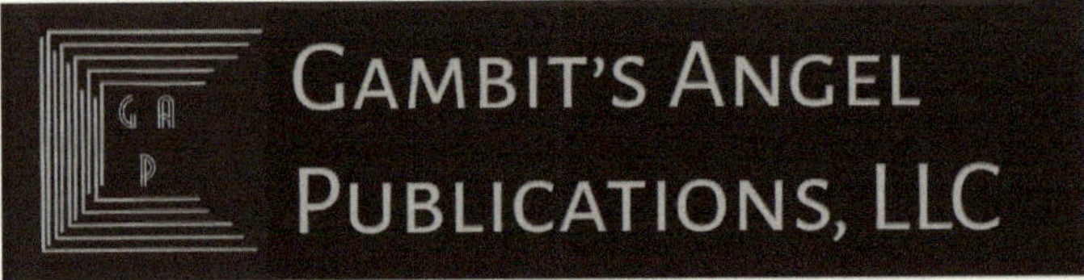
G A P
Gambit's Angel
Publications, LLC

www.ingramcontent.com/pod-product-compliance
Lightning Source LLC
LaVergne TN
LVHW090550110826
845146LV00001B/94

9798989668137